VENGEANCE

ALSO BY RICK CAMPBELL

The Trident Deception
Empire Rising
Ice Station Nautilus
Blackmail
Treason
Deep Strike
The Bin Laden Plot

VENGEANCE

RICK CAMPBELL

ST. MARTIN'S
PRESS
NEW YORK

First published in the United States by St. Martin's Press, an imprint of St. Martin's Publishing Group

EU Representative: Macmillan Publishers Ireland Ltd, 1st Floor, The Liffey Trust Centre, 117–126 Sheriff Street Upper, Dublin 1, DO1 YC43

www.stmartins.com

The Library of Congress Cataloging-in-Publication Data is available upon request.

ISBN 978-1-250-27712-1 (hardcover)
ISBN 978-1-250-27713-8 (ebook)

Our books may be purchased in bulk for specialty retail/wholesale, literacy, corporate/ premium, educational, and subscription box use. Please contact MacmillanSpecialMarkets@macmillan.com.

First Edition: 2025

10 9 8 7 6 5 4 3 2 1

MAIN CHARACTERS

-Complete cast of characters is provided in Addendum-

UNITED STATES ADMINISTRATION

KEVIN HARDISON—chief of staff
MARCY PERINI—secretary of state
TOM GLASS—secretary of defense
PETER SEUFFERT—acting secretary of defense
SHEILA McNEIL—secretary of the Navy

RUSSIAN ADMINISTRATION

DMITRY EGOROV—president

CENTRAL INTELLIGENCE AGENCY

CHRISTINE O'CONNOR—director (DCIA)
MONROE BRYANT—deputy director (DDCIA)
FRANK McKINNON—deputy director for operations (DDO)
JAKE HARRISON—paramilitary operations officer
KHALILA DUFOUR—specialized skills officer, National Clandestine Service

OTHER U.S. GOVERNMENT AGENCIES

BILL GUISEWHITE—director of the Federal Bureau of Investigation

USS *THEODORE ROOSEVELT* (NIMITZ-CLASS AIRCRAFT CARRIER)

RYAN NOSS (Captain)—Commanding Officer

USS *MICHIGAN* (OHIO-CLASS GUIDED MISSILE SUBMARINE)—BLUE CREW

MURRAY WILSON (Captain)—Commanding Officer
TOM MONTGOMERY (Lieutenant Commander)—Executive Officer

K-328 *LEOPARD* (AKULA-CLASS NUCLEAR ATTACK SUBMARINE)

MAKSIM SIDOROV (Captain Second Rank)—Commanding Officer

K-571 *KRASNOYARSK* (YASEN-CLASS NUCLEAR ATTACK SUBMARINE)

GAVRIIL NOVIKOV (Captain Second Rank)—Commanding Officer

MEDINA FALLS

SARAH GREENWOOD—waitress at Irina's Diner

OTHER CHARACTERS

LONNIE MIXELL—former Navy SEAL
BRENDA VERBECK—CEO, Snyder Industries / former secretary of the Navy
ANGIE HARRISON—Jake Harrison's wife (deceased)
MADELINE (MADDY) HARRISON—Jake Harrison's daughter

1

WASHINGTON, D.C.

This would be her big break, Bonni told herself again.

Under a clear blue sky on a peninsula in Southwest D.C. where the Potomac and Anacostia Rivers converge, local CBS television reporter Bonni Shuff stood on the sidewalk with a microphone in one hand, talking with her cameraman beside her. They were outside Lincoln Hall, one of the main buildings within the National Defense University complex inside the Army's Fort McNair. Parked along the street were three black SUVs with tinted windows, and stationed nearby were several Defense Security Service agents in their dark-gray suits.

Earlier this morning, Bonni had received a tip that she hoped would propel her career to the next level. In the aftermath of the recent Russian presidential election, Secretary of Defense Tom Glass was delivering a speech today that would supposedly serve as a warning to the new Russian president. After the speech, instead of leaving via Lincoln Hall's front entrance as was customary, Secretary Glass would depart via the rear exit, attempting to slip away quickly to his next engagement. Bonni, who had learned of the secretary's planned covert exit, would be waiting to get the scoop she needed: exclusive additional details about today's speech.

At least, that had been the plan.

Only moments after she had arrived behind Lincoln Hall, another news van had appeared, and there were now over a dozen vehicles parked nearby, the sidewalk crowded with reporters and cameramen. Apparently, the tip Bonni had received from her contact inside the National Defense University hadn't been exclusive. Exacerbating her irritation had been the arrival of Nicole Fleming, the CBS network reporter covering the presidential administration.

After Nicole arrived at Lincoln Hall with her cameraman—Bonni noted with a twinge of jealousy that she also had a makeup assistant—Nicole had wasted little time pointing out that Bonni was merely a local reporter who covered for her whenever she was otherwise occupied. That not being the case today, Nicole demanded Bonni's spot directly in front of Lincoln Hall's rear exit, and even had the gall to tell Bonni that she could pack up and depart—she'd take it from here.

Ed Lipska, Bonni's cameraman, had intervened as Nicole and her crew tried to muscle their way into the front row of reporters, displacing Bonni. Standing six feet, four inches tall and weighing well north of two hundred pounds, Lipska had stood his ground, glaring at Nicole and her cameraman. The situation had eventually ended in a draw, with Nicole and Bonni positioned beside each other after Nicole had displaced another crew.

As they awaited the secretary of defense's departure, Bonni found herself hoping that Nicole would suddenly break out in an unsightly rash, something that affected only pretentious, story-stealing network reporters. Better yet, maybe the woman would be afflicted with an uncontrollable stutter if she was called upon to question Glass this afternoon. Bonni brightened at the thought, but knew she was asking too much. Nicole was a seasoned professional with over twenty years of experience handling the pressure of televised journalism.

Still, Bonni told herself that this would be her big break. She had occasionally filled in for the national broadcast reporters assigned to cover the White House, but promotion to a network job had eluded her. She had the right qualifications: she had her bachelor's and master's degrees in journalism, she was attractive, and she had the requisite experience and talent. All she lacked was the video clip that would catch the attention of senior management at the national news agencies.

Inside the Lincoln Hall auditorium, Secretary of Defense Tom Glass was introduced by the president of the National Defense University. Bonni listened on her earpiece as Glass began his speech, which was being broadcast by the NDU.

"Good morning, everyone. Thank you for joining me today, and thank you to Lieutenant General Collins and his staff here at the National Defense University for hosting today's event."

As Glass continued, Bonni concentrated on the secretary's remarks, searching for the juicy morsel that would lead to an interview clip that would be broadcast to millions of viewers. Finally, Glass revealed the nugget she was looking for—the U.S. president had worked out an agreement with Congress on preapproved economic sanctions designed to cripple the Russian economy if Russian troops invaded Ukraine or any other country. If she could obtain exclusive details of those sanctions, somehow beating Nicole to the scoop, it might be her big break.

The secretary of defense completed his speech, which was followed by audience applause until Glass exited the auditorium, his departure announced by the radio broadcast narrator. Two DSS agents moved toward Lincoln Hall's rear exit, signaling that the secretary's emergence from the building was imminent.

"Let's get you for a few seconds introducing yourself," Lipska said. "Then, if you're called upon, I'll get footage of you and the SecDef, and we'll edit in the van."

Bonni turned and faced the camera, transitioning to her on-air presence: shoulders back, chin up, and an engaging—but not too enthusiastic—smile. She looked into the camera lens as Lipska counted down.

"You're on in three, two, one—"

The red recording light on the camera energized, and Bonni delivered her introduction, finishing as the exit door behind her opened. She turned as Secretary Glass, accompanied by two DSS agents, emerged from the building.

Glass stopped near the exit as his eyes swept over the crowd, no doubt surprised by the cadre of reporters awaiting his supposedly clandestine exit from Lincoln Hall, their voices erupting in a deluge of unintelligible questions.

Bonni surged forward, as did Nicole, the two women drawing the secretary's attention.

"I have time for one question," he said.

Nicole blurted her query, but Glass raised his hand, stopping her.

"It's good to see you again, Nicole. But let's go with someone new this time."

Before Nicole could respond, Glass shifted his gaze to the local TV reporter beside her.

Bonni was momentarily at a loss for words, seemingly afflicted by the stutter she had wished upon her competitor. Her mind raced as she felt today's opportunity slipping away. But then the fog cleared and the questions came.

"What are the specific sanctions the president is prepared to invoke in the case of Russian aggression?"

As Glass took a few seconds to compose his response, Bonni glanced over her shoulder, confirming that the camera was recording and that Lipska had a clear shot.

She focused again on Glass as he began to answer, but he stopped mid-sentence. Bonni wasn't sure which registered first—the small hole appearing in his forehead just above the bridge of his nose, or the reddish-gray puff materializing behind his head. It took a short moment to realize that a bullet had passed through his skull.

It was pandemonium outside Lincoln Hall after the secretary of defense collapsed onto the pavement. Bonni instinctively turned in the direction of the gunshot, spotting a man standing between two pillars on the third floor of the parking garage across the street, lowering a rifle as he surveyed the scene below. Lipska also turned, aiming his camera toward the garage. It might have been her imagination, but Bonni thought she saw the man across the street smile as he brought the rifle scope to his eye again.

Another shot rang out as a bullet struck Lipska's camera, followed by another round into his head.

As Lipska and his camera tumbled to the ground, Bonni realized she might be the next target—she had seen the assassin and could identify him. As she turned to flee toward the nearest cover, a bullet entered her left temple, exiting the other side of her head.

WASHINGTON, D.C.

Darkness was falling across the District as CIA Director Christine O'Connor entered the West Wing of the White House, descending to the Situation Room in the basement. The last to arrive for this evening's impromptu meeting aside from the president, Christine took one of two empty seats at the table, then took note of tonight's attendance. Seated around the table were Secretary of State Marcy Perini, Secretary of Homeland Security Nova Conover, FBI Director Bill Guisewhite, National Security Advisor Thom Parham, and Kevin Hardison, the president's chief of staff.

Christine had been invited because the perpetrator of this morning's assassination had been identified: a man the CIA had tracked down twice but who had slipped away on both occasions. Now that Christine had arrived, Hardison contacted the president's secretary, informing her that they were ready for the president, who arrived a moment later. All stood as he entered, returning to their seats after the president settled into his chair at the head of the table.

"What have you got?" he asked.

Hardison replied, "Director Guisewhite has the lead on the investigation and will brief you on what we know."

After the president nodded, Guisewhite began.

"Good evening, Mr. President. As you're aware, Secretary of Defense Glass was assassinated this morning after his speech at the National Defense University. Although the sniper sent a bullet through the lens of a local TV reporter's camera, the images of the assassin had already been recorded in the camera's digital memory. His picture was run through all available databases—there was initially no result, until regression analysis identified the perpetrator: a disguised Lonnie Mixell."

The president's eyes shifted momentarily to Christine O'Connor, whose organization had previously been tasked to track down the former U.S. Navy SEAL who had been incarcerated for killing several prisoners during a tour of duty in the Middle East. After his release from prison, Mixell had turned on the country that he believed had betrayed him, helping America's enemies and even attempting to assassinate the president a year ago.

Additionally, he harbored a vendetta against the fellow SEAL who had reported his transgressions in the Middle East—Jake Harrison, his former best friend. Three months ago, Mixell had obtained revenge for his eight-year incarceration, slaying Harrison's wife and wounding Harrison and his daughter.

Complicating the matter, Christine was from the same town as Mixell and Harrison, and the three had been close friends until Mixell's imprisonment. Christine had sided with Harrison, which infuriated Mixell, and Christine had also been wounded in the confrontation between Mixell and Harrison.

Christine had left Mixell's body in the barn, believing he was dead. But when law enforcement searched the barn, they found no body, just a bloody trail leading to a broken window. They had used dogs to track him through the Northwest wilderness, but they had lost his trail in a heavy rain.

The president turned back to Guisewhite. "You're sure it was Mixell?"

"Yes, Mr. President. We have video from a local television station that was filmed during the assassination."

"What kind of security was in place?" the president asked, irritation evident in his tone. "This man is number one on the FBI's most wanted list and there's an Interpol red notice on him. How did Mixell get onto an Army base to begin with and escape afterwards?"

"Mixell was disguised with a beard and colored eye contacts," Guisewhite replied, "plus he had an official ID. The surveillance video at the entrance gate shows the guard scanning Mixell's ID card, and his entry onto the base was approved. As far as Mixell's escape, there was initial confusion after the assassination, and it took a few minutes to lock down the base. By that time, Mixell had already exited."

"Do you have any leads on him?" the president asked.

"Not at this time," Guisewhite replied, "but we're monitoring all transportation hubs and the cameras at every Metro, train, and highway toll, and have law enforcement searching for the suspect's vehicle."

The president nodded curtly. "What about the other deaths? Two civilians and two DSS agents?"

"That's correct. Bonni Shuff, a reporter for a local station, plus her cameraman, Ed Lipska, were the civilian casualties. Mixell was partially concealed from his vantage point in the parking garage across the street, but Bonni and Lipska had a clear view from their position on the sidewalk, in line with Mixell's shot on Secretary Glass. It looks like Mixell took out anyone able to identify him. However, I don't think he expected to be captured on video during the assassination.

"Regarding the DSS casualties, two agents were killed as they moved across the street from Lincoln Hall toward the parking garage, which discouraged pursuit. The other DSS agents took cover, and Mixell used their reluctance to cross the street to his advantage, buying enough time to escape."

"Are there any other details I need to be aware of?" the president asked.

After Guisewhite replied no, the president turned to Hardison. "What's the plan?"

"The deputy secretary of defense, Peter Seuffert, will be the acting SecDef until a replacement is nominated and approved. Regarding Mixell, the FBI will coordinate with the CIA again to track him down."

The president shifted his gaze back to Christine. "You've tracked down and supposedly killed Mixell twice, and both times he's slipped through your fingers. This time, make sure he's dead," he said tersely. "Put his head on a stick if you have to."

"Yes, Mr. President."

A report from the Situation Room speakers interrupted their discussion. "Mr. President, the new Russian president is delivering his inauguration speech. Do you want us to broadcast it on the Situation Room display?"

The president declined the offer, and there was a momentary silence in the Situation Room as everyone reflected on the change in Russian leadership.

After the United States had assisted the previous Russian president, Yuri Kalinin, in thwarting a military coup, Kalinin's relationship with America had turned conciliatory—or soft, as his political enemies had framed things. Kalinin's hard-liner opponent in the recent presidential election had seized on this perceived weakness, blaming Kalinin for Russia's declining influence on the world stage.

The U.S. had lost a quasi-ally in Yuri Kalinin, and the relationship with the new Russian president would undoubtedly be more strained.

Thom Parham, the president's national security adviser, broke the silence. "Negotiating preapproved sanctions with Congress was a wise decision. Hopefully, they will send a strong enough signal to the Kremlin to deter any aggressive moves."

"Without Kalinin," Secretary of State Marcy Perini added, "Russia will likely strengthen its relationship with Iran, which could seriously undermine the international sanctions in place to deter Iran's quest for nuclear weapons."

"Perhaps we could send a more direct message to Russia than just the SecDef's speech," Parham replied.

"We need to tread carefully," Hardison said. "The last thing we need, right before *our* presidential election, is another confrontation with Russia."

The president mulled his options, then announced his decision.

"We'll sit tight for now and see what initiatives the new Russian president pursues."

LANGLEY, VIRGINIA

Christine O'Connor used the ride from the White House back to CIA headquarters to evaluate how best to proceed with the assigned task—track down and apprehend or kill Mixell. Under normal circumstances, the answer would have been obvious. The task would have been assigned to Jake Harrison and Khalila Dufour, who had led the two previous efforts. However, the circumstances at the moment were far from normal. Khalila was in the proverbial doghouse, to describe it mildly, and Harrison had disappeared.

Harrison had dropped off the grid because of what had occurred three months ago, when Mixell murdered Harrison's wife. Christine would never forget the sight of Harrison holding Angie as she died in his arms. The conflict with Mixell that night had been brutal, leaving Harrison with two bullets in his chest while Christine suffered two knife wounds, with Harrison's twelve-year-old daughter, Maddy, knocked unconscious and bleeding after Mixell slammed a shovel into the side of her head.

At the time, Christine had believed Mixell was dead, lying on the barn floor as blood spread out slowly beneath him. After hearing the faint sound of approaching police and medical vehicles, Christine had carried Maddy to the house for immediate medical attention, leaving Mixell's body behind.

By the following morning, when she stood beside Harrison's hospital bed after he awoke from surgery to repair the two bullet wounds, Christine had learned that Mixell had survived. But she had lied to Harrison, telling him Mixell was dead. As he lay in bed, grieving for his wife, Christine had decided that he had enough to deal with. She had planned to wait a few days before revealing that Mixell had survived. But by then, her lifelong relationship with Harrison—who had been her best friend as a child, had dated her for over a decade, and had proposed to her twice—had been shattered.

Harrison blamed Christine for everything. In the hospital room after his surgery, he told Christine that he never wanted to see or hear from her again. If she hadn't pulled him into the CIA the first time, leading to the death of Mixell's girlfriend, Mixell wouldn't have taken his revenge out on Angie; it would instead have been just between the two men.

Christine had tried to meet with Harrison while he was recovering, but he refused to see her each time. She had tried one last time at Angie's funeral, which had been delayed until Harrison was healthy enough to attend. She recalled the funeral, only two weeks ago . . .

Christine had known she wasn't welcome, but had decided to attend anyway. Jake had refused to share the funeral details with her, sticking to the proclamation he had delivered in his hospital room.

I don't ever want to see or hear from you again.

However, she didn't need to be the CIA director to sleuth the details. There had been notices in the Baltimore newspapers and on the internet.

When Maddy spotted Christine's arrival, she had moved to greet Christine, but Jake pulled her close, then whispered in her ear. Maddy stared at Christine for a moment, then subtly waved at her, and Christine waved back.

Harrison and Maddy were standing graveside with family members from both sides, including Jake's parents, who had cared for Maddy while Jake was in the hospital. Under normal circumstances, Christine would have been beside Jake, offering her support. But it was clear that he still blamed her for Angie's death, so she stood off to the side, watching from a distance.

Following the funeral, Harrison left Maddy with her grandparents. After arranging for a protective detail for his daughter, he had disappeared. Harrison seemed convinced that Mixell would attempt to track him down again and didn't want Maddy anywhere near him when that happened.

Christine's SUV passed through the entrance gate at Langley and stopped outside the Original Headquarters Building. After entering her seventh-floor office, she approached her secretary.

"Have the DD, DDO, and DDA meet me in my office."

Deputy Director Monroe Bryant and Deputy Director for Analysis Tracey McFarland were the first to arrive, taking a seat at the conference table in Christine's office, followed by Frank McKinnon, the agency's new deputy director for operations. The position had opened up three months ago when PJ Rolow, the former DDO, had been slain by one of the agency's own officers—Khalila Dufour. There were unusual circumstances involved, and Christine had left it up to the new DDO to recommend what to do about Khalila.

McKinnon was ten years older than Rolow, which wasn't unusual given that Rolow had been the youngest DDO in the history of the agency. Rather than mirroring Rolow's meteoric rise through the ranks, McKinnon had percolated his way to the top, spending notable time in various leadership roles after twenty years as a field officer. McKinnon was still feeling his way as DDO, leaving Rolow's policies in place so far, and had not yet decided how best to handle the Khalila issue.

"How'd it go?" Tracey asked, empathetic to Christine's uncomfortable position as CIA director and also Mixell's childhood chum, along with the CIA's failure to put Mixell away the two previous times.

"As best as can be expected," Christine replied. "It's the same drill as before—find Mixell before he does more harm." She turned to McKinnon. "We'd normally assign Harrison and Khalila, but neither is an option at the moment. Any suggestions?"

"Khalila might be available," McKinnon replied. Monroe and McFarland seemed surprised, but Christine had seen this coming.

"The president has tied our hands," McKinnon explained. "His directive was clear—no one except the four of us, plus the president and his chief of staff, is to learn that Khalila killed Rolow; the official story is that he died of a heart attack. That limits the punitive measures we can take against Khalila. Anything too drastic will generate unwanted questions. Besides, Rolow had it coming, one way or another. Khalila saved the taxpayers a lot of money, skipping the expensive trial and freeing up a cell in federal prison."

McFarland replied, "Spoken like a true DDO—just get the job done; dispense with the legalities." McFarland meant it as a compliment. She smiled and added, "I think you're going to fit in just fine as DDO."

"Let's not get too carried away," Christine said. "I realize the rules get bent around here on occasion, but I need to be the one who authorizes it." She directed her gaze at Deputy Director Bryant. "I know there are matters you hide from me, making the decision at your level, leaving me out of the loop. That needs to stop. I get a vote on anything that might violate the law."

Bryant and McFarland exchanged glances.

Turning to Christine, Bryant said, "I do that for a reason—to insulate and protect the director from any fallout regarding those matters."

"No," Christine replied. "You do it because you believe that *you,* with four decades of agency experience, are more qualified than a newbie wet-behind-the-ears director who could barely spell CIA when she got appointed to the job."

"Well, there's that," Bryant agreed.

"Going forward," Christine replied, "you'll bring *all* of these sensitive matters to me, and I'll decide which ones get managed at your level."

"As you wish," he said, with no hint of resentment.

"Regarding sensitive matters," Christine said as she shifted back to McKinnon, "what's the plan for Khalila and Mixell?"

"I plan to reinstate Khalila next week. As far as rehabilitation goes, there's been none and there won't be. Her outlook on matters is firm, and I'm confident that if Khalila were to find herself in a similar situation in the future, she'd respond the same way. Frankly, I don't blame her. If I had been in her shoes, I would have done the same thing."

"So, Khalila will lead the effort to track down Mixell?" Christine asked.

"I'd prefer to have Harrison as well," McKinnon replied. "I realize he's trying to lay low, but if you approve, we'll try to locate him and invite him back."

Christine hesitated, considering what hiring Harrison the first time had cost him. But Mixell would eventually track down and attempt to kill Harrison, and the outcome would likely be better if Harrison was part of the team, hunting down Mixell instead.

Plus, if they located Harrison, it would give Christine an opportunity to at least talk with him. Give her a chance to clear the air and hopefully begin the effort to repair their relationship.

She nodded. "Find him."

MEDINA FALLS, ARKANSAS

"Thanks, Nicholai."

Twenty-year-old Sarah Greenwood smiled as she picked up the tip, then wiped the diner counter as Nicholai Gherkin pushed himself to his feet, then hobbled toward the door. Sarah watched through the diner's large front windows in sympathy as the elderly man worked his way down the sidewalk, aided by his cane. It wouldn't be much longer, she thought, before he would need one of those fancy motorized scooters. But the folks in Medina Falls didn't have a lot of money, and Nicholai would probably have to make do with a used wheelchair.

Medina Falls was a town with only a few hundred residents situated in the vast expanse of southern Arkansas, or as most of the town's residents preferred to say, *in the middle of nowhere.* The diner's clientele were almost exclusively locals—they didn't get many visitors in Medina Falls—but the patronage was steady and the income enough to keep the diner afloat. Sarah not being a paid employee helped make ends meet; her dad owned and managed the diner.

Sarah occasionally wondered what her life would have been like if she had gone to college, or at least moved to a big city, but she felt obligated to help her dad out. After all, he had fed and clothed her, and put a roof over her head her entire life. Helping him make a living running the diner was the least she could do.

As Sarah took additional orders and delivered the food, she lost track of time, realizing it was 1 p.m. when a Greyhound bus coasted to a halt across the street. Medina Falls was a small town with only a few stores along the main street, and not even one traffic light. But it was significant enough to warrant a bus stop once a week, something the townsfolk took pride in. The bus pulled away, leaving behind a lone passenger who had disembarked—a tall, well-built man standing with a backpack on the sidewalk beside him.

As he gazed across the street toward the diner, surveying the town buildings, something about the man caught Sarah's attention. There was a darkness in his eyes, the look of someone who had suffered a terrible loss. He had also lost a good deal of weight, it seemed. His clothes hung on his frame, a size too large. Despite his lean appearance, however, he still had a strong, athletic build. She noticed the muscles in his arm as he heaved his backpack over his shoulder, then moved across the street toward her.

The man entered the diner, quickly surveying the establishment— Sarah and four customers—before stopping by the counter.

"Welcome to Medina Falls," Sarah said as she approached. "What can I get to drink for ya?" She placed a menu on the counter before him.

"Just information," the man replied in a northern accent. He was definitely going to stick out in Medina Falls, whose inhabitants spoke with a southern drawl.

"Surely, you must be hungry after your long ride. Perhaps a burger. I recommend the bacon cheese, a town favorite."

"I'm looking for a place to stay," the man replied. "I understand there's a room for rent by Gloria Potter."

"Miss Potter? Yep, she has a guesthouse that she rents out on occasion. There's no hotel in town; Miss Potter's is pretty much all we got. Her house is a few blocks that way," Sarah said, pointing to her left, "on the other side of the street. A big white house with blue shutters. Is she expecting you? She was in here the other night and didn't mention anything about a new guest."

"Thanks," the man said. His eyes surveyed the diner's occupants again, and Sarah got the impression he was about to leave. And he hadn't ordered anything to eat yet.

"Is there anything you'd like to eat or drink? I'm Sarah, by the way. What's your name?"

The man nodded politely. "It's nice to meet you, Sarah."

Then he turned and headed toward the door.

Sarah watched as the man exited the diner, then stopped on the sidewalk, looking both ways pensively before heading toward Miss Potter's. When the man disappeared from view, she realized that he hadn't answered a single question, and she hadn't even learned his first name.

What a strange man, Sarah thought.

MOSCOW, RUSSIA

Russian President Dmitry Egorov entered the Kremlin conference room, joining his advisors seated around the table. To the president's right were newly appointed Defense Minister Andrei Grigorenko and Foreign Minister Marat Trutnev. On the other side of the table sat Egorov's Chief of Staff Anton Kravtsov and Chief of the General Staff Nikolai Volkov, the senior officer in the Russian military.

Egorov had assembled his senior civilian and military advisors to hear their proposals. Upon his election, he had issued an edict to develop plans to fulfill the primary campaign promise he had made to the Russian people: to return Russian prestige and influence on the world stage to the levels of the Soviet Union. Egorov turned first to his new minister of defense.

"Proceed."

Grigorenko began. "The plan we have developed will fulfill not one, but two of your campaign promises. Not only will the West learn to respect and fear Russia again, but we will solve the issue of an isolated Crimea by establishing Russian control of a land corridor connecting Crimea with mainland Russia."

"You're talking about invading Ukraine," Egorov said.

"In a matter of speaking," Grigorenko replied. "The Donbas region has already declared its independence from Ukraine, and its pro-Russian governments have confirmed that they will not object to their residents becoming Russian citizens. That leaves the Zaporizhia and Kherson oblasts, which connect the Donbas with Crimea. All told, we're talking about transitioning only two of Ukraine's twenty-four oblasts to Russia, plus the small region of the Donbas that remains in Ukrainian control."

Grigorenko continued, "We prefer to think of this not as an invasion, but a realignment of territory to its rightful owner. History is on our side. Not only have European borders changed numerous times throughout history, but these oblasts were Russian territory in the eighteenth and nineteenth centuries. The argument can be made that these four oblasts, which have a significant ethnic Russian population and whose populations speak primarily Russian, belong in Russia, not Ukraine."

Egorov canvased the other three men at the table. "Are you in consensus on this matter?"

"We are," Foreign Minister Trutnev replied. "The limited scope of this territorial *realignment* is an attractive element. The problem with our previous invasion of Ukraine is that it was too ambitious, forging onward into NATO countries. Keeping this military conflict limited to only a small percentage of a non-NATO country, over territory that was once part of Russia, will deter NATO from intervening. With only Ukraine to combat, we can seize the desired territory and dig in until the Ukrainians grow weary of war."

Anton Kravtsov, the president's chief of staff, asked, "What about the sanctions the American secretary of defense threatened in his speech?"

President Egorov replied, "Let them try. The American president may think his threat of economic sanctions has us by the throat, but we have Western Europe by the balls. Their governments were foolish enough to let their economies become dependent on Russian oil and natural gas. The West will squeeze us only so hard, because we can squeeze harder. And when we squeeze, it'll hurt a whole lot more."

There were nods of agreement around the table.

"One last issue," Egorov said. "The assassination of the American secretary of defense. I realize that I had asked you to send a message to the United States—that our new administration would not respond kindly to American intervention in Russian matters—and you were accommodating enough to implement this plan before I was inaugurated. However, the secretary of defense was killed moments after threatening sanctions against our country. I was hoping for something less obvious regarding our culpability."

The four other men cast uneasy glances around the table until Egorov's chief of staff responded. "The method was chosen by Josef Hippchenko,"

Kravtsov replied, referring to the director of Russia's Foreign Intelligence Service—the successor to the First Chief Directorate of the KGB—"although we were aware and approved the plan. We thought that something obvious and direct would be the most effective method of dissuading the United States from meddling in our affairs."

Egorov nodded. "I understand."

The topic then turned back to the proposed invasion of Ukraine.

"What are your wishes?" Kravtsov asked.

Egorov contemplated the matter, then replied, "Begin preparations to seize control of the southeastern oblasts in Ukraine."

POTOMAC, MARYLAND

In an affluent neighborhood just north of the Potomac River, Vance Verbeck turned onto Highland Farm Road, passing several twenty-thousand-square-foot mansions. The last to arrive in preparation for today's event, Vance stopped before a black iron gate blocking the entrance to his wife's East Coast home.

After Vance identified himself, the gate slid aside and he pulled up to the mansion's entrance. He handed the car keys to a house attendant, who parked the vehicle inside the home's six-car garage, hiding it from sight to preclude giving away today's planned surprise birthday party for his wife, Brenda. Considering the events of the last few months, Vance and Brenda's brothers had decided she could use a private, but festive, occasion to lift her spirits.

Three months ago, Brenda had been forced to resign as secretary of the Navy. After learning that her brother, Dan Snyder, had sold high-speed centrifuges to Iran that would accelerate the regime's enrichment of uranium to weapon-grade purity, Brenda had used her influence as secretary of the Navy to protect her brother's plot from discovery. The effort had failed and Dan had struck a plea deal, landing him in federal prison for fifteen years.

Brenda should have been pleased that the only consequence of her actions was resignation; her transgressions had been far worse than Dan's. She could have spent decades in prison for arranging the murder of two men who had learned too much about Dan's ill-advised scheme to earn a quick billion dollars. But with the president up for reelection later this year, the fact that a senior member of his administration had likely been involved in a murder plot had been swept under the rug. Instead of being thankful for the president's decision to limit the repercussions to her resignation, Brenda had spent the last three months fuming.

As Vance was escorted through the richly appointed mansion toward the back patio, he pondered the current state of affairs, with him living in San Diego while Brenda remained in Maryland. Her move to the Washington, D.C. area, while Vance remained in San Diego as technical director of the U.S. Navy's Arctic Submarine Laboratory, had made sense following her appointment as secretary of the Navy. Since her resignation, however, she hadn't yet made plans to move back to California. That told Vance much—that his beautiful, rich, and ambitious wife was planning something.

Vance reached the patio, inhaling the savory scent of chateaubriand and lobsters roasting in the ovens along the way. He was greeted by Brenda's three other brothers: Bob, Ray, and Tim Snyder, drinks in hand. After ordering one for himself, Vance joined the men at the patio railing overlooking Brenda's estate, ten acres of sprawling Maryland countryside. The conversation covered nothing of importance, mostly catching up on what everyone had been up to since the last time they were together—while avoiding the recent events that were undoubtedly on their minds—until a member of Brenda's staff interrupted the discourse.

"Mrs. Verbeck has arrived. She just passed through the front gate."

Vance and Brenda's brothers moved to the sides of the balcony, hidden from Brenda's view until she stepped onto the patio, supposedly to talk with a neighbor who had stopped by for a visit. A moment later, she arrived and was greeted instead by her husband and brothers.

Brenda's face lit up in delight. She acted surprised, but Vance could tell she had somehow deciphered their plan ahead of time. She offered Vance a brief but passionate kiss. It had been several months since they had been together.

Dinner was soon served, and they took their seats at a round patio table covered with a white tablecloth, with place settings of porcelain china and crystal glasses. The conversation throughout dinner was jovial, as Brenda's brothers recalled childhood stories and antics, attempting to keep their sister's spirits high. At the end of the meal, Brenda's birthday dinner was punctuated by her favorite dessert, cheesecake topped with strawberries and drizzled with caramel.

After the sun dipped beneath the horizon, they sipped drinks around a fire pit. However, despite the best efforts of the four men accompanying her, as the night chill seeped in and the flames danced in the pit, Brenda slipped into a gloomy mood.

"He shouldn't be allowed to get away with it," she said.

"Who?" Vance asked. "Get away with what?"

"The president. Forcing me to resign. I would have beaten any charges. They had nothing on me besides another person's word."

"That person happened to be the director of the CIA."

"It would have been hearsay! Rolow made the arrangements to kill those two men and he told that CIA bitch that he did it for me. The third-person hearsay wouldn't have held up in court."

As Vance debated how to respond, he couldn't help but notice that Brenda hadn't once, in the last three months, denied the accusation—that she had arranged the death of two men in her effort to protect her brother. Family loyalty was an admirable trait, but Brenda had taken it too far.

Brenda added, "The president swept everything under the rug to keep his poll numbers up."

"You *do* realize that you benefited from the president's leniency?" Bob said. "He didn't want a scandal involving his secretary of the Navy to mar his reelection campaign."

"No," Brenda replied. "He didn't have the guts to charge me."

"The president was smart," Ray remarked. "If they had charged you, the outcome would have been unclear. And if the jury had agreed with the prosecution, you would have ended up in jail, just like Dan."

"Dan didn't deserve jail," Brenda replied. "They made an example out of him. He agreed to a plea deal and still got fifteen years. For what! Selling forbidden merchandise? I've seen murderers get lighter sentences."

Brenda slowly swirled the wine in her glass. "The president has forgotten who put him in the White House. When he decided to enter politics, it was people like us who financed his campaigns. Now that he's president, he doesn't need us anymore. We can't let him get away with treating me . . . us, this way."

"You should let it go," Tim said.

"Let it go?" Brenda replied, her face turning red. "I will *not* let it go!"

As Brenda's features flickered in the firelight, Vance knew that she was plotting something.

MEDINA FALLS, ARKANSAS

Sarah Greenwood stood beside the table in Irina's Diner, pen and pad in hand, as a customer perused the menu. While she waited for him to place an order, another patron entered the crowded restaurant, and Sarah mentally updated the growing list of those waiting to be served, prioritized by their arrival time. It was busy this weekend, as usual, with Sarah helping her mom out in the evenings while her dad handled the cooking duties all day, assisted at night by an ever-changing list of teenage assistant cooks looking to make a few bucks.

After waiting on the same customers for several years now, Sarah could take most orders without asking. However, Leonid Romanko rarely ordered the same meal in succession, and tonight the elderly gentleman was particularly indecisive, flipping the single-sheet menu from back to front.

My goodness! There really aren't that many options to choose from!

"How about the borscht, Mister Romanko? Or perhaps the pelmeni dumplings? Some authentic Russian food tonight?"

It was an appropriate recommendation. Irina's Diner was named after Sarah's mom, a first-generation immigrant from Russia, and the menu included several popular dishes from her homeland. Many of the customers enjoyed the food, given that fifteen percent of the town's population were Russian immigrants.

"I'll have the borscht," Romanko decided.

Sarah scribbled down the request and hurried toward the kitchen, where she added the order to the dozen slips hanging from the cook's clip line. As she moved to the next customer waiting to be served, she glanced at the stranger sitting at the counter. A week after his arrival, he was a regular at the diner now, stopping by for lunch and dinner each day. He was staying in Miss Potter's guest cottage, earning money by doing odds and ends around her house and yard: repairing gutters and fences, and even fixing some of the stubborn windows that had warped and stuck shut over time.

The mystery man was a topic of conversation at the diner, with patrons wondering who he was and what had brought him here. The only thing anyone had learned thus far was his first name—Jake. Not even Miss Potter had learned his last name or anything noteworthy about him. However, Sarah had drawn her own speculative conclusion. He was half Russian. One-third of Sarah's friends were half Russian, and while it was difficult to determine their other ethnicities, she could spot the Russians in the crowd. Perhaps Medina Falls' high percentage of Russian immigrants was what had drawn the stranger to town.

There was something more, though. The man seemed wary for some reason, always sitting at the counter on a stool offering a clear view of the front door, surveying the customers as they entered. His eyes occasionally swept across the entire diner, taking everything in. He had eaten in the diner more than a dozen times now and despite her repeated attempts, Sarah had learned nothing about him, as the man routinely deflected or ignored her questions.

Sarah's attention was caught by a louder than normal conversation at the counter. Mikhail Goergen was haranguing Irina about the food he was waiting on. He and Irina were good friends, both from the same region in Russia, and the two would occasionally banter back and forth about one topic or another. Tonight, Goergen was complaining in Russian about the slow service.

Irina fired back, also in Russian. "When we lived in the Soviet Union, you remember what we called a four-hour breadline? Fast food!"

Sarah, who also spoke Russian, laughed at the joke, as did Goergen. But what caught Sarah's attention was that the stranger, sitting at the counter nearby, broke into a grin. Her hunch had been correct. Jake spoke Russian, and was likely at least half Russian.

After dropping off her latest order, Sarah stopped by the stranger, speaking in Russian. "Your smile gave yourself away, Jake. You understood what my mom said. Are you full-blooded or half Russian?"

He didn't immediately answer, so she added, "My guess is half Russian. Mom or dad?"

He finally answered. "Mom."

"That means you probably don't have a good Russian last name," she said, shifting back to English. "What is it, again? I don't recall."

She caught a flicker of a smile on the man's face. "Nice try, Sarah."

For some reason, his smile made her feel good. Most of the time, the man seemed lost in his thoughts, a distant look in his eyes as he seemed to be recalling painful memories. Tonight was the only time she had seen him smile the entire time she had been around him.

"This is a monumental moment," she said. "I've learned something about you." She leaned closer to him. "Care to share any other tidbits tonight, like where you're from, what brought you here, and how long you plan to stay?"

The man surveyed the diner's patrons, then returned his gaze to Sarah. "It looks like you've got several customers waiting to place orders."

Sarah sighed. Jake was right. She had already dawdled too long.

"Some other time, then," she said, "when you're in a more talkative mood." She smiled and said, "Don't make me wait too long."

She hurried to her next customers, quickly taking their orders. When she looked back toward Jake, his stool was empty. Just some folded-up money on the counter, paying for dinner. Each time, she hoped he would pay with a credit card, so she could at least learn his last name and begin unraveling the mystery, but he always paid with cash.

The curiosity gnawed at her.

BUTNER, NORTH CAROLINA

It was midafternoon, under a clear blue sky, when a silver Mercedes-Benz SL Roadster, the top down, pulled into a visitor's parking lot inside Federal Correctional Complex, Butner. Brenda Verbeck stepped from the vehicle, headed toward one of four prisons within the FCC—Butner Low, a low-security facility considered by many to be the crown jewel of the federal prison system, where white-collar criminals vied for placement.

After Brenda presented her ID to the Front Entrance Officer, who verified she was on the approved visitor list, she was escorted to the visiting room, where she sat at a table awaiting her brother's arrival. Although Dan Snyder had been handed an extraordinarily harsh sentence as far as Brenda was concerned, he had hit the inmate lottery by being assigned to Butner's low-security lockup. With a look and feel of a college campus instead of a prison, Butner Low was a popular request by nonviolent criminals such as Bernie Madoff, convicted for perpetrating the largest Ponzi scheme in history.

While she waited for her brother, she examined the Spartan room, filled only with several metal tables and chairs, plus a few snack and drink vending machines. Dan finally arrived, presenting an uncharacteristic image. Instead of a fifty-thousand-dollar bespoke Desmond Merrion suit, he wore institutional-issued clothing: khaki pants and shirt with matching black belt and boots. After a long hug, Brenda and her brother sat opposite each other at a table.

Their initial conversation covered the expected topics of how Dan was handling his incarceration and what his daily routine comprised: up at 6 a.m., followed by eight hours of work each day at various tasks that included groundskeeper, food service employee, and commissary worker. The revelation that Dan was actually paid for his work—fifty cents an hour—generated a shared laugh between Brenda and her billionaire brother.

The conversation eventually turned from personal to professional matters.

"How are you and the company doing?" Dan asked.

Following his conviction, Brenda had taken over as CEO of Snyder Industries.

"I'm getting the hang of things, and we're doing well. Surprisingly, orders and profits are up. It seems the adage of *There's no such thing as bad publicity* holds true."

Dan smiled sadly and lowered his eyes to the table.

Brenda reached across and placed her hand on his.

"You didn't deserve this. The president could have intervened, but he threw both of us under the bus. Now that he's president, he no longer needs us. There's no loyalty these days. It's all about *what can you do for me now?*"

Dan nodded glumly, then looked back up. There must have been something in her eyes or tone of voice, because Dan picked up on it.

"What are you planning?"

She leaned toward him. "Revenge."

"How so?"

"The man you contracted to ship the centrifuges to Iran—what's your assessment? Competent or not?"

"Quite competent. That the centrifuges didn't reach their destination wasn't his fault. It was mine."

One of Dan's communications with his Iranian contact had been intercepted by American electronic surveillance in the Persian Gulf, which had culminated in the U.S. Navy sinking the merchant ship carrying the centrifuges as it approached the Iranian port.

"Do you recall the contact information for this man?"

Dan nodded.

Brenda pulled a pen and notepad from her purse and pushed it across the table.

Her brother hesitated a moment, then scribbled the requested information.

After Brenda slipped the pen and pad back into her purse, she smiled.

"The president will pay for what he's done to us."

LANHAM, MARYLAND

Seated at a desk in his hotel room a block from the Capital Beltway carving its way through Maryland and Virginia, Lonnie Mixell perused the encrypted employment offers on his laptop computer, deciding which task seemed most interesting. After the agreed-to fee for the assassination of America's secretary of defense had been deposited into one of his accounts, Mixell's thoughts had turned to his former best friends Jake Harrison, who had betrayed him, sending him to prison for eight years, and Christine O'Connor, who had sided with Harrison against him.

Harrison was next on Mixell's personal to-do list, but he had disappeared after his wife's funeral. Although Mixell was confident that he would eventually locate Harrison, he would need something else to keep him occupied in the meantime.

Mixell was about to respond to an offer when a new encrypted message arrived.

I'm looking for a man who goes by Mitch Larson.

"Who's asking?"

A friend of Dan Snyder.

Mixell contemplated who had contacted him, and it didn't take long to reach a conclusion.

It was Dan's sister, Brenda Verbeck. While surveilling her during his previous assignment, Mixell had wondered if she would be a suitable replacement for Trish, whom Harrison had killed during their confrontation six months ago. He had to admit that Brenda was a tantalizing candidate: beautiful, conniving, and ruthless. And very rich. That she was married hadn't prevented her from engaging in a recent affair, plus her husband could always be removed from the equation if necessary.

He typed a response. "Hello, Brenda."

Hello, Mitch. Or whatever name you're going by now.

"Mitch is fine. How can I help?"

There's a delicate task I want you to accomplish.

"Which is . . . ?"

Meet me in person. Nothing in writing.

"Fee?"

One hundred million.

Mixell's hands froze over the laptop keyboard. Although he was occasionally paid eight-figure sums, he had encountered a nine-figure fee only once before.

"I assume the desired task is not only delicate, but difficult?"

Very.

"Where and when do you want to meet?"

When can you make it to Baltimore?

"Tomorrow."

An address appeared on the laptop screen, plus a time. *6 p.m.?*

"I'll be there."

NOVOSHAKHTINSK, RUSSIA

Under the cover of darkness, a column of mechanized vehicles sped down Highway E50 toward the Russia–Ukraine border. In the passenger seat of a GAZ Tigr all-terrain infantry vehicle, Major General Alexei Sokolov, commanding Russia's 2nd Guards Motor Rifle Division, peered at the wooded landscape ahead through night vision goggles. Behind him, stretched out on the highway, was a regiment of T-90 main battle tanks and fifteen thousand infantry troops divided into two more regiments: one aboard BTR-90 armored personnel carriers and a second aboard BMP-3 infantry combat vehicles, sometimes referred to as light tanks. As Sokolov's division approached its destination, he wondered whether its unusual repositioning was simply political posturing, or the precursor to an imminent invasion.

The 2nd Guards Motor Rifle Division was one of the most famous and decorated formations in the Russian military, having seen extensive combat during World War II and also played prominent roles in two of the major political crises in recent Soviet and Russian history. In 1991, during the hard-line coup attempt against Soviet President Mikhail Gorbachev, one of the division's tank units surrounding the Russian parliament building had switched sides, opposing the coup. It was atop one of the division's tanks that Boris Yeltsin had delivered his rousing speech, condemning the traitorous attempt to depose Gorbachev.

Two years later during the 1993 Russian constitutional crisis, the division again played a decisive role. The Russian military had initially remained neutral, and with the country on the brink of civil war, the 2nd Guards Motor Rifle Division had thrown its support to Yeltsin once more, its tanks opening fire on Moscow's House of Soviets building.

Continuing its journey down Highway E50, Sokolov's division reached its prescribed destination northwest of Novoshakhtinsk, only a few kilometers from Ukraine's border, where he ordered his unit to halt. The sound of his tank and infantry fighting vehicles' engines faded, leaving his unit stretched out along a desolate road cutting through the silence of the serene forest. In another two hours, after sunrise, the presence of Sokolov's unit poised on the highway and aimed toward Ukraine would be visible to a plethora of photo-reconnaissance satellites, not to mention the occasional infrared version passing overhead, able to detect the heat from the tank and personnel carrier engines.

Sokolov resolved himself to the next phase of the modus operandi that seemed to permeate all Army operations—*hurry up and wait*. Less than a day ago, his unit had been ordered to hastily mobilize and reposition. As Sokolov resolved himself to patiently await new orders in a rather unusual location—in the middle of a highway in plain sight—the forest on both sides of the road ahead came to life with the deep rumble of diesel engines.

A moment later, tanks and armored personnel carriers emerged from the trees, assembling into formation along the highway. On the digital tactical display inside Sokolov's vehicle, new units appeared. The 4th and 47th Guards Tank Divisions were joining the 2nd Guards Motor Rifle Division, completing the amalgamation of the formidable 1st Guards Tank Army.

Sokolov's unit had been ordered to hastily mobilize, not for the standard hurry-up-and-wait scenario, but because it was the last major component of the 1st Guards Tank Army moved into place. Now that Sokolov's unit had arrived, the 1st Guards Tank Army was ready to commence its strike into Ukrainian territory.

WASHINGTON, D.C.

It was just past midnight when the president entered the Situation Room in the West Wing, taking his seat at the head of the table, joining members of his staff and cabinet on one side and the Joint Chiefs of Staff on the other. Acting Secretary of Defense Peter Seuffert began his hastily prepared brief.

"We're still analyzing the data, Mr. President, but here's what we know." Seuffert opened a presentation on his computer, which displayed a map of Ukraine and western Russia on the flat-screen display on the far wall, with four red arrows thrusting into Ukrainian territory.

"At four thirty a.m. local time, Russian military units invaded Ukraine. There are four main incursions, one into each of the southeastern Ukrainian oblasts. The First Guards Tank Army has invaded Luhansk, the Eighth Guards Combined Arms Army has entered Donetsk, and the Fifty-eighth Guards Combined Arms Army is surging westward through southern Donetsk toward Zaporizhia while Russian forces from Crimea are moving north into the Kherson oblast.

"We expect the First Guards Tank Army to quickly overwhelm Ukrainian forces in Luhansk, where it will be backfilled by several smaller units moving in behind it, then the First Guards Tank Army will likely serve as a reserve unit employed against difficult Ukrainian resistance or counterattacks. With the lack of incursions elsewhere in Ukraine, it appears that the aim of Russia's invasion is to seize control of a corridor between Russia proper and Crimea, which Russia annexed from Ukraine in 2014."

Seuffert reviewed the relevant details of the earlier conflict. "Russia's annexation of Crimea was a unique situation. Its population is two-thirds ethnic Russian and the province was part of Russia for two hundred years before it was gifted to Ukraine by Nikita Khrushchev in 1954. From a Russian perspective, now that Ukraine is no longer an ally, they simply took back what was rightfully theirs. Ukraine protested, but eventually ceded the region without conflict.

"Crimea's isolation from the rest of Russia has been a sensitive issue, particularly since Russia's Black Sea Fleet is based in Sevastopol, Crimea. Needing the approval of Ukrainian authorities to move military personnel and equipment to and from Crimea has been a thorn in the side of the Russian government. With Russian separatists already controlling portions of Luhansk and Donetsk, it seems that Russia is intent on expanding its foothold in those oblasts while also seizing portions of Zaporizhia and Kherson."

"How did Russian preparations for this invasion go undetected?" the president asked.

"The troop movements were done piecemeal over the last few days and occurred only in a single Russian oblast. Some movements were detected, but not significant enough to raise concern to our level. We were expecting a more expansive mobilization and assault, similar to Russia's last invasion of Ukraine.

"The crux of the issue," Seuffert continued, "is that Ukraine cannot repel Russian forces without NATO assistance, but Ukraine isn't a NATO member. The United States could intervene unilaterally, but without NATO support, our casualties could be high, plus there's a significant risk when engaging an opponent with nuclear weapons. The situation could escalate."

Chief of Staff Kevin Hardison added to Seuffert's observation. "Intervening in this conflict is not only high risk, but it will be a hard sell to Congress and the American people. With the presidential election only a few months away, entering into a war with Russia could be an extraordinarily bad decision."

Turning to Secretary of State Marcy Perini, the president asked, "What's your assessment of the situation?"

"Based on what we're seeing, Russia has learned from their past mistake of venturing into NATO territory, triggering a defense response from the allied countries. Also, Russia appears to be limiting its invasion to a relatively small corridor of land instead of the entire country."

"What's your appraisal of NATO's willingness to intercede?"

"Essentially zero," Perini replied. "After the last two conflicts with Russia, NATO members are weary of war. There will be no appetite to intervene on Ukraine's behalf. At least not militarily. Fortunately, you've already publicly outlined the repercussions of Russian aggression, and there will likely be support within NATO for extensive sanctions. Several countries may pose a challenge, however, due to their dependence on Russian energy. Our attempt to hit Russia where it hurts will also harm many of our allies."

"Resistance to harsh sanctions against Russia by some NATO members isn't a surprise," the president replied. "We've been working the issue, and hopefully we'll have a solution soon. When can we expect a NATO member-nation meeting?"

Perini replied, "An emergency meeting of the North Atlantic Council will occur within the hour, and the council representatives will likely recommend an immediate meeting with the heads of state from all thirty-two nations. I'll keep you informed as I learn more, but you should plan to travel to Brussels within the next twenty-four hours."

The president nodded his understanding. "We've got a lot of work ahead of us on the diplomatic front. Promulgate our proposed list of sanctions against Russia, plus military aid to Ukraine, to each NATO country by noon, and have our ambassadors begin liaising with their respective governments."

12

BALTIMORE, MARYLAND

Standing outside the entrance to Camden Yards, home of the Baltimore Orioles, Lonnie Mixell checked his watch: 5:58 p.m.

Brenda Verbeck had provided an unusual meeting address, which Mixell assumed was where she planned to pick him up. With the Baltimore Orioles in spring training in Sarasota, Florida, the area around Camden Yards was sparsely populated, with only occasional passing pedestrians. The mostly empty sidewalk would be helpful, Mixell surmised, since Brenda likely had no idea who she was meeting—he was just a faceless name and alias on the dark web.

Even if she knew who he was, he had altered his appearance before venturing into public. His hair had been dyed black and his eyes were blue due to a pair of contacts. His cheekbone structure had been altered by implants wedged high in his mouth on both sides, and his jawline was more pronounced because of additional implants outside his lower teeth—on the sides and in the front. Despite the altered appearance, the face in the mirror in his hotel room had still been quite handsome, he had to admit.

At exactly 6 p.m., a black limousine cruised to a halt before him. The front passenger window slid down and the driver called out to him.

"What's your name?"

"Mitch Larson."

The rear passenger door opened automatically. Mixell approached the vehicle and peered inside, finding the limousine unoccupied aside from the driver.

"Get in," the driver said. "I'll take you to Mrs. Verbeck."

After Mixell slid into the back seat, the door closed and the limo pulled back into traffic. Following a ten-minute drive deeper into Baltimore, the driver stopped alongside a block of small dilapidated storefronts.

The rear door opened again.

Mixell cast a curious look toward the driver, who pointed to a narrow stairway between two of the stores. He exited the car and made his way to the second floor, reaching the entrance to a restaurant. He entered a small foyer where he was greeted by an attractive Vietnamese woman wearing a red silk dress. After informing her that he was meeting Mrs. Verbeck for dinner, he followed the hostess through a busy dining area to a row of small rooms in the back, where he found Brenda waiting at a table for two, examining a menu.

The hostess handed Mixell a menu and departed, softly sliding the door closed behind her. Mixell took the seat across from Brenda, noting that it was quiet in the small alcove, with the only sound penetrating the door being the barely audible murmur of customer conversations.

Sitting across from Brenda, Mixell examined his potential employer. Before today, his closest view of her had been through the scope of his Steyr SSG 69 rifle. Up close, she was even more attractive, and there was a seductive quality to her that he couldn't put his finger on. Perhaps it was the confidence exuded by a woman who always got what she wanted. Her forced resignation as secretary of the Navy must have stung.

"Before we get into the details," Mixell said, "I want to ensure the payment amount wasn't a typo. One hundred million?"

"Not a typo. Ten million up front, ninety upon task completion."

There was a tap on the door, and it slid aside, revealing a waitress. She smiled demurely and placed two cups on the table, then filled them with tea. Brenda recommended several menu items, and after they placed their orders, the waitress departed, closing the door behind her.

"Do you eat here often?" Mixell asked.

"Not recently. But I used to eat here on occasion with my parents when I was a teenager."

"I like the place," Mixell remarked. "Nice ambiance, and I look forward to the food you recommended. In the meantime, how can I help you?"

"I must admit," Brenda said, "that I have reservations about hiring you, considering your failure to complete my brother's task."

"That's your brother's fault, not mine. The ship carrying the centrifuges was sunk because your brother slipped up, letting U.S. intelligence decipher what he had sold to Iran."

"True," Brenda conceded.

"However, I did accomplish *your* previous task, eliminating the Navy Pentagon chief and your military aide when you were secretary of the Navy, plus making the murder of your protective agent look like an attempt to assassinate you."

Brenda's eyes widened, which caught Mixell by surprise—she apparently hadn't known who had been contracted for the jobs.

"I didn't make those arrangements," she admitted. "An associate of mine did."

"A mutual friend of ours?"

"Not anymore. He took a bullet to his head."

"I see," Mixell replied, wondering who the friend had been.

"Well, Lonnie," Brenda said, using his real name, "I must commend you on your disguise."

Brenda had pieced the information together, although they weren't clues he had intended to provide. Authorities had identified Lonnie Mixell as the man who had attempted to assassinate the secretary of the Navy, and he had just revealed that he had been the man contracted for that job. Brenda knew she was sitting across from the most wanted man on the planet, but the revelation seemed not to faze the woman. Mixell's thoughts returned to her concern about his failure to complete her brother's task.

"I'll admit that I don't always succeed, and that my track record is about fifty-fifty. However, if you bat .500, you'll make it into the Baseball Hall of Fame."

"Quite true," Brenda replied.

She reached into her purse and withdrew an envelope, which she handed to Mixell. Inside was an itinerary.

"Hopefully, this will aid your endeavor."

It didn't take long for Mixell to realize whose itinerary it was, with occasional departures from Joint Base Andrews aboard Air Force One.

"You want me to assassinate the president of the United States?"

"Can you do it?"

Mixell leaned back in his chair. He had tried once before and failed. He'd been only seconds away from success, thwarted only by the unexpected arrival of Harrison and his sidekick Khalila. Given a second chance, he was confident he could do it. But the plan would have to be a novel one, something unexpected that could penetrate the president's protection.

"Getting even?" he asked.

Brenda nodded.

"I'm all about getting even," Mixell remarked. "I'm working a similar task at the moment."

"That's the most satisfying type of endeavor, isn't it?"

"It is," Mixell agreed. Brenda was truly a woman after his own heart.

The waitress returned, bearing food. After she placed the dishes on the table and departed, Mixell waited for Brenda to start before digging in. After Brenda placed the first forkful in her mouth and swallowed, she smiled.

Mixell grinned in return. Perhaps, after he was finished with Brenda's task plus his own, it would be time to settle down. Brenda's husband might be an issue, but it was a problem that could be easily dealt with.

13

MEDINA FALLS, ARKANSAS

Another weekend, another busy night at Irina's Diner.

Sarah Greenwood wrote down the latest order, dropping it off at the kitchen, returning with several plates of food balanced on one forearm. Her eyes briefly met Jake's as she passed by him, seated at a booth tonight. The counter had been full, but he still sat in a seat with a view of the front door, as usual.

For some reason, Sarah thought about Jake frequently, looking forward to their interactions during lunch and dinner. Thus far, however, no information had been pried from the stranger aside from his first name. Not even Miss Potter had been able to strike up a revealing conversation with him. Jake simply asked what she wanted done around house and yard and was paid in cash upon each task's completion. As far as Sarah could tell, Jake kept a low profile, leaving Miss Potter's property only to eat at the diner.

Although Jake was much older than her—in his forties, Sarah guessed—she found him quite handsome. At first, she had admonished herself for being attracted to someone so old. However, she had noticed that men had no qualms about dating much younger women, as long as they weren't *too* young. She was plenty old enough, she told herself again—she was in her twenties now.

At the moment, she wasn't in a relationship, having broken up with her previous boyfriend two months ago. She knew she was attractive enough to have had her pick of almost any of the available men around town, but her last choice had been an unwise one, selecting the handsome and popular former starting quarterback on their high school's football team. He had turned out to be the jealous and domineering type, monitoring where she went and with whom, even at times telling her what she could wear.

Unfortunately, Trent had trouble taking no for an answer. He was here tonight at a table with two of his buddies, pounding down Saturday night's half-priced beers after their dinner. His eyes were constantly on her, monitoring her movement through the diner. Trent had been polite and conciliatory at first tonight, commenting on how beautiful she looked and how much he missed her. She had smiled politely and kept her responses limited to what they wanted to order and nothing more.

She stopped by Jake's table. "Can I getcha anything more tonight?"

"A cup of coffee would be great."

Sarah was about to get Jake his coffee when she remembered it was half-priced beer night. Perhaps a few drinks would loosen his tongue.

"How about a beer? They're half-priced tonight."

"I'll stick with coffee."

"No problem," she replied, attempting to conceal her disappointment.

As she headed to the counter to get Jake's coffee, passing by Trent's table, he grabbed her wrist.

"What do you say we get together after work tonight?" he said, slurring his words slightly.

"You've had too much to drink," she replied. "Go home and sleep it off." She tried to pull away, but Trent clamped down on her wrist.

"Why so unfriendly tonight?" he asked.

"It's over, Trent," she said quietly, hoping not to cause a scene, as she tried to pry his hand off her wrist.

"It's over when I say it's over!" he said angrily, squeezing even tighter.

"You're hurting me," she said. "Please, Trent. Not here."

"Then hang out with me tonight."

"Stop it, Trent!"

Someone standing behind her spoke. "How's my coffee coming?"

She turned, spotting Jake.

Before she could respond, Trent replied, "She's busy! Have Irina get your coffee!"

"If I were you," Jake replied, his voice lowering a notch, "I'd take your hand off the lady."

"Oh, she's no lady, trust me. Besides, who's gonna make me?"

Trent glanced at his two friends, then stood, confronting Jake, while still gripping Sarah. Although Trent had been a quarterback, weighing around one hundred sixty pounds, his buddies were former football linemen, over two hundred pounds each. However, standing a few inches over six foot and also around two hundred pounds himself, Jake didn't back down.

He grabbed the hand holding Sarah, prying Trent's fingers away. Despite Trent's best effort, Jake freed Sarah from his grip.

As Sarah stepped back, Trent punched Jake, landing a blow squarely on his jaw.

Jake barely flinched, then responded with lightning-quick speed, decking Trent with a powerful blow to his face. Trent knocked over a table and some chairs as he fell, landing on his back as blood oozed from his nose.

His friends stood suddenly to engage Jake, but he stared both of them down.

Sarah's dad emerged from the kitchen, a meat cleaver in hand. "What's the commotion out here about?"

"It's nothing, Daddy," Sarah replied. "Trent just slipped and fell."

Sarah's dad eyed the bloodied man lying on the floor in front of Jake, with Sarah standing closely behind him.

"You should be more careful, Trent," he said. "Why don't you and your friends move along."

One of Trent's friends helped him up from the floor, while the other grabbed some napkins from the table to help stem Trent's nosebleed.

They helped Trent from the diner, where once outside, he shoved his friends away, yelling at them. After they moved down the sidewalk, disappearing from view, Sarah's dad locked eyes with Jake, then nodded slightly.

Jake reciprocated the nod, then returned to his seat.

Sarah tried to regain her composure, realizing tonight's event would be the topic of tomorrow's gossip. After all, nothing much ever happened in Medina Falls.

A few minutes later, Sarah delivered Jake's coffee, her hand shaking slightly.

"Have a seat," Jake said.

"Yeah, I could use a break," Sarah replied. She signaled her mom, informing her she'd be taking a break for a few minutes, then slid into the booth across from Jake.

"I'm sorry you had to step in like that," she said. "But thank you. It's just that . . . Trent's my ex-boyfriend, and he doesn't take rejection well. He's such a hothead."

"I know the type," Jake replied. "A former girlfriend of mine has a similar temperament."

He didn't elaborate, taking a sip of his coffee instead. Not for the first time, Sarah glanced at his left hand, which lacked a wedding ring, and wondered if there was a significant other in his life. Tonight was the first time Jake had said anything to her aside from what he wanted to eat or drink, and she hoped he might reveal more about himself.

"Relationships are hard," she said. "You have to work at them, I guess. Not that I have much experience." Her eyes searched his as she prepared to ask the question that had been on her mind lately.

"Are you in a relationship with anyone?"

Pain registered in the man's eyes instantly, the same look she'd seen the day he stepped off the bus in Medina Falls. Sarah immediately regretted prying into his personal life. But at least she knew what haunted him. Something horrible must have happened to his wife or girlfriend.

Without thinking, she placed her hand on his, caressing the back of his hand gently with her thumb. "If there's any way I can help, let me know."

A long silence ensued before Jake replied. "You can't help me. But thank you."

He gently removed her hand from his.

14

BRUSSELS, BELGIUM

Seven hours after departing Joint Base Andrews, Air Force One descended through gray, overcast skies, landing at Brussels-Zaventem Airport. The president was met on the tarmac by the U.S. ambassadors to Belgium and NATO, plus senior NATO staff and Belgian government representatives.

After the requisite greetings, the president slipped into the back of Cadillac One, which had been transported to Brussels during the night with the rest of the president's motorcade and backup vehicles. The motorcade traveled into Brussels, arriving at NATO's headquarters, identified by a twenty-three-foot-tall oxidized steel star, symbol of the North Atlantic Treaty Organization, in front of the building.

The president and his entourage were escorted to a lobby outside the Alliance's main conference room, where the leaders of NATO's other thirty-one countries were gathered. British Prime Minister Susan Gates was the first to greet the president.

"I've reviewed your proposal," Gates said. "We are of the same mind when it comes to sanctions and military aid. I've spoken with Chancellor Klein, and she affirmed that Germany shares the sentiment."

German Chancellor Lidwina Klein maneuvered her way across the lobby, joining the American president and British prime minister. The diminutive woman, barely five feet tall, shook the president's hand firmly.

"Gaining approval for the sanctions will be difficult," Klein said, "given that several member nations are highly dependent on Russian energy. While Germany has almost completely weaned itself from Russian oil and natural gas over the last decade, other countries have actually increased their dependence." She cast a glance at French President François Loubet.

"I'm conscious of the predicament created by my proposed sanctions," the president replied. "I've been working on the issue and believe I have a solution."

Before either Gates or Klein could inquire, the clock struck the appointed hour and the conference room doors opened. The thirty-two NATO leaders took their seats at a large round table with thirty-three chairs: one for the leader of each NATO country, and the final chair for the secretary general. The president inserted a wireless earpiece into his ear, listening to the English translator as the secretary general, Johan Van der Bie, a well-respected diplomat from the Netherlands, gave a short introductory speech. An update on Russia's invasion of Ukraine followed, with the information displayed on video screens mounted around the conference room perimeter.

Russian units surging southwest from Russia and north from Crimea had linked up, establishing a Russian-controlled corridor in the southeastern region of the country, bordering the Sea of Azov to the south. Fighting along the northern edge of the corridor was more intense than expected, with Ukrainian forces responding quicker and more effectively than during Russia's two previous invasions.

Following the secretary general's update, Van der Bie recognized Lithuania's president, ceding the floor to her. After a brief greeting, Dalia Grybauskaitė delivered a passionate plea for NATO intervention.

"Once again, Russia has trampled upon the sovereignty of a neighboring country. Much like Russia's attempt to annex part of Lithuania two years ago, Russia is attempting the same in Ukraine. I want to express my gratitude again to my fellow members who responded to our call for aid. Ukraine is not so fortunate, lacking membership in our powerful alliance. However, the international community has an obligation to assist Ukraine's effort to repel its invaders. NATO is a member of that international community, with the resources and proximity to lend that aid swiftly and effectively."

A glance around the table told the American president that there was little appetite for direct military intervention this time, specifically because Ukraine was not a NATO member. If any country could benefit from Alliance assistance, what was the point of being a NATO member?

Secretary General Van der Bie recognized a motion from French President François Loubet, who had requested to speak.

"To a large extent," Loubet began, "the conflict between Russia and Ukraine can be considered a territorial squabble, similar to Pakistan and India's dispute over Kashmir. Around the world, there are dozens of other territorial disputes that erupt into armed conflict. Does NATO get involved in each of these disputes? No, we *do* not, and *should* not. NATO refrains from military conflict unless the sovereignty of one of our member nations is infringed upon."

Loubet's eyes canvassed the leaders of his fellow NATO countries, stopping briefly on the U.S. president before continuing.

"I have reviewed the list of sanctions proposed by the United States. They are substantial, but there is no guarantee they would produce the desired effect. We have tried sanctions in the past—although not as comprehensive as these—and they have failed to influence Russian behavior. Additionally, we must consider the effect these sanctions will have on our own countries, many of which remain significantly dependent on Russian oil and natural gas. Succinctly stated, I do not have sufficient alternative energy resources or public support to confront Russia over this relatively minor transgression."

The French president ended his soliloquy with, "Unless a solution is presented that ensures a sufficient and uninterrupted supply of energy to France and other NATO countries, I cannot endorse sanctions that will do as much harm, or more, to my country than they do to Russia."

Numerous council members looked to the American president, who had taken the floor after Russia's invasion of Lithuania, pledging the United States' support. Britain and Germany had privately signaled their intention to support the proposed sanctions, but the president knew it would be a tough sell to other NATO members. The president had foreseen the resistance months ago, when he had decided to propose sanctions in response to Russian aggression, and had carefully prepared.

The American president requested to speak, and the secretary general turned the floor over to him.

He pulled the microphone in front of him closer. "Thank you, Mr.

Secretary General. Ladies and gentlemen, I'll keep my remarks short. Russia has invaded a sovereign nation again, and we have another decision to make. NATO's dependence on Russian energy is a threat to the viability of our Alliance, one that must be dealt with more effectively than we've done to date. That, however, is a long-term issue. In the short term, Ukraine requires—and *deserves*—our assistance.

"Regarding the proposed military equipment and financial aid to Ukraine in my proposal, there are no hard requirements. Each country will be free to determine the extent of equipment and funding provided, so I suspect there are no objections to this provision."

The president paused, offering the other leaders the opportunity to signal their disagreement. None did.

Continuing, the president confronted the key issue. "Regarding the economic sanctions, the goal is to throttle Russia's income and change their calculus, making it more beneficial for the Russians to withdraw from Ukraine than to occupy part of it. I realize that these sanctions will also curtail the flow of critical energy resources to NATO members, which is a repercussion that some governments find untenable. To address this, I have just reached an agreement with OPEC. While NATO's economic sanctions remain in place against Russia, OPEC will increase output sufficiently to offset the reduction in Russian imports. NATO countries will be able to obtain the energy we need, and without a significant price increase."

There were murmurs around the table; the president's revelation was being favorably received.

"Details of the agreement with OPEC will be provided to each member nation following this meeting."

The president shifted his gaze to French President François Loubet. After a long moment, Loubet nodded tersely.

Wrapping up his speech, the president finished with, "I request a vote on the proposed sanctions against Russia and aid to Ukraine by the close of business tomorrow."

General Secretary Van der Bie replied, "The United States has requested a vote on its proposal in thirty hours. Does anyone object?"

When no one did, the meeting was adjourned with a thud of Van der Bie's gavel.

15

MOSCOW, RUSSIA

In a Kremlin conference room, Chief of Staff Anton Kravtsov leaned back in his chair, waiting for President Dmitry Egorov's fury to run its course. The red-faced leader of the Russian Federation had just been briefed on the sanctions approved by NATO, along with their predicted impacts on government revenue and the country's economy. Oil and natural gas sales accounted for forty-five percent of federal government revenue each year—over fifteen trillion rubles.

NATO sanctions would cut that revenue by two-thirds, leaving a ten trillion ruble deficit unless sales to other customers could replace the lost demand, an unlikely event due to OPEC's agreement to supply the extra oil and natural gas that Western Europe and Turkey would need.

"I have to give the American president credit," Egorov said after his anger faded. "He followed through on his threat. Additionally, his agreement with OPEC insulates NATO countries from the impact their sanctions would have had. We must respond in a way that forces NATO to relax these sanctions. What options do we have?"

There was silence around the table until Defense Minister Andrei Grigorenko spoke.

"The agreement with OPEC presents an unexpected opportunity."

"How so?" Egorov asked.

"OPEC agreeing to increase output is only one part of the equation. Transporting that oil and natural gas to Western Europe is the other critical part. Pipelines into NATO countries are limited and already at full capacity. The additional energy must travel by ship, and ninety percent of oil and natural gas leaving the Persian Gulf passes through the Strait of Hormuz. At its narrowest point, the merchant ship transit lanes constrict to a six-mile-wide swath for the deep-draft oil and natural gas tankers. With the necessary intervention, we can strangle NATO's energy supply in repayment for their attempt to strangle our finances."

"How would we accomplish this?"

"Our surface Navy was ravaged during the battle with the American carrier task force in the Arabian Sea, but our submarine force remains a potent asset. With appropriate orders, we can sink every oil and natural gas tanker transiting the Strait of Hormuz until NATO acquiesces and terminates these economic sanctions."

"We need to think this all the way through," Foreign Minister Marat Trutnev remarked. "NATO will not sit idly by while we sink merchant ships in the Persian Gulf. The Americans will assign Navy assets to escort these tankers, which may neutralize our effort."

"I like the plan," Egorov interjected, "but I concede you have a point, Marat. The Americans will undoubtedly respond, but this presents us with an even better opportunity." Turning to Grigorenko, he asked, "With advanced planning, can we be prepared to defeat any American military attempt to thwart our plan?"

"We have sufficient assets, plus we also have an ally in the region— Iran. During our battle with the Americans in the Arabian Sea, Iran agreed to host Russian aircraft and missile batteries in their country, providing us with a critical advantage. Iranian assistance may again prove valuable. With your permission, I'll see what I can arrange."

"The Iranian alliance also provides us with an interesting option," President Egorov said. "To use an American idiom, blockading the Strait of Hormuz can be the stick, and our relationship with Iran can be the carrot."

Egorov was greeted by confused looks, so he explained. "We have the opportunity to create a crisis for the West that we are uniquely able to resolve. Iran desperately wants advanced high-speed gas centrifuges to speed up uranium enrichment for nuclear weapons. If Iran were to obtain these centrifuges, Russia would be uniquely positioned to influence Iran's use of these centrifuges, or perhaps activate a fatal flaw in their hardware or software. Of course, we would do so only in return for appropriate concessions by America and its allies."

His idea was met by several grins around the table.

To Grigorenko, the Russian president said, "During your discussion with the Iranians, offer these centrifuges to them as a token of our appreciation for their past—and future—assistance."

16

K-571 *KRASNOYARSK*

Vladivostok, with jagged snow-capped mountains rising in the background, is the largest Russian port on the Pacific Ocean. The eastern terminus of the Trans-Siberian Railway, the city is often envisioned by foreigners as an ice-covered Russian outpost in the Far East. However, the opposite is true, with titanic merchant vessels anchored in emerald-blue water and sleek white yachts rocking gently at their moorings. Vladivostok, which translates to "Ruler of the East," is also home to the Russian Navy's Pacific Fleet.

This morning, as a light mist crept down green knolls toward the submarine berths, Captain Second Rank Gavriil Novikov strode down the pier toward the pride of the Russian Fleet—K-571 *Krasnoyarsk*—the newest Yasen-class nuclear attack submarine. Commissioned only three months ago, it was manned by a handpicked veteran crew that had distinguished itself during sea trials in preparation for its maiden deployment. With ten bow-mounted torpedo tubes and ten vertical launch tubes, *Krasnoyarsk* was loaded with the newest and most advanced weaponry in the Russian Navy: forty Futlyar wire-guided torpedoes in the submarine's torpedo room and a mix of forty anti-surface and anti-air missiles in its vertical launch tubes.

Much of Novikov's crew was topside this morning preparing for the submarine's deployment next week. Several work parties were assisting with the food and spare parts loadouts, transferring the pallets of material from the pier into the submarine. *Krasnoyarsk*'s First Officer, Captain Third Rank Anton Topolski, was topside, supervising the loadout.

Novikov crossed the brow onto his submarine, where he was saluted by the topside watch, who announced the Captain's arrival over the shipwide intercom. Novikov was greeted by Topolski, the submarine's second-in-command.

"Good morning, Captain. All preparations are proceeding smoothly, but we are expecting a courier from Pacific Fleet within the hour."

"Do we know what information the courier will bring?"

"New orders, supposedly."

Novikov nodded his understanding, wondering why there would be a late change to *Krasnoyarsk*'s mission profile. The current plan took Novikov's crew east toward Hawaii, where *Krasnoyarsk* would undoubtedly encounter American warships striving to trail Russia's newest and most advanced submarine. Novikov's mission orders were clear and simple—detect and trail whichever American submarines crossed *Krasnoyarsk*'s path without being counter-detected, proving the superiority of Russian technology and submarine crew training.

After deciding to wait topside for the pending courier, Novikov monitored the stores loadout while Topolski dropped down into the submarine's interior via a nearby hatch. Not long thereafter came the Topside Watch's announcement:

"Commander, Pacific Fleet, arriving."

The report caught Novikov by surprise. It seemed *Krasnoyarsk*'s new orders were being delivered not by a standard courier, but by Admiral Pavel Klokov himself.

Novikov saluted Klokov after he crossed the brow onto the submarine.

"Welcome aboard *Krasnoyarsk*, Admiral."

Klokov returned the salute. "Your stateroom," was all he said.

A few minutes later, the two men entered Novikov's stateroom, a three-by-three-meter room containing only a narrow bed, a small desk, and a table seating two persons. Klokov closed the door, then settled into one of the chairs, motioning Novikov into the other with a wave of his hand. The admiral retrieved a manila envelope from his inside coat pocket, which he handed to Novikov.

Novikov unsealed the envelope and read his new orders. *Krasnoyarsk* was no longer traveling east; it was now headed west into the Persian Gulf.

The new destination was a surprise, but *Krasnoyarsk*'s revised mission profile was even more unexpected. Novikov looked up in shock.

"Do you have any questions?" Klokov asked. "I believe the orders are quite clear."

Admiral Klokov was correct. The orders were succinct and easily understood. Additionally, their deployment date was being moved up.

"Underway in two days?" Novikov asked.

"At the latest. Tomorrow, if possible."

17

USS *MICHIGAN*

A thick layer of fog clogged the Strait of Juan de Fuca as USS *Michigan* plowed through dark green water, the seas spilling over its bow before rolling down the sides of the long black ship. With Canada to the north and the Olympic Peninsula of Washington State to the south, Lieutenant Keith Ressler stood on the Bridge in the submarine's sail, assessing a fishing boat materializing from the fog ahead.

The submarine's commanding officer, Captain Murray Wilson, stood beside Ressler, binoculars to his eyes, likewise studying the contact that had been reported by the radar operator a few minutes ago. Standing behind them atop the sail, a lookout searched the fog for other contacts. But the fishing boat crossing in front of the submarine was the pressing concern, and Ressler decided to alter *Michigan*'s course to pass safely behind it.

Pressing the microphone in his hand, Ressler passed his order to the Control Room below.

"Helm, left ten degrees rudder, steady course two-six-zero."

Ressler turned aft to verify the order was properly executed, watching the top of the rudder, poking above the ocean's surface, shift in the desired direction. Behind the ship, the submarine's powerful propeller churned a frothy white wake as *Michigan* began its gentle turn to port.

Less than a week ago, *Michigan* had completed its maintenance refit, and resupplied with food, spare parts, and crew replacements, the former ballistic missile submarine had slipped from the Delta Pier at Naval Base Kitsap earlier this morning. After transiting the quiet waters of Hood Canal, *Michigan* had passed Port Ludlow and the Twin Spits before entering the Strait of Juan de Fuca.

The submarine's rudder returned to amidships, and Ressler monitored the fishing boat until it was no longer a collision threat, then altered course back to starboard. *Michigan* returned to its prescribed track through the strait, headed to the western Pacific for what would likely be a more suspenseful deployment than normal. Subsequent to Russia's invasion of Ukraine, *Michigan* had received new orders. It would enter the Black Sea, where its armament might play a decisive role.

Although *Michigan* had been built as a ballistic missile submarine, it was a far different ship today than when it was launched four decades ago. With the implementation of the Strategic Offensive Reductions Treaty, the Navy had converted the four oldest Ohio-class submarines into guided missile and special warfare platforms. Twenty-two of *Michigan*'s twenty-four missile tubes had been outfitted with seven-pack Tomahawk launchers—154 missiles total—with the remaining two tubes providing access to two Dry Deck Shelters attached to the missile deck, each one containing a mini-sub used to transport Navy SEALs miles underwater for clandestine operations. There were multiple scenarios where *Michigan*'s Tomahawk missile or two platoons of Navy SEALs might play a role in the Russia–Ukraine war.

After *Michigan* cleared the Strait of Juan de Fuca and entered the Pacific Ocean, a report from below echoed from the Bridge communications box.

"Bridge, Nav. Passing the one-hundred fathom curve."

Ressler acknowledged the report, then glanced at the Bridge Display Unit, checking *Michigan*'s progress toward the Dive Point.

"Shift the watch below decks," Wilson ordered. "Prepare to dive."

Ressler acknowledged the Captain's order as Wilson ducked down into the ship's sail, descending the ladder into Control. Ressler squinted at the sun, peeking through a break in the fog. It'd be six long months before he saw it again, aside from the occasional view through the submarine's periscope. Six months of fluorescent lighting and artificially controlled days and nights. Six months before *Michigan*'s crew returned home, greeted by their families waiting on the pier.

With his thoughts lingering on his wife and two daughters, Ressler flipped the switch on the Bridge box, shifting the microphone in his hand over to the shipwide 1-MC announcing circuit.

"Shift the watch below decks. Prepare to dive."

18

TEHRAN, IRAN

Russian Foreign Minister Marat Trutnev peered out the side window of his black sedan as it wound through the center of Tehran, home to a population of over nine million. Joining Trutnev in the back of the car was the Russian ambassador to Iran, Danil Morozov, who would translate during this afternoon's meeting with Trutnev's Iranian counterpart.

The sedan glided to a halt in front of Iran's foreign ministry building, where the Russians were greeted and escorted by Iranian diplomatic aides into Shahrbani Palace, which spread across twenty-one thousand hectares. Trutnev admired the building's architecture, inspired by the Apadana reception hall in Persepolis, where Achaemenid kings had greeted visitors and foreign dignitaries. He was escorted past a decorative frieze of ancient Persian soldiers and into the vaulted entrance supported by immense stone columns topped with ornately carved capitals. Despite the ancient heritage imbued in its exterior, the palace was commonly referred to as simply Building 9 of the House of Commons.

Trutnev and Morozov were led through the building, which was decorated with artistic mirrors and intricate stucco designs, entering a conference room belonging to the Iranian minister of foreign affairs. Minister Koorush Shirvani and a single aide joined the two Russians for the small, private meeting Trutnev had requested. Considering the topics of today's meeting, Trutnev found it fortunate that Iran's ministry of foreign affairs was now responsible for negotiations concerning Iran's nuclear weapons program, which had previously been carried out by Iran's Supreme National Security Council. Shirvani would be keenly interested in the arrangement Trutnev would propose today.

After the standard diplomatic pleasantries, with Morozov and his Iranian counterpart translating, Shirvani shifted to business. "I understand that your government has a proposal for us. What is the topic?"

Trutnev decided to delay a direct answer, providing instead a meandering response designed to stroke Shirvani's ego. "I must first reiterate Russia's sincere appreciation for your country's assistance during our recent conflict with the United States in the Arabian Sea. Providing access to Iranian territory and military bases for Russian air and missile forces created the advantage we needed while engaging the American Pacific Fleet." Trutnev avoided discussing the battle's outcome, which had eventually swung in America's favor.

Shirvani nodded his appreciation for Trutnev's words, and he also did not comment on the devastating losses Russia had incurred in the battle. All four of America's heavily damaged aircraft carriers had completed repairs and were back in service, while the bulk of the Russian Pacific Fleet's surface ships still rested on the bottom of the Arabian Sea.

The Iranian foreign minister replied, "Iran values and appreciates the support Russia has provided to our country in the past, and allowing Russian forces onto our land was the least we could do. Our assistance did not go unpunished, however. American and European sanctions were intensified, and we still feel those effects today. If you are here to discuss a similar arrangement as before, it is unlikely that your proposal will be well-received."

"I am aware of the potential difficulties my proposal may face," Trutnev replied. "But we request only a small task, and the reward will be great."

The promise of great reward elicited a raised eyebrow. "How can we assist?" Shirvani asked.

Trutnev went on to explain the single task Iran would need to complete and its timing. "Of course," he added, "we will provide the necessary equipment to conduct the effort."

The Iranian minister of foreign affairs considered Trutnev's request, then replied, "The Americans will eventually determine that Iran was responsible and will undoubtedly strike back militarily or economically. Russia will need to provide significant incentive for us to execute this task."

"How about one thousand gas centrifuges, the newest Russian design?"

Shirvani's eyes brightened at the offer. "What are the specifications?"

Trutnev looked to Ambassador Morozov, who opened a black leather satchel and retrieved a folder, which he gave to Shirvani.

"The centrifuge details are contained therein," Trutnev said. "I'm certain that you'll find these centrifuges far superior to anything you have in inventory or are designing."

Shirvani perused the first sheet in the folder, then leaned back in his chair, studying Trutnev. After a long moment, he replied, "I will see what I can arrange."

19

MEDINA FALLS, ARKANSAS

It was late in the afternoon on an unseasonably warm spring day when Sarah Greenwood, holding a plate in each hand, passed through the front gate of Miss Potter's antebellum-era estate. But instead of heading toward the front door, framed by two majestic white columns rising toward the portico roof, Sarah turned toward the cottage where Jake was staying.

Last weekend, Jake had intervened at the diner, freeing her from Trent's grip and knocking him to the ground. After her busy weekend shifts at the diner, Sarah had finally found time to prepare a thank-you gift for Jake. Unsure whether she should bake a pie or cookies, she had settled on both, and one hand held a still-warm cinnamon apple pie while in the other rested a platter of chocolate chip cookies.

Sarah had initially been embarrassed at how forward she had been with Jake that night, caressing his hand. But after further reflection, she decided she had done nothing wrong. She liked Jake and wondered if there was a possibility they might get together once Jake worked through whatever had happened in his previous relationship.

After debating whether she should let the matter take its natural course or attempt to influence its outcome, she had decided on the latter. There was nothing wrong with working toward something she wanted. To that end, her mom had mentioned on occasion that there were two ways to a man's heart, and that one of them was through his stomach. She had never mentioned the other way, but Sarah had figured that part out on her own. For now, however, she would focus on food.

When she reached the cottage door, she balanced the plate of cookies on one forearm, then knocked. There was no response. She knocked again, and still no one answered. Disappointed, she went to Miss Potter's house to drop off the food, but she wasn't home either.

Sarah didn't want to head back home with the pie and cookies, and wondered if it would be okay if she left them in Jake's cottage, leaving a note saying they were from her. After returning to the cottage, she turned the doorknob—it was unlocked—and called inside for Jake. There was no response.

She entered the small cottage, which featured a combined living room, dining room, and kitchen in the front, and a bedroom and bathroom in the back. After placing the pie and cookies on the dining room table, she looked around, searching for a pen and piece of paper. Or even better, something that might provide a clue to Jake's identity and what had brought him to Medina Falls. After spotting nothing noteworthy, she decided to check the bedroom. At the diner, Jake always paid with cash, pulling the bills from a pocket; he didn't seem to even carry a wallet. But he must have one, and if she could find it, there would undoubtedly be a driver's license or credit card with his name on it.

The bed was neatly made up and there were a few shirts and pairs of pants hanging in the closet, plus a shaving kit in the bathroom. But there was no sign of the backpack he had stepped off the bus with. As she stood with her hands on her hips, wondering where it might be, she heard sounds coming from outside, behind the cottage. Through the bedroom window, she spotted Jake in the backyard, replacing a section of Miss Potter's fence.

Sarah approached the bedroom's back wall, being careful to stay out of Jake's view in case he happened to look her way, then peered at him from the side of the window. He had his back to her, digging holes for new fence posts. It was a warm day and he had taken his shirt off. Sarah couldn't help but notice his muscular back and shoulders, slim waist, and nice butt. What caught her attention even more, though, were the scars on his back. She had never seen anything like them in real life, but she had in the movies: two bullet wounds, one behind each shoulder.

She sucked in a sharp breath, wondering what type of man Jake really was. He clearly lived on the more dangerous side of the tracks, but was he a good guy—maybe a policeman or military veteran—or a criminal? Maybe even a highly wanted fugitive, hiding out from the law in

Medina Falls. Her curiosity had spurred her desire to learn more about Jake, and now her concern provided extra motivation. If only she could find his wallet.

Turning around, she scanned the bedroom again for his backpack; it was nowhere to be found. She searched the closet more closely, finding nothing, then decided to check under the bed.

Jackpot.

She pulled the backpack out and unzipped the top, revealing more clothes stuffed inside. She searched through the garments until her hand touched something cold and hard. Pulling the item from the backpack, her eyes went wide as she stared at a semiautomatic pistol in her hand. Placing it carefully on the bed beside her, she searched further, finally locating Jake's wallet. Inside was a driver's license, which she pulled out and examined.

At last, Sarah had a name to go with his face.

Jake Edward Harrison.

As she stared at his photo on the ID, Sarah's sixth sense gnawed at her. It took a few seconds to realize that the sound of Jake digging postholes in the backyard had ceased. She hurried to the window, spotting Jake walking toward the cottage; he was already halfway there.

She stuffed Jake's wallet and pistol into the backpack and shoved it under the bed, then, after a quick glance to ensure she hadn't disturbed anything else in the bedroom during her search, returned to the dining room. With her pulse racing, she stopped beside the table just as Jake entered the cottage.

He stopped suddenly after spotting her, his eyes skimming the cottage before settling back on Sarah.

"What are you doing here?"

"I was just—" She tucked a curl of hair behind one ear, then pointed to the plates on the table. "I baked something for you. To thank you for helping me with Trent at the diner. You and Miss Potter weren't home, so I thought I'd drop it off. Your door was unlocked . . ." She stopped talking and forced a smile.

Jake glanced at the pie and cookies, then shifted his gaze back to Sarah. It looked as if he was debating how to respond, and Sarah waited tensely as her heartbeat pounded in her ears. She fought the urge to flee the cottage, realizing it was hopeless if the situation took a sinister turn; he was still at the door, blocking the only escape point.

After a long moment, he finally spoke. "Thank you."

He stepped aside, gesturing toward the door.

Relief washed over Sarah. "I hope you enjoy them," she managed to say as she moved toward the door.

As she passed by, Jake gently grabbed her arm, stopping her.

"A word of advice," he said. "In the future, don't be so . . ." He paused, searching for the right word. ". . . *unguarded* around strangers. Understand?"

There was a darkness in his eyes again.

Sarah nodded, then he released her.

After she exited the cottage and reached the street, her heart rate slowly returned to normal.

After returning home, Sarah immediately sat down before the computer, typing Jake's name into the internet browser. The search returned only a few results.

The first few were local news snippets concerning Jake's performance on a high school football team in Fayetteville, Iowa, which is where he appeared to have grown up. Then an article about him enlisting in the Navy after graduation. Sarah felt relieved, learning that he had served in the U.S. Navy, which must have been how he received the bullet wounds.

There was nothing more on Jake until sixteen years ago: an engagement photo in the local Fayetteville newspaper, with Jake beside an attractive woman. Then another gap until a few months ago, when he was mentioned in an obituary for his wife, Angeline. There was no mention, however, of how she had died.

Sarah pondered the newfound information, convinced she had solved the mystery of Jake Edward Harrison—a military veteran hiding out in Medina Falls as he dealt with the tragic loss of his beloved wife.

Her heart went out to him.

20

LANGLEY, VIRGINIA

"We got a hit."

It was almost quitting time when Tracey McFarland, the CIA's deputy director for analysis, stopped by Christine O'Connor's seventh-floor office, delivering the news.

"Someone did an internet search for Jake Edward Harrison this afternoon."

"From where?" Christine asked, looking up from her desk.

"A small town in southern Arkansas. Medina Falls."

"Who did the search?"

Tracey pulled a sheet from a folder in her hand, providing it to Christine as she explained.

"Someone at the residence of George Greenwood. The options are George, his wife Irina, or daughter Sarah. All three work at a restaurant in Medina Falls called Irina's Diner. Looks like Jake stopped by for a bite to eat and left enough of an impression to spark someone's curiosity."

Christine's eyes narrowed. "Something's not right. There's no way Jake would provide his full name to someone after dropping off the grid, and he certainly isn't stupid enough to let someone see a credit card or ID with his name on it." After pondering the issue, she asked, "Do you have anything else on these Greenwoods and Medina Falls?"

Tracey smiled as she handed the folder to Christine. "The top sheet has photos of the Greenwoods. The rest is pretty dry stuff about their backgrounds and the town."

As Christine perused the information, Tracey provided the highlights.

"The Greenwoods own a family diner. Dad's the cook and the mom and daughter serve the customers. The town's population is nine hundred twelve. Russian ethnicity thirty-two percent, with first generation immigrants comprising fifteen percent."

Christine looked up as Tracey added, "I thought you'd find the town statistics interesting, given that you and Jake are from a small town in Iowa about the same size as Medina Falls, also with a sizeable ethnic Russian population."

"He's not passing through the town," Christine concluded. "He's hiding out there. Feels like home."

Tracey agreed. "That's my assessment as well. Should I send someone to present our employment offer?"

After considering the suggestion, Christine decided otherwise. "I'll go. There are a few things that Jake and I need to iron out before he'll agree to return to the agency. Can you have Support make travel arrangements? I'll clear my calendar and depart tomorrow morning."

Tracey grinned. "I've already got Becky working on it. When it comes to Jake, you're far too predictable."

Christine leaned back in her chair, assessing Tracey's observation.

"Yeah, I suppose you're right."

21

LANHAM, MARYLAND

As Lonnie Mixell stepped from the hotel room shower, his cell phone on the desk vibrated. He unlocked the screen, and a notification appeared, informing him he had received an encrypted message. After drying off with a towel and pulling on underwear and a pair of shorts, Mixell launched the application and read the message:

The package you're interested in has been located.

Mixell typed his response. "Where?"

Medina Falls, Arkansas.

Mixell smiled. After Angie's funeral, Mixell had decided that Harrison had suffered enough and it was time to put him out of his misery. But Harrison had disappeared the next day, seemingly knowing that Mixell was coming for him.

Making oneself disappear was a challenging endeavor, and Mixell had been confident that it would only be a matter of time before Harrison surfaced somewhere. One of Mixell's former business partners had the necessary capabilities, and for a modest cost, Mixell had arranged for the surveillance of every transportation hub and internet post, searching for the face or name of his former best friend. Mixell was surprised, however, that Harrison had slipped up so soon, only a few weeks after disappearing following Angie's funeral.

Mixell had been there, watching the funeral from under a tree across the street, wearing a gray overcoat and wide-brimmed hat, his eyes fixed on Harrison as Angie was lowered into her grave.

He had paid Harrison back for killing Trish.

Even now, Mixell could clearly remember the night he killed Angie. The look of utter despair and helplessness on Harrison's face had been priceless. As satisfying as that had been, the best part had been the way Angie had trembled in his grasp like a frightened rabbit, the way her body had stiffened in shock and horror when the knife sliced into her neck . . .

Mixell looked up, catching his reflection in the wall mirror, and noticed he was smiling. The smile faded, but the memory remained.

Trish had been avenged, but there were still two more debts to collect: from Harrison, for the betrayal that had put him in prison for eight years, and from Christine, for aligning with Jake and thwarting his recent plans, costing him fifty million dollars in unpaid fees, since he had not completed the assigned task. Taking care of Harrison would be a straightforward task once he was located. Being the CIA director, Christine was more problematic, but Mixell was confident that an opportunity for revenge would eventually present itself.

Mixell's thoughts returned to Angie's funeral, where he had spotted Christine off to the side instead of near Harrison as he had expected. The two had been inseparable in high school. Even when Christine left for college and Harrison joined the Navy, they managed to return home at the same time and were rarely seen apart. There had been no doubt in Mixell's mind that they would end up together.

He now felt obliged to arrange it; not in marriage, but together in a shallow grave.

22

MEDINA FALLS, ARKANSAS

It was just after ten in the morning, during the lull between breakfast and lunch, as Sarah Greenwood finished rolling the last few sets of silverware inside their napkins. As she placed the utensils in their bin in preparation for lunch, a shiny black SUV stopped outside the diner. A man wearing a black suit emerged from the front passenger seat and opened the rear passenger door.

An attractive woman in her forties stepped onto the sidewalk, carrying a brown leather satchel. She wore a business suit—a dark blue jacket and skirt, tailored to accent her figure, paired with a light blue blouse. The woman looked around for a moment, studying the storefronts along the street, then entered the diner, accompanied by the man who had opened the car door for her. She stopped just inside the restaurant, waiting a moment while her companion's eyes scoured the diner, then walked toward Sarah.

As the woman approached, Sarah examined her closely. Sarah had known since she was a teenager that she was attractive, but in a plain-Jane sort of way compared to the woman before her. Sarah was pretty, while the woman was *beautiful*—elegant and refined. The perfect haircut and highlights, wearing tailored clothes and designer shoes. The outfit she was wearing probably cost more than Sarah's entire wardrobe.

When the woman reached the counter, she pulled a photograph from the satchel and placed it on the counter. It was a picture of Jake.

"I'm looking for this man. Do you know where I can find him?"

Throughout Sarah's interactions with Jake, he had given the distinct impression he didn't want to be found.

She examined the photograph. "I can't say that I do, ma'am. He doesn't look familiar."

The woman pulled a sheet of paper from her satchel and placed it on the counter beside the photo. On the paper were three pictures—of Sarah, her mom, and her dad.

"One of these three," the woman said, "did an internet search for this man, Jake Edward Harrison, yesterday from your home. Based on the websites that were visited after this search—a trendy makeup site followed by a women's clothing store, which included a search for size four dresses—my guess is that it was you. Would you like to answer my question again?"

Sarah swallowed hard. How did this woman know the websites she had visited?

Who was she?

The woman tapped a finger on Jake's picture.

"Now that I think about it, ma'am"—Sarah cleared her throat—"he does look familiar. Jake . . . yeah, Jake. That's his name, I think."

Looking up from the photo, Sarah glanced at the man who had entered the diner with the woman. He had settled onto a counter stool near the back—the same seat that Jake selected whenever it was unoccupied, one which offered a clear view of the front door. A second man, dressed identically to the first, had stepped from the SUV and was standing outside, surveying the street in both directions.

"Do you know where I can find him?" the woman asked.

Sarah decided to provide an indirect answer, hoping she could somehow slip away and warn Jake that someone was looking for him.

"He normally comes in for lunch at around noon."

"I'd rather not wait until then," the woman said. "Where is he staying? There's no hotel in town, so he must be staying with a local."

Sarah hesitated, trying to concoct another evasive answer, but the woman interrupted her thoughts.

"I know how things work in a small town like this. Everybody knows everyone else's business, and I have no doubt that you know where Jake is staying." She glanced at the two men with her. "We'll eventually find him, and if it turns out you knew where he was staying and refused to tell me, there's a legal term for the charge—*obstruction.*"

Sarah's stomach knotted at the implication, being charged for obstructing justice somehow, although it didn't seem like the woman and her two companions were police officers.

"There's no need to be concerned," the woman said in a softer tone. "I'm a friend of Jake's and have known him his entire life. I know he's hiding out here, getting away from things for a while, but something important has come up and we need to talk."

Unsure whether the woman was telling the truth, Sarah searched for a way to confirm her story—that she had supposedly known Jake his entire life—then recalled the two bullet wounds she had seen on his back when she had dropped off the pie and cookies at his cottage.

"You've known Jake his entire life? Then what kind of scars does he have on his back?"

Her question elicited a raised eyebrow from the woman, followed by a wry smile, as she probably wondered how Sarah had seen Jake's bare back. Then the woman took a step back from the counter and pulled her skirt up a few inches, exposing a scar on her right thigh.

"Two bullet wounds, like this," she said. "One behind each shoulder."

Sarah let out a slow breath. Clearly, she knew Jake well. *Very* well. Sarah also realized that she was dealing with a woman who had been shot at least once, and might have shot others.

"He's staying in Miss Potter's guest cottage. Her house is a few blocks that way," Sarah said, pointing to her left, "on the other side of the street. A large white house with blue shutters."

"Thank you," the woman said as she slid her skirt back down, then collected the photos on the counter, returning them to her satchel.

The woman and her two companions returned to their SUV, which did a quick U-turn and headed toward Miss Potter's house.

Despite the woman's assurance that she was Jake's friend, Sarah wanted to warn him, but there was no way she could get to Miss Potter's before the woman. She would have called, but Jake had never provided his phone number, and now that she thought about it, she had never seen him use a mobile phone, nor had she discovered one while searching his cottage.

With a protective agent beside her, Christine O'Connor knocked on the cottage door. She noticed one of the front curtains pulling back slightly as a man inside examined his unexpected guests. A moment later, Jake Harrison opened the door.

Christine considered asking if she could come inside, but based on her most recent interactions with Jake, there was a high probability he'd say no. Instead, she chose not to give him that opportunity.

"Something has come up," she said as she moved past him into the cottage. She stopped and faced him. "We need to talk."

Harrison stared at Christine's protective agent, who had moved forward when Christine stepped inside, but was still at the front door.

"Jake and I will talk in private," she said to her agent.

The man nodded and returned to the SUV, but Jake kept the door open, his hand still on the knob. She met his gaze without flinching. One way or another, this conversation was *going* to happen.

Finally, he closed the door and gestured toward a dining room chair, then took one opposite her.

As Jake settled into his seat, Christine noted his lean appearance. Physically, he had lost a good deal of weight while recovering from the two chest wounds and the subsequent surgery. From a psychological standpoint, Christine didn't need to be a counselor to know that Jake had been damaged in a significant way by Angie's death. She could only imagine the visions, anguish, and guilt he had to deal with.

"What do you want?" he asked.

"Hello to you, too, Jake."

"Dispense with the pleasantries, Chris. I didn't ask you to come here, and I don't want you here."

"Alright, I'll get straight to the point. Lonnie has resurfaced. He was the assassin who killed the secretary of defense."

"You *lied* to me," he said. "You told me Lonnie was dead when you knew he was alive and had escaped."

"What did you expect me to do? While you were lying in a hospital bed grieving for Angie, did you really want to know that the man who killed your wife had escaped? I was planning to tell you later—I wasn't trying to hide it from you. I just wanted to give you some time."

"How did Lonnie get away? Why did you let him live?"

Christine pulled back; she couldn't believe what she was hearing. "*Let* him live? Is that what you think? That I let Lonnie go?" She leaned forward, tamping down on her rising anger. "I realize you lost a lot of blood that night, but that's no excuse for your deranged accusation."

Jake waved her response away. "If you're here to ask me to return to the agency, I'll save you the spiel—I'm not interested."

"You can't keep hiding like this."

"I'm not hiding. I'm keeping Maddy safe."

"The best way to ensure her safety is to kill or imprison Lonnie."

"I already tried that. Angie warned me about returning to the agency to help hunt him down. I told her not to worry. I *promised* her that she and Maddy would be safe. See how that turned out? I should have listened to Angie, but you just couldn't let me be. You had to drag me back into the agency. As far as I'm concerned, you're the reason Angie is dead. I meant what I said in the hospital—I don't ever want to see or hear from you again. You apparently have a comprehension problem."

It was clear that Jake was still in an irrational state of mind, blaming Christine for Angie's death when it was Mixell who had driven the knife into her neck. But she had to admit that he was partially right. If she hadn't convinced him to join the CIA, enlisting his help to track down Mixell, Trish wouldn't have died at Jake's feet, and Angie wouldn't have died in Jake's arms. Christine decided to concede his point.

"You're right," she replied. "It's my fault for dragging you into this. We've had some unfortunate setbacks, but we need to finish this."

Harrison's face lit up in anger. "Angie's death was an unfortunate *setback*?"

"That's not what I meant."

He leaned forward, his voice dropping a notch. "You destroy everything you touch."

"Could you be more specific?" Christine asked tersely.

"Dave, dead on your kitchen floor. Brackman, dead at Ice Station Nautilus. And Angie—" His voice choked with emotion.

Harrison's words evoked images of the confrontation with her ex-husband a few years ago, culminating with him straddling her waist while she lay on the kitchen floor, trying to drive a knife through her neck. Then of Captain Steve Brackman aboard a submarine torpedoed beneath the polar ice cap, sacrificing his life while closing a watertight compartment door, trapping him on the wrong side as the submarine flooded.

His accusation cut into her. "That's so unfair, Jake, blaming me for their deaths. None of them were my fault."

"What about Huan in Beijing and Gorev in Russia? I've known you my entire life and witnessed it many times—your tendency to turn vicious in the heat of the moment, remorseful for your actions the next morning."

Images flashed in Christine's mind, one of her putting a bullet into the head of a defenseless man kneeling at her feet in China's Great Hall of the People. Then a scene on the coast of the Black Sea, where she had jammed a pistol into the mouth of Semyon Gorev, director of Russia's Foreign Intelligence Service, then pulled the trigger, blowing his brains out. In both cases, there had been alternatives. But in the first case, killing Huan had seemed the most effective, and the option chosen in the second case had been the most gratifying. Later, she had regretted her actions, taking the lives of defenseless men.

Jake's words hit close to home, igniting Christine's rage. Her voice followed her temper as it rose.

"If you want to play the blame game, the blood I've spilled is *your* fault!" She jabbed a finger at him. "*You* started it in China. *You* put a flash drive in one of my hands and a pistol in the other, then shoved me onto a ledge to finish the job. Everything I've done from that point on is *your* fault!"

She set her jaw and looked away. He had hit her where it hurt; he knew she was ashamed of what she had done.

There was a strained silence between them until Harrison replied in a softer tone. "I'm sorry, Chris. I shouldn't have said that."

Jake waited quietly as Christine's temper ran its course. When she turned to face him, his eyes searched hers. As her anger faded, she noticed the plate of homemade chocolate chip cookies and the pie on the table.

"You've taken up baking?"

"A friend dropped them off."

"Let me guess—Sarah from the diner?"

"Yeah. She had an altercation with her ex-boyfriend and I helped her out. This was her thank-you."

Christine considered asking him how Sarah knew about the scars on his back, but decided otherwise. What Jake did in his personal life was none of her business.

"How's Maddy?" Jake asked.

"As well as can be expected. She misses her dad."

"It's safer this way. When Lonnie finds me again, I don't want Maddy anywhere near me."

"Hanging out in Medina Falls isn't the best way to handle the issue. Do you plan to spend the rest of your life hiding while Maddy grows up without her father? She's already lost her mother. She *needs* you."

Christine waited a few seconds for her last comment to sink in, then continued. "The faster we find Mixell and plant him six feet under or behind bars, the sooner Maddy can have her dad back. Come back to the agency. Help us find Mixell."

He seemed to be considering her offer, so she added, "Help me track Lonnie down, and when we do, I swear this to you—if it's within my power, we aren't going to take him alive."

Jake contemplated Christine's job offer a moment longer, then nodded. "Give me a few minutes to pack."

Christine stood and started toward the door, then stopped beside him and placed a hand on his shoulder. "It'll be good to have you back."

MEDINA FALLS, ARKANSAS

Walking home in the dark after her evening shift, Sarah's thoughts dwelt on Jake and the woman who had come to town looking for him. That the woman was someone important and powerful was obvious, but her relationship with Harrison, and for what reason she had come to see him in Medina Falls, was unclear.

Sarah looked around at the strange houses along the street, suddenly realizing she wasn't on her way home. While lost in her thoughts, she had subconsciously headed toward Jake's cottage. She was only a block away now, so she decided to stop by, attempting to conjure a reason for her visit. Perhaps she could ask if he liked the desserts she had baked for him.

As the cottage came into view, she noticed that the only illumination inside was a night-light, faintly illuminating the kitchen and dining room. Perhaps Jake was already asleep or out somewhere. She knocked on the door in case he was home and still awake, reading or watching TV in his bedroom. But there was no answer. Peering through the window, she spotted her pie and cookies on the dining room table. He hadn't touched the pie and it looked like he hadn't eaten a single cookie.

There were several lights on inside Miss Potter's house, so Sarah knocked, hoping she knew where Jake was. The elderly woman answered the door.

"Hi, Miss Potter. I was wondering if you knew if Jake was home or out somewhere."

"Oh, he's gone. He left this afternoon with another woman. He said he wouldn't be back."

Sarah's heart sank, accompanied by a knot in her throat and ache in her chest. The physical reaction must have been evident, because Miss Potter's face softened.

"My dear, I'm certain that Jake was quite fond of you. He gave me a message for you."

Sarah brightened at the news. "What did he say?"

"He wanted me to thank you again for the pie and cookies, and tell you he was sorry that he didn't have time to enjoy them."

Jake's message didn't really help. He was gone and wasn't coming back.

After bidding Miss Potter goodnight, Sarah headed home, fighting back tears of disappointment. She tried to turn her grief into anger, telling herself that her interest in Jake had been a fool's errand. What had she been thinking, being interested in a man twice her age? She'd been fortunate that nothing had come from it. In fact, she wished that Jake had never come to Medina Falls.

A few blocks from home, Sarah spotted a strange car parked alongside the curb, in the shadows between the two nearest streetlights. A man emerged from the vehicle as Sarah approached.

"Excuse me, miss," he said. "I'm looking for a friend of mine named Jake. Can you tell me where he is?"

As Sarah prepared to answer, Jake's last words to her flashed in her mind: *In the future, don't be so unguarded around strangers.*

"I'm sorry," she said. "I don't know anyone named Jake."

"That's strange," the man said as he moved onto the sidewalk, blocking the path to her house. "Several people told me that you knew him well. He stopped by the diner every day. A new guy in town, tall, about my build. Ring a bell?"

Sarah felt a deepening uneasiness, and seriously doubted the man was Jake's friend. After pretending to think for moment, she replied, "Nope. I don't know anyone named Jake or matching your description."

The man offered a tight smile.

It was at this moment that Sarah realized the man was wearing a light jacket, even though it was a warm evening. Looking closer, she spotted a bulge under the jacket on his left side. She had seen enough movies to realize the bulge might be a pistol in a shoulder holster. The man followed her eyes, then his smile faded as he reached inside his jacket.

Sarah bolted to her left, running from a man who likely had nefarious intentions. Glancing over her shoulder, she spotted him sprinting after her.

She cut through a neighbor's yard, hurtling over a low chain link fence, hoping to reach her house before the man caught up to her. But she hadn't had much of a head start and he was gaining on her. He was only a few paces behind her when she realized it was hopeless—there was no way she could escape him. She started screaming for help, but seconds later, the man tackled her on the grass and pinned her body beneath his, clamping one hand over her mouth as he placed the pistol barrel against her head.

"I only want information," he said. "Nothing more. Understand?"

As her heart thumped inside her chest, she nodded.

"I'm going to ask you one more time. Where is Jake? I stopped by Miss Potter's cottage and he wasn't there. Where is he?"

He removed his hand.

"I don't know," she said. "A woman arrived today and he left with her."

"This woman, what did she look like?"

"A white woman in her forties. Beautiful, with auburn hair and blue eyes."

The man scowled. "Chris," he said under his breath.

He stood, offering his hand to help Sarah up.

Afraid to decline his assistance, she took his hand and he pulled her to her feet.

"Listen up," he said. "You're going to forget everything that happened tonight. That I came looking for Jake. Understand?"

Sarah nodded vigorously. "Never saw you," she said.

"Good. Now why don't you run along?"

She stood there for a second until he gestured with his hand. "Get going."

Sarah started toward her house, only a block away. After a few steps, she began running, hoping to put distance between her and the man as soon as possible.

As Sarah sprinted away, Mixell pulled a suppressor from its holster, screwing it onto the pistol barrel.

There was only one way to ensure Sarah told no one about what happened tonight—that he was hot on Harrison's trail.

He straightened his arm, aiming at his prey. Just before the woman disappeared into the darkness, he pulled the trigger. The woman's head jolted forward as the bullet drilled through the back of her skull. Her limp body hit the ground face-first, leaving a bloody smear on the grass as she slid several feet.

It had been a quick and painless death, Mixell noted to himself. And Harrison had once accused him of being a heartless killer.

24

NATANZ, IRAN

On the western side of the new Natanz Underground Complex, Behrouz Khavari watched a stream of transport trucks passing through one of the facility's entrances. Beside him stood Saeed Masud, director of the sprawling complex built deep beneath the Kūh-e Kolang Gaz Lā mountain peak. Although Masud wore a stoic expression, Khavari could sense the excitement radiating from the sixty-year-old man.

They were standing at one of four entrances to Natanz's newest and most protected complex, built in response to several successful attempts to sabotage Iran's nuclear weapons program. Within the complex were two critical facilities: the replacement Centrifuge Fabrication Center and a new Fuel Enrichment Plant, the latter of which would process uranium to weapon-grade purity.

Several years ago, the previous centrifuge assembly center, an aboveground facility in the main Natanz complex to the north, had been destroyed by an explosive device planted by saboteurs. Combined with the introduction of a computer virus that had caused thousands of Iran's gas centrifuges to overspeed, tearing themselves apart, leadership had concluded that a more secure and protected nuclear complex was required—one that was immune to even the most potent cyber or conventional weapons.

After the last truck entered the underground complex, the massive steel doors slowly rumbled closed, encasing Khavari and Masud in a concrete tunnel illuminated by harsh white fluorescent lighting. The two men entered into a two-person transport vehicle and followed the trucks to the lower of two main levels in the underground complex, where the truck contents were being unloaded: one thousand Russian gas centrifuges, significantly more advanced than any centrifuge Iran had built to date. Iran's uranium enrichment efforts, which had slowed to a crawl after the destruction of the aboveground centrifuge facility, would be jump-started by the Russian centrifuges.

Khavari and Masud's vehicle stopped at the unloading dock, and the two men entered the main hall on the fuel enrichment level where they watched the installation of the first batch of Russian devices. On the concrete floor, spaced every five feet, were hexagon-shaped holes that would anchor the sixteen-foot-tall centrifuges. While Masud stood beside him filled with excitement, Khavari did his best to hide the dread gnawing at him. With these new centrifuges, Iran could process uranium to weapon-grade purity eight times faster than before.

Turning to Masud, Khavari asked, "How long before we have enough weapon-grade uranium for our first nuclear weapon?"

Masud didn't reply, smiling instead.

25

OWINGS MILLS, MARYLAND

In the back of Christine's armored SUV, neither she nor her companion said much during the trip north toward Baltimore. Moments earlier, she had picked up Jake Harrison after his arrival at Baltimore/Washington International Airport. Although they were back on speaking terms, their relationship remained strained. Despite their conversation in Medina Falls, Christine could tell that Harrison still blamed her for Angie's death, at least in part. It would take time, Christine told herself again, to fully repair their relationship. To that end, she had offered to pick Jake up upon his arrival in Maryland and join him as he attended to his most important mission upon returning to the East Coast—visiting Maddy.

Thus far, Mixell had shown no interest in taking his vengeance out on Harrison's daughter. The night Mixell killed Angie in her home, he had first sent Maddy upstairs, ordering her not to leave her bedroom until morning. However, Maddy had ventured downstairs after hearing the shots Mixell fired, putting two bullets into Harrison. When Maddy intervened as Mixell was about to slay Christine, Mixell had knocked the young girl unconscious in a fit of rage, fracturing her skull in the process.

Even though Mixell had displayed no intent to include Maddy in his retribution, Harrison wasn't taking any chances, ensuring his daughter would be nowhere near him during his next confrontation with his former best friend. Prior to Harrison's disappearance a few weeks ago, he had arranged for Maddy to stay with his parents inside a gated, guarded community. Christine had assisted, assigning a four-person team to watch over the girl.

Upon reaching I-695, Christine's SUV traveled clockwise around the Baltimore Beltway until speeding outward on I-795 toward Owings Mills, eventually stopping before a tall metal gate. After the guard verified Harrison was on the visitor list, the CIA vehicle pulled forward, parking in front of a four-story condominium. As Christine and Harrison headed toward the building, Christine knew that two members of Maddy's protective detail were somewhere nearby, monitoring the approach to the condominium entrance.

After knocking on the second-floor door, Harrison's father answered, embracing his son in a short but firm hug. Jake had called ahead, letting his parents know he was coming, but it appeared they hadn't told Maddy in case the planned meeting fell through. Sitting on the couch watching television, the young girl's eyes went wide upon seeing her dad. She raced across the living room, jumping into her father's arms. Harrison lifted her off her feet, holding her tightly for a while before lowering her back to the floor.

Harrison greeted his mother with a long hug, then Christine and Jake joined Maddy and her grandparents at the dining room table. At first, the four adults barely got a word in as the girl rattled on about how much she missed her dad, what her new school was like and the new friends she had made there, ending with a series of questions: where had her dad been, how long would he back, and when would they move back home together?

"Soon," Jake replied to Maddy's last question. "There's one thing I need to take care of, and then we can be a family again."

Jake's words were meant to soothe his daughter, but tears formed in Maddy's eyes instead.

"We're not a family anymore. Mom's dead! And you're never home!"

Christine's heart went out to the young girl. She had essentially lost both parents, at least until Jake returned home. To assuage Maddy's grief in the meantime, Christine offered encouraging words.

"Your father is working on a critical assignment, one that gets briefed to the president himself."

Maddy brightened at the revelation, so Christine enhanced Jake's role. "Your father is a very important person. If you want, I'm sure he can arrange a tour of the White House and maybe even for you to meet the president himself."

Maddy's eyes grew wide, her gaze shifting to her dad. "You can do that?"

Technically, Jake didn't have the connections, but Christine did. And there was an easy opportunity only a few weeks away. Easter was approaching, and the White House would be open for tours that weekend and on Easter Monday.

"Actually," Jake replied, "Christine will make the arrangements, not me. She knows the president very well. She's practically on a first name basis with him. In fact, her last job was in the White House itself."

"Really?" Maddy asked.

"Really," Christine replied. "I tell you what—I'll take you on a personal tour of the White House." She leaned toward Maddy and whispered, "I'll even show you some of the special places most people never see. Sound good?"

"Sounds great!"

Maddy beamed with excitement, and Christine even caught a glimmer of a smile from Jake. It felt good to see Maddy excited and Harrison smiling. It had probably been a long time for both of them.

26

NATANZ, IRAN

Not far from the Jameh Mosque in Natanz, Behrouz Khavari sat alone in a booth at the back of Charsooq, a small, family-owned restaurant specializing in traditional Persian cuisine, savoring a cup of chai tea while he waited. It was early for dinner, with only one other table filled with patrons, and Khavari's eyes studied the restaurant guests, convincing himself that there was nothing to worry about. After all, he had met his *friend,* as he preferred to think of him, on many occasions in this restaurant without being discovered.

As he took another sip of tea, Khavari spotted Karim Rashidi, a tall, thin man wearing a light sports jacket in the day's heat, entering the restaurant. After spotting Khavari, he joined him in the back of the restaurant, sliding into the seat on the opposite side of the booth. Neither man greeted the other, instead waiting silently for Ariana, the owner's daughter and waitress, to approach and take their dinner order. Once their order was placed and Ariana entered the kitchen, Rashidi spoke.

"What information do you have?"

"We received a shipment of advanced Russian gas centrifuges this week."

Rashidi's eyes widened.

"How many?"

"One thousand."

Khavari's friend, a CIA field agent, brought his hands up to his head, rubbing his temples, his eyes staring down at the table. Looking back up at Khavari, Rashidi asked, "How long until they're operational?"

"A few days."

Rashidi muttered something unintelligible under his breath.

"Tell me everything," he said.

Dinner was soon served, and Khavari spent the time while they ate conveying what he knew about the centrifuge design, their uranium purification rate, current Iranian stockpiles of low-grade and purified uranium, and the status of the new facilities being built within Kūh-e Kolang Gaz Lā.

"I need to know more about the mountain complex."

After surveying the restaurant customers and staff, verifying that no one was watching them, Khavari pulled a folded envelope from his back pocket and slid it across the table to Rashidi, who quickly concealed it inside his jacket.

"Everything I know about the facility layout and security is in the envelope." Khavari leaned toward Rashidi. "You must act swiftly."

27

WASHINGTON, D.C.

The journey from CIA headquarters into the District was only a few miles. During the short trip, Christine O'Connor pulled a folder from her satchel and reviewed the information related to Russia's shipment of advanced centrifuges to Iran. The president's administration had been wrestling with the issue—how best to deter Iran's pursuit of nuclear weapons—but had been convinced they had time to sort things out. Iran's centrifuge fabrication facility at Natanz had been destroyed and its replacement was not yet producing new centrifuges, handicapping Iran's enrichment effort with an insufficient quantity of older and less efficient centrifuges. That assessment had changed earlier this morning.

After Christine's SUV rolled to a stop beneath the West Wing's north portico, she passed between two Marines in dress blues guarding the White House entrance, then descended to the West Wing basement and entered the Situation Room. Inside the conference room, seated at the rectangular table, were Secretary of State Marcy Perini, acting Secretary of Defense Peter Seuffert, and Thom Parham, the president's national security advisor. Also attending today's meeting were Chief of Staff Kevin Hardison and Vice President Bob Tompkins. Hardison buzzed the secretary, informing her that they were ready for the president, who arrived a moment later for the meeting Christine had requested.

"How serious is this?" the president asked after taking his seat, having been notified of the meeting's topic—Iran's ability to enrich uranium to weapon-grade purity.

Christine understood the issue and its impact quite well, having spent two years as the Director for Nuclear Defense Policy prior to her assignment as the president's national security advisor. Given that today's situation involved agency intelligence gathered on a foreign country, Christine was involved due to her current assignment as CIA director.

"Iran has just received a shipment of one thousand advanced gas centrifuges from Russia," she explained. "It triggers the breakout-time trip wire."

Christine passed out paper copies of her brief to the attendees, then took a moment to recap the efforts to limit Iran's ability to build nuclear weapons, since the current cabinet members might not have been familiar with the details.

"The president and several previous administrations adopted a policy and implemented sanctions to limit the breakout time—the time it would take Iran to produce enough weapon-grade uranium for a single nuclear weapon—to a minimum of twelve months. Despite sanctions, Iran's enrichment efforts had significantly reduced that time interval. To reset the breakout time back to the one-year requirement, George W. Bush authorized a cyber-warfare operation code-named *Olympic Games,* which sabotaged Iran's uranium enrichment efforts by infecting Iran's centrifuge-control software with a virus called Stuxnet. The virus caused the rotors to overspeed, destroying the centrifuges.

"President Obama continued the program, destroying over one thousand of Iran's most advanced centrifuges before the Iranians eventually detected and deleted the software virus. With Stuxnet neutralized, more direct action was taken by the first Trump administration with Israeli assistance, planting an explosive device in Iran's centrifuge fabrication facility at Natanz, which destroyed their centrifuge manufacturing capability.

"These measures kept Iran's breakout time at greater than twelve months and bought us enough time, we believed, to deal with Iran's construction of a replacement centrifuge fabrication facility in their new underground complex at Natanz. That assessment has just changed with Russia's shipment of one thousand gas centrifuges to Iran. Not only is the quantity a concern, but these centrifuges are eight times more efficient than anything Iran has fabricated to date. The quantity and quality of these new centrifuges, once fully operational, will reduce Iran's breakout time to approximately two weeks."

"My God!" Secretary of State Perini exclaimed. "Twenty-six nuclear weapons per year."

"That's correct," Christine replied, "assuming Iran has a sufficient stockpile of low-grade uranium to enrich. We believe they have enough uranium for fifty nuclear weapons."

"What are our options?" the president asked.

"Another cyberattack such as the Stuxnet virus is unlikely to succeed. The Iranians have implemented significant cyber-warfare prevention measures that have eliminated all known virus-introduction mechanisms. Destroying the new centrifuge fabrication facility will be much harder than before since the new facility is being built inside Iran's new underground complex at Natanz, as opposed to the previous aboveground facility."

"What about the MOP?" Vice President Tompkins asked, referring to the Air Force's thirty-thousand-pound bunker-busting bomb with a unique fuze design, detonating only after coming to a stop, allowing the ordnance to penetrate deep below the surface before exploding.

Acting Secretary of Defense Seuffert replied, "That depends on how deep underground the new Iranian complex is."

"Turn to page five," Christine said, directing the group to a satellite view of the mountain complex.

"The new complex is built into Kūh-e Kolang Gaz Lā, sometimes referred to as Pickaxe Mountain. Based on the location of the entry tunnels in the side of the mountain, we believe there are two main levels within the complex. If the entrance tunnels are built horizontally, that places one level at two hundred fifty feet beneath the mountain surface and a lower level almost five hundred feet deep. The two levels could be even deeper if the tunnels slope downward from the entrance instead of staying level."

Seuffert shook his head. "Not even a one-two punch with the MOP would destroy a reinforced concrete complex that deep."

"What other options do we have?" the president asked. "We can't let these centrifuges operate for long."

There was momentary silence in the Situation Room. The issue of Iran's uranium enrichment had come up during previous White House meetings, and the president's position had been consistent up to now. He had been reluctant to implement sabotage, preferring diplomacy instead, since Iran could just replace whatever had been destroyed, simply delaying the inevitable unless a diplomatic solution was forged. However, Iran seemed intent on developing nuclear weapons, and Russia's supply of advanced centrifuges had changed the calculus.

"I think it's time for direct intervention," Seuffert offered, "but a covert mission. Something that can't be directly traced back to the United States." He glanced at Christine, who took the cue.

"We can put together a CIA mission with former special operations personnel—all civilians, no active-duty military. A clandestine insertion into the Natanz facility to destroy the centrifuges."

The president canvassed the others present, obtaining their opinion on the recommendation. After receiving universal concurrence on a covert sabotage mission, the president announced his decision.

"Draft a plan and brief me when you're ready."

28

LANGLEY, VIRGINIA

The morning traffic in the District had already begun to thicken when Jake Harrison pulled out from the parking garage near his temporary agency-provided lodging at the Hotel Washington, only a block from the White House. After heading north on the George Washington Parkway in Virginia, he took the exit for the George Bush Center for Intelligence, where a gate guard verified he was on the authorized visitor list, then waved him through.

Harrison pulled into the main parking garage, then entered the lobby of the CIA Original Headquarters Building, taking the elevator to the seventh floor. After informing the director's secretary that he had arrived, he was asked to wait in a conference room down the hall. Three others soon arrived: CIA Director Christine O'Connor, Deputy Director Monroe Bryant, and the new member of the seventh-floor oligarchy whom Harrison was meeting for the first time—Deputy Director for Operations Frank McKinnon.

"Welcome back, Jake," Christine said as she took her seat at the head of the table.

Bryant and McKinnon likewise welcomed him back to the agency. The conference room door opened again and two women entered. The first was Deputy Director for Analysis Tracey McFarland, carrying two manila folders. The second was a woman Harrison hadn't expected to see again—his previous partner, Khalila Dufour—an attractive six-foot-tall Arab with straight black hair falling across her shoulders.

Khalila had been assigned to assist Harrison during his two previous stints in the CIA, accompanying him whenever leads took him to the

Middle East. Khalila's contacts in the region and linguistic skills were the best the agency had to offer.

McFarland greeted Harrison after taking her seat, but Khalila said nothing after settling into her chair, offering only a brief glance in his direction. It seemed that her typical aloofness hadn't changed, but Harrison detected a notable improvement in her demeanor. Instead of sitting with her arms folded across her chest, projecting a why-am-I-here attitude as she had done in previous meetings, she presented a respectable, business-like persona. He followed her gaze toward the new DDO.

Four months ago, Khalila had put a bullet into the previous DDO's head, acting as judge, jury, and executioner in response to his treason. But instead of tension between the new DDO and Khalila, McKinnon exuded a calm confidence in the presence of the woman who had slain his predecessor. The DDO apparently didn't know Khalila as well as he did. Harrison was convinced that Khalila was a sociopath who had killed several previous partners—ones who had learned too much about her true identity.

When the conversation resumed, the deputy directors expressed their condolences for Angie's death. Harrison nodded his appreciation and silence in the conference room followed, eventually broken by Christine.

"Your primary goal is to locate Mixell. He assassinated the secretary of defense, and we're also concerned about what else he's up to. You two are being teamed up again due to your previous experience tracking Mixell down. Here's a summary of what we've got regarding the SecDef's assassination."

Christine turned to McFarland, who handed Harrison and Khalila the folders she had brought to the meeting. The folders held identical contents, and Tracey walked Harrison and Khalila through the material.

"But first," Christine said after McFarland finished, "we have a higher priority mission for you. Iran has just received a shipment of one thousand advanced gas centrifuges from Russia." Christine went on to explain how Iran would now be able to produce enough weapon-grade uranium for a nuclear bomb every two weeks instead of every twelve months.

When she finished, Harrison said, "I understand the problem, but not where Khalila and I come in."

Christine answered, "The president wants to avoid a direct military attack on Iranian facilities. We'd prefer something stealthy, such as the Stuxnet virus that was discreetly injected into the computer software controlling Iran's previous centrifuges. Unfortunately, the Iranians have significantly improved their defenses against cyber strikes, so a more direct approach is required."

McKinnon took over from Christine. "You'll team up with several other agency members. Mission details will be provided upon your arrival in the Middle East. Your qualifications are obvious, Jake; you'll be joining several former U.S. special operations force personnel. Khalila will accompany the team due to her linguistic skills, as she is fluent in Farsi and the other prevalent languages in the region."

"When do we leave?" Harrison asked.

"This afternoon. Your travel arrangements to the Middle East have already been made. The details are on the last sheet in your folders."

After a momentary lull, the DDO added, "You know the drill, Jake. You're being assigned to the special operations group within the special activities center. Pick up your ID and check out a weapon and any other gear you need. Any other questions?"

"Not at the moment."

"Well, then," McKinnon said, "we'll let you and Khalila get started."

After wishing them good luck, Christine and her deputy directors left the conference room, leaving Harrison and Khalila behind.

Harrison turned to his former—and present—partner, but she spoke first, keeping their conversation perfunctory as usual.

"Get your gear and I'll pick you up at the entrance."

29

WOODMORE, MARYLAND

Far from bustling Washington, D.C., and its nearby suburbs, beyond the traffic jams on the Capital Beltway and its arteries, lies Maryland's true nature—winding country roads offering scenic views of farms and heavily forested land that remains largely unaffected by the blight of humanity. In a rented green Jeep Grand Cherokee, Lonnie Mixell turned onto a narrow gravel driveway that snaked through the trees, ending beside a small single-story home. According to the rent-by-owner ad, it was a twelve-hundred-square-foot house available on a month-to-month basis for a reasonable price.

After turning off the engine, Mixell checked his watch. He was ten minutes early. While he waited, he lowered the driver's side window and closed his eyes, listening to the birds, crickets, and the brisk wind blowing through the foliage. But his thoughts soon turned to the task for which Brenda Verbeck had paid an initial ten million dollars.

To that end, a white Ford F-150 appeared in the rearview mirror, grinding to a halt on the gravel road behind him. From the truck stepped a woman in her fifties who approached Mixell's car. Stepping from the sedan, Mixell extended his hand to the owner of the nearby residence.

"George Banks, I assume?" she asked as they shook hands. "I'm Cheryl Payne. It's a pleasure to meet you."

After quickly sizing up the six-foot-tall man who had expressed interest in renting her vacant property, her eyes went to the house.

"I think you'll find this to be exactly what you're looking for," she said as she led Mixell toward the front door.

Mixell had already decided that the property would suit his needs. It was a small farm situated on several acres that Cheryl had inherited when her father had recently passed away. Located in a semi-rural area, the closest house was a half-mile away, but it was also less than ten minutes from Route 50 and the Capital Beltway.

"As you can see," Cheryl said after she unlocked the door and they stepped inside the fully furnished home, "the house and furniture are a bit worn, but together create a homey ambiance. The main level isn't very big," she said as they moved through the house, "but the basement is large and fully finished. Every room has hardwood floors, plus there's a fireplace in the living room for the cold winter nights. Perhaps the best part of the property is the privacy. Perfect for you and . . . is there a Mrs. Banks?"

Mixell held up his left hand, which lacked a wedding ring.

Cheryl nodded. "This place holds a lot of memories," she said. "Not just for me, but for my children and grandkids as well."

After the quick tour of the house, Mixell had already formed an opinion. *What a shithole.* He wouldn't be caught dead living in a place like this, but for a few weeks, he could suffer. Besides, he was interested in the property primarily for its privacy, plus another reason.

"Can I take a look at the barn?"

Not far behind the house, Cheryl unlocked and pushed aside a large sliding door and they entered the barn. Although the structure was in comparable condition to the house, Mixell was pleased with what he saw. The barn was hidden from the road and the roof seemed intact—there were no indications of leaks from the recent rainy weather. More important, the entrance was wide enough to accommodate a large commercial van.

"How soon can I move in?"

"Any time you'd like."

Three hours later, as the sun slipped toward the horizon, Mixell's car stopped beside a dilapidated warehouse on the bank of the Potomac River. Bordered on one side by Oronoco Bay and the other by Founders Park, the warehouse was in a fairly secluded location considering it was in the heart of Alexandria, Virginia. As he sat in the car and stared at the warehouse, his thoughts drifted into the past to the night Jake Harrison had killed his soulmate.

He recalled the event vividly, both in his waking moments and nightmares. Jake hiding behind Trish, one arm wrapped around her body and a pistol against her head. Both men had been wounded moments earlier, with Mixell taking one bullet and Harrison two, leaving Jake in far worse shape. Mixell recalled the desperation in Jake's eyes as he hid behind Trish, searching for a way out. But there was no way he was letting Jake leave the warehouse alive.

As Jake gradually made his way toward the exit, doing his best to keep Trish between them, he eventually exposed enough of himself for a viable shot. Mixell adjusted his aim and exhaled slowly, then squeezed the trigger.

But Harrison jerked Trish sideways a few inches at the last second, and Mixell had watched in horror as her head snapped back and her body went limp, then crumpled to the floor after Harrison released her.

Technically, his bullet had done the deed. But Trish was dead because the coward Harrison had chosen to hide behind a defenseless woman.

Mixell stepped from his car, parked on the river side of the warehouse, and approached the industrial-sized garage door. Even if it was unlocked, he knew the door was too heavy to lift, so he stopped beside one of the grimy windows and broke an opening large enough to fit through.

After climbing through the window, he scanned his surroundings. It looked like the warehouse had a new tenant, as it was filled now with several dozen stacks of crates. There was nothing blocking the area he was interested in, so he moved forward, illuminating the floor with his cell phone's camera light. He eventually found what he was looking for.

He knelt and placed a hand on the red stain from Trish's blood, which had soaked into the concrete.

Trish's death had been avenged, with Angie dying in Harrison's arms. In a perfect world, Harrison would also be forced to watch while Mixell slayed Christine, knowing that his traitorous actions—turning Mixell in for killing a few despicable terrorists—had determined her fate as well. Before Mixell's knife or bullets ended Harrison, he would suffer, knowing that the two women he had loved in his life were dead because of him.

30

K-571 *KRASNOYARSK*

In the Strait of Hormuz, K-571 lurked beneath the water's surface, its periscope poking four feet above the waves. In the submarine's Central Command Post, Captain Second Rank Gavriil Novikov pressed his right eye against the scope optics, turning slowly as he examined the surface ships transiting the narrow waterway, searching for a desirable target.

There were few places more hazardous for submarines at periscope depth than the Strait of Hormuz. The opening to the Persian Gulf was only thirty-five miles wide at its narrowest point, and the shipping lanes in the center were even narrower—only two miles wide—separated by a two-mile buffer zone. In the middle of the buffer zone, where the water was deepest and in a position that offered an ideal view of merchant ships exiting the Persian Gulf, Novikov deftly maneuvered his submarine, dodging ships that failed to adhere to the stipulated transit zones.

Twelve days ago, with his submarine tied up alongside a pier in Vladivostok, homeport of the Russian Pacific Fleet, Novikov had received the orders he had yearned for since joining the Navy—the directive to use the skills of his crew and the devastating weaponry at his disposal to sink ships. After all, what was the purpose of building such magnificent submarines and the thousands of hours spent training their crews, if they were never used? He had hoped to engage Russia's true adversary in underwater warfare—the American Navy—but would have to be content, for the moment, to focus on the initial targets specified in his operational order.

Novikov's crew typically used the submarine's ears, rather than its eyes, to track and then avoid or engage a target. But in the busy Strait of Hormuz, the men monitoring the submarine's hydrophones suffered from sensory overload, unable to efficiently process the numerous contacts scurrying through the narrow waterway. With no enemy surface warships—and their periscope detection radars—in the area, Novikov had decided to remain at periscope depth, using one of the submarine's two scopes to examine the transiting ships.

Just over the horizon, Novikov detected a likely target. The ship was still *hull-down,* partially hidden due to the curvature of the Earth; only its superstructure was visible. Gradually, as the ship approached *Krasnoyarsk,* Novikov gained a clear look at the merchant.

"Man Combat Stations," he directed Captain Lieutenant Petr Dolinski, the submarine's Central Command Post Watch Officer, who was standing nearby.

The general alarm reverberated throughout the submarine, followed by the announcement directing all personnel to report to their assigned stations. Three minutes later, *Krasnoyarsk* was ready for combat, with every console in the Central Command Post energized and manned.

"Captain, Combat Stations are manned," Dolinski reported, "with the exception of the Conning Officer."

Novikov acknowledged Dolinski's report, then announced, "This is the Captain. I have the Conn. Captain Lieutenant Dolinski retains the Watch. Standby for observation, aft scope."

"Ready," reported the michman manning the nearest fire control console.

After aligning the periscope to the desired merchant ship, Novikov pressed the red button on the right periscope handle and announced, "Visual one. Bearing, mark. Range, twelve thousand meters. Angle on the bow, port ten."

The fire control michman entered the data into his console, then reported, "Hold Visual one bearing two-three-two, course zero-five-zero."

Novikov announced, "Visual one is classified merchant, an oil tanker."

Merchant ships were easy prey in almost any scenario and, within the maneuvering confines of the Strait of Hormuz, easier to shoot than fish in a barrel. No further periscope observations were required.

Novikov ordered, "Open muzzle door, tube One. Prepare to Fire, Visual one, tube One."

In preparation for their mission in the Strait of Hormuz and the Persian Gulf, Novikov had already ordered tubes One through Five loaded.

Captain Third Rank Anton Topolski, *Krasnoyarsk*'s First Officer, stopped behind the michman who had entered the periscope observation. After a quick survey of the target's solution—its range, course, and speed—he ordered, "Send solution to Weapon Control." The michman complied, and Topolski announced, "Captain, I have a firing solution."

The Weapons Officer announced, "Ready to Fire, tube One."

Satisfied that all parameters were acceptable, Novikov ordered, "Fire tube One."

The Weapons Officer sent the command to the Torpedo Room, and Novikov felt a tremor in the deck as one of the submarine's forty wire-guided torpedoes was launched.

With his eye still pressed against the periscope optics, Novikov listened to reports on the progress of his torpedo, although the events were anticlimactic. The unsuspecting merchant had no way to detect the incoming weapon and lacked the maneuverability to avoid it or the countermeasures to deceive it.

A few minutes later, after the torpedo had closed sufficiently to detect its prey with the sonar built into the torpedo's nose, the Weapons Officer announced:

"Detect!"

The next report came soon thereafter. "Torpedo is homing!"

On the Weapon Launch Console, the parameters updated as the torpedo increased speed and made a slight adjustment in course, angling toward its target.

"Loss of guidance wire!" the Weapons Officer announced.

Simultaneously, a geyser engulfed the merchant ship, the water shooting high into the air. Seconds later, the sound of the explosion rumbled through *Krasnoyarsk*'s hull.

A cheer arose from the men at their stations in the Central Command Post; their submarine and its weapon had performed admirably.

Novikov ordered, "Reload tube One."

After verifying the merchant had sustained sufficient damage—it was soon listing twenty degrees to starboard—Novikov resumed his periscope search, scouring the approaching ships for his next target. Another large merchant ship caught his attention. This one had four bulbous domes rising from the ship's main deck—a natural gas tanker.

"Standby for observation, forward scope," Novikov announced.

Even if the tanker's crew now understood the peril and reversed course, it could not outrun *Krasnoyarsk*'s torpedoes.

31

WASHINGTON, D.C.

In the West Wing basement, the president was joined in the Situation Room by Chief of Staff Kevin Hardison, National Security Advisor Thom Parham, Secretary of State Marcy Perini, acting Secretary of Defense Peter Seuffert, and Sheila McNeil, who had replaced Brenda Verbeck as secretary of the Navy. The information coming in from the Persian Gulf was alarming, with the casualties climbing by the hour. The president turned to Sheila for the latest update.

"How bad is it?"

"So far, eight merchant ships—all of them oil or natural gas tankers—have been sunk in the Strait of Hormuz or the Persian Gulf. The sinkings began six hours ago, commencing in the strait, and have moved into the Persian Gulf. All shipping through the strait, both into or out of the Persian Gulf, has come to a standstill."

"Do we know who's responsible?"

"We have nothing concrete at the moment, but the circumstantial evidence points heavily toward Russia. Twelve days ago, several Russian nuclear-powered attack submarines sortied from Vladivostok. We had only one American submarine on station in the area, and it trailed one of the Russian submarines as it traveled southwest. It lost the Russian sub in the dense shipping lanes northwest of Malaysia, but it was headed toward the Persian Gulf. Based on the Russian submarine's average speed while it was trailed, extrapolations have it reaching the Strait of Hormuz about an hour before the first sinking occurred. We're analyzing sonar recordings of the torpedo explosions to determine the type of torpedo employed, but so far, the quality of the recordings has been inadequate for a confident assessment."

"I have a suspicion about what's going on," the president said, "but what are your thoughts?"

Secretary of State Marcy Perini replied, "It's likely the Kremlin's response to our aggressive sanctions imposed after their invasion of Ukraine. The sanctions are designed to throttle their oil and natural gas sales, starving their government of funding, and it appears Russia is attempting to neutralize our effort by cutting off natural gas and oil shipments to Western Europe, forcing our NATO allies to rely on Russian resources instead."

The president nodded. "That's my assessment as well. Are there any other opinions?"

There were headshakes around the table, so the president turned again to Sheila McNeil. "We'll need to defend these merchant ships from attack. What are our options?"

"We have Fifth Fleet assets in the Persian Gulf, which could be assigned to escort oil and natural gas tankers, but we'll need more ships to escort every tanker. The Theodore Roosevelt strike group is in the Red Sea, on its way back to the West Coast after being relieved in the Mediterranean by the Eisenhower strike group. We could divert the Roosevelt strike group into the Persian Gulf instead. If so, the strike group would arrive in the gulf in two days."

"What about submarines?" the president asked.

"We have one fast attack in the vicinity—the one that was trailing the Russian submarine—which we can assign to the Roosevelt strike group. We have five submarines homeported in Guam and two squadrons in Hawaii. Three of the Guam boats are in a ready-to-deploy status, and if assigned, can be in the gulf in about a week. Submarines from Pearl Harbor would take another week. However, *Michigan* is in the Arabian Sea at the moment, currently en route to the Black Sea to give you the option to provide Tomahawk missile support to the Ukrainians, if desired. Instead, we could divert *Michigan* into the gulf until the submarines from Guam arrive."

"What do you recommend?" the president asked.

McNeil replied, "We'd like to reroute the Roosevelt strike group into the Persian Gulf, accompanied by *Michigan* and the nearby fast attack, and sortie the three available submarines from Guam. In case there are more Russian submarines in the gulf, we also plan to order the Pearl Harbor submarine squadrons to prepare for deployment."

The president nodded his understanding. "I concur with your plan. Begin escorting oil and natural gas tankers in the Persian Gulf."

Turning to acting Secretary of Defense Peter Seuffert, the president asked, "What's the latest status on Russia's invasion of Ukraine?"

"It appears that President Egorov has achieved his primary objective, seizing control of a corridor of land along the southeast border of Ukraine, connecting mainland Russia with the Crimean Peninsula. The situation has stabilized somewhat, partly due to the inflow of NATO funding and military equipment to Ukraine, and Egorov seems content with the territory seized thus far. The Russian Army is fortifying its front line and has not launched offensives into other parts of Ukraine. It appears that Egorov is digging in for a prolonged war until Ukraine gives up and cedes the territory under Russian control."

"I understand," the president said. "Keep me informed on any changes in status in Ukraine or the Persian Gulf."

32

USS *THEODORE ROOSEVELT*

In the Red Sea, seven hundred miles southeast of the Suez Canal, USS *Theodore Roosevelt* headed into the wind as an F-35C Lightning II moved forward on the Flight Deck, locking into the starboard bow catapult. Seated in his chair on the Bridge, Captain Ryan Noss watched as the jet blast deflector behind the fighter tilted up, shielding another F-35C, following behind, from the lead aircraft's single-engine exhaust. A moment later, the Lightning II raced forward, angling up and to the right after clearing the bow, headed out to relieve one of the fighters in *Theodore Roosevelt*'s combat air patrol.

The next Lightning II also launched successfully, completing this launch cycle. In another thirty minutes, the fighters on Combat Air Patrol would land aboard *Theodore Roosevelt*. In the meantime, Noss's eyes scanned the displays mounted below the Bridge windows. Earlier today, he had received reports of merchant ship sinkings in the Strait of Hormuz and the Persian Gulf, followed by an update on the Navy's Common Operational Picture, a fused tactical database, which had placed a Russian Yasen-class guided missile submarine in the Persian Gulf, exact location unknown.

USS *Theodore Roosevelt* had been at sea for seven months, and the grind had worn down the crew and equipment. Aircraft carriers had tremendous repair departments, well stocked with spares and well-trained technicians, and *Theodore Roosevelt* was no exception. However, the seven-month deployment had taken its toll and the failures requiring depot-level repair had mounted.

There had been a collective sigh of relief after the aircraft carrier had been relieved by USS *Eisenhower* and had begun its journey home. After receiving the startling news from the Persian Gulf, however, followed by a review of the location of the U.S. Navy's assets, Noss had seen the writing on the wall; *Theodore Roosevelt*'s journey home would likely be delayed. During this afternoon's department head meeting, he had directed the maintenance department to return to round-the-clock repair efforts, ensuring every possible aircraft aboard was fully operational.

The ship's Communicator approached, handing Noss the message board. He read the OPORD, then reflected on his new operational orders. As expected, *Theodore Roosevelt* and the other warships in the strike group were being sent into the Persian Gulf to assist Fifth Fleet's mission to protect merchant ships from attack. However, their new mission required a different mindset. For the last seven months, the strike group had focused on being prepared for attacks with their strike fighter squadrons. Now, *Theodore Roosevelt* would employ its squadron of MH-60R anti-submarine warfare helicopters, along with the MH-60Rs carried aboard *Theodore Roosevelt*'s escort warships.

Noss directed his Communicator, "Have the Navigator lay out a track into the Persian Gulf with the strike group at thirty knots."

33

USS *MICHIGAN*

Five hundred feet beneath the ocean's surface, USS *Michigan* was traveling toward its operating area in the Black Sea. Seated in the Captain's chair on the Conn, Captain Murray Wilson surveyed the watchstanders in the Control Room as they prepared for a trip to periscope depth.

The submarine's Officer of the Deck, Lieutenant Brittany Kern, stood on the Conn between the two lowered periscopes as she initiated the routine procedure.

"All stations, Conn. Make preparations to come to periscope depth. Helm, ahead two-thirds. Dive, make your depth two hundred feet."

The submarine tilted upward, slowing as it ascended to ordered depth. The sonar technicians on watch adjusted the sonar lineup, beginning a detailed search for surface contacts.

Michigan was in the northern Indian Ocean, having completed three-fourths of its journey to the Black Sea. After Russia's transgression against Ukraine, the United States was moving as much firepower as possible within striking distance of Russian forces, with *Michigan* joining another SSGN, USS *Georgia*, from the Atlantic Fleet, which was already on station in the Black Sea.

After *Michigan* leveled off at two hundred feet, Lieutenant Kern ordered, "Sonar, Conn. Report all contacts."

A few minutes later, Sonar reported, "Conn, Sonar. Hold no contacts."

Kern briefed Wilson on the ship's status and contact picture. After obtaining permission to proceed to periscope depth, Kern announced, "Raising Number Two scope," then reached up and twisted the periscope ring above her head.

After the periscope finished its silent ascent, she lowered the handles and placed her right eye against the scope optics.

"All stations, Conn," Kern called out. "Proceeding to periscope depth."

Sonar, Radio, and the Quartermaster acknowledged, then Kern ordered, "Helm, ahead one-third. Dive, make your depth eight-zero feet."

The Diving Officer directed the two watchstanders seated in front of him, "Ten degrees up. Full rise, fairwater planes."

Aside from periodic depth reports from the Diving Officer, it was silent in the Control Room as *Michigan* tilted upward and rose toward the surface.

As the Diving Officer called out eight-zero feet, the scope broke the water's surface and Kern started circling with the periscope, searching for nearby contacts. After several revolutions, she announced, "No close contacts."

Conversation in Control resumed, and Radio reported over the 27-MC, "Conn, Radio. Download in progress." The Quartermaster followed with, "GPS fix received."

Kern acknowledged the reports, and a moment later, Radio reported *Michigan* had received the latest round of naval messages. "Conn, Radio. Download complete."

With both objectives for their trip to periscope depth completed—a satellite navigation fix and receipt of the latest batch of messages—Kern called out, "All stations, Conn. Going deep. Helm, ahead two-thirds. Dive, make your depth two hundred feet."

Each station acknowledged and *Michigan* tilted downward, leaving periscope depth behind as Kern lowered the scope back into its well. After *Michigan* leveled off at two hundred feet, a radioman entered Control, delivering the message clipboard to the submarine's Captain. Wilson began reviewing the messages, studying the one on top. *Michigan* had received new operational orders, which caught Wilson by surprise.

Michigan was being diverted to the Persian Gulf, where it would be attached to the Theodore Roosevelt strike group. *Roosevelt* had just been relieved by *Eisenhower* and was supposedly on its way home to San Diego. Why were *Michigan* and the Roosevelt strike group being sent into the Persian Gulf? Although *Michigan*'s new operational orders were clear, the reason for the change in plan was not explained.

Wilson flipped to the next message on the clipboard—*Michigan*'s new waterspace assignment—which allocated a new corridor for *Michigan* to travel within, plus a higher transit speed, taking the submarine into the Persian Gulf. Unfortunately, like the operational order, no reason for the new destination or accelerated transit was provided. However, the third message, a tactical picture update, answered Wilson's question.

Michigan had been out of communication for the last twelve hours, traveling deep, ascending to periscope depth to copy the broadcast only twice each day. As a result, *Michigan*'s crew had been unaware of the recent events in the Persian Gulf. Only now was Wilson learning of the merchant ship attacks.

He turned to Lieutenant Kern. "Come down to five hundred feet, course three-four-zero. Increase speed to ahead flank."

34

NSA BAHRAIN

Jake Harrison reclined in his seat as the Dassault Falcon executive jet began its descent toward the Kingdom of Bahrain. Sixteen hours earlier, the jet had lifted off from Ronald Reagan Washington National Airport with Harrison and Khalila as its only passengers. As the aircraft descended, Harrison examined the archipelago nation comprising fifty natural islands and thirty-three artificial ones.

Bahrain Island, where they would land, was the largest island by far, making up over eighty percent of the country. Located on the northern tip of the island was Naval Support Activity Bahrain, home to U.S. Naval Forces Central Command and the United States Fifth Fleet, an area advertised as the busiest 152 acres in the world, hosting seventy-eight military commands.

It had been a long and quiet flight. Khalila's behavior hadn't changed since their last mission together. She kept her thoughts to herself and rarely spoke, but Harrison detected no hint of the tension that had permeated their relationship during the two previous assignments. The source of that tension—her true identity—had been resolved, along with her need to eliminate those who discovered who she really was.

During their first mission together, Harrison had forged an agreement with Khalila. She would take no action as long as he didn't discover her true identity. That truce had held until four months ago, when Khalila had pressed her pistol against his head seconds after he had learned who she was. She had refrained from pulling the trigger, and Harrison had subsequently been authorized knowledge of her true identity, which remained a closely guarded agency secret.

After touching down, the Falcon taxied to a halt under the midday sun. Harrison and Khalila descended the aircraft staircase onto the tarmac, where they were met by representatives from U.S. Naval Forces Central Command. The two CIA officers were taken to Central Command's secure operations center, where they were introduced to the other four team members: former SEAL Team Six member Robert Wilson, two former Delta Force operators—Steve Hile and Eric White—plus Bob Lesher, their Black Hawk helicopter pilot.

Joining the group today was Karim Rashidi, the CIA Middle East field officer who had obtained the critical information: the delivery of advanced Russian centrifuges, plus an internal layout of the new Natanz mountain complex. Rashidi began his brief, progressing through slides on a large-screen video display at the front of the operations center.

"Your objective tonight is the destruction of equipment inside the underground complex within Pickaxe Mountain. There are two main levels inside the complex. The upper level is a centrifuge fabrication facility that is nearing completion. The lower level houses a uranium enrichment plant, where several thousand centrifuges purify uranium gas, increasing Uranium-235 concentration to weapon-grade level. The upper level is two hundred fifty feet beneath the mountain surface and the lower level is almost five hundred feet deep, which means the complex can't be destroyed by a conventional munitions strike. That's where you come in. You'll infiltrate the facility and plant explosives on both levels."

With the mission objective clear, Rashidi shifted to the complex's exterior defenses. "Natanz is protected by anti-aircraft batteries, perimeter fencing, and a contingent of Iran's Revolutionary Guard. There are four entrances into the mountain complex, two to the east and another two to the west, and all are guarded and normally sealed. Covert ingress into the complex via a standard entrance isn't feasible, so you'll be trying something different."

The presentation shifted to the next slide, a satellite infrared view of Pickaxe Mountain. "There are four vertical ventilation shafts: two induction and two exhaust. These are the exhaust vents." Rashidi pointed to two small dark blotches on the satellite photograph indicating the exhaust of cool facility air. "You'll travel to the complex tonight aboard a CIA Black Hawk helicopter, which should enable a clandestine approach to within a few hundred meters of this exhaust vent." He pointed to one of the two dark spots.

"It's likely that there are surveillance devices near the vent, so you'll have to identify and neutralize them, then gain access to the vent and rappel down to the upper level. Once you've entered the facility, the plan is straightforward—plant explosives and depart."

Rashidi moved through the next several slides, which contained hand-drawn layouts of the two levels inside the complex. In addition to the centrifuge fabrication facility, the upper level contained supply storerooms, a security control room, and accommodations for the complex's security detachment. Rashidi walked through the drawings his contact had provided, highlighting the best locations for explosives.

"Since the complex is deep within the mountain, you won't be able to detonate the explosives on the lower level remotely. It's possible you can trigger the charges on the upper level after returning to the mountain surface, but to ensure they detonate, the explosives on both levels will be set with synchronized timers. That means once you set the timers, you'll be living on borrowed time. Any questions so far?"

Steve Hile, one of the former Delta Force operators, asked, "What about a possible nuclear explosion when we destroy the uranium enrichment plant?"

"That won't happen," Rashidi replied. "To achieve a nuclear detonation, you have to compress the uranium into a fraction of its size, which initiates the nuclear chain reaction. Your sabotage will just create a giant mess of radioactive material, highly contaminating the facility. The Iranians will have to abandon the complex or spend years decontaminating it.

"As you're aware," Rashidi said, "in case any of you are captured or killed, it is essential that you cannot be directly tied to the U.S. government. In support of this directive, your fingerprint and DNA signatures have been erased from every database, both domestic and international. We've also deleted any social media profiles and other internet records. You are now officially ghosts. Although"—he glanced at Khalila—"you're already a ghost, aside from your recent employment as a translator for Bluestone Security."

Khalila offered no response, either verbally or physically, simply staring back at Rashidi.

Rashidi then asked, "Any more questions?"

There were none, so he continued, "During tonight's mission, you'll refer to each other using code names, in case any of your communications are intercepted."

He looked at Wilson, a six-foot-four, barrel-chested guy. "You'll go by Leviathan."

Rashidi shifted his gaze to Eric White, a tall, thin, wiry man. "You're Cutlass."

To Steve Hile, he said, "You'll be Pile Driver," and Harrison was code-named Riptide.

"Your pilot," Rashidi said, referring to Bob Lesher, "will go by Falcon."

That left Khalila, to whom he said, "You'll go by Translator."

Khalila frowned as she folded her arms across her chest. "They get fancy names and I get Translator? You're kidding, right?"

Rashidi grinned. "I am. You'll be Stingray. Is that suitable?"

"Quite."

"Great," Rashidi said. "Try to get some sleep. You depart at midnight."

35

TIMONIUM, MARYLAND

A block from the Carver Construction worksite on the outskirts of Timonium, Lonnie Mixell waited in his SUV as the day drew to a close and workers headed home. When only a single car remained in the parking lot, Mixell put his car into drive and entered the expansive complex, parking behind a large warehouse. A man was waiting at the rear exit.

Craig Daniels unlocked and pushed the door open for Mixell, and the two men strode silently down a hallway. Few words would be required today. The deal had been previously arranged via secure messaging and the price agreed upon—a hefty sum for Daniels but peanuts considering the fee Brenda Verbeck was paying.

Daniels swiped his badge and pushed open a set of double doors, and the two men entered a secure storage room. Carter Construction specialized in building roads through mountainous regions, the type of work that required a large quantity and variety of explosives. The two men stopped as Mixell took in the scene: several rows of explosives stacked floor to ceiling.

"I have what we agreed to over here," Daniels said as he grabbed a hand trolley leaning against the wall. From a chest-high shelf, he transferred two large wooden crates and a smaller one onto the trolley.

"I appreciate your business and the payment, of course," Daniels said. "I've verified the funds have been deposited. Here's fifty pounds of C-4 and three dozen detonators, as requested."

Mixell could see the curiosity in the man's eyes, but Daniels wasn't the type to ask questions. The only real question was in Mixell's mind—should he kill Daniels?

Fifty pounds of C-4 doesn't just get up and walk away. However,

Daniels had assured him that the missing C-4 wouldn't be discovered; he had already ordered a replacement batch, which would arrive before the next inventory. The computer record of the order would be deleted the moment the explosives arrived, ensuring the computer and stock-on-hand quantities agreed. Still, things could go wrong, and if the discrepancy was discovered, authorities could tie Daniels to Mixell.

Perhaps it was better if he killed Daniels, eliminating any possibility of connecting the fifty pounds of C-4 to himself. On the other hand, Daniels's death might prompt an inventory when responsibility for the explosive material was transferred to his replacement.

Neither solution was foolproof, and after having debated the issue for the last few days and moments, he made his decision.

"Thanks, Craig," Mixell said as he tilted the trolley back on its wheels. "It's been a pleasure doing business with you."

36

NATANZ, IRAN

The faint beat of a helicopter's four-bladed rotor dissipated in the darkness as an MH-60M Black Hawk skimmed fast and low through a ravine in the Karkas Mountains, attempting to avoid detection by the Natanz complex's air radar system. Harrison was confident in this endeavor; he had been aboard one of two Black Hawks that had penetrated Pakistan's military defense radars without being seen, with his helicopter landing inside Osama bin Laden's compound walls without being heard.

Although the Black Hawk could carry nine combat-equipped troops, there were only five aboard the helicopter, plus the pilot, Bob Lesher, code-named Falcon, who was a former Night Stalker—a member of the U.S. Army's 160th Special Operations Aviation Regiment.

As they neared their destination, Harrison checked his equipment one last time. Like Khalila and the three men beside him, he was dressed in black gear, outfitted in commercial body armor, night vision goggles, and a headset. Rather than the standard MP-7 easily associated with U.S. Navy SEALs, all five team members carried commercially available Sig Sauer MCX Rattler short-barreled machine guns with suppressors.

The Rattlers were small and light, weighing only six pounds each, which had been a crucial factor in their selection since the team would be maneuvering in tight spaces at times tonight. As usual, Khalila also had a spring-loaded knife strapped to each forearm. The explosives required for tonight's mission had been evenly divided between the five team members, each carrying a black backpack.

The unit's makeup resembled that of a SEAL four-man-fire team plus Khalila. Whoever had selected the personnel for tonight's mission had thought through the scenario. Two of the men were explosives experts—

Leviathan and Pile Driver—since they would split into two teams after gaining access to the facility. A master rappeler, Cutlass, had been assigned due to the team's planned descent through a vertical ventilation shaft. Harrison, as the only former military officer, had been tagged as the fire team leader.

Falcon's voice came across Harrison's headset, announcing they were approaching their destination. Harrison and the rest of the team pulled their night vision goggles over their eyes. The Black Hawk airframe shuddered as the pilot pulled back on the cyclic and adjusted the collective, and the helicopter angled toward the bottom of the ravine. The Black Hawk slowed to a hover, then the wheels settled into the dirt.

Harrison led his team from the helicopter, stopping beside a nearby rock outcropping where he examined the GPS display on his wrist. They were three hundred yards from their planned entry point, although the journey would cover more distance. They would have to climb the adjacent ridge then drop into the next ravine before beginning their ascent of Pickaxe Mountain.

As the Black Hawk rotor spun down to a halt, Harrison led the team up the ridge, where they got their first look at Pickaxe Mountain rising before them. The Black Hawk had landed inside the perimeter fencing, so their first obstacle was the covert mountain ascent, avoiding any surveillance cameras. Harrison and the others had each been issued a handheld electrical current detector capable of sensing the presence of nearby powered equipment such as cameras or other electronic devices. None had been detected thus far.

They ascended the mountain in single file, eventually reaching their planned ingress location—the ventilation exhaust shaft from the upper level—which was located within a small crescent-shaped depression in the mountain surface. As the team peered over the nearest outcropping at the covered ventilation shaft, Harrison's current detector indicated the presence of electronic equipment. As he scanned the area, Leviathan spotted it first.

"Surveillance camera at two o'clock, embedded in the rock wall."

It was a small device, only about four-by-four inches, painted to blend into the mountain, and was mounted in a location almost impossible to approach without being seen.

Almost impossible.

"Cutlass," Harrison said softly into his headset, unsure if the camera had audio capability in addition to video.

"On it," the wiry rappeler said. "Leviathan and Pile Driver, I'll need your help."

The two men joined Cutlass as he circled around and climbed the ridge behind the camera, stopping atop the crescent-shaped outcropping twenty feet above it. Not wanting to hammer a spike into the mountain rock, which would have been a noisy event, he handed one end of a rope to Leviathan and Pile Driver.

Cutlass was already wearing a rappelling harness, which was nothing more than a waist strap attached to loops that encircled his thighs. He hooked the rope via carabiners to the loops in a manner that would allow him to stop his descent at the desired location, but more important, enable free use of both hands.

Standing with his feet on the edge of the precipice, he leaned forward and loosened his grip on the rope. He descended headfirst for twenty feet, pinching the rope between his feet along the way before stopping just above the camera where he locked himself in place.

Cutlass then reached into a breast pocket and retrieved a thin two-inch-diameter disk. He placed the disk near the camera lens, facing in the same direction, and pressed a button on the disk's side, taking a video recording. After a few seconds, an indicator on the disk flashed green.

He pressed the button again, sending an electronic signal that scrambled the camera's video, then slipped the disk in front of the camera and pressed it against the lens, where it stuck in place. He pressed the button a third time, activating the disk. The camera would now see a video clip played in a loop instead of a live feed, allowing the CIA team to approach the ventilation shaft unnoticed.

With the disk covering the camera lens, Cutlass flipped around and dropped down onto the mountain surface, joined by the other four team members. After examining the ventilation shaft covering, they determined it was welded in place, providing only narrow slits for the air to escape. However, they had come prepared, and Leviathan and Cutlass retrieved handheld plasma torches from their backpacks. It took only a few minutes before the torches cut through the metal, and the ventilation lid was lifted out of the way.

It would be a long descent to the first level, requiring a thin but strong line, which was fastened to the base of the ventilation shaft. Cutlass went first as the team descended two hundred feet before reaching a large spinning exhaust fan blocking their way. He placed a small device on the fan casing and energized it, causing a current surge through the fan motor, shorting it out.

After the fan stopped spinning, the team squeezed past the blades and reached the ventilation shaft intake cover, where Cutlass used his plasma torch to cut through the cover fasteners. Holding the cover in place with one hand, he cut the final fastener with the torch, then lowered himself and the cover silently into the upper level of the Natanz complex.

37

NATANZ, IRAN

Harrison was the last to drop onto the floor in the center of the facility's upper level. The other team members were crouched, each facing outward in a different direction. It was mostly dark in the upper level; the main lights were off, with a few perimeter lights illuminating the area, which was filled with a dozen centrifuge fabrication and assembly centers.

They surveyed the expansive area, searching for the security guard who supposedly patrolled the level during the night shift. Khalila spotted the man first.

"Security guard, north side."

In the distance, Harrison spotted an armed guard appearing from behind one of the fabrication centers, moving along the facility perimeter.

"Cover," Harrison ordered, and the team moved behind nearby equipment as they monitored the guard's movement.

The guard continued his perimeter route for a while, then turned into a center corridor that would take him within ten feet of the team's present location. Leviathan was in the best position, with a clear shot once the guard approached within twenty feet, so Harrison ordered Leviathan to neutralize the guard while the others remained concealed.

Leviathan took aim, awaiting the guard's arrival, then squeezed the trigger of his MCX Rattler with attached noise suppressor, putting a round between the man's eyes. Cutlass and Pile Driver moved quickly, dragging the guard behind a nearby equipment console.

After determining there were no other guards on this level, Harrison directed Cutlass and Pile Driver to begin setting charges, with the timers set for one hour, which should give them enough time to place the explosives on both levels and ascend back through the ventilation shaft. Everyone set the timers on their watches, then Harrison led Leviathan and Khalila toward stairs and elevators on the west end.

Not wanting to risk taking an elevator in case there were cameras inside, they took a staircase cut from the mountain rock. After descending several hundred feet, they reached the lower level. They stopped to survey the uranium enrichment plant, which contained row upon row of tall centrifuges stretching into the distance. On the south side was a small, well-lit control room with glass panels. Inside was another security guard, talking with a female technician wearing a white lab coat and black hijab, sitting at a control panel.

Assuming the guard patrolled this level similarly to the upper-level guard, Harrison decided to wait until the man resumed his patrol, which would bring him to within striking range. However, the guard seemed more interested in the woman than his patrol, and Harrison couldn't afford to wait. They had only fifty minutes left and they hadn't yet placed any charges on this level.

Harrison directed Leviathan and Khalila to wait at the staircase while he took care of the guard and technician. He moved from centrifuge to centrifuge, working his way toward the control room. When he reached the last row, he peered around the centrifuge he was hiding behind. The woman was facing the centrifuges while the guard leaned against the console, his back to Harrison. Although the woman could spot Harrison if she looked in his direction, she was focused on the guard.

Slowly, Harrison brought the MCX Rattler to his shoulder and peered through the sight. Taking aim at the back of the guard's head, he pulled the trigger.

The man's head snapped forward and Harrison surged toward the control room as the man slumped to the ground. The woman's face clouded in confusion at first, then she screamed once she realized what had happened. Harrison entered the control room as the woman shifted his gaze toward him, and it was at that moment that he realized he should have sent Khalila instead. He wanted to spare the woman's life, informing her that she would be safe as long as she cooperated. Unfortunately, he didn't speak Farsi.

It may not have mattered. The woman immediately lurched toward the control panel, her hand reaching toward a large red button. Harrison reacted instinctively, putting a bullet into the woman's head.

With the guard sprawled on the floor and the woman slumped in her chair, Harrison directed Leviathan and Khalila to join him. The two arrived as he pulled the woman to the ground, hiding her and the guard from sight on the floor.

He checked his watch. Forty-five minutes left.

Looking out from the control room, Harrison examined the enrichment plant. There were more than two thousand centrifuges in operation, and they had three dozen explosive charges between them. After assessing the centrifuge plant layout, he decided they would split up, with Khalila and Leviathan placing their charges along the perimeter while he attached his to centrifuges down the center.

They moved out and Harrison placed his first charge, heading deeper into the centrifuge labyrinth.

In the security surveillance cell on the upper level, Amer Sarsour looked up from his magazine, giving the console displays a cursory survey. He stopped on a feed from one of the lower-level cameras, fixed on the centrifuge control room. Ahmad had been talking to Fatima the last time he checked, but neither were visible now. He grinned at first, concluding the two were up to no good on the control room floor. But on second thought, that didn't seem like something Fatima would entertain.

Sarsour also noted that the upper-level security guard hadn't checked in at the prescribed time, five minutes ago. Something seemed amiss. He scanned the upper- and lower-level cameras, spotting movement on one of them. A black-clad man was moving along the perimeter of the fuel enrichment plant. Sarsour zoomed in on the man, who was wearing body armor and was armed. The man stopped and placed something at the base of a centrifuge, then moved on.

Sarsour slammed his hand on the red security alarm button on his console.

Harrison had just set his last charge and was headed toward the centrifuge control room, where he would rendezvous with Leviathan and Khalila, when a loud wailing siren cut through the silence. The enrichment plant lighting energized, illuminating the level in bright white light. He cursed under his breath, then contacted Khalila and Leviathan. Khalila had finished placing her explosives and had just reached the control room, while Leviathan was setting his last explosive charge now.

Harrison joined Khalila in the control room, and Leviathan was sprinting around the corner toward the control room when a team of four Iranian security guards emerged from one of the elevators. Leviathan was still in the open when the guards turned the other corner, obtaining a clear shot at the former SEAL. Harrison and Khalila provided firing cover, distracting the security guards and forcing them to take cover behind the centrifuges, but not before Leviathan was hit with a burst of gunfire. Two bullets impacted harmlessly on his body armor, but a third round entered his left thigh.

Leviathan made it to the control room, sliding to a halt beside Harrison and Khalila, who were hunkered down behind the control console. Harrison peered above the console, monitoring the Iranian guards who were working their way down the nearest row of centrifuges toward the control room. Harrison considered the wisdom of engaging in a firefight with uranium centrifuges between them. They appeared sturdily constructed, with an outer metal surface, but he had no idea if they were impervious to MCX Rattler bullets.

He preferred not to find out. Neither he nor the other team members had protective breathing gear, and the prospect of puncturing the centrifuges, filling the level with uranium gas, wasn't appealing. The Iranian guards also seemed concerned, as none had fired on the control room as they worked their way toward them. Had the control room still been sealed he would have considered puncturing a few centrifuges. Unfortunately, his shot on the first guard had pierced one glass panel, and the initial exchange with the guards had shattered another panel.

Harrison tried communicating with Cutlass and Pile Driver, but failed to contact them. However, he heard the faint sound of gunfire over his headset, indicating the two former Delta Force operatives were engaged in a shoot-out in the upper level. As he contemplated their situation, he turned to Leviathan.

"How bad is it?" he asked.

"It's just a flesh wound," Leviathan replied with a grin. "I'm good to go."

Harrison returned his attention to their predicament. The Iranian guards had stopped maneuvering and were hiding behind the nearest row of centrifuges in front of the control room. They seemed content to simply wait, firing upon the intruders if they emerged from behind the control room console, attempting the exposed hundred-foot-long sprint toward the staircase and elevators. Harrison surmised why— reinforcements were likely on the way.

They were trapped.

38

NATANZ, IRAN

Harrison checked his watch: *twenty minutes.*

It had taken them fifteen minutes to set the explosive charges, and they had wasted another five minutes debating how to fight their way from the centrifuge control room to the staircase. Opinions vacillated between a sprint toward the staircase and a direct charge toward the Iranian guards, hoping to reach the centrifuge maze before incurring serious injury. Each option had a greater than zero chance of success, since they were wearing body armor and would be moving fast. Harrison was about to give the order to charge the centrifuges, which would minimize their time in the open, when Khalila began removing her body armor.

"What are you doing?" he asked.

"Both options suck," she said.

"You've got a better idea?"

"I do," she replied as she finished shedding her body armor, then crawled to the female technician.

She removed the blood-stained white lab coat and hijab from the dead woman, then pulled them on.

After reaching the control room door on her hands and knees, she lay prone on the ground and crawled on the floor, crying out in Farsi. She emerged from the control room, moving in a slow Army crawl toward the Iranian guards, keeping her face tilted toward the ground as she begged for help.

The Iranian guards took the bait. There were two guards behind the nearest centrifuge, and one of the guards responded to her cry for assistance, guiding her toward him. When she approached the centrifuge he was hiding behind, he crouched down and extended his hand, pulling her to safety between himself and the other guard.

Khalila held onto the man's arm, thanking him profusely for his help between feigned sobs of relief and cries of pain. She pulled herself slowly to her feet, staying close to the man so he couldn't get a clear look at her face until she stood erect.

His eyes narrowed as he stared at the strange six-foot-tall woman, realizing his peril too late.

Flexing her wrists, Khalila released both knives, hidden beneath her lab coat sleeves, into her hands. She drove one knife up beneath the man's jaw and into his brain, then turned and stabbed the other guard through an eye. As the second man collapsed, she pulled the carbine from his hand and put a bullet into the head of the guard on her left, then swiveled to her right, putting a round into the fourth guard's face.

She emerged from behind the centrifuges, sprinting back toward the control room, where she shed her lab coat and donned her body armor again, then retrieved her firearm. After stepping from the control room, she joined Harrison and Leviathan in a sprint toward the staircase. Leviathan, running beside her, had stopped to check on the guards while Khalila put on her body armor.

"Nice work," he said.

They reached the staircase without further incident, ascending to the upper level as the sound of gunfire grew louder. Harrison stopped at the staircase exit, surveying the ongoing firefight. Unlike on the lower level, there seemed to be no concern about the effect of stray bullets. Cutlass and Pile Driver had killed two of four Iranian guards, but the remaining two had the former Delta Force operators pinned down, unable to reach the ventilation shaft in the middle of the level. However, the two guards had their backs to the staircase.

Harrison took aim, putting three bullets into each man.

As all five members of the fire team headed toward the ventilation shaft, Khalila checked her watch.

Ten minutes.

When they reached the ventilation shaft, Cutlass retrieved the end of the rope they had used to descend into the facility, then each team member retrieved a small motorized winch from their backpack. Khalila went first, feeding the end of the rope through the device, then she engaged the clutch and activated the drive. Holding onto the winch with both hands, she rose into the ventilation shaft, slowing her ascension speed as she approached the disabled exhaust fan. Once past the blades, she increased speed to maximum.

Even with the motorized ascent, it was a long journey to the surface. After reaching the top of the ventilation shaft, she slowed the winch to a halt, then pulled herself from the vent. She checked her watch.

Three minutes.

Khalila waited impatiently as the other team members exited the ventilation shaft, her anxiety growing as the time ticked down. After helping Leviathan from the vent, only Harrison remained.

Thirty seconds.

She peered into the dark shaft, detecting the sound of Harrison's winch pulling him upward.

"Hurry!" she shouted.

"The winch is at max speed," was the faint reply.

Twenty seconds.

Harrison reached the top of the ventilation shaft with only ten seconds remaining. Leviathan helped Khalila haul him from the opening as time reached zero.

As Harrison tumbled to the ground, the mountain trembled, followed by a fiery plume shooting upward from the vent, streaking skyward.

"Time to get moving," Harrison said as he regained his feet and glanced at the plume. "That's a calling card we don't want to be anywhere near."

"We got a bigger problem," Cutlass said, pointing up the mountain slope, illuminated by the fiery ventilation exhaust.

The explosion had dislodged a portion of the mountain surface, which was sliding down toward them.

"There's a ledge along the cliff, directly below us," Cutlass shouted, "if we can get there in time!"

He led the way, sliding down the mountainside as quickly as possible.

Khalila and the others joined him, and after a few seconds, two things became apparent. The first was that the cliff edge wasn't far away. The second was that they were moving too fast; there was no way they could stop their descent before they reached the cliff. Cutlass seemed unfazed, descending toward the cliff edge at breakneck speed. Apparently, falling off the cliff was preferrable to being buried beneath a landslide.

Cutlass reached the edge of the cliff, then disappeared from view. The ground slipped away from Khalila a moment later, and she fell through the darkness for several seconds before she hit the ground, landing on her side. She lay stunned on a ledge for a few seconds until strong hands grabbed and pulled her closer to the mountainside. As rocks and dirt cascaded over them from above, Harrison covered her body with his own.

She lay beneath him until the mountain raining down upon them ceased. Thankfully, they were close enough to the mountain face that most of the rubble passed harmlessly a few feet farther out from them.

"You okay?" Harrison asked.

"I'm fine."

He adjusted his headset and contacted the other team members. They were scattered on the ledge, but everyone had survived, although Cutlass had broken an arm.

Khalila was lying on her back with Harrison still atop her, so Khalila whispered, "This isn't the time or place, Riptide."

She spotted Harrison's faint smile as he rolled off of her. Then he contacted Falcon, informing their Black Hawk pilot that they were on their way back.

39

WASHINGTON, D.C.

It was midafternoon on a bright sunny day in the heart of the District, the sidewalks along Connecticut Avenue NW crowded with pedestrians, as Lonnie Mixell entered the lobby of the Capitol Talent Agency, five minutes early for his meeting with agent Fred Rogers. Stopping at the front desk, he was greeted by an attractive woman in her twenties.

"May I help you?" she asked.

"It's a beautiful day and I happened to find myself in Mister Rogers's neighborhood, so thought I'd stop by to see him."

He waited to see if the woman caught his reference to the kids' television show, but nothing flickered in her eyes. She simply replied, "Do you have an appointment?"

Mixell sighed inwardly, then replied, "One p.m."

"I'll let him know you're here." She smiled and gestured toward an alcove. "Please make yourself comfortable."

The waiting area was sparsely furnished, containing only a few plush chairs and sofas, plus a watercooler and paper cups. There weren't any magazines to peruse—it seemed most of the agency's clientele kept themselves occupied by scrolling through their cell phones. Mixell had only a burner phone, which he didn't intend to use except in an emergency or at the designated time.

As he looked around, he caught the reflection of a man in a wall-mounted mirror display. He smiled at the handsome stranger, which was himself, of course. Before venturing into Washington, D.C., he had dyed his hair blond and inserted blue contacts, plus implants on both sides of his mouth that modified the structure of his jaw and cheekbones.

Fred Rogers eventually arrived, a tall man in his forties wearing dress slacks and a pressed blue silk shirt.

"Welcome to Capitol Talent Agency." He shook hands as Mixell stood, then escorted him to a glass-encased office with a desk and small conference table. Both men took their seats at the table, and after a few rounds of small talk, Rogers got down to business.

"I understand you're looking for a male model. What physical characteristics do you have in mind, and for what type of endeavor?"

"The primary characteristic is . . . he needs to look like me. The same build and height would be great but neither are essential, as long as they're reasonably close."

"What type of work will the model be engaged in?"

"Nothing difficult—he'll need to be stationed at a designated place and time for an hour."

"Can you be more specific?"

"I'm having an important business event, and I need a stand-in for a while. But he won't need to engage with anyone. He'll just need to hang around and pretend to be me."

"All right, then," Rogers replied. "Let me snap an image and get going."

He pulled his cell phone from his pocket and took a picture of Mixell, which he transferred to a software application. Then he pulled a keyboard on the table closer to him and energized a flat-panel display on the wall. After waiting a moment for the software algorithms to search the Capitol Talent Agency database, ten headshot portraits appeared on the display, with each man's characteristics—age, height, and weight—listed beneath his picture.

All ten were reasonably close matches, but three stood out from the rest. From a distance, any of the three would do, but a man named Robert Keeshan was the closest match, Mixell decided.

Rogers concurred.

After discussing the agency fee, which Mixell agreed to, Rogers asked, "When do you need him?"

Mixell provided the date and time. "As far as the location goes, it's not yet set. I'll call him the day before and let him know. But it'll be in the D.C. area."

"Fair enough," Rogers replied. "Let me confirm that Robert is available and interested," he said. "Then I'll draw up the contract and call you when it's signed and payment has been made. You and Robert can then work out the details of your event."

Rogers handed Mixell his business card. "Let me know if there's anything else I can do for you."

40

NSA BAHRAIN

After boarding the Black Hawk helicopter at Natanz, it had been a quiet trip back to Bahrain for Harrison and the other team members. Upon landing, Leviathan's wound had been tended to and confirmed not to be life-threatening. The mission debrief took several hours, after which the team was released for the rest of the day, with Harrison and Khalila scheduled to begin their return trip to Langley the next morning.

It was 1 p.m. by the time Harrison opened the door to his room, an upgrade from standard barracks but not by much—about half the size of a standard hotel room—but at least it had an adjoining bathroom with a shower, plus a window offering a view of the warships tied up along the waterfront. It had been a long night in Natanz and he hadn't gotten much rest during the return trip; he had kept an eye on Leviathan in case his wound was more serious than it appeared. After being awake for more than twenty-four hours, he crashed on the bed for a few hours.

He slept fitfully, his dreams filled with images of Angie, Maddy, and Christine, until he woke late in the afternoon. As he lay in bed, he tried to make sense of the fragmented images. Angie, Maddy, and Christine were the three persons he had loved most in his life, but instead of love and warmth, pain and anguish had permeated his dream.

In Angie's case, it had been another twisted nightmare where he had tried another strategy to save her from Mixell's insanity, convinced that this time it would work. Instead, Angie ended up dying in his arms again; he would never forget those last moments as she looked up at him, the light fading from her eyes until they froze in place. His dreams of Maddy were frequently the same, starting with his daughter sitting on Mixell's lap at the dining room table, Mixell's knife hovering near her neck. The outcome each time was far worse than what had actually happened, with Maddy ending up on the floor beside her mother, her neck slit, or lying on the barn floor, her head cracked open by Mixell's shovel.

In his dreams, Christine never died. Instead, she took pleasure in inflicting pain. In this afternoon's dream, he was back in his house again with Angie lying beside him while Christine tried to extract the gun from Mixell's hand. She was successful, as she had been that night, but this time, instead of attacking Mixell, she had aimed the pistol at Harrison and fired.

In each nightmare, the scenario involving Christine was either a perversion of what had happened that night or a snippet from their past that had previously held a promise of happiness, only to be replaced with pain and anguish. For some reason, her rejections of his marriage proposals were frequently replayed in his dreams.

As kids, they had been almost inseparable, primarily because both had first-generation Russian mothers who frequently got together, leaving Christine to play with Jake and his two older brothers. Jake always got saddled with the *girl*, whether they were playing board games or running around outside. As they grew older, Christine chose to hang out with the boys in the neighborhood, even deciding to go by Chris instead of Christine. Her mom's exasperated efforts to transform her from a tomboy into a proper girl had repeatedly failed. However, nature had eventually taken care of things, and as she matured into a woman, the boys who used to consider her just one of the gang began to look at her differently. By the time they were freshmen in high school, Jake and Christine had started dating.

He had proposed to her twice, and she had rejected both proposals. The first time, they had both just graduated from high school and Christine had been on her way to college on a gymnastics scholarship. She hadn't been ready to be a wife yet, and certainly not a mother. He waited another four years until she graduated from college and proposed again, but by then Christine had landed a job in Washington, D.C., on Congressman Tim Johnson's staff, beginning her meteoric rise through the ranks until she ended up with a corner office in the White House barely twenty years later. She'd be ready to get married soon, she kept saying.

Christine was an intelligent and beautiful woman who was intent on climbing the professional and social ladders in Washington, D.C., and it eventually became obvious that she didn't want to be encumbered by a Midwestern farm boy. After waiting ten years, he realized that he would never be good enough for her and moved on, proposing to Angie a year later. Christine had called the following month, saying she was finally ready. She hadn't heard the news. He loved Angie, but he sometimes wondered how different things would have been if he had waited just a little longer.

As he lay in bed, memories of his time with Christine flitted through his mind until a knock on the door interrupted his reverie. He opened the door to find Khalila dressed in gym shorts and a sports bra.

"I'm going for a run. Want to come along?"

He considered her offer for a moment, his thoughts still filled with snippets of Angie, Maddy, and Christine. "Yeah, I could use a run."

She stepped inside and waited while he changed into running clothes. After working closely together during their previous missions, she didn't seem fazed as he stripped down and changed, and he didn't mind her presence either. Although they had shared the same bed on occasion, she had made it clear each time that the sleeping accommodations were a "hands-off" arrangement, which suited him just fine, since he'd been married to Angie at the time.

"Do you have a route picked out?" he asked after he finished dressing.

"Along the base perimeter on the way out, then back along the waterfront. Five miles sound good?"

Harrison nodded.

Daylight had begun to fade by the time they began their run, with the temperature in the Middle East country easing below ninety degrees. He let Khalila set the pace, which was brisk for the average woman and provided a decent, but comfortable workout for Harrison. True to her usual aloof nature, she said nothing while they ran. His thoughts focused on Mixell, envisioning various scenarios where his former best friend would meet his demise in the most excruciatingly painful way possible.

Halfway through their run, they cut across the base toward the waterfront, then began their journey back toward their rooms. Khalila had previously proven to be a fast runner, almost keeping up with Harrison while chasing down a suspect in Sochi, Russia. As far as long-distance runs went, he didn't know what speed she could maintain, but decided to find out.

He picked up his pace, pulling away from her. It wasn't a blistering speed, considering the heat, at least not for a recently retired Navy SEAL, but there were few women, he reckoned, who would be able to keep up. A moment later, she pulled up beside him. When he glanced at her, he noticed a smile she quickly erased once she noticed his glance. She kept up, but he could tell she was straining. Only two more miles to go.

By the time they returned to the barracks, the sun had begun slipping below the horizon. They stopped at Harrison's room, where he unlocked and opened his door, then turned to Khalila.

"I'm gonna jump in the shower, then grab a bite to eat. Want to join me?"

"Sure."

"I'll be ready in a half hour. You?"

"I'm ready now."

Her response confused him for a second, then he figured she was comfortable heading out for a bite to eat still in her workout clothes, which meant they'd be hitting the base cafeteria rather than venturing out in town. Although Bahrain wasn't as conservative as other Middle Eastern countries, it was still an Islamic nation with dress standards that residents and tourists were expected to observe. Her exposed shoulders and bare legs and midriff would not have been well received. Her next words, however, clarified her previous response.

"I said I'd join you, but I wasn't talking about dinner. I was referring to the shower."

She pushed Harrison backward, following him into his room, then closed the door behind her.

"I no longer have to keep you at arm's length," she said, "hiding my true identity from you. Plus, you're no longer married. Our previous personal rules of engagement no longer apply." She leaned back against the wall. "I can either leave or join you in the shower. Your call."

Harrison was stunned by the sudden turn of events. Until this moment, Khalila had been clear that their partnership would remain purely professional. Now, she had unexpectedly offered to take their relationship to the next level.

But it was too soon.

Angie had been dead for only a few months, and becoming romantically involved with another woman so soon after her death felt like a betrayal.

Khalila seemed to read his mind. "I realize that your heart still aches for Angie. But at some point, you need to move on. One day, when you're ready, you'll find the right woman to spend the rest of your life with. Today, however, I'm the woman who wants to be with you, no strings attached."

As Khalila leaned against the wall, he couldn't keep his eyes from surveying her body. Six foot tall with an athletic build and attractive face, her beauty was undeniable.

And difficult to refuse.

"Stay."

Khalila approached him and offered a passionate kiss, then kicked off her shoes and stripped the clothes from her body. She headed toward the shower.

"Don't be long."

It was dark when Harrison awoke. Khalila lay beside him beneath a thin bedsheet, her eyes open, staring at the ceiling. She eventually rose and he watched her sleek form, faintly illuminated by the waterfront lights, as she picked her bath towel up from the floor and wrapped it around her body, then sat on the window ledge. He watched her for a while, her knees pulled up against her chest as she stared into the darkness. He sat up and pulled on a pair of shorts, then stopped beside the window facing her, leaning against the wall. She seemed not to notice.

"Still wrestling with demons?" he asked.

Khalila nodded, then turned, her eyes locking onto him. "I thought things would be better after I killed the DDO. But nothing has changed." She fell silent for a short while. "I fight for honor," she finally said, "but whose honor? My family's or my own? In my attempt to obtain redemption for the evil perpetrated by my family, I myself have done evil. I've killed many, hoping for resolution, but the guilt and shame remain. Yet I've seen you kill men time and time again without a flicker of remorse. How do you do it?"

"I fight for my country," Harrison replied. "I think it's as simple as that. I've committed evil, as you say, but good has come from every one of those evil acts. For people like us, I think what matters is—at the end, which way do the scales tip?"

She considered his words, then nodded subtly. "By the way, tonight was a one-time deal. If you recall, I don't get attached to my partners. Besides, when I said that one day you'd find another woman to spend your life with, I lied. You've already met that woman."

"Who's that?"

"Tonight, you talked in your sleep. *Chris*. Is that Christine's nickname?"

Harrison pulled back slightly, unsure whether he was more surprised that he talked in his sleep or that he had mentioned Christine. "There's no telling what I was dreaming about when I mentioned her name. But what's certain is that I want nothing to do with Christine."

Khalila smiled. "I've known since the first meeting with you and Christine at Langley that there was something special between you two. You can deny it if you want, but you were still in love with her when you were married to Angie."

Harrison looked away.

"Interesting," Khalila said.

"What?" Harrison turned back toward her.

"You kill without remorse, but the fact that you were in love with Christine while you were married fills you with guilt and shame."

"I moved on from Christine years ago. I loved *Angie*, and she's dead because of Christine!"

"I didn't say you didn't love Angie. Only that you still love Christine."

"You're grossly mistaken. As Angie died in my arms, I promised her that I would make those responsible pay for what they've done. I will end Mixell's life, and although I can't hurt Christine, my relationship with her, even as friends, is over."

"You can't put Christine's actions in the same category as Mixell's. I think I can say with certainty that if she had known your involvement in Mixell's case would have led to your wife's death, she would not have brought you into the agency."

"It's too late now, isn't it? And why are you such a fan of Christine all of a sudden?"

"Because Mixell deserves your hate. Christine does not."

Harrison folded his arms across his chest. "We're done talking about Christine."

His statement hung in the air until Khalila stood. "In that case . . ." She pulled the towel from her body, letting it fall to the floor.

As she approached him, Harrison said, "I thought tonight was a one-time deal."

"It is. The night's not over."

41

LANGLEY, VIRGINIA

Not long after landing at Ronald Reagan Washington National Airport, Jake Harrison and Khalila Dufour were seated at the table in the seventh-floor conference room, joined by the usual CIA leadership—Christine O'Connor, DD Monroe Bryant, DDO Frank McKinnon, and DDA Tracey McFarland—wrapping up their discussion of the Natanz mission. Events had transpired as planned when it came to the issues that mattered: the centrifuge fabrication and uranium enrichment facilities had been destroyed, and no team members had been left behind, alive or dead, which would have provided incontrovertible evidence that the United States had been involved. The topic then shifted to Mixell.

"We still don't have any leads," McFarland explained. "At this point, we think it's best you help out at the NCTC; see what you can find."

The National Counterterrorism Center, located in the Liberty Crossing Building in McLean, Virginia, was staffed by fourteen government agencies, including the FBI and CIA, serving as the logistical hub for the collation and dissemination of terrorist-related information within the U.S. intelligence community. During their previous attempts to track down and thwart Mixell's plans, Harrison and Khalila had discovered critical leads while at the NCTC.

Harrison and Khalila were soon on their way to McLean in Khalila's car. Their trip was a quiet one, as had been their return journey from Bahrain. Khalila had resumed her typical aloof persona, with not a single mention of anything that had happened between them the last night in Bahrain. For Harrison's part, he felt guilty, as if he had soiled Angie's memory. It had been too soon to be with another woman and Angie deserved better, he told himself. Thankfully, Khalila appeared true to her word—the night in Bahrain was a one-time deal—as she had offered no indication that she was further interested.

After arriving at the NCTC, they worked their way across the main floor, filled with sixty analysts at their desks while supervisors observed from glass-enclosed offices on the second floor, until they reached the two workstations that had been freed up for them.

To help track Mixell down, the NCTC had released his image, captured as he left Fort McNair after assassinating the secretary of defense. It was clear that Mixell was either lying low or traveling with an effective disguise, because not a single shred of his existence had been detected since the assassination. Although law enforcement agencies had been directed to be on the alert for Mixell, the effort was suffering because the search for him hadn't been designated a National Special Security Event by the Department of Homeland Security. There had been no determination on what Mixell's next target was—person, place, or event—or even that there was a follow-on target. As a result, the NCTC wasn't entirely focused on Mixell, spreading its resources across several potential terrorist actions.

Nonetheless, potential leads had been flowing into the NCTC from various law enforcement agencies and the public. Harrison sat beside Khalila and pulled up the files on Mixell, then began reviewing the evidence collected from the scene of the Secretary of Defense's assassination and the leads that had been investigated thus far. Despite the lack of a focused NCTC effort, several hundred leads had already been run to ground, producing nothing. After categorizing those that remained, Harrison and Khalila each took half.

None of the leads seemed promising or even interesting. Harrison was trained to work out in the field, not pore over data scrolling across a computer screen for days or even weeks on end. He could tell that Khalila was similarly unenthused.

Harrison pushed back from the desk. "I'm getting some coffee. Want some?"

Khalila nodded. "Yeah. This is gonna be brutal."

42

USS *THEODORE ROOSEVELT*

Dusk was creeping across the Middle East, the sun sinking beneath the horizon as the Theodore Roosevelt strike group entered the Strait of Hormuz, headed into the Persian Gulf. It had been an uncharacteristically rainy day in the strait, with visibility out to only a few hundred yards in the waning light. Rather than monitor the small displays on the ship's Bridge, Captain Ryan Noss had decided to monitor the strike group's status from the aircraft carrier's Combat Direction Center, located three levels below the Flight Deck.

On watch as the Operations Officer was Captain Dolores Gonzalez, her eyes scanning the Video Wall, a collection of two eight-by-ten-foot displays mounted beside each other, with a half-dozen smaller monitors on each side. With the apparent threat being only one or more Russian submarines, only the standard Combat Air Patrol was aloft, but an E-2C Hawkeye was at twenty-five thousand feet, its radar searching the skies for hostile aircraft or missiles in case the Russians had more nefarious intentions.

Although Noss was relatively new aboard *Theodore Roosevelt*, having relieved the former Captain, Rich Tilghman, only a few months ago, Gonzalez was near the end of her tour of duty aboard the carrier and one of the veterans of the brutal battle in the Arabian Sea against the combined Russian Pacific Fleet and Indian Navy, occurring at the apex of Russia's *Blackmail* operation against its NATO foes. By the time *Roosevelt* joined the conflict, black smoke had been billowing upward from the other four American carriers engaged in the battle, with *Eisenhower* and *Bush* forced to terminate flight operations due to the extensive damage, while *Truman* and *Reagan* limped along, somehow retrieving, rearming, and launching aircraft while fires raged in compartments damaged by missile strikes.

Theodore Roosevelt had entered the battle late, still scarred from an earlier engagement with the Russian Pacific Fleet. Its Island superstructure was still a molten mass of steel and her hangar bays were scorched black from the fires that had raged inside. But her flight systems—catapults, arresting wires, and elevators—were operational again. Shipyard tiger teams had done an admirable job, beginning the carrier's repairs in Pearl Harbor, then continuing their efforts as the carrier sailed across the Pacific, with the ship navigated from Secondary Control located beneath the Flight Deck, instead of the mangled Bridge.

After the battle in the Arabian Sea, *Theodore Roosevelt*'s Island superstructure had been rebuilt, and now one would have to know where to look to spot the residual scars in the Hangar Deck. Noss knew that those who had participated in the vicious engagement—especially Captain Gonzalez, who had been the Operations Officer in CDC—would never forget what *Theodore Roosevelt* and the other American carriers had endured during the devastating battle.

After scanning the Video Wall displays and failing to note anything unusual, Noss shifted his thoughts to the aircraft positioned on the strike group's perimeter. Three MH-60R anti-submarine warfare helicopters were approaching bingo fuel and would head back to the carrier shortly. His eyes moved to the Flight Deck display; three replacement MH-60Rs were preparing to take off and would be on their way to relieve the on-station helicopters in a few minutes.

While the battle in the Arabian Sea had been primarily an air battle, the potential upcoming engagement with the Russian submarine in the Persian Gulf would be a test of the carrier strike group's anti-submarine capabilities. *Theodore Roosevelt* had four surface ship escorts: USS *Chosin,* a Ticonderoga-class cruiser, and three Arleigh Burke–class destroyers: USS *Halsey,* USS *O'Kane,* and USS *Paul Hamilton.* Each of those ships had two triple-tube torpedo launchers, but Noss figured that no Russian submarine captain would approach close enough to be sunk with torpedoes launched from surface ships. Russian heavyweight torpedoes had sufficient range to sink their target while the firing submarine remained outside counterfire range.

Instead, the strike group would rely on its anti-submarine aircraft. The squadron of MH-60R helicopters aboard *Theodore Roosevelt* was augmented by several more helicopters aboard the aircraft carrier's escorts. But the most potent anti-submarine platforms had recently joined the Theodore Roosevelt strike group. The fast attack submarine USS *Asheville* and the guided missile submarine USS *Michigan* had joined the strike group a few hours ago as it passed through the Gulf of Oman. *Asheville* was traveling in front of the strike group, searching the water ahead, while *Michigan* trailed the strike group in case the Russian submarine attempted to sneak up from behind.

Thus far, there had been no detection of the expected threat that lurked beneath the water's surface.

43

IRIS *JAMARAN*

Night had settled over the Strait of Hormuz, light rain falling from clouds hidden in the darkness above, as IRIS *Jamaran,* a Moudge-class frigate in the Islamic Republic of Iran Navy, moved swiftly across the waterway. The ship's captain, Commander Behzad Ahmadi, monitored the frigate's position as it approached the designated starting point for tonight's mission. A few hundred yards out, Ahmadi ordered engines to all stop, and his ship coasted until it halted and then loitered in the desired spot.

He went aft to the ship's fantail, where he monitored the progress of tonight's mission. *Jamaran's* stern was filled with black spherical objects, each one a few feet in diameter with spikes jutting out from its smooth metallic surface. In the distance, Ahmadi spotted the other Iranian ships that had been outfitted with Russian mines for the night's task, likewise making their way across the Strait to their designated starting points.

Ahmadi's assignment was straightforward but painstaking, releasing the mines at a predetermined distance apart as *Jamaran* journeyed across the strait. When the Iranian ships completed their task, hopefully before the sun rose across the Middle East, the Strait of Hormuz would be closed for business, with several barriers of mines stretching across the waterway, the mines floating at multiple depths so that not only would surface ships be threatened, but submarines as well.

The frigate's Executive Officer approached Ahmadi and reported that all preparations had been completed; the mines and their anchor chains were ready to deploy. *Jamaran* would lay mines that would float a few meters beneath the water's surface in the first tier across the strait, while other ships would lay mines at deeper levels and in the second and third tiers.

"Are the mine timers set?" Ahmadi asked.

"Yes, sir. All mines will activate simultaneously at the designated time."

Ahmadi nodded his understanding, then returned to the frigate's Bridge, where he commenced the night's operation.

"Helm, ahead one-third. Come to course one-six-zero."

To his Executive Officer on the fantail, he ordered, "Commence minelaying."

44

TIMONIUM, MARYLAND

Beth Walters, seated at her desk at the Carver Construction headquarters building, finished printing the last approval form for Mr. Carver just as his pickup truck coasted into his reserved parking space by the front door. The printing had been a last-minute task, since Jack and his wife had returned unexpectedly from their planned two-week vacation in the Ozark Mountains. Something had happened to Jill that had necessitated a trip to the hospital, cutting their trip short.

The portly man with a scruffy beard and his usual attire—worn jeans paired with a long-sleeve button-up dress shirt, plus a pair of boots that likely dated back to the previous century—stopped by the desk of his longtime secretary.

"Welcome back, Jack! I'm sorry to hear about Jill. What happened?"

"Thanks, Beth. A hiking trail got the best of her. Sprained her ankle pretty bad. She ended up in a boot and on painkillers, and we decided she'd be more comfortable at home."

"I'm sorry to hear that. Please give Jill my best." Beth slid the form into a clipboard, which she handed to Jack. "I've got an explosives procurement authorization form for you to sign. The Catoctin Mountain project needed fifty pounds of C-4 and some detonators, which Craig issued a few days ago. He's already ordered the replacement material. All that's left is your signature for our records."

Carver perused the form, but before he signed it, Beth added, "The odd thing is, when one of the foremen on the Catoctin Mountain project stopped by the office yesterday and I asked him what they needed those fancy detonators for, he had no idea about what I was talking about."

"What kind of detonators?"

"Wireless micro MEMS."

Carver scratched his beard, reviewing the order form in more detail. "Hmm . . . Micro MEMS detonators . . . Who's the chief engineer?"

"Frank Dougherty."

"Get him on the line."

Beth pulled up his number, dialed, and put the call on speakerphone. A man with a baritone voice answered. "Frank here."

"Hey, Frank, this is Jack. I've got an explosives order from your outfit—fifty pounds of C-4 and several dozen wireless micro MEMS detonators. What do you need this for?"

"C-4 and micro detonators? Why would we need that?"

"My thought exactly. That's not the type of stuff you'd need to blast through those mountains, but I thought maybe you ran into some demolition work. I want to know who placed the order and what for. Check with your foremen and get back to me."

"Got it. I'll be back in touch in a bit."

45

KENSINGTON, MARYLAND

Lonnie Mixell eased his Jeep Grand Cherokee to a stop alongside the curb on Webster Road, shifting his gaze to the storefront across the street—Gordon's Wholesale, a family-owned operation. The most delicate part of the plan he had devised to accomplish Brenda Verbeck's goal was the delivery, and he had a few options. Gordon's Wholesale offered the lowest risk and highest probability of success, but there was no guarantee he could arrange it.

He glanced at his face in the rearview mirror. His hair was now blond again, his eye contacts and mouth implants were in place, and he had deliberately donned a pair of worn jeans and the oldest sweatshirt he owned. Sufficiently disguised and presentable for the day's mission, he crossed the street and entered the store, asking the nearest worker if Dave Gordon was on the premises. He was directed to an office in the back of the main warehouse, where he was greeted by Gordon's secretary, who looked up from her computer when he entered the office.

"Can I help you?"

"I have an appointment with Mr. Gordon."

She squinted her eyes a bit, then looked back at her computer display. A few clicks on the keyboard followed, then she replied, "I don't see anything on his calendar. Are you sure you have the right day and time?"

"Wednesday at 4 p.m."

"Well, I'll let him know you're here, Mister . . ."

"Banks. George Banks."

The woman smiled and moved down a short hallway, knocking on one of the doors. After opening the door and poking her head in the office for a moment, she returned to her desk.

"He'll see you now," she said.

Gordon's office door was partially open, but Mixell knocked nonetheless, pushing it open wider before introducing himself.

"Have we met," the man replied, "or talked on the phone? I don't recall making an appointment to meet with you."

"Actually, we've never met, nor do I have an appointment today."

A perplexed look crossed the man's face. "Then why are you here?"

"I need a job, and I was hoping you had an opening."

"I'm sorry, Mister—what's your name again?"

"George Banks."

"I'm sorry, George, but I don't have any openings right now."

The man's response had been a likely outcome of today's task, but Mixell wasn't yet ready to concede defeat.

"I'm looking for weekend work. I've already got a weekday job, but I don't make much money and not enough to support my family, so I was hoping to pick up some work on the weekends. I imagine you've got to pay your employees extra for weekend deliveries. I'll work for the standard rate, minimum wage even. And I can start this weekend."

"Minimum wage? Every Saturday and Sunday?"

Mixell nodded.

"All right, George. You've got yourself a job. Minimum wage plus five extra dollars an hour." He gestured toward the woman at the desk. "Carole will provide the paperwork you need to fill out."

He stood and approached Mixell, offering his hand. "Welcome to Gordon's Wholesale."

The paperwork was quickly filled out and Mixell returned to his Jeep, pulling the SUV out into traffic for the second of the day's errands.

Less than half an hour later, Mixell stopped by a local grocery store. Pushing a cart through the aisles, he quickly found what he needed—at least from this store—and entered a self-checkout lane. Had anyone bothered to peruse the items in his cart, they would have concluded that he was either very hungry or had a lot of mouths to feed.

He made a few more stops at different stores to prevent anyone from noticing the unusual quantities he was purchasing, and eventually headed toward his rental home in Woodmore.

46

WOODMORE, MARYLAND

Cheryl Payne parked her truck on the gravel driveway near the front door of her father's home. After visiting a nearby friend, she had decided to stop by and check on her new tenant, see if there was anything that needed repair or improvement. George's Jeep wasn't at the house, so she assumed he was out and considered returning another time. But she decided to knock, just in case a friend had borrowed the car.

After receiving no response, she started back toward her truck, then stopped to peer through the living room window. Everything appeared as it had during her walk-through on the day George had decided to rent the house—not a single piece of furniture had been moved, nor was there any sign that George had moved in. Perhaps he had only a few belongings, which were probably in his bedroom.

As she walked toward her truck, she noticed a set of tire tracks through the grass leading to the barn. George had been keenly interested in the barn for some reason, and she wondered why. After retrieving the keys from her purse—she had given George the spare keys to the property—she headed into the backyard. The barn was locked, as expected. Looking over her shoulder to ensure George wasn't pulling into the driveway, she unlocked the door and slid it aside. After she flipped the switch by the entrance, yellow light illuminated several unexpected items.

In the center of the barn, a small worktable had been set up, and clamped to it was one of those extendable desk lamps frequently found in college dorms. On the table was a single tool—a metal X-Acto precision knife. As she wondered what George was up to, Cheryl spotted what appeared to be a stack of boxes or crates covered with a blanket.

She pulled the blanket away and examined two large wooden crates and a small one on top, each with unusual markings. The markings on the front of the large crates caught her attention.

CHARGE DEMOLITION M112

She pondered the words, wondering if the crates contained what she thought they did, then spotted another marking.

HIGH EXPLOSIVES

Cheryl sucked in a sharp breath, her pulse quickening when she heard the sound of an approaching car.

She threw the blanket back over the crates and hurried to the barn entrance, quickly pulling the door closed behind her, fumbling to slide the padlock shackle through the hasp and into the hole in the padlock body. Finally, the shackle went in and she turned around just as George's Jeep came into sight. As the SUV ground to a halt, Cheryl hoped—and prayed—that there was a simple explanation for her new tenant's possession of several crates of explosives.

After turning off the engine, Mixell kept his eyes fixed on Cheryl Payne. The woman was standing in front of the barn door frozen in place, her eyes wide with fright. It took only a second to process what had occurred—that she had another set of keys and had seen what was inside the barn. Mixell took a deep breath and let it out slowly. There was only one way this could play out. He reached into the glove compartment and slid his pistol into one back pocket of his pants and the suppressor into the other.

He stepped from the Jeep and waved to Cheryl as he casually strode toward her.

"Hi, Cheryl. What brings you around? Is there something you need from the barn?"

It took her a second to latch onto the lifeline he had thrown.

"Yes . . . actually, yes. There's, ahh, some tools in the back I need for a project at my house. I was hoping you'd be home, and when you weren't I tried to get into the barn, but the door was locked."

"Not a problem. Just show me what you need and I'll put 'em in your truck."

"That'd be great, George."

She forced a smile, but Mixell noticed the slight quiver of her lips.

He unlocked the barn door and pushed it aside. The lights were on. His eyes went to the crates, noticing that the blanket was draped over them in a haphazard manner, not neatly like he had left it.

Cheryl Payne had clearly seen too much.

She accompanied him into the barn, and Mixell stopped when they reached the crates. Cheryl took a few more steps before she also stopped and turned. Offering a disingenuous smile, Mixell straightened the blanket, returning it to how it had been previously placed. Then he waited for Cheryl's inevitable realization—that he knew what she had seen, and that she would likely not leave the barn alive.

Her eyes went to the crates. "I . . . I don't need to know what you need that for. I really don't care. It's none of my business."

Cheryl continued on as Mixell reached behind his back with both hands, retrieving the pistol and suppressor.

A trained opponent would have reacted instantly after spotting the firearm, attempting to disarm him. But your average civilian . . .

Cheryl stood frozen as he screwed the suppressor onto the barrel, processing what she was seeing and what was about to happen. She took two stilted steps backward, then fled toward the door.

Too late.

He finished attaching the suppressor and put two bullets into her back, dropping her to the ground.

Mixell was sometimes mesmerized by what a human body could do when sufficient adrenaline entered its bloodstream. As red stains spread across her back from the bullet wounds, Cheryl pushed herself to her feet and staggered toward the door.

He aimed and put a round into the back of one knee, the bullet shattering her kneecap as it exited. She collapsed to the ground and Mixell put another bullet into her other knee.

She wouldn't be moving anywhere now. At least not very fast.

Cheryl crawled slowly toward the door, another few feet before finally halting. She lay on the barn floor, whimpering, as Mixell approached.

He aimed the pistol at her head, holding it steady for a moment. Then he unscrewed the suppressor and returned it and the gun to his back pockets. Cheryl wasn't going anywhere, and she'd be dead in a few hours.

Mixell checked her pockets, verifying she didn't have her phone on her, then retrieved her keys so he could move her truck.

Stopping at the barn entrance, he turned the lights off, then closed and locked the door.

K-571 *KRASNOYARSK*

In the Persian Gulf, the Yasen-class submarine lurked just beneath the water's surface as Captain Second Rank Gavriil Novikov's crew manned Combat Stations. Hydroacoustic had detected the American carrier strike group shortly after it entered the Persian Gulf, and it was passing by to starboard now, just within range of *Krasnoyarsk*'s torpedoes. Novikov knew that the strike group had deployed an anti-submarine warfare helicopter screen; the rhythmic beat of the helicopter rotors on the water's surface had been detected by Hydroacoustic. What Novikov didn't yet know was—how far away were the torpedo-carrying helicopters?

Thus far, there had been no indication *Krasnoyarsk* had been detected. The strike group maneuvered at random intervals, a wise tactic in the vicinity of enemy submarines, but was still maintaining a north-westerly course. More indicative of whether *Krasnoyarsk* had been detected was the lack of attack by the helicopters. Instead, they continued their leapfrog searches, the aircraft in the rear retrieving its dipping sonar, then flying to the front and dropping its hydrophone back into the water. Once an initial search had been conducted, the next helicopter at the rear performed the same maneuver, leapfrogging over the other aircraft to the front of the line as the helicopters kept pace with the carrier strike group.

"Captain, Combat Stations are manned," the submarine's Watch Officer, Captain Lieutenant Petr Dolinski, reported, "with the exception of the Conning Officer."

Novikov acknowledged Dolinski's report, then announced, "This is the Captain. I have the Conn. Captain Lieutenant Dolinski retains the Watch. All stations, make preparations to proceed to periscope depth."

After every station acknowledged, Novikov ordered, "Diving Officer, make your depth twenty meters."

The Diving Officer acknowledged, and *Krasnoyarsk* tilted upward, rising toward periscope depth. Novikov had his face pressed to the attack periscope, the aft of the submarine's two scopes. Despite the crowded Central Command Post, now at full manning, it was quiet while the submarine rose from the deep.

Shortly before the Diving Officer reported that the submarine had reached the ordered depth, Novikov announced, "Scope clear," as the periscope pierced the water's surface.

He started turning the scope swiftly, completing several sweeps in search of nearby ships. "No close contacts!"

Normally, conversation would have resumed in the Central Command Post once the hazardous ascent to periscope depth had been safely conducted, but they were in the vicinity of an American carrier strike group with its anti-submarine screen deployed. Plus, the strike group was likely accompanied by one or possibly two submarines.

Now that Novikov had confirmed that there was no threat of imminent collision or attack, he completed a more detailed visual scan, searching for the American ships and aircraft. To starboard, he spotted five gray specks on the horizon. Although Hydroacoustic could hear the anti-submarine helicopters, they were too small and distant to be seen, even with the periscope on high power.

Reaching up, he pressed the periscope *Down* button, retracting the scope back into its well. The American surface ships, and potentially the anti-submarine helicopters, were outfitted with periscope detection radars. Expose too much of the periscope or leave it up too long, and the radar algorithms would detect the static object protruding above the relatively calm surface of the Persian Gulf.

Now that Novikov had verified the American anti-submarine helicopters weren't close enough to attack *Krasnoyarsk,* he examined the contact fusion plot. The five American surface ships were traveling close together, with the aircraft carrier in the middle and two escorts on each side. There were six anti-submarine helicopters aloft, three on each side of the carrier, but no aircraft ahead or behind. That meant that the carrier strike group indeed had a submarine escort, one in front and another trailing; the MH-60Rs would not be allowed into areas where friendly submarines were operating.

The tactical picture was clear. The question now was—attack with torpedoes or missiles?

Several years earlier, an American aircraft carrier—ironically, USS *Theodore Roosevelt*—had been attacked by a Russian submarine, which had launched its entire complement of twenty-four anti-ship missiles. The carrier had been seriously damaged and knocked out of service. But temporary repairs had been quickly made, returning the ship to action in time for the climactic battle in the Arabian Sea.

Novikov would not make that same mistake. He had only sixteen anti-ship missiles loaded, plus *Theodore Roosevelt*'s escorts would not be taken unaware, like they had before, with a surprise attack. Although *Krasnoyarsk* carried fewer missiles than the previous Russian assailant, it was loaded with forty wire-guided heavyweight torpedoes, and a single torpedo would send any surface combatant, aside from an aircraft carrier, to the bottom. A ship the size of their primary target, a Nimitz-class aircraft carrier, would be more difficult to sink, requiring two or more torpedoes to break its keel.

Complicating the attack was the engagement range. To avoid detection by the carrier strike group's helicopters, Novikov had kept *Krasnoyarsk* at the very limit of the submarine's Futlyar torpedoes. At this distance and against a closely packed group of ships, the Futlyar torpedoes could not be guided past the escorts to hit the aircraft carrier instead with certainty. Plus, *Krasnoyarsk*'s torpedoes, as they sped toward their targets, would be detected by the anti-submarine helicopters, and the surface ships would likely begin maneuvering before the torpedoes reached them. As a result, there was no guarantee that each torpedo would hit its designated target.

That, however, was a complication Novikov was happy to deal with. To get to the aircraft carrier, he'd likely have to sink its escort ships.

"Prepare to fire, Hydroacoustic two-five through two-nine, horizontal salvo, tubes One through Five. Tube One fired first."

In preparation for today's task, Novikov had loaded torpedoes in all ten of *Krasnoyarsk*'s tubes. If the tactical situation allowed, he'd send another five-torpedo salvo after the first one.

Captain Third Rank Anton Topolski, Novikov's First Officer, stopped behind the two men seated at their fire control consoles. He tapped one michman on the shoulder. "Send solutions to Weapon Control."

The michman complied, and Topolski announced, "Captain, all contacts remain steady on course. I have a firing solution."

Krasnoyarsk's Weapons Officer reported, "Ready to Fire, tubes One through Five."

The Watch Officer followed. "Countermeasures are armed."

Novikov gave the order. "Fire tubes One though Five!"

As each torpedo was impulsed from the submarine, Novikov felt the tremor in the deck, then his ears popped as all five tubes were vented, releasing the pressurized air that had shot the torpedoes from their tubes.

"Raising aft periscope," he announced.

The attack periscope rose swiftly from its well, and Novikov pressed his right eye against the optics, searching for any sign that the torpedo launch had been detected. In the distance, the five surface ships remained on course. But that was not a surprise. It would take a moment for the American helicopters to detect the incoming torpedoes and inform the strike group's Anti-Submarine Warfare commander, who would relay the information to each ship.

Novikov scanned the water's surface, spotting the five faint torpedo trails. Soon, the helicopter crews would also see the trails and speed toward their source.

"Command Post, Hydroacoustic. Upshift in frequency, Hydroacoustic two-five through two-nine. All contacts are increasing speed and maneuvering."

In the distance, Novikov spotted the American ships turning away from the torpedoes.

"All contacts are maneuvering, turning to starboard," he said.

Novikov waited until the surface ships steadied on their new course, then did the mental calculation. "Weapons Officer. Send torpedo steer, sixty degrees right, to all torpedoes."

The Weapons Officer sent the course correction, turning the torpedoes back onto an intercept course with the evading targets. Each torpedo had a built-in sonar, so the task was to simply steer the torpedo close enough to detect the target, and then its internal software would take over, guiding the weapon until it reached its target and detonated, or the torpedo ran out of fuel. Novikov had factored in a twenty-five-percent fuel reserve to allow the torpedoes to chase down their targets while receiving new steering commands, which Novikov would send as long as *Krasnoyarsk* could remain at periscope depth and the American surface ships remained within visual range.

Novikov shifted back to an air search, spotting three small specks growing quickly larger. The American anti-submarine warfare helicopters were streaking toward *Krasnoyarsk,* either due to spotting the torpedo trails or detecting its periscope.

At this point, Novikov would normally have gone deep and attempted to evade the helicopters and their air-dropped torpedoes. But he wanted to remain at periscope depth, sending additional steer commands to his torpedoes as the American warships maneuvered.

"Raise radar mast and radiate," he ordered.

The Watch Officer complied and the mast popped above the water's surface, then began searching for contacts.

Krasnoyarsk's presence and location were now being blatantly broadcast, lighting up radar detectors on the American surface ships and helicopters. But that was okay. The Americans knew an enemy submarine was nearby, and the helicopters were heading straight for it. However, *Krasnoyarsk* was safe for the moment, inside the minimum attack range of the U.S. Navy's Vertical-Launch ASROC—a torpedo atop a rocket—and the torpedoes carried by the helicopters were simply dropped, which meant the American helicopters would have to approach to within a few hundred yards of their target.

Perfect.

Krasnoyarsk was an improved Yasen-class guided missile submarine, and in addition to sixteen anti-surface missiles, it also carried twenty-four anti-air missiles on this deployment.

Novikov glanced at the radar display, then announced, "Set radar contact zero-one, zero-two, and zero-three as the targets of interest. Prepare to Fire, three missiles."

The Missile Officer acknowledged and prepared to launch three of *Krasnoyarsk*'s Pantsir-M short-range anti-air missiles.

"All three missiles are energized," reported a watchstander seated at one of the fire control consoles. He soon followed up with, "Anti-air missiles starboard One-one, One-two, and One-three have accepted targeting."

Novikov initiated the next step. "Open starboard missile hatch One."

"Missile hatch One is open," the Missile Officer reported. "Ready to Fire."

Novikov surveyed the approaching helicopters—they were almost within range of their air-dropped torpedoes—then gave the order, launching three of the four missiles housed in vertical launch tube One.

"Fire."

The three missiles were launched from the submarine, streaking upward and then veering toward their targets. The helicopter crews realized their peril and began evasive maneuvers, launching chaff and infrared flares, but the missiles were only seconds away from their targets when launched and only the farthest of the three helicopters was able to evade the incoming weapon. The other two missiles ignored the flares and plowed through the chaff, detonating after slamming into the helicopters. Two fireballs of twisted metal plummeted into the ocean.

The third missile missed, but the Pantsir-M radar system guided it back toward its target. The missile veered into a sharp turn, lining back onto an intercept path with the helicopter. Seconds later, a third fireball fell from the sky.

With *Krasnoyarsk* no longer threatened, Novikov refocused on the surface warships. They were shrinking into the distance, and Novikov figured he'd be able to send one more steer command to his torpedoes before the ships were beyond visual range.

After surveying the trajectory of the fleeing ships, Novikov ordered, "Weapons Officer. Insert steer, thirty degrees right, all torpedoes."

The Weapons Officer sent the commands as Novikov lowered the periscope.

"Diving Officer, make your depth fifty meters. Steersman, right full rudder, steady course zero-four-zero. Ahead flank."

The American warships were on the run. But they would not get away.

48

USS *THEODORE ROOSEVELT*

Seated in the Captain's chair on the Bridge, Captain Ryan Noss's first indication that *Theodore Roosevelt* was in jeopardy had been when the MH-60Rs on the port side of the ship had begun streaking outbound. Seconds later, a report from the strike group's ASW commander emanated from the Bridge speakers, delivering the unwelcome news—incoming torpedoes.

Noss's eyes were drawn to several thin streaks of light green water traveling toward the carrier strike group, one torpedo angling toward each ship. The situation coalesced quickly in Noss's mind. The MH-60Rs had detected an enemy submarine and were en route to sink it. But the submarine had already fired several heavyweight torpedoes at the strike group.

Theodore Roosevelt's Officer of the Deck, Lieutenant Commander Michael Beresford, assumed the Conn from the more junior Conning Officer and bellowed out, "Ahead flank! Right full rudder!"

The Helm acknowledged and Noss felt the vibration in the ship's deck as the carrier's four propellers accelerated. The ship's rudders dug into the water, turning *Theodore Roosevelt* sharply to starboard. After assessing the torpedo's approach angle, Beresford ordered, "Steady course one-zero-zero!"

Roosevelt steadied up on its new course and Noss watched as the torpedoes kept traveling on a straight path; they were still too far away and hadn't detected the strike group's ships with their built-in sonars. Unless new steer commands were sent to the torpedoes, the carrier strike group would easily evade all five torpedoes. *Theodore Roosevelt*'s four escorts were likewise turning to starboard, maintaining their formation around the aircraft carrier.

Through the Bridge windows, several bright flashes in the distance caught Noss's attention. As he contemplated what they were, the ASW commander's voice came across the Bridge speaker, confirming Noss's fear. Three MH-60Rs had been shot down by submarine-launched anti-air missiles. His attention shifted to *Theodore Roosevelt's* survival when the five incoming torpedoes veered sharply to the right. The enemy submarine crew had apparently detected the strike group's evasive maneuver and steered the torpedoes onto a new intercept course.

Lieutenant Commander Beresford responded immediately, turning the carrier to a new course that would result in the torpedoes passing behind *Roosevelt* and her escorts. Noss shifted his Bridge speaker to the dedicated ASW channel just in time to learn that torpedo pings had been detected, with their frequency correlated to Futlyar torpedoes, the newest heavyweight torpedo in the Russian Navy's arsenal. Noss's concern increased when the ASW commander reported that two of the torpedoes had begun homing.

Roosevelt and its escorts began another round of evasive maneuvers, but the torpedoes altered course toward the strike group again, and a moment later on the starboard side of the carrier, a plume of water jetted two hundred feet into the air, whipsawing the destroyer USS *Paul Hamilton* like a rubber toy. Seconds later, another explosion engulfed the cruiser USS *Chosin,* seawater shooting upward, then falling like rain onto the stricken ship. Both ships lost propulsion and slowed, and as the mist cleared, it was obvious that the torpedo explosions had broken the keel of each ship. It was a gut-wrenching sight, watching each ship split in half and take on water, the stern and bow tilting upward as *Theodore Roosevelt* and her two remaining surface ships sped away.

Noss monitored the three remaining torpedoes, which drew steadily aft, with no sign of receiving another steer command. He breathed a sigh of relief before recalling that the Futlyar torpedoes had a wake-homing capability. As one of the torpedoes crossed the carrier's wake, Noss watched tensely through the rear Bridge windows. The torpedo continued on, then suddenly turned back toward the turbulent trail of water. It snaked back and forth before settling into *Theodore Roosevelt's* wake. It steadily closed on the carrier, and the ASW commander soon reported that the torpedo was homing.

Roosevelt was already at maximum speed and evasive maneuvers were far more complicated when dealing with a wake-following torpedo. As Noss considered his options, the bright trail through the water faded, and the ASW commander reported that the torpedo had shut down. It had been fired from a very long range and had finally run out of fuel. A visual check confirmed the other two torpedoes chasing the strike group had also shut down.

As the remaining strike group ships sped eastward, Noss evaluated the current scenario. They had lost two surface ships and three of their MH-60R anti-submarine warfare helicopters, and the remaining MH-60Rs aloft were being withdrawn until the tactical situation was better understood—why had the helicopters' missile defense systems failed?

The inability to employ the strike group's MH-60Rs was a significant concern. That there was an enemy submarine in the area was obvious, but how to sink it was the critical issue. It was inside the minimum range of the strike group's ASROC rocket-launched torpedoes, and the MH-60Rs, at the moment, couldn't approach close enough to drop their lightweight torpedoes within attack range. That left *Theodore Roosevelt's* escort submarines—*Asheville* and *Michigan*—to deal with the assailant.

49

USS *ASHEVILLE*

"No close contacts!"

Commander Gary Watson stopped circling on the periscope, his gaze settling on the remnants of two U.S. Navy warships, each sheared in half, their bows and sterns pointing skyward as they slipped beneath the water's surface. Watson and his crew listened to the ships' death throes as the severed sections sank deeper—the groans and sudden bangs as sealed compartments imploded from the increasing ocean pressure.

Swiveling toward the surviving surface ships, Watson shifted the periscope to high power and pressed the doubler, zooming in on the sterns of *Theodore Roosevelt* and the two remaining surface escorts as they sped away.

Moments earlier, while searching the water ahead of the carrier strike group, *Asheville*'s sonar technicians had detected a salvo of torpedoes headed toward the surface warships, followed by the strike group's evasive maneuvers. Watson had ordered his crew to Battle Stations, then waited in frustration, unable to assist.

Anti-submarine warfare was a complicated process when coordinating surface, air, and submarine assets. To prevent blue-on-blue engagements—air or surface ships accidentally sinking one of their own submarines—surface ships and ASW helicopters were not allowed to attack contacts in areas assigned to U.S. submarines. Conversely, American submarines could not travel into an unauthorized area to assist for fear of being attacked, since the surface and air assets were *weapons-free*, allowed to attack any submerged contact detected in their area.

The submarine that had fired the torpedo salvo was operating in water owned by the MH-60Rs, and although *Asheville*'s sonar technicians had detected the torpedoes speeding toward the strike group, the location of the firing submarine remained unknown. *Asheville* needed to approach closer in order to detect and attack the enemy submarine, but couldn't, at least not until it received new orders, which is why Watson had brought *Asheville* to periscope depth to download the latest radio messages. He finally heard the announcement he was waiting for.

"Conn, Radio. Download complete."

Watson acknowledged the report, then asked, "Have we received a new OPORD?"

"Conn, Radio. Yes, along with a corresponding change in waterspace. We're printing the messages now."

While Watson waited for the messages, he ordered *Asheville* down from periscope depth, to a quieter realm away from the noisy surface.

"Dive, make your depth one-five-zero feet. Helm, ahead two-thirds."

Watson lowered the periscope as *Asheville* tilted downward, and a radioman soon arrived in the Control Room with a message clipboard, which he handed to the submarine's Captain.

Asheville's new operational order was on top, followed by the associated waterspace assignment. The MH-60Rs had been removed from the equation, perhaps because they couldn't adequately search the water at a pace that kept up with the strike group traveling at ahead flank. Instead, the waterspace had been divided between *Asheville* and *Michigan*. The torpedo salvo had been fired from within *Asheville*'s new operating area, which meant that Watson and his crew now had sufficient leeway to track down and sink the offending submarine.

In concert with his thoughts, Sonar completed its initial search following the descent from periscope depth.

"Conn, Sonar. Hold a new contact on the towed array, designated Sierra four-five, classified submerged, bearing one-eight-two. Analyzing."

Watson glanced at the nearest combat control display. The submerged contact was to the south and was held passively on the towed array, which meant the only concrete information available to the crew was the contact's bearing. It would take a while for the combat control system algorithms to determine the contact's parameters—range, course, and speed. However, Sonar helped out.

"Conn, Sonar. Contact is classified as Russian Yasen-class nuclear submarine, traveling at high speed. Estimate contact is traveling in excess of thirty knots based on screw blade rate."

The Russian submarine had increased speed to flank, attempting to chase down the evading carrier strike group.

Watson replied, his voice carrying through the Control Room and also into adjacent areas via the microphone above the Conn. "All stations, Conn. Designate Sierra four-five as Master one. Track Master one. I want a firing solution as soon as possible."

Torpedoes had already been loaded into all four tubes, leaving one more preparation remaining. "Flood down and open outer doors, all tubes."

Asheville was still at low speed, maximizing the range of its sensors. Without knowing how far away the Russian submarine was, it was better to remain stealthy at a lower speed while determining the target's course and range. However, maneuvering *Asheville* would help the combat control system algorithms calculate the target's approximate course and range. Watson guessed that the Russian submarine was chasing down the strike group, so he turned *Asheville* in the same direction.

"Helm, left full rudder, steady course zero-nine-zero."

A few minutes after completing the turn, the towed array stopped snaking back and forth, and reliable bearings began arriving. It didn't take long to confirm Watson's guess—the Russian submarine was headed eastward. The estimated range was problematic, near the limit of *Asheville*'s MK 48 torpedoes.

"Weapon Control, report fuel remaining to Master one."

Lieutenant Rusty Idleman, supervising the Weapon Launch Console, reported, "Estimated fuel remaining is four percent."

Watson's crew would have to react quickly. Their torpedoes had barely enough fuel to catch the Russian submarine, and the fuel remaining would decrease rapidly with the target at ahead flank and *Asheville* still at ahead two-thirds. He was about to increase speed and begin torpedo launch procedures when Sonar's report interrupted his thoughts.

"Conn, Sonar. Hold a new contact on the towed array, designated Sierra four-six, classified submerged, bearing one-five-zero. Analyzing."

Watson glanced at the geographic plot. The new contact wasn't

Michigan—its new operating area was to the northeast, not southeast—which meant there was a second Russian submarine in *Asheville*'s area. Its range was currently unknown, and the Russian submarine would be a significant threat if it was close enough to detect *Asheville*'s torpedo launch toward Master one and fire in response.

"Conn, Sonar. Sierra four-six is classified as Russian Akula-class submarine."

Watson announced immediately, "All stations, Conn. Designate Sierra four-six as Master two. Track Master two."

"Conn, Sonar. Hold Master two on the spherical array. Estimated range is ten thousand yards based on spherical array range-of-the-day for an Akula."

Asheville and other American submarines' sonar search plans were multifaceted, and one parameter updated daily was the initial detection range of various contacts by the submarine's sensors, taking into account the current environmental conditions and the estimated radiated noise of each contact. At ten thousand yards, the Akula submarine to the southeast was much closer than Master one and a clear counterfire threat. It would have to be dealt with first.

"All stations, Conn. Master two is the target of interest."

As the fire control technicians manning the combat control consoles shifted their emphasis to the closer submarine, Sonar made another report.

"Conn, Sonar. Hold a new contact on the towed array, designated Sierra four-seven, classified Akula, bearing three-five-five."

There was a third Russian submarine to the north. Whether it was traveling south toward *Asheville* or chasing the surface ships was unknown. Then Sonar's report clarified the matter.

"Conn, Sonar. Gained Sierra four-seven on the spherical array."

The submarine to the north was also closing on *Asheville*. The situation then turned drastically worse with Sonar's next report.

"Conn, Sonar. Hold a new contact on the towed array, designated Sierra four-eight, classified Akula, bearing two-six-zero."

Watson evaluated the deteriorating situation. *Asheville* was boxed in by three Russian submarines, two of which were closing on them, and he was fairly certain the third submarine was headed their way as well. The Russians were hunting in a pack, like the Germans had done in World War II, apparently disregarding the American philosophy of one submarine per operating area while weapons-free. Watson was about to give new course and speed orders to the Helm when he was interrupted by the Sonar Supervisor's voice blaring over the Control Room speaker.

"Torpedo launch transients, bearing one-five-five!"

Seconds later, Sonar reported, "Torpedo in the water! Bearing one-five-five!"

Turning toward the sonar display on the Conn, Watson examined the monitor. A bright white trace had appeared at the reported bearing.

Watson responded immediately. "Ahead flank! Left full rudder, steady course three-four-zero! Launch countermeasures!"

The Helm twisted the rudder yoke to left full as he rang up ahead flank on the Engine Order Telegraph, while the submarine's Junior Officer of the Deck flipped up the protective cover on the countermeasure launch panel, ejecting a torpedo decoy into the water.

Watson followed up, "Quick Reaction Firing, Master two, tube One!"

As Watson's crew executed the order, bearing lines to the incoming torpedo appeared on the nearest combat control console, updated every ten seconds. With the crew already at Battle Stations and tracking the designated target, that should be more than enough time to shoot back. But the more important issue was whether *Asheville* could evade the incoming torpedo. The situation turned worse, however.

"Second torpedo in the water, bearing three-five-zero!"

A new bearing trace appeared on the Conn Sonar display, followed by another report blaring across the Control Room speakers. "Third torpedo in the water, bearing two-six-two!"

There were now three torpedoes inbound toward *Asheville*. Watson stared at the Sonar display, searching for a solution. No matter which way he turned, he'd be headed toward one of the torpedoes. For *Asheville* to survive, he would have to maneuver his submarine expertly and correctly guess the ranges and courses of the incoming torpedoes.

The torpedo to the south was likely the closest, having been fired from the first Russian submarine detected on the spherical array. *Asheville* was well positioned to evade the first-fired torpedo, having turned to a different course after being fired upon and leaving countermeasures behind that the torpedo would have to deal with. The challenge now was to thread the needle between the other two torpedoes.

Unfortunately, events were proceeding so rapidly that combat control could not accurately determine the range and course of each incoming torpedo in the time required, which meant guesswork—and luck—would be required.

After assessing the likely firing range and trajectory of each torpedo, Watson made his decision. "Helm, left ten degrees rudder. Steady course three-one-zero. Launch countermeasures!"

Asheville had already turned to the northwest, and a slight maneuver to the left appeared to provide the optimal path between the other two torpedoes, maximizing the distance to both, one on each side of the submarine.

It grew silent in the Control Room as the crew realized what their Captain was attempting to do. Through the submarine's hull, they began hearing the high-pitched pings—like bird chirps—growing louder as the Russian torpedoes searched the water for a target that met the engagement parameters.

Suddenly, one of the ping rates increased.

"Conn, Sonar. Torpedo to the southwest is range-gating! Torpedo's homing!"

The torpedo had increased the rate of its sonar pings to more accurately determine the range to its target, so a refined intercept course could be calculated. It had locked onto *Asheville*. Then the rate of pings from the second torpedo also increased.

"Conn, Sonar. Torpedo to the north is also homing!"

After analyzing the latest information, Watson concluded that the situation was almost hopeless. There was nowhere to evade. Turning left or right would head toward a homing torpedo, exacerbating the situation. The only hope was to eject more decoys and pray.

"Launch countermeasures!" Watson ordered. "Alternate a decoy and jammer every fifteen seconds!"

The Junior Officer of the Deck complied, ejecting the first decoy as Sonar made its next report.

"Nearest torpedo range is one thousand yards!"

Watson did the mental calculation, using the estimated closing speed of a Russian heavyweight torpedo and *Asheville*'s speed at ahead flank.

One minute left.

Sonar's report echoed in the quiet Control Room. Maybe they'd get lucky and the incoming torpedoes would lock onto the decoys, with the jammers providing cover for *Asheville*'s escape.

The Executive Officer's voice broke the silence. "Firing solution to Master two has been sent to Weapon Control. Solution ready!"

"Weapon ready!" the Weapons Officer announced.

"Ship ready!" Lieutenant Idleman reported.

Watson had temporarily forgotten that they were in the middle of a Quick Reaction firing, his thoughts focused on torpedo evasion. At a minimum, they'd send a torpedo back down the throat of one of the Russian submarines, hopefully sending it to the bottom.

"Shoot tube One!" he ordered.

Watson felt the ship shudder as it ejected the three-thousand-pound weapon, then returned his attention to the critical issue.

"Range to nearest torpedo is five hundred yards!"

Thirty seconds left.

His eyes were glued to the Sonar display, trying to discern whether their decoys had distracted the torpedoes. If so, the torpedo bearings would start falling rapidly behind them. But the bearings to both torpedoes remained steady.

"Nearest torpedo's range is two hundred yards! Both are still homing!"

Ten seconds.

Their fate was sealed. There was nothing more Watson or his crew could do.

He counted down the seconds in his mind, and when he reached zero, *Asheville* jolted as a deafening explosion filled his ears. The wail of the flooding alarm soon emanated from the speakers, and the lights in Control fluttered, then went dark momentarily before the emergency lights kicked on.

Watson ordered an Emergency Blow, hoping to offset the flooding, but the submarine slowed and its stern began to squat from the weight of the ocean flooding the Engine Room. As Watson watched the red numbers on the digital depth display swiftly increase, he knew that *Asheville* would not reach the surface.

50

IRIS *JAMARAN*

Along the northern shore of the Strait of Hormuz, the Iranian frigate IRIS *Jamaran* loitered in the shoals just south of Larak Island. As the hot sun beat down on the warship's metal structure, the ship's captain, Commander Behzad Ahmadi, leaned back in his chair and checked the clock mounted to the Bridge bulkhead, waiting in anticipation as time counted down.

Two nights ago, Ahmadi's ship had participated in a clandestine operation, laying mines provided by a military ally across the entire width of the Strait of Hormuz. It didn't take much for Ahmadi to decipher that the ally was Russia, since the mines were marked with Cyrillic inscriptions. While Ahmadi didn't care much about the markings nor who their covert ally was, he was keenly interested in the carnage the ordnance would inflict. Before laying each mine, an activation timer had been set. Ahmadi glanced again at the clock, his eyes remaining focused on the minute hand until it reached the designated time.

Ahmadi's gaze shifted to the busy strait. A large container ship was less than a thousand yards away from the nearest layer of mines. His eyes followed the ship, his body tensing in anticipation as the unsuspecting merchant sped toward its demise.

Seconds after the ship reached the first mine layer, a billowy waterspout shot upward, engulfing the ship's bow, and the sound of the muffled explosion rolled past *Jamaran.* When the mist cleared, Ahmadi could tell that the ship's bow was already sinking lower into the water.

The merchant turned suddenly, heading north. It took Ahmadi a moment to realize what was happening. The merchant ship's captain had quickly deduced what had occurred—the ship had hit a mine and was taking on water—and he had turned the ship toward the nearest shoal water, which was to the north, hoping to ground the merchant ship before it sunk. A wise move, Ahmadi concluded.

A moment later, another merchant ship reached the first mine layer to the west, suffering a similar fate, except this ship started taking water on faster and was unable to reach shoal water before slipping beneath the waves. On both sides of the strait, backing bells were ordered aboard the ships, and traffic through the Strait of Hormuz ground to a halt.

Ahmadi smiled. Their mission had been accomplished.

51

WASHINGTON, D.C.

In the Situation Room in the West Wing, the president took his seat at the table, joining Chief of Staff Kevin Hardison, Secretary of State Marcy Perini, acting Secretary of Defense Peter Seuffert, Secretary of the Navy Sheila McNeil, and Chief of Naval Operations Admiral Joe Sites. The information coming in from the Persian Gulf was grim, with the near-term outlook alarming. The president turned to his secretary of the Navy, Sheila McNeil, for the latest update.

"We're certain it's Russia?"

"Yes, Mr. President," Sheila replied. "The sonar frequency of the fired torpedoes correlates to the Russian Futlyar heavyweight torpedo, plus the signature of the radar guiding the missiles that shot down our helicopters matches the maritime version of the Russian Pantsir missile system. There is no doubt, Mr. President. We've been attacked by Russian submarines."

"How many?"

"Four that we know of. *Asheville*'s crew launched its emergency SEPIRB buoy after their submarine was sunk, which included a message informing us that they were engaged by three Russian submarines in addition to the one chasing the strike group."

"Is it possible that there are even more submarines?"

"Four is our best guess at the moment. Based on the submarines that sortied from Vladivostok, five is the max, but the fifth submarine departed later than the other four, and we don't know its destination."

"How bad is the situation?"

"We've lost three warships: the destroyer *Paul Hamilton*, the cruiser *Chosin*, and *Asheville*. The Russians have also shot down seven MH-60Rs:

three during the initial attack, plus another four in a subsequent engagement. The strike group initially evaded to the east, but eventually had to turn around—much of the gulf is only about one hundred and thirty miles wide. The strike group had to circle back to the west, away from Iran's shoreline, which allowed the Russian submarine to catch up. We lost those four additional helicopters, but they slowed down the Russian submarine sufficiently to allow P-8A assets to arrive on station. The MH-60Rs have been withdrawn, and the strike group is now protected by a screen of sonobuoy fields laid by and monitored by the P-8As."

"Will the P-8As be safe from the Russian submarine anti-air missiles?"

"We think so. The P-8As are militarized versions of Boeing 737 jets, which can monitor their sonobuoys at a high altitude and distance. They'll launch torpedoes using the HAAWC wing kit," Sheila explained, referring to the High Altitude ASW Weapon Capability provided by a wing kit, which flew the torpedo to its desired water entry point, "which should keep them beyond the range of the Pantsir missiles."

"Where is the strike group now?"

"It's temporarily safe, just off the Kuwaiti shore on the western side of the gulf."

Shifting topics somewhat, the president inquired on the new complication. "What's the status of the Strait of Hormuz?"

"The strait has been heavily mined across its entire width. Two merchant ships have hit mines so far, one sinking and the other running aground. Initial analysis indicates there are several layers of mines, each with mines at various depths, not just near the surface."

"So, the Russians are attempting to prevent us from sending additional forces into the Gulf or extracting the carrier and its escorts?"

"It appears so. With four submarines in the gulf, they have the advantage and want to keep it that way."

"How do you recommend we respond?" the president asked.

Sheila looked to Admiral Sites, who took over the brief.

"Our first priority is to rescue the crews of the sunk surface ships and *Asheville*. Civilian and Fifth Fleet ships are pulling our surface ship crew members from the water. Not everyone is accounted for yet, and the rescue effort continues. Regarding *Asheville*, most of the crew is likely alive. The Persian Gulf is very shallow, typically two to three hundred feet, well above *Asheville*'s crush depth. Those who made it into an intact compartment would be safe for now, and they should have enough air to last for at least a week; longer if they can access the reserve oxygen banks and have enough emergency carbon dioxide absorbers. Within the hour, submarine rescue assets should depart San Diego for the Persian Gulf, and we should be able to rescue all surviving members of *Asheville*'s crew."

"That's good news," the president remarked.

"The next, and equally important, priority is to sink these Russian submarines before they inflict more damage. The basic strategy is to protect our surface ships until we can flow more submarines into the gulf. The P-8A sonobuoy fields should provide sufficient warning if any Russian submarine tries to approach close enough to launch torpedoes. If one does try to stick its nose where it doesn't belong, the P-8As have an ample supply of our latest and most effective lightweight torpedo— the MK 54 MOD 1—outfitted with HAAWC wing kits.

"As far as long-range missile strikes from the Yasen-class submarine, it has a maximum loadout of forty missiles, which is likely split between anti-surface and anti-air. The carrier and its remaining escorts are well equipped to defend against anti-surface missiles. So, the plan is to keep the Russian submarines beyond torpedo launch range until our submarines arrive."

"When do you expect that?"

"This is where the plan gets sticky. Submarines from Guam will arrive before the mines are cleared, and it's entirely possible the squadron from Hawaii will also arrive before a path through the minefield has been created. We have assets that can identify and target mines near the surface, but we can't clear the deeper mines to allow passage of deep-draft surface warships or submarines traveling on the surface. Also, the mines are laid at multiple depths to prevent submerged submarines from entering the Gulf. The necessary deep-water mine-clearing assets are on their way, but it will take a while for them to arrive. This is where *Michigan* factors in."

"*Michigan,* a guided missile submarine?"

"Correct. In an ASW role, *Michigan* would be outmatched by four

Russian attack submarines. She's available to engage if necessary, but we think she'll have a more significant impact clearing mines."

The president raised an eyebrow. "How is she going to clear mines?"

"We've speculated, but haven't figured that out yet. We're leaving it up to *Michigan*'s crew and its SEAL detachment. They've got two minisubs in their Dry Deck Shelters, plus sixty tons of SEAL-related ordnance aboard. We're reasonably confident they'll figure something out. It's worth a shot, at least." Admiral Sites paused momentarily. "Subject to your questions, this concludes my brief."

The president nodded his understanding. "I concur with your recommendations. Keep me informed of any significant changes in status."

52

MCLEAN, VIRGINIA

At the National Counterterrorism Center, on the main floor amongst sixty other employees of the fourteen-agency center, Jake Harrison sat beside Khalila Dufour, staring at his computer display as he searched for potential links to Lonnie Mixell. Harrison took a sip of lukewarm coffee as the next set of FBI reports loaded on his display, while Khalila scoured reports from other agencies. They had been at it since their return from the Middle East, but thus far their efforts had yielded no clues to Mixell's whereabouts or next plan.

"I've got something," Khalila announced.

Harrison glanced at her computer display, which listed reports from ATF—the Bureau of Alcohol, Tobacco, Firearms and Explosives. Khalila had expanded one of the reports, which provided the details.

"We've got fifty pounds of missing C-4," she said. "Want to check it out?"

Harrison perused the report, focusing first on the amount of C-4. One pound of C-4 could demolish a car or wreck an average-sized house. Fifty pounds could take out a medium-sized office building. Then his gaze stopped on the associated report of missing detonators.

"Three dozen wireless micro detonators," Harrison read the information out loud. "Looks like whoever has this C-4 intends to hit a lot of small targets. Maybe simultaneously, if the wireless detonators can be set off at the same time from a single signal."

He glanced at the report location—Carver Construction, Timonium, Maryland—which was just north of Baltimore, not far away.

"Do you have any other leads?" he asked.

"This is it."

"Let's check it out. Even if it's not Mixell, someone's up to something. It's worth looking into it now, rather than letting the ATF and NCTC wheels churn before this onion gets peeled apart."

Khalila picked up the phone, calling the number on the report for Carver Construction.

Ninety minutes later, after a short drive north on Interstate 95 and up the western side of the Baltimore Beltway to Timonium, Harrison and Khalila pulled into the parking lot for Carver Construction. Calling from the NCTC, Khalila had connected with the office manager, who was aware of the C-4 and detonator issue, but didn't know all of the details. However, the company's owner, Jack Carver, was expected back in the office in about an hour, so Harrison and Khalila had decided to meet with him at Carver Construction.

The office manager, Beth Walters, escorted Harrison and Khalila into a nearby office, closing the door behind her as she left. Carver, seated at his desk, rose to greet his visitors, and after a quick examination of Harrison's and Khalila's identification cards, returned to his desk while the two CIA officers settled into chairs facing him.

After reviewing the ATF report with Carver, Harrison asked, "Do you have any idea what might have happened to the missing C-4 and detonators?"

"I don't know what their intended use is, but I know where you can start. Our supply manager admitted that he had sold the material, pocketing a hefty sum. He even tried to bribe me and my office manager to keep quiet about the issue, offering to split the payment he received with us. I fired him on the spot."

"How long ago was that?"

"Yesterday."

"His name?"

"Craig Daniels."

"Did he mention who he sold the explosives to?"

Carver shook his head. "He wouldn't provide the name. He said ratting the guy out would likely be detrimental to his health. Plus, his customer was probably using an alias anyway."

"So, Daniels interfaced with a single person. Did he provide a description of the man?"

"Nothing. He clammed up when it became clear I wasn't going to go along with his plan to sweep the issue under the rug."

"Do you have any idea where we might find him?"

"We have his home address and other basic information on file. That's it."

Khalila, who had been taking notes, said, "We'd like all of the personal details you have on him: full name, address, phone numbers, etcetera."

"Not a problem. I'll have Beth print out everything we have."

"Thank you, Mr. Carver," she said, then turned to Harrison. "I'll have NCTC put out a bulletin for Daniels and identify potential locations he might be at."

53

FREDERICKSBURG, VIRGINIA

Traveling south on Interstate 95, Craig Daniels glanced at the backed-up traffic in the standard lanes a short distance to his right. He was traveling in the center Express Lanes stretching from the Capital Beltway south to Fredericksburg, Virginia, pleased with his decision to pay the $39.80 toll for the Expressway rather than take the normal lanes, which were bogged down with Easter weekend holiday traffic. After all, he could afford the toll; his bank account balance now exceeded two million dollars.

His car was packed with suitcases and several boxes containing everything of value from a life he intended to leave behind. However, this hadn't been his plan until yesterday, when he had been called into his boss's office at Carver Construction to discuss why he had placed an order of replacement C-4 and detonators, when nothing had been issued to the Catoctin Mountain project, as he had claimed on the reorder form. When Jack Carver had refused to turn a blind eye to the matter, even when offered half of the proceeds, it had become apparent that a change in plans was required.

When his thoughts turned to his predicament, he was overcome with anger—not for the first time in the last twenty-four hours—pounding both hands on his steering wheel for a few seconds.

That nosy old bat, Beth Walters.

No one should have noticed the missing C-4 and detonators. Beth should have had Jack Carver simply sign the order form, like he'd done hundreds of times before, then filed it away. No one would have noticed the missing items once Daniels deleted the new entry in the database. During the routine inventory checks in the past, the inspectors had never riffled through the paper orders and issues—the database was what mattered. Instead, Beth had piqued Jack's curiosity and the meeting with his boss hadn't gone well. He'd been given his walking papers yesterday, and it was apparent that a report would be filed with the ATF by the close of business.

Instead of discreetly tapping into the two million dollars on occasion, with no one wiser about the missing explosives or the payment he had received, he now had to disappear and start a new life. He wasn't sure exactly how to accomplish the feat—it hadn't been his plan until yesterday—but he figured he ought to vacate the premises in case authorities came looking for him, buying time to figure things out. He had contacted a retired friend in Miami, who said he might be able to help. So, off to Florida it was, and the quicker he arrived, the better.

However, Daniels hadn't thought everything through, particularly when it came to databases. There were no toll booths on the Express Lanes. Instead, electronic sensors detected passing cars at the entrances and exits, and when Daniels reached the end of the Expressway and merged into the normal lanes, one of the cameras snapped a photo of his car's license plate, so the bill could be mailed to the driver or transferred to the associated E-Z Pass toll account.

The Express Lane database also happened to be one of several thousand monitored by the FBI and other law enforcement agencies.

Thirty minutes after merging onto the normal Interstate 95 traffic lanes, Daniels was just north of Richmond when he noticed flashing red and blue lights in his rearview mirror, rapidly approaching. He checked the speedometer, verifying he wasn't speeding. He tensed as the state trooper approached, hoping the vehicle would speed by. Instead, it slowed and swerved into the lane behind him. He waited a moment, praying that the trooper would soon be on his or her way again. But the vehicle closed the gap, following only a few car lengths behind.

Daniels finally pulled onto the right shoulder and stopped, then opened the glove compartment, retrieving the folder with his car insurance and registration. After he pulled his wallet out for his driver's license, he checked on the state trooper via the rearview mirror. He was sitting in the driver's seat, staring ahead. As Daniels wondered what the trooper was waiting for, another sedan with flashing red and blue lights approached, stopping in front of Daniels's car. The two troopers stepped from their vehicles at the same time and approached Daniels.

It was at that moment, as each man unfastened his pistol holster retention strap and withdrew his firearm, that Daniels realized he was in a world of trouble.

54

USS *MICHIGAN*

In the submarine's quiet Control Room, Captain Murray Wilson stood on the Conn between the two lowered periscopes, his eyes surveying the various sonar and combat control displays as *Michigan* headed toward the Strait of Hormuz. Following the Russian attack on the Theodore Roosevelt strike group, *Michigan* had received two new orders. The first had directed *Michigan* to protect the strike group's northern side as they sprinted away from danger. However, that order had been short-lived, since the former ballistic missile submarine couldn't match the speed of the evading aircraft carrier and its remaining surface ship escorts. Even with *Michigan* at ahead flank, the surface ships had steadily pulled away.

A second order had subsequently been received, sending *Michigan* southeast. Now, an hour after the northeastern turn at the bottom of the gulf, Wilson's crew was approaching its destination—the minefield stretching across the Strait of Hormuz. Although *Michigan*'s slower speed had been a handicap earlier, the guided missile submarine's new capabilities might now come in handy. It would take over a week for mine-clearing assets capable of dealing with the deeper mines to arrive at the strait. In the meantime, Wilson had been ordered to devise a way to utilize the SEAL detachment and their equipment aboard to clear a path through the minefield.

Wilson glanced at the navigation display; *Michigan* was fifteen nautical miles from the strait, still traveling at ahead full, with the turbulent water flowing past the hydrophones blunting the detection range of the submarine's sensors.

"Slow to ahead two-thirds," Wilson ordered Lieutenant Brian Resor, the Officer of the Deck.

Resor relayed the order to the Helm, slowing the ship to ten knots. He followed up, "Sonar, Conn. Report all contacts."

Two minutes later, after shifting their equipment lineup to take advantage of the longer detection range of the submarine's sensors at the slower speed, Sonar reported, "Hold a new contact on the towed array, designated Sierra eight-five, ambiguous bearings zero-zero-five and zero-nine-five."

With the towed array being a single string of cylindrical hydrophones, the sonar algorithms couldn't determine which side of the array the sound had been received on. A maneuver would be required to determine whether the contact was to the north or east. More important, however, was the contact's classification—surface ship or submarine. Sonar quickly completed its initial assessment.

"Conn, Sonar. Sierra eight-five is classified submerged. Analyzing."

No other American or NATO submarines were authorized in *Michigan*'s new operating area, which meant Sierra eight-five wasn't friendly.

Wilson turned to his Officer of the Deck. "Man Battle Stations Torpedo silently."

55

K-328 *LEOPARD*

Captain Second Rank Maksim Sidorov, seated in the Captain's chair in the submarine's Central Command Post, listened intently to Hydroacoustic's report.

"Command Post, Hydroacoustic. Hold a new contact on the towed array, a sixty-point-two Hertz tonal, designated Hydroacoustic two-five, ambiguous bearings one-one-zero and two-five-zero. Sixty-point-two Hertz frequency correlates to American nuclear-powered submarine."

Interesting, Sidorov thought.

The commanding officer of *Leopard,* a second flight Akula nuclear attack submarine, and his crew had waited patiently at their assigned station just west of the minefield stretching across the Strait of Hormuz. The explosive barrier had done its job thus far, preventing additional American warships from entering the Persian Gulf to assist the Theodore Roosevelt strike group, helping to ensure that the preeminent symbol of U.S. naval power—the potent aircraft carrier—did not escape its doomed fate.

Sidorov's assignment was less glamorous than that of the other four Russian submarines hunting the aircraft carrier. *Leopard*'s task was to assist in keeping the minefield in place, sinking mine-clearing ships that attempted to clear the obstacles. What he hadn't expected was the arrival of the lone American submarine in the gulf. Why was it headed toward the strait instead of protecting the aircraft carrier?

The next report Sidorov received was even more perplexing. "Command Post, Hydroacoustic. Contact tonals correlate to American ballistic missile submarine, Ohio class."

The report confused Sidorov. What was a ballistic missile submarine doing in the Persian Gulf? They normally prowled the depths of the Atlantic and Pacific Oceans, far away from the busy shipping lanes, hiding during their months-long patrols. Then he realized the new contact wasn't a ballistic missile submarine at all. It was one of America's four guided missile submarines—Ohio-class submarines converted to carry Tomahawk missiles and a SEAL detachment.

During the recent engagement with the Theodore Roosevelt strike group, two submarine escorts had been detected. The lead submarine had been sunk, but the second had faded from the sensor screens as it accompanied the evading aircraft carrier. That submarine had now been located, approaching the strait for some reason. The American submarine's mission was unclear, but its fate was not.

"Man Combat Stations silently," he ordered.

The two Command Post Messengers sped through the submarine, and three minutes later, *Leopard*'s Central Command Post was fully manned.

"This is the Captain," Sidorov announced, capturing the attention of the Command Post watchstanders. "I have the Conn and Captain Lieutenant Yegorov retains the Watch. The target of interest is Hydroacoustic two-five, an American guided missile submarine. Track Hydroacoustic two-five."

As his crew set to their initial task—determining their target's course, speed, and range—Sidorov knew he had the advantage over his adversary, even if *Leopard* had been detected.

The contact had been gained on the towed array, but even though two ambiguous bearings had been reported, Sidorov already knew which one was the true one and which one was false. With the minefield barrier on *Leopard*'s starboard side, the approaching American submarine was clearly to port, bearing two-five-zero. No maneuver would be required to resolve the bearing ambiguity.

Additionally, Sidorov's crew already had a rough target course to work with, since the Persian Gulf slanted northeast as it met the Strait of Hormuz. It would not take long to lock down a firing solution for the approaching American submarine. A single maneuver should provide *Leopard*'s fire control algorithms with the information necessary.

Sidorov ordered, "Steersman. Ahead standard. Left full rudder, steady course one-nine-zero."

56

USS *MICHIGAN* • K-328 *LEOPARD*

USS *MICHIGAN*

"Conn, Sonar. Master one is classified Akula."

Wilson acknowledged Sonar's report, then surveyed the watchstanders in the Control Room. *Michigan* was at Battle Stations Torpedo, every station manned with his crew communicating via headsets, augmented by occasional reports from Sonar coming across the Conn speaker. The submarine's Executive Officer, Lieutenant Commander Tom Montgomery, hovered behind the three combat control consoles, examining their displays.

The console operators—two fire control technicians and one junior officer—adjusted Master one's estimated solution: its course, speed, and range, analyzing how the combat control system reacted. It was a complicated process combining complex algorithms and the operator's ability to fuse the myriad data available—frequency shifts and bearing changes over time, geographic constraints, and target characteristics—using the data to guide the algorithms more quickly to an accurate target solution.

Montgomery stood erect, alerted by a report coming across his headset. After acknowledging, he announced, "Possible contact zig, Master one, due to upshift in frequency."

Wilson glanced at the nearest time-frequency plot. The target's tonals were increasing. He checked the contact's bearing drift; the bearings were drifting to the left of those projected by combat control, indicating a maneuver to port.

Montgomery's eyes shifted between the combat control displays, coming to the same conclusion. "Confirm target zig. Contact has turned to port. Set anchor range at ten thousand yards. Master one has turned to a southern course and has increased speed."

Wilson folded his arms across his chest. *Michigan* had been counter-detected, making the tactical situation significantly more challenging. Instead of sneaking up on unsuspecting prey, their enemy had been alerted. It was now a race to determine which crew would be the first to determine a firing solution.

K-328 *LEOPARD*

"Command Post, Hydroacoustic. Towed array is stable. Sending bearings to fire control."

Leopard had completed its turn to the south, headed toward the American submarine as Sidorov's crew refined the target's course, speed, and range. Their initial estimate of the American submarine's solution had been fairly accurate, and two minutes after the towed array stabilized, the michmen manning the fire control consoles settled on nearly identical parameters.

Captain Third Rank Lev Ivanov, Sidorov's First Officer, hovering behind the fire controlmen, announced, "I have a firing solution."

Sidorov quickly ordered, "Prepare to Fire, Hydroacoustic two-five, single weapon from tube Two, tube Four as backup."

Ivanov tapped a fire controlman on the shoulder. "Send solution to Weapon Control."

Leopard's Watch Officer followed, reporting they were ready for counterfire from the American submarine. "Torpedo countermeasures are armed."

The Weapons Officer reported, "Ready to Fire, tubes Two and Four."

Sidorov stopped beside his First Officer, evaluating the solution to Hydroacoustic two-five. The American submarine remained steady on course and speed.

He retreated to the aft section of the Command Post, where he had a clear view of all stations, and examined the displays one final time.

Satisfied that all parameters were optimal, he ordered, "Fire tube Two."

USS *MICHIGAN*

In *Michigan*'s Control Room, a report blared from the Conn speaker. "Torpedo in the water, bearing three-five-seven!"

A red bearing line appeared on the combat control displays, signaling the detection of an incoming torpedo.

Wilson responded immediately. "Helm, ahead flank! Left full rudder, steady course two-four-zero! Launch countermeasures!"

An acoustic decoy was ejected to maintain the incoming torpedo focused on where *Michigan* had been, instead of where it was going, as the eighteen-thousand-pound submarine's screw churned the water, accelerating the submarine to maximum speed.

"Quick Reaction Firing," Wilson ordered, "Master one, tube One! Flood down and open all torpedo tube outer doors, tube One first!"

Wilson had skipped the normal torpedo firing process, implementing the more urgent version, which forced his Executive Officer to send his best solution to the torpedo immediately. The Russian captain wouldn't know how well-aimed the torpedo was, and it was better to give him something to worry about, distracting his crew while they attempted to monitor *Michigan*'s evasion maneuver and send updates to their torpedo over its guidance wire.

Montgomery shifted his gaze between the three consoles, then tapped one of the fire control technicians on the shoulder. "Promote to master."

After the solution was updated, Montgomery reported, "Solution ready!"

The submarine's Weapons Officer followed. "Weapon ready!"

"Ship ready!" Lieutenant Resor announced, reporting the submarine was ready to launch more decoys and jammers.

Wilson ordered, "Match Sonar bearing and shoot!"

He heard the whir of the torpedo ejection pump, verifying that the starboard torpedo bank had operated as expected, then listened to the sonar technicians as they monitored their torpedo.

"Own ship's unit is in the water, running normally."

"Fuel crossover achieved."

"Turning to preset gyro course."

"Shifting to medium speed."

Michigan's torpedo was headed toward its target.

K-329 *LEOPARD*

"Torpedo in the water, bearing one-seven-two!"

Sidorov turned toward the nearest fire control console. A red bearing line appeared on the display, accompanied by a bright white trace on the sonar monitor.

"Steersman, ahead flank!"

The Steersman rang up maximum propulsion as Sidorov determined the best evasion course. He decided to place the torpedo twenty degrees aft of the beam, so Leopard could open range while evading. The more optimal course was to port, but the minefield was on that side. He'd have to turn in the more dangerous direction.

"Steersman, right full rudder, steady course three-one-zero."

To his Watch Officer, Sidorov ordered, "Launch torpedo decoy!"

Leopard swung around as it increased speed, and a decoy was launched in its wake, which would hopefully distract the torpedo long enough for *Leopard* to slip away.

Once they had put enough distance between the submarine and the decoy, Sidorov ordered, "Launch jammer!"

A broadband sonar jammer was ejected from the submarine, which would hopefully mask *Leopard* as it sped away, leaving the decoy as a tantalizing target for the torpedo.

USS *MICHIGAN*

"Possible contact zig, Master one," Montgomery announced. "Downshift in frequency. Contact is turning away."

Wilson glanced at the nearest time-frequency plot. The Russian submarine crew had detected *Michigan*'s incoming torpedo and was attempting to evade.

A moment later, Montgomery announced, "Confirm target zig. Contact has turned to the northwest."

Michigan's crew was now faced with two tasks: evade the incoming torpedo, and guide their torpedo onto a new intercept course with the Russian submarine.

Wilson examined the incoming torpedo bearings, which were drifting steadily aft, indicating the torpedo had remained on its original firing course. *Michigan* was safe, unless a new steer command was sent to the torpedo or another torpedo was launched. Wilson needed to keep the Russian crew focused on its survival and not on sinking *Michigan*.

"I want to send a steer command now," Wilson announced. "Give me the best solution update you've got."

Montgomery quickly surveyed the solutions on the three combat control displays, picking the one that was tracking most closely to the bearings coming in from Sonar. He tapped one of the fire control technicians on the shoulder.

"Send to Weapon Control."

The fire control technician pressed the appropriate icon on his console, then Montgomery announced, "Updated solution sent to Weapon Control."

Lieutenant Ryan Jescovitch studied the display on the Weapon Control Console as the fire control technician manning it determined the steer command that would turn *Michigan*'s torpedo onto a course that would intercept the evading Russian submarine.

"Recommend left forty degrees," he announced.

"Insert steer, tube One, left forty!" Wilson ordered.

The command was sent to *Michigan*'s torpedo over the thin guidance wire spooling from dual dispensers, one inside the torpedo and another mounted at the back of the torpedo tube.

"Command accepted!" the Weapons Officer reported.

Wilson watched as *Michigan*'s torpedo veered onto its new course, then turned his attention to the incoming Russian torpedo. Its bearings were still drawing aft, indicating it hadn't received a new steer command. Either the Russian crew was focused primarily on evading *Michigan*'s torpedo or it wasn't as efficient as Wilson's crew while executing the dual actions of torpedo evasion and submarine prosecution.

Michigan's torpedo steadily closed on the Russian submarine, and when it was within a few thousand yards, the Weapons Officer announced, "Detect!"

A moment later, he reported, "Homing!"

The Russian submarine maneuvered shortly thereafter, but *Michigan's* torpedo also changed course. The torpedo had locked onto its target and would now independently maneuver until it closed the distance. No further assistance from *Michigan's* crew was required. The next announcement indicated the torpedo had intercepted its target.

"Loss of guidance wire!"

The sound of an explosion rumbled through *Michigan's* hull. Wilson put broadband sonar on the Conn speaker, and not long thereafter, a deep rumbling sound indicated the Russian submarine had plowed into the ocean floor.

A final glance at the bearings to the Russian torpedo revealed that it had passed by too far away to detect *Michigan*. Without receiving a new steer command, it would continue on the same course until it ran out of fuel. *Michigan* was safe, at least for the moment.

Wilson stopped by the navigation table, wondering if there might be another Russian submarine lurking nearby.

"Sonar, Conn. Report all contacts."

"Conn, Sonar. Hold no contacts."

With the minefield straddling the Strait of Hormuz, traffic through the narrow waterway was at a standstill.

"Helm, ahead two-thirds," Wilson ordered. "Left ten degrees rudder, steady course zero-nine-zero."

Michigan turned east as it slowed, headed toward the minefield.

57

GLEN ALLEN, VIRGINIA

Jake Harrison swerved his car into a parking spot in front of the Virginia State Police Division One, Area 1 office. Harrison and Khalila had been notified shortly after Craig Daniels's detention, and the CIA's National Resources Division had requested Daniels be held at a local Virginia State Police office for interrogation. The state troopers had been happy to comply, and Khalila and Harrison had made the trip down Interstate 95, using the Express Lanes, of course.

Inside the office, they were met by state trooper Alex Martin, who escorted them to the interrogation room where Daniels was being held. Along the way, he passed on what little they had discerned thus far.

"He hasn't told us anything about the C-4 and detonators yet. Daniels knows he's screwed and is still trying to figure out what to do about it. Basically, he's out of his depth. Just a guy with an occasional side hustle who thought he'd never get caught, as far as we can tell." When they reached the door to the interrogation room, Martin added, "Put the pressure on, and he'll crack."

Khalila and Harrison entered the room, which contained only a table and three chairs. Daniels sat in one chair, his hands in cuffs attached to a fixture on his side of the table. Harrison and Khalila took their seats in the other two chairs, across from Daniels.

During the drive from the NCTC, Harrison had agreed to let Khalila take the lead interrogating Daniels, since he hadn't received any training in that area. Harrison had made one stipulation: Khalila would not employ the interrogation tactic she had used in Sochi, Russia, when she had driven one of her knives through the suspect's forearm, pinning it to the table while she pressed her other knife against the man's neck, threatening to slice it open if he didn't start talking.

However, they had been in a CIA safe house in Sochi, not a Virginia State Police office, and Khalila armed herself with knives only when on a field assignment. Like Harrison, she carried only a single pistol today, strapped to her hip. She had offered to pick up some knives along the way to the state police office, mostly in jest, Harrison figured.

Khalila commenced the interrogation. "Craig, I'm agent Khalila Dufour and my partner is agent Jake Harrison. We're here to help you understand the mess you've gotten yourself into, and what's going to happen unless you cooperate with us."

Daniels did his best to pretend he was unconcerned while Khalila continued. "We know what you've done, selling C-4 and detonators on the black market. With your assistance and a quick resolution to this matter, you could be looking at a few months in a minimum security prison—practically a college campus. But if you fail to help us and the man you sold the explosives to commits a crime with that material, you can be charged with those crimes as well. If anyone dies, you'll be charged with murder, and you'll end up doing time in a maximum security prison with hardened criminals and gang members—large, burly blokes enjoying bedtime benefits with their new cellmate each night, if you catch my drift. Is that what you want?"

Daniels swallowed hard, and Harrison could tell Khalila was getting to him. A thin sheen of perspiration appeared on his face.

"Cooperate with us," Khalila said. "Help us catch whoever you sold the explosives to before anyone gets hurt. Tell us everything you know about this transaction, and we'll ensure you don't spend the rest of your life in prison."

Harrison could see the indecision in Daniels's eyes and considered engaging the man, but Khalila was doing an admirable job, employing psychological coercion instead of her typical brute-force tactics.

Finally, Daniels responded. "I don't know much."

"Tell us what you know," Khalila replied.

The dam broke and the information flowed, with Daniels describing how he had connected with a man named George Banks, to whom he had sold the fifty pounds of C-4 and three dozen wireless detonators.

"Did he say what he planned to do with the material?" Khalila asked.

Daniels shook his head. "He didn't offer and I didn't ask."

"Can you describe him?"

Daniels glanced at Harrison. "A well-built guy about the same size as your partner. I got the impression he was former special forces, but he never said, either way."

Harrison pulled his phone from his pocket, then selected a photograph of Lonnie Mixell.

"Is this who you sold the explosives to?"

Daniels squinted his eyes, studying the photograph. "I don't think it's him, but it could be his brother. The guy I made the deal with had a different hair and eye color, and his facial structure was a bit different."

Khalila turned to Harrison, their eyes meeting. She was probably thinking the same thing—hair and eye color were easy to change, and Mixell could be using temporary facial implants to alter his appearance; he'd done so before.

Harrison asked Daniels, "Can you help generate a sketch of what this guy looks like?"

Daniels nodded.

Khalila stood and knocked on the door. After Martin answered, she asked for a forensic artist, and one soon arrived. Not long thereafter, Harrison and Khalila were examining a sketch of the man Daniels had sold the explosives to.

Harrison locked eyes with Khalila. "That's Mixell," he said.

58

WOODMORE, MARYLAND

A heavy rain was drenching the countryside as Lonnie Mixell sat at a small table in the barn behind the house. In the short time since he had rented the property, the contents of the house and barn had remained largely unchanged aside from the additional items stored inside the barn. One of the crates of C-4 was empty and the second one was open, with several blocks of the explosive stacked neatly on the table before Mixell. Illuminated by the lamp clamped to the table, the X-Acto knife in his hand moved slowly, carefully carving the C-4 into the desired shape.

As the steady rain pattered the barn roof, Mixell's mind wandered to a popular saying his mother used to utter each spring: *April showers bring May flowers*. If Mixell's plot executed according to plan, there would be many people who would experience April showers, but not live to see May flowers.

One of them, unfortunately, was the homeowner who had rented the property to him, the woman who had stumbled across the barn's new contents. Mixell had disposed of her body and car, leaving no trace of her visit to the property on the day she was killed.

Mixell's cell phone in his pocket beeped, indicating an encrypted text message had been received. After placing the C-4 and knife on the table, he retrieved his phone and launched the app. Mixell recognized the encoded address of the sender—Brenda Verbeck.

What is the status of your task? she asked.

"It's progressing."

I've paid you a lot of money. I'd like more details.

"You don't need to know the details. However, everything is set, aside from a few things I'll finish by tomorrow."

His eyes went to the remaining blocks of C-4, along with several items he had purchased from a paint store.

When will you execute your task?

"In two days."

Will it be dramatic?

"Very."

Mixell smiled at the thought. He figured Brenda did as well.

59

USS *MICHIGAN*

As *Michigan* hovered at one hundred fifty feet, several hundred yards from the minefield stretching across the Strait of Hormuz, Murray Wilson entered the guided missile submarine's Battle Management Center, located aft of the Control Room. The former Navigation Center had been transformed during *Michigan*'s conversion from ballistic to guided missile submarine, and was now crammed with twenty-five consoles used for Tomahawk missile mission planning and overseeing SEAL operations.

Aboard *Michigan* during this deployment were two platoons of Navy SEALs, plus sixty tons of munitions stored in two of *Michigan*'s missile tubes: small arms, grenade launchers, limpet mines . . . anything a SEAL team might need. Stored inside each of the two Dry Deck Shelters attached to *Michigan*'s Missile Deck was a SEAL Delivery Vehicle (SDV), a mini-sub capable of transporting four SEALs, or various combinations of SEALs and equipment, to their destination.

Several *Michigan* crew members and SEALs were in the Battle Management Center, occupying consoles on the starboard side: *Michigan*'s Executive Officer and four department heads, plus Commander Jon Peters, the commanding officer of the SEAL detachment aboard *Michigan*. Also present were five other SEALs: Senior Chief Russ Burkhardt and Special Warfare Operators Michael Keller, Kurt Hacker, and Dave Narehood. Lieutenant Tracey Noviello, the officer-in-charge of one of the SEAL detachment's two platoons, stood at the front of the Battle Management Center beside a sixty-inch plasma display mounted to the bulkhead.

Wilson settled into the lone vacant seat, beside Peters, and the SEAL commander nodded in Noviello's direction.

Lieutenant Noviello began the mission brief, starting with a summary of the information provided in *Michigan*'s operational order.

"As you're aware, *Michigan* has been tasked with devising a way to clear a path through the minefield that is preventing shipping from entering or leaving the Persian Gulf."

Noviello went on to explain that the SEALs planned to use their SDVs to attach limpet mines, which were normally used to sabotage ships in port, to the mines instead.

"There are a few potential problems," he said. "The first is that we have only two dozen limpets, and we don't know how many mines we'll have to destroy to clear a path large enough for a surface warship or submarine to pass through. The second issue is that the limpets have a magnetic base, which is used to attach them to a ship's hull during a sabotage mission. The question is whether this magnetic base will set the mine off once it makes contact when we attach it.

"The initial intel from the mine-clearing community is that we should be fine. The types of mines employed in the scenario we're looking at are typically set off by forceful contact or by the magnetic field of a large ship—or they could have both types of sensors. In either case, the mine shouldn't be triggered by our limpets. Assuming the experts are correct and we don't blow ourselves up, we'll set the limpet timer and depart the minefield before it detonates.

"That's the basic plan, but the first order of business is a recon mission through the minefield, to determine the type of mines we're facing and to map out which mines need to be cleared. Senior Chief Burkhardt and Hacker will take one SDV, while Keller and Narehood will be in the other one. Subject to your questions, we plan to launch the SDVs as soon as we're geared up and *Michigan* is ready."

After a few questions and a short discussion, the mission brief concluded.

Thirty minutes later, Michael Keller and Dave Narehood, outfitted in standard dive gear for this mission, stepped through the circular hatch in the side of Missile Tube One. Keller shut the hatch and spun the handle, sealing the two men inside the seven-foot-diameter missile tube. Narehood climbed a steel ladder up two levels as Keller followed, entering the Dry Deck Shelter bathed in diffuse red light.

The Dry Deck Shelter was a conglomeration of three separate chambers: a spherical hyperbaric chamber at the forward end to treat injured divers, a spherical transfer trunk in the middle, which Keller and Narehood had entered, and a long cylindrical hangar section containing the SEAL Delivery Vehicle, a black mini-sub resembling a fat torpedo—twenty-two feet long by six feet in diameter. The hangar was divided into two sections by a Plexiglas shield dropping halfway down from the top of the hangar, with the SDV on one side and controls for operating the hangar on the other side.

Narehood stepped into the hangar, which was manned by five Navy divers: one on the forward side of the Plexiglas shield to operate the controls, and four divers in scuba gear on the other side. Keller sealed the hatch behind him, then the two SEALs ducked under the Plexiglas shield, stopping at the forward end of the SDV, which was loaded nose first into the Dry Deck Shelter. The SDV had two seating areas, one in front of the other, each capable of carrying two persons. The back seat would be empty this time, but would carry a limpet once they began clearing a path through the minefield.

After donning their fins and face masks, the two men climbed into the front seat of the SDV. Keller manipulated the controls and a contour of the Strait of Hormuz appeared on the navigation display. He rendered the *okay* hand signal to the diver on the other side of the Plexiglas shield. Water surged into the hangar, gushing up from vents beneath them. The DDS was soon flooded except for a pocket of air on the other side of the Plexiglas shield, where the Navy diver operated the Dry Deck Shelter. There was a faint rumbling as the circular hatch at the end of the shelter opened, and two divers on each side of the SDV glided toward the chamber opening with a kick of their fins.

The divers pulled rails out onto the submarine's missile deck, and the SDV was extracted from the hangar. Keller manipulated the controls and the SDV's propeller started spinning. The submersible rose slowly, as did the second SDV after emerging from the other Dry Deck Shelter. Both SDVs moved forward, passing above the shelters and along each side of *Michigan*'s sail, cruising over the submarine's bow into the dark water ahead.

Not long thereafter, several mines materialized in the murky water. Keller eased back on the throttle and the mini-sub slowed as it approached the nearest one, while the second SDV, piloted by Burkhardt, stopped to examine the next closest mine. Each was a sphere three feet in diameter with a dozen contact spikes sticking out from the its spherical surface, attached to an anchor chain disappearing into the darkness below. Above and beneath them, Keller spotted more dark spheres; mines had been anchored to at least three different depths in this layer.

After Keller logged the first mine's location and depth, he adjusted the SDV's buoyancy, descending to the mine below it to determine and log its depth. Beside him, the second SDV did the same. It was going to take a while to map a path through the minefield, much less destroy each mine one by one.

60

K-571 *KRASNOYARSK*

"Scope clear!" the Watch Officer announced as *Krasnoyarsk's* forward periscope pierced the water's surface.

Captain Lieutenant Petr Dolinski turned the scope swiftly, completing several sweeps in search of nearby contacts. A moment later, he declared, "No close contacts!"

Conversation resumed in the Central Command Post, now that the hazardous ascent to periscope depth had been safely conducted. The crew shifted its focus to executing the tasks directed by their commanding officer: obtain a satellite fix, and more important, download the latest satellite reconnaissance on the American carrier strike group.

While Captain Second Rank Gavriil Novikov awaited the update, he reviewed the Russian submarine task force's plan to hunt down and sink the American carrier strike group. Thus far, three of the six strike group escort ships had been sunk, leaving only two destroyers and a lone submarine. However, the most potent American ASW asset, the remaining submarine, had abandoned the carrier strike group for some reason. Not that it would matter.

The three Akulas were pursuing the carrier strike group, while the more heavily armed *Krasnoyarsk* had headed in a different direction. Based on the pending satellite recon, Novikov's decision to head south instead of east, abandoning his initial chase of the strike group, would prove either foolish or brilliant.

As expected, the speedy aircraft carrier was proving a challenge to catch and sink. As fast as the Akulas were, the American aircraft carrier could outrun them. It might have to leave its surface warship escorts behind—and Novikov didn't doubt that it would if necessary—making them easy prey for the Akulas. Novikov knew that to achieve success, he needed a plan that somehow countered the American aircraft carrier's speed.

"Command Post, Communication. Message broadcast download is complete. Satellite intel message has been received."

The Watch Officer acknowledged the report, then Novikov ordered his submarine down from periscope depth.

As *Krasnoyarsk* settled out at fifty meters, Communication followed up. "Command Post, Communication. Intel update has been transferred to fire control."

Novikov stopped behind one of the michmen at his fire control console. "Load the latest satellite recon," he directed.

The michman did as directed, and his display populated with numerous symbols and markers. The American carrier strike was to the east as expected, but it had turned south, still a short distance ahead of the pursuing Akulas. The strike group was headed toward the U.S. Navy's Fifth Fleet's main base in Bahrain. Additionally, American ASW resources were being repositioned to Bahrain.

The American strategy seemed clear. The plan was to create a formidable ASW screen across the entrance to the Gulf of Bahrain, behind which the American aircraft carrier and other surface warships would be safe.

Novikov smiled. The Americans were reacting as he had expected.

He turned to his Watch Officer. "Come to course one-eight-five. Increase speed to flank."

61

MCLEAN, VIRGINIA

Seated beside Khalila on the main floor of the National Counterterrorism Center, surrounded by sixty other men and women focused on their computer displays, Jake Harrison leaned back in his chair and rubbed his eyes. It had been a fruitless two days as he and Khalila looked for clues to Mixell's whereabouts, scouring law enforcement reports and databases. It was obvious that Mixell was planning something major, with the target likely in the Baltimore/Washington, D.C., area, but thus far the man had remained a ghost.

Mixell's updated appearance had been fed to the automated surveillance databases, but personnel resources assigned to tracking him down remained scarce because the issue still hadn't been designated a National Special Security Event by the Department of Homeland Security. They hadn't yet determined what Mixell's target was nor the timing of the attack. As a result, only a handful of NCTC analysts had been assigned to assist Harrison and Khalila.

Khalila noticed Harrison taking a break, leaning back in his chair. "Want another cup of coffee?" she asked.

It was only 8 a.m., but they had already been at it for two hours. After Craig Daniels had helped generate the sketch of Mixell's updated appearance, Harrison and Khalila had redoubled their efforts to track him down, working nonstop the last few days aside from six hours of sleep each night.

"Yeah, I could use more coffee," Harrison answered.

"Great," Khalila said. "While you're at it, get me another cup, too."

She gave him a deadpan stare, having turned what had seemed to be an offer to get him a cup of coffee into Harrison getting one for her. Then she broke into a grin.

"Just kidding," she said as she stood, placing a hand on Harrison's shoulder as she passed behind him, headed toward the coffee station at the back of the main floor.

Harrison's eyes followed her, his thoughts flitting back to the night they had spent together in Bahrain. Since then, her demeanor had softened considerably, and a subtle, dry sense of humor had surfaced. True to her word, she had displayed no further interest in a romantic relationship with him, which suited Harrison. He still felt guilty about what happened, ending up in another woman's arms so soon after Angie's death.

His computer monitor began flashing, drawing his attention to the display. Facial recognition algorithms had identified a match in one of the secondary surveillance systems. In addition to federal and state camera networks, the NCTC had access to thousands of private security surveillance systems, subject to each company's agreement to participate in the government program.

A visual match for Mixell had been identified on a surveillance system installed at a Giant Food store, the largest grocery chain in Maryland. As Harrison studied the video frame supposedly capturing Mixell's image, Khalila returned with coffee, handing him a cup.

The image was somewhat grainy, but Harrison was convinced it was Mixell.

"What do you think?" he said, turning to Khalila.

Before she could respond, Harrison's display filled with three more alerts, also from the Giant Food surveillance system. Mixell had been spotted three more times.

"It's him," Khalila concluded.

Harrison scanned the surveillance photo details, searching for the location of the Giant Food store. However, each surveillance photo had come from a different store. That made sense, Harrison figured. Mixell was altering his routine, not shopping at the same place each time. But then he noticed an oddity. The surveillance cameras had detected Mixell at four different grocery stores on the same day.

He pointed to the dates. "Is this correct?" he asked Khalila. "Are these when he was spotted on the cameras, or the processing date? It doesn't make sense that he'd visit four different grocery stores on the same day."

"I don't know. It could be dependent on the surveillance system."

Khalila picked up the phone and contacted the supervisor overseeing their section of analysts. Jessica Del Rio descended from her second floor office overlooking the main floor, stopping behind Harrison and Khalila.

After Harrison posed his question, Jessica replied, "All surveillance systems are designed to input the capture date, not a processing or delivery date to us. This means Mixell visited four different stores on the same day. I admit it seems odd, but let's put that aside for the moment and focus on finding him. Do you know how to identify the store locations?"

Harrison nodded, then dragged the address of each store onto a locator app, and a map appeared on his display showing the location of each Giant Food store. All were located in Eastern Maryland between Washington, D.C., and the Chesapeake Bay, within a ten-by-ten-mile area.

"A hundred square miles," Khalila muttered.

"It's a start," Jessica replied, "and we can narrow his location substantially if we can get a license plate number."

She assigned four analysts to assist, one to each Giant Food store, and they downloaded video from every camera at the stores during Mixell's visits. Harrison waited tensely as each analyst viewed multiple video streams simultaneously.

"Got it," one of the analysts reported.

Harrison and Khalila gathered around his computer monitor, which displayed video from a parking lot surveillance camera, showing Mixell placing his groceries in a green Jeep Grand Cherokee. The analyst zoomed in on the license plate and froze the video. After clicking on the image, the details appeared in a text box nearby.

"It's a rental," the analyst announced, "to a John Fonda. The vehicle was rented from Dulles Airport a few weeks ago, with a home address in California."

"Pull up all hits after the rental date," Jessica ordered. The analyst complied, and a map appeared on his display, populated with dozens of drop-pins. Jessica explained, "These are license plate detections from speed and traffic light cameras."

The bulk of the drop-pins were clustered in the city of Woodmore at two intersections along Enterprise Road: Lottsford Road and Central Avenue. Along the 1.5-mile stretch of Enterprise Road between those intersections were nine entrances into housing developments plus several small farms.

"I'll coordinate with law enforcement and have checkpoints established at both intersections," Jessica said. "We can then conduct a door-to-door search."

62

OWINGS MILLS, MARYLAND

The metal security gate guarding a condominium complex on Wordsworth Way slid slowly aside, making way for a black Lincoln Navigator with dark tinted windows, which entered the complex and parked in front of a four-story building. Christine O'Connor stepped from the back seat of the vehicle and entered the condominium, accompanied by two protective agents. On the second floor, Christine knocked on the door to Apartment 203. Nadia Harrison, Jake's mother, answered the door, welcoming Christine into the apartment while the protective agents waited in the hallway.

"Maddy's almost ready," Nadia said.

It was Easter Sunday, the day Christine had arranged a White House tour for Maddy, following up on her promise to Harrison's daughter a few weeks ago. Additionally, Christine had arranged a short meeting with the president himself, who had just returned from Europe in time for the annual Easter Monday celebration held on the White House South Lawn.

While they waited for Maddy, Christine joined Nadia at the breakfast table in the kitchen.

"Can I get you anything to drink?" Nadia asked.

There was something comforting about Nadia's accent, reminding Christine of her mother, who was also a first-generation Russian. When they had lived in Fayetteville, the two women had often gathered for social visits while the kids played, although that meant Christine had to deal with the antics of Nadia's three boys. It had been over twenty years since Christine had heard her mom's voice; she had died from cancer when Christine was in her early twenties. Christine had been dating

Jake at the time, and she recalled his arm wrapped around her, offering support as her mother was lowered into her grave at Arlington National Cemetery, joining her father.

Nadia must have noticed the distant look in her eyes as she recalled the event, because she said, "With everything that's happened, I'm glad you're back in Jake's life. He needs a good friend right now."

Christine forced a quick smile. It seemed that Jake hadn't explained things to his parents—that he wanted nothing further to do with her, interfacing with her to the minimum extent possible while tracking down Mixell.

She shifted her gaze away from Jake's mom, ostensibly to check on Maddy, hoping her face didn't convey the emotion she felt. Fortunately, Maddy appeared around the corner, entering the kitchen beaming with excitement. She greeted Christine with a hug.

As Christine rose from her chair, Nadia asked, "When do you expect to return?"

"Probably just before dinner. I've arranged the White House tour and meeting with the president this afternoon."

Nadia stood and joined them, giving Maddy a goodbye kiss. "Enjoy the tour, and be on your best behavior when you meet the president!"

"I will," Maddy replied as she took Christine's hand in hers.

"I'm sure she'll do fine," Christine added.

63

WOODMORE, MARYLAND

At the intersection of Enterprise Road and Central Avenue, Harrison's car was waved through the checkpoint after the police officer examined his ID. Thirty minutes ago, Harrison and Khalila had departed the NCTC, speeding along the Capital Beltway toward Woodmore. Harrison was pleased that law enforcement had responded quickly, blocking both ends of Enterprise Road where Mixell's residence was suspected. Whether Mixell was currently within the checkpoint area was the salient question that no one could answer.

Most of the residences in the cordoned area were single-family homes, which would take quite a while to inspect, depending on how many personnel were assigned to the task. After conferring with Khalila during the trip around the Beltway, Harrison had decided to inspect the handful of small farms along Enterprise Road, which would have provided Mixell with more privacy than the housing developments.

They came up empty at the first three homes, conversing with the residents who had never seen anyone matching Mixell's description. At the fourth stop, no one answered the door, and there were no vehicles parked outside. After a quick inspection through several windows, it appeared that no one was home. They were about to head to the next house when Harrison spotted tire tracks in the grass, leading from the end of the driveway into the backyard, which seemed a bit odd. They followed the tracks, which ended at the entrance to a barn.

The doors were secured with a padlock, so Harrison and Khalila circled around the barn, searching for another entrance. There wasn't one, but there was a small window on one side. Through the window, Harrison spotted a worktable and three open crates, but couldn't make out the markings on the crates. They warranted further inspection, given that Mixell had procured two crates of C-4 and a third containing detonators.

Returning to the entrance, Harrison examined the padlock.

"Do you know how to pick a lock?" he asked Khalila.

"Most types. But I don't have the right tools."

"We've got the only tool we need," he replied as he pulled his pistol from its holster.

After looking around, verifying there was no one in sight, he used his pistol as a hammer, smashing the bottom of the pistol grip into the padlock hasp. The barn was old, and after a few whacks, the hasp screws tore from the aged wood.

He slid the door aside and Khalila illuminated the interior with her cell phone flashlight in one hand, wielding her pistol in the other. The beam of light swept across the barn, stopping on the crates. Stenciled on the side of two crates, in large black letters, was:

CHARGE DEMOLITION M112

Each crate was big enough, Harrison estimated, to hold twenty-five pounds of C-4.

They had found Mixell's lair.

An inspection of the crates, however, revealed no explosives. Only the empty packaging from the individual blocks. The crate of wireless detonators was likewise empty.

Harrison turned around, inspecting the tire tracks again. They stopped just inside the barn entrance.

"Mixell loaded a vehicle with the C-4," Harrison concluded.

Khalila nodded her concurrence.

WASHINGTON, D.C.

Lonnie Mixell checked the side mirrors of his van again, searching for any indication that his plot had been discovered and law enforcement was closing in on him. It was an instinctive precaution, which he considered an unnecessary one, confirmed again by his latest observation—he spotted only standard traffic. Everything had gone according to plan so far, culminating with the preparations for this morning's trip.

The van he was driving was properly marked and loaded with fifty pounds of C-4. He was also wearing a different disguise—one he had specifically chosen for today's occasion—another prudent precaution. He'd been wearing his previous disguise for the last week traveling in and out of Woodmore, where the odds of his discovery were low. Today, however, he'd be evaluated by professionals up close, and he couldn't take the chance that his previous disguise had been compromised.

Completing this morning's charade was the new identification card in his wallet, matching his new face and the van markings. He carried no weapons with him, since he would likely be searched. Rather, he carried no typical weapons. His cell phone was all he needed, plus the app he had loaded that would send the signal to all thirty-six wireless detonators. Only a single task remained.

In the distance, his destination appeared through a break in the District's buildings.

K-571 *KRASNOYARSK*

Gavriil Novikov stood behind the fire controlman's shoulder, studying the geographic display on his console. *Krasnoyarsk* was lurking at three knots, the minimum speed possible for bare steerageway, at a depth of fifty meters. The Russian submarine was stationed just outside the Gulf of Bahrain, ten miles east of a sonobuoy barrier the American P-8As had laid across the entrance to the gulf.

If the American aircraft carrier made it to the other side of the sonobuoy field, it would likely survive. Although *Krasnoyarsk* could penetrate an open-ocean sonobuoy field, defending itself in the process, there were too many ASW forces concentrated near the entrance to the Gulf of Bahrain. Novikov would not attempt to follow the aircraft carrier into the gulf. That meant that USS *Theodore Roosevelt* would have to be sunk before it reached the Gulf of Bahrain.

That, of course, was the plan.

This close to the sonobuoy fields, stealth was paramount. Novikov had shifted propulsion to the much quieter electric drive, and *Krasnoyarsk* was rigged for ultra-quiet, limiting crew activity and movement throughout the submarine. Novikov's crew would wait until the American aircraft carrier arrived, which should be any time now.

A few minutes later, a report came across the Central Command Post speakers.

"Command Post, Hydroacoustic. Hold three new surface contacts, designated Hydroacoustic seven-two, seven-three, and seven-four, approaching from the north. High blade rate accompanied by low broadband signature indicates all three contacts are warships, approaching at high speed."

Novikov acknowledged, then ordered his crew to Combat Stations.

As additional watchstanders streamed into the Central Command Post, Novikov took control of the Conn and ordered his crew to prepare to come to periscope depth.

Shortly after Combat Stations were manned, *Krasnoyarsk*'s periscope broke the water's surface. After completing a rapid surface and air sweep, Novikov turned the periscope to the north. Three gray warships were approaching, with the middle one much larger than the others.

Novikov decided to dispense with the often laborious process of determining a target solution before shifting to torpedo launch preparations. The courses of the approaching targets were obvious—all three were bow-on, headed directly toward *Krasnoyarsk*—and on that trajectory, range and speed didn't matter.

With his eye still pressed to the periscope, monitoring the approaching American warships, Novikov ordered, "Prepare to Fire, six-torpedo horizontal salvo. Tubes One and Two against Hydroacoustic seven-two, tubes Three and Four against Hydroacoustic seven-three, and tubes Five and Six against Hydroacoustic seven-four. Tube One fired first."

Novikov had decided to fire a tight salvo of six torpedoes, which should result in one or two torpedoes locking onto each target.

"Set courses for all three contacts to one-seven-zero."

The expected reports soon flowed from his watchstanders.

The submarine's First Officer called out, "All solutions updated."

"Torpedoes ready, tubes One through Six," the Weapons Officer announced.

The Watch Officer reported, "Countermeasures are armed."

Krasnoyarsk was ready.

Novikov gave the order. "Fire tubes One through Six!"

The torpedoes were impulsed from their tubes, then Novikov turned the scope toward the Gulf of Bahrain and the optics skyward. The Americans would likely detect the sound of the torpedo launches or the thin, light green trails streaking out from *Krasnoyarsk* and counterattack. However, the threat to Novikov's crew wouldn't come from the approaching warships. They would have their hands full, plus *Krasnoyarsk* was beyond the range of the lightweight torpedoes loaded in their deck-mounted torpedo tubes.

Instead, the threat would come from the air—torpedoes dropped from the P-8A aircraft circling high above, out of sight and beyond range of *Krasnoyarsk*'s anti-air missiles. From their current altitude, the lightweight torpedoes would be carried to their aimpoints by HAAWC wing kits, with the wing kit releasing the torpedo just prior to water entry.

"Watch Officer, raise the radar mast. Do not radiate."

Krasnoyarsk's crew would be ready when the HAAWCs arrived.

In the meantime, it was time to slip away as quietly as possible, in case *Krasnoyarsk* had somehow avoided detection following the torpedo launch.

"Steersman. Ahead two-thirds. Right full rudder, steady course zero-nine-five."

Krasnoyarsk turned to the east, and as Novikov searched the sky, he spotted two specks streaking down toward him. The American P-8As had launched two HAAWCs.

"Watch Officer, begin radiating."

After the radar began its search, quickly detecting the descending targets, Novikov glanced at the radar display. "Set radar contacts zero-one and zero-two as the targets of interest. Prepare to Fire, two missiles."

The Missile Officer acknowledged and prepared to launch two of *Krasnoyarsk*'s Pantsir-M short-range anti-air missiles. A watchstander seated at one of the fire control consoles reported, "Anti-air missiles Three-four and Five-one have accepted targeting."

Novikov initiated the next step. "Open starboard missile hatches Three and Five," he ordered, preparing to launch the last missile in tube Three and the first missile in tube Five.

"Missile hatches Three and Five are open," the Missile Officer reported. "Ready to Fire."

Novikov surveyed the approaching HAAWCs—they had almost completed their descent and were beginning to level off as they approached their torpedo release points.

"Fire!"

Two missiles were launched from the submarine, streaking upward and then veering toward their targets. Unlike the ASW helicopters, the HAAWCs had no defensive measures and no way to even detect the incoming weapons. Both missiles slammed into the HAAWCs and exploded, sending two small fireballs spiraling into the ocean.

Novikov searched the sky and checked the radar monitor for additional HAAWCs or ASW helicopters—there were none—then checked on the American warships. All three had changed course to the east, attempting to evade the torpedoes chasing them.

He lowered the periscope, then ordered, "Diving Officer, make your depth fifty meters." Turning to his Watch Officer, he ordered, "Shift propulsion to the main engines."

The Watch Officer complied, and a moment later reported that the shift was complete.

"Steersman, ahead flank," Novikov ordered. No new course was required; he had already ordered *Krasnoyarsk* onto the optimal pursuit path.

If an American warship survived the current torpedo attack, it would make the final encounter all the sweeter. Three Akulas were inbound from the north, not far behind the American ships, with *Krasnoyarsk* pursuing from the west. On the other side of the evading warships, the Strait of Hormuz was blocked by mines.

There would soon be nowhere for the Americans to run.

USS *THEODORE ROOSEVELT*

As USS *Theodore Roosevelt* surged through the dark green water at ahead flank, Captain Ryan Noss looked over his shoulder through the aft Bridge window, his gaze settling on the torpedo that had just finished snaking back and forth into the aircraft carrier's frothy white wake. On each side of the hundred-thousand-ton ship, the Arleigh Burke–class destroyers USS *Halsey* and USS *O'Kane* kept falling behind, each with a torpedo also in its wake, steadily closing. Three other torpedoes had failed to latch onto their assigned targets and had continued north, while *Theodore Roosevelt* and her escorts sped east.

Moments ago, after the incoming torpedoes had been spotted and *Theodore Roosevelt* had turned to evade them, Noss had watched two HAAWCs get shot down, similar to the loss of the MH-60R helicopters the previous day. The Russian submarine that had fired the torpedoes was still out there and had undoubtedly begun its pursuit. The knowledge that three more Russian submarines were closing from the north and that the carrier and her escorts were headed toward a minefield stretching across the Strait of Hormuz hovered in the background of Noss's thoughts, but he pushed that concern aside for the moment. The far more urgent issue was how to shake the trailing torpedo that was steadily gaining on his ship.

Maybe, if *Theodore Roosevelt* increased speed, the carrier could keep the torpedo chasing it at bay until it ran out of fuel. But the aircraft carrier was already at ahead flank. Noss needed more speed, and the only option was to increase reactor power above the authorized limit.

Noss picked up the 23-MC, issuing orders to DC Central. "RO,

Captain. Override reactor protection and increase shaft turns to one hundred and twenty percent power."

The Reactor Officer acknowledged, and Noss felt vibrations in the deck as the main engines strained under the increased steam load. *Theodore Roosevelt* surged forward as the carrier's four screws churned the water more rapidly, and Noss watched his ship slowly increase speed.

Stepping close to the aft Bridge window, he studied the incoming torpedo. It was still gaining on the carrier, but not as rapidly.

Both destroyers, having fallen notably behind the aircraft carrier, were in dire straits. The torpedoes had almost closed the remaining distance. Both ships began an evasive maneuver called an Anderson turn—essentially a turn forming a complete circle. The torpedoes would follow the destroyers, and once each ship crossed its wake where it began the turn, each torpedo would be forced to choose which wake to follow. Hopefully, it would choose the wrong one.

Each destroyer crossed its wake and Noss watched tensely, hoping the torpedoes would be tricked into following the original wake. But he was observing from a distance, unable to discern what the torpedoes had done. Both ships turned sharply away from their original wakes, steadying up as they increased speed, having slowed down during the sharp turn due to the immense rudders digging into the water.

As both ships returned to flank speed, Noss was about to breathe a sigh of relief when USS *Halsey* was engulfed in a geyser shooting two hundred feet into the air. Seconds later, USS *O'Kane* was similarly shrouded as a water plume shot up from beneath the warship, falling back down in a misty rain. As the air cleared, Noss hoped that neither ship had suffered a mortal wound. But both destroyers slowed down, and Noss noted that in each case, the ship's bow was no longer aligned with its stern. The keel on each ship had been broken. It would only be a matter of time before each warship went to the bottom.

Noss's attention returned to the torpedo chasing *Theodore Roosevelt*, which had continued to close. The torpedoes chasing the destroyers had ignored the decoys trailing behind the warships—the new Russian Futlyar torpedoes were superior to the previous model indeed, able to ignore the small countermeasures trailed behind the massive warships. He concluded that the torpedo chasing *Roosevelt* would not be fooled either.

Their only hope was to either outrun the torpedo or successfully confuse it with an Anderson turn. Lieutenant Commander Michael Beresford, the aircraft carrier's Officer of the Deck during General Quarters, decided to give the Anderson turn a try.

"Helm, left full rudder!" Beresford called out.

He kept the rudder on as the carrier circled around, and *Roosevelt* crossed its original wake a minute later, the torpedo not far behind.

"Shift your rudder!" Beresford ordered, "Steady course one-two-zero."

Beresford steered the carrier onto a thirty-degree tangent from its original course, hoping the torpedo chose the wake heading to the left rather than the right. All eyes on the Bridge turned aft, watching the torpedo reach the intersecting wakes. Noss momentarily lost the light green trail as the torpedo traveled into the dual wakes, his hope rising each second the torpedo failed to reappear. Finally, a light green trail emerged, snaking within the starboard wake.

The torpedo hadn't been fooled.

By now the torpedo was only a thousand yards behind *Theodore Roosevelt*. Noss estimated they had less than a minute before the torpedo reached the carrier's stern, the last place he wanted to get hit by a torpedo. It would destroy the rudders and propellers, reducing the carrier to a drifting hunk of metal, awaiting the coup de grâce that would send it to the bottom.

Noss approached the Officer of the Deck. "You cannot let the torpedo hit us in the stern! Do whatever you have to, but protect the screws and rudders!"

Beresford nodded his understanding, his eyes shifting back to the torpedo for a second. Then he called out, "Helm, hard right rudder. Starboard engines, back emergency!"

The Helm complied and the hundred-thousand-ton carrier tilted to port as the twin twenty-by-thirty-foot rudders dug into the ocean and the starboard screws quickly slowed, then began churning the water in reverse. Beresford was using the starboard engines to help twist the carrier around faster. But as a result, the carrier slowed down rapidly as it made the sharp turn, while the torpedo sped toward its target.

Whether Beresford's bold maneuver would succeed depended on

which of the torpedo's homing algorithms was dominant. As modern torpedoes closed on their targets, they depended on the magnetic field of the large metal ship to determine when to detonate; heavyweight torpedoes didn't run into a ship. They ran below the ship and detonated beneath the keel, with the explosion creating a huge bubble void, followed by a water jet that shot upward when the bubble collapsed. The weight of the unsupported ship in the bubble void, combined with the water jet cutting through the hull and compartment decks, was usually enough trauma to break a warship's keel.

However, *Theodore Roosevelt* was not an ordinary warship, and the carrier could likely survive a single torpedo explosion without incurring fatal damage, as long as propulsion and the rudders were spared. The question in Noss's mind was whether the torpedo would continue spiraling toward the carrier by following the ship's wake, or, when it was close enough and sensed the ship's magnetic signature, would it cut through the water directly toward it?

The torpedo reached the point where Beresford had begun the sharp turn, and Noss's stomach tightened as the torpedo remained in the ship's wake. *Roosevelt* kept turning, its rate rising rapidly now that the starboard engines had reached back emergency speed.

Suddenly, the torpedo veered sharply, speeding out of the wake, traveling directly toward *Roosevelt*'s starboard side.

It was an odd sensation—the relief spreading through Noss's body—as he realized his ship was about to be torpedoed. But *Theodore Roosevelt* was going to take it in the side instead of the critical stern.

The torpedo trail disappeared as it ran beneath the carrier, and a second later, Noss felt and heard the explosion as a water plume shot a hundred and fifty feet above the carrier, dousing the tower and flight deck as it fell.

The Flooding Alarm sounded, followed by emergency announcements reporting flooding in several starboard compartments amidships. Noss listened tensely for any indication that the ship's keel had been broken, but . . . there was no indication it had. Just flooding, plus the damaged equipment and injured personnel from the water jet slicing through the hull. A query to Engineering confirmed that the ship was ready to answer all bells; there had been no damage to the rudder, screws, or nuclear reactor plants.

"Your orders, sir?" Beresford asked.

Noss evaluated his options, which weren't many. Actually, with four Russian submarines in pursuit, only one plan came to mind. Head east and coordinate with the ASW commander to have the P-8A squadrons lay down a sonobuoy field stretching across the Persian Gulf behind the aircraft carrier, just west of the strait.

"Head east," Noss ordered, "at ahead flank."

Soon, *Roosevelt* would be protected by mines to the east and sono-buoys to the west. Noss's ship would be safe, as long as the Russian submarines didn't penetrate the sonobuoy field.

67

WOODMORE, MARYLAND

Standing beside Khalila on the gravel driveway beside the farmhouse, Harrison sifted through the limited clues, attempting to determine what Mixell was planning. Local law enforcement and FBI agents had swarmed the property after Khalila had called the NCTC, and the initial search of the house had revealed nothing noteworthy. After assessing what little they knew, Harrison decided to focus on the C-4.

"Let's take a closer look at the barn."

Harrison and Khalila entered the barn, joining a team of four FBI agents scouring the area. Someone had found the light switch and the barn was now well illuminated. Harrison first inspected the three empty crates. As suspected, the markings on the third crate indicated that its contents were the wireless detonators that would be inserted into the C-4.

The table nearby contained an odd assortment of items. One side of the work area contained white C-4 shavings that had been swept into a small pile next to a carving knife, and on the other side of the table were several cans of spray paint: red, green, yellow, blue, pink, purple, and orange—a rainbow of colors. At the back of the table were several colored patches indicating that objects had indeed been spray painted. A small trash can beside the table was filled with the empty C-4 packages.

Harrison quickly surmised what Mixell had done, sharing his assessment with Khalila. "It looks like Mixell carved the C-4 into specific shapes, then painted them to blend into wherever the explosive was placed."

"It seems that way," Khalila agreed. "But why the different colors? Mixell placed the C-4 into different objects?"

Harrison folded his arms across his chest. Despite the clues they had gathered, they were no closer to determining the plot Mixell was about to hatch. He turned to the lead FBI agent, Ken Singleton.

"Have you found any additional evidence?"

"Nothing related to the explosives or that indicates the potential target—just the usual assortment of farm tools and equipment. But there is one rather unusual item."

He led Harrison and Khalila to a large trash can with a lid. With a gloved hand, he lifted the lid, revealing a trash can half-filled with eggs, some whole and others broken. "Any idea why Mixell would buy and then discard enough eggs to feed a small army?"

No answer came to Harrison, but Khalila had a question. "Where are the egg cartons?"

Singleton scratched his head. "Good question. Not in this barn."

Harrison examined the work table again, his eyes settling on the pile of C-4 shavings. Mixell had been shaping the C-4 into something.

"Eggs," he said. "Mixell carved the C-4 into eggs and placed them in the egg cartons."

"What would Mixell do with cartons of C-4 eggs?" Singleton asked.

"Return them to the stores," Khalila postulated. "Walk into a store with an egg carton hidden in a reusable shopping bag, put the eggs back on the shelf when no one is watching, then leave. With wireless detonators, Mixell could simultaneously detonate the C-4 in several dozen stores. Or he could detonate them in sequence over a longer period of time, sowing mayhem and panic across the region."

"It's plausible," Harrison replied, "but that's not Mixell's MO. What would he achieve by blowing up grocery stores?"

"Alright," Khalila replied, "let's set that theory aside for the moment. What else could he do?"

Harrison's gaze returned to the work table, this time focusing on the cans of spray paint. "What horrific thing could Mixell do with several dozen brightly colored C-4 eggs?" He asked the question more to himself than to Khalila and Singleton.

As he stared at the brightly colored splotches where the eggs had been painted, things started falling into place.

"Mixell didn't carve the C-4 into ordinary eggs. He painted them too. He made Easter eggs."

After assessing Harrison's claim, Khalila replied, "Assuming you're correct, I'm not sure how that helps us. Instead of just grocery stores, Mixell could have placed them wherever there's an Easter bunny or candy display."

"I know," Harrison replied, aggravated that his revelation had made tracking down the C-4 eggs even harder.

Singleton mumbled, "Talk about a veritable Easter egg hunt . . ."

"That's it!" Harrison said.

"What is?" Singleton asked.

"What day is today?"

"Sunday."

"I mean, what holiday is today?"

"Easter."

"And what happens every Easter Monday at the White House?"

Singleton's and Khalila's eyes widened in understanding. "The annual Easter Egg festivities," Khalila answered. "Each year, they ship thousands of dyed eggs to the White House for the games."

"That's where the C-4 eggs are headed," Harrison said, "if they're not already there."

Singleton pulled out his phone and called the information in while Khalila contacted the NCTC. Harrison also made a call, his pulse racing as he dialed.

Maddy was at the White House today for the tour with Christine.

68

WASHINGTON, D.C.

Since 1878, American presidents and their families have celebrated Easter Monday by hosting an "egg roll" party. Held on the South Lawn, it is one of the oldest annual events in White House history. More than forty thousand adults and children participate in the event each year, which includes over thirty thousand hard-boiled eggs, half of which are dyed and used for games and the other half consumed as egg pops. Although Braswell Farms in North Carolina provides most of the eggs each year, Gordon's Wholesale provided the remainder for this year's festivities.

At the apex of the South Lawn, a white Gordon's Wholesale van coasted to a halt behind several other vehicles parked on the curved driveway behind the White House. In the driver's seat of the van, Lonnie Mixell surveyed the bustling activity as supplies for tomorrow's event were unloaded. Thus far, everything had gone according to plan.

After being hired a few weeks earlier as a weekend delivery driver for Gordon's Wholesale, his assignment to assist with the egg deliveries to the White House this weekend had occurred as expected. The security check at the entrance to the White House grounds had been uneventful; the physical disguise he had chosen for today matched the picture on his Gordon's Wholesale identification card, and a check of Mixell's cargo had yielded no weapons or anything suspicious—just a large crate of dyed eggs.

After stepping from the van, Mixell pulled the crate from the back, then approached a supervisor with a clipboard, informing her of his cargo.

"I've got a shipment of egg pops for the White House."

The supervisor checked her clipboard, then looked up with a confused look on her face. "We've already received all of the egg pops."

Mixell shrugged his shoulders. "I just deliver what they load in the van." He nodded toward a note taped to the crate. "They said it was an extra order for the White House staff."

The supervisor considered the matter, then looked around for a place to deposit the egg pops.

"They need to be refrigerated," Mixell reminded her.

"Oh, right." She captured the attention of one of the dozen police officers nearby, a member of the Secret Service Uniformed Division, responsible for protecting the White House and foreign diplomatic missions in the District of Columbia, who was providing security during the Egg Roll event and its preparations. "Can you escort this man to the kitchen?"

The officer agreed and Mixell joined him as they entered the White House.

On the main floor of the West Wing, Christine waited with Maddy beside the closed door to the Oval Office. They had almost completed their White House tour, with Christine even showing Maddy the Situation Room in the basement of the West Wing. The only space left to explore was the Oval Office, which would include a meeting with its occupant. Christine could tell Maddy was nervous, fidgeting as she waited to meet the president of the United States.

The president's secretary approached. "He'll see you now."

Christine knocked, then entered the Oval Office with Maddy alongside her.

The president, seated at his desk, rose to greet his guests.

"Christine, it's good to see you, as always." Then he turned his attention to the young girl accompanying her, extending his hand. "It's a pleasure to meet you, Maddy. I've heard a lot about you," he said as they shook hands.

"You have?"

"Actually, I've heard a lot about your dad." He gestured toward the two sofas at the other end of the Oval Office, which faced each other.

As the president sat on one sofa while Christine and Maddy settled into the other one, the cell phone in Christine's purse vibrated. Considering the circumstances—an audience with the president—she ignored the call.

"I understand that you haven't spent much time with your dad the last few months," the president said. "I know it's hard not being together, but your father is a very important man, and he's been assigned to a critical mission."

When scheduling today's meeting with the president, Christine had explained to him that Maddy was Jake Harrison's daughter, and had reminded the president that Harrison and Khalila were the two CIA employees who had tracked Mixell down months earlier, preventing him from launching surface-to-air missiles at Air Force One as it took off from Joint Base Andrews. After learning what had happened to Harrison's wife, followed by Maddy's subsequent separation from her father, the president had agreed to amplify Harrison's role while steering clear of Angie's death.

Christine's cell phone vibrated, and she ignored it again.

Maddy simply nodded as the president spoke, awestruck in his presence. The Oval Office door suddenly opened and Special Agent Ashley Tobin, this afternoon's shift leader for the President's Protection Detail, burst into the room, accompanied by three other Secret Service agents.

"We have an imminent bomb threat, Mr. President. We need to get you to safety immediately."

The president stood, quickly surveying Christine and Maddy. He extended his hand to Maddy. "Come with me. You'll be safe." Turning to Ashley, the president said, "Christine and the girl will join me."

Ashley acknowledged the president's order, then led them toward the elevator that would take them to the hardened underground bunker deep beneath the White House. Along the way, Christine's phone vibrated again, and this time she answered.

Harrison was on the other end, informing her that Mixell had shaped the C-4 into Easter eggs, and that they were already at the White House or on their way, being delivered for Easter Monday's festivities.

They had almost reached the elevator when Christine hung up, deciding she'd be more useful tracking Mixell down than hiding in a bunker. There were dozens of lives at stake if fifty pounds of C-4 were detonated in the White House, and even if he had altered his appearance, she could likely spot him if he was here. There shouldn't be too many six-foot-two men who looked somewhat like Mixell in the White House or on its grounds.

Christine explained her plan and the president nodded his concurrence as he stepped into the elevator with Maddy, directing one of his Secret Service agents to accompany Christine as she searched the White House.

Mixell was loading the C-4 eggs into one of the large White House refrigerators when an announcement blared from a speaker in the kitchen ceiling.

"Lockdown in progress. No personnel may enter or exit the White House until further notice. All personnel shall remain in their current location until directed otherwise."

It took Mixell only a few seconds to analyze the situation and come to a conclusion: somehow, his plot had been discovered. Even if he was wrong and the lockdown had been ordered for a different reason—although what were the odds of that—he would likely be discovered if his delivery to the White House was scrutinized.

He had completed the most difficult part of his mission, delivering the C-4 eggs to the White House. What remained was straightforward—depart and detonate the C-4. He briefly considered pulling his cell phone out and detonating the eggs beside him; the president was in the White House and assassinating him would be a monumental achievement, whether Mixell lived to celebrate it or not. But he decided not to give up so easily.

His Secret Service Uniformed Division escort had a hand to his earpiece, listening to a transmission, his attention temporarily distracted from the Gordon's Wholesale delivery man standing nearby. Mixell moved swiftly, levying a vicious blow to the man's Adam's apple with one hand as he unfastened the security strap of the pistol holster at his waist with the other. As the man staggered backward a step, grabbing his throat, Mixell pulled the pistol from its holster, leveling it at the man.

There was one other person in the kitchen—an assistant cook, it seemed. She stood frozen in place as Mixell backed up to keep her and the officer in view. Mixell gestured toward the walk-in freezer.

"Inside."

Neither person moved.

"Now," Mixell snarled, "unless you want to eat a bullet."

The officer moved slowly toward the freezer and the cook joined him. The freezer was opened and the officer and cook stepped inside, staring at Mixell as the door was closed. Then he jammed the handle with a kitchen utensil to ensure the door couldn't be opened from inside.

Mixell attempted to slide the officer's pistol into his pants pocket, but the pistol grip wouldn't fit, which was fine with Mixell. He decided to hide the grip with his hand wrapped around it, which kept it ready for any encounters as he worked his way toward the nearest White House exit.

There was no one in the hallway, so Mixell moved swiftly, backtracking his path through the White House. He was only a few strides from turning into an adjacent corridor when a man and woman burst into the hallway at the next intersection. He immediately recognized the woman—Christine O'Connor—plus what looked like a Secret Service agent accompanying her.

He decided to keep moving toward the intersection, hoping Christine wouldn't realize who he was and that he wouldn't be challenged for not staying in place as ordered over the White House speakers. He'd just pretend to be a dumb delivery man, wanting to stay on schedule with his next delivery. Unfortunately, when Christine's gaze settled on him, he noticed a flicker of recognition in her eyes.

The jig was up.

Mixell withdrew his pistol and fired at the Secret Service agent, putting a bullet in his head. As the man collapsed to the ground, Mixell shifted the pistol toward Christine, who froze in place.

"Hello, Chris," he said. "Fancy meeting you here."

"Lonnie, we know what you're planning. Don't do this."

Mixell ignored her plea as he moved toward her, keeping his pistol aimed at her head. When he reached Christine, he grabbed her by the neck and slammed her into the wall.

"I've laid awake at night, plotting how to get past your protective agents. And today, you waltz into my grasp." He placed the pistol barrel against her head. "How many bullets did you put into me at Jake's house?"

"Not enough."

Mixell smiled. "True. Very true."

Their conversation was interrupted as two more Secret Service agents entered the hallway from the next intersection, their weapons drawn. Mixell jerked Christine in front of him, keeping the pistol barrel pressed against her head, with one arm wrapped around her body. Both agents halted, their weapons aimed in Mixell's direction, while one of the agents reported the situation over the microphone inside his shirt sleeve cuff.

Mixell backed up toward the intersection leading to the exit, keeping Christine between him and the agents, occasionally glancing behind him.

"Who's the coward now," Christine asked, "hiding behind a woman? Didn't you chastise Jake for doing the same thing with your soulmate?"

Christine's question—accusing him of being a coward—made Mixell's blood boil. There wasn't anyone besides Jake who knew him better, and she was pushing his buttons. He did his best to let the anger dissipate.

"Shut up, Chris. Every time you open your mouth, you make your death more painful."

She pressed her lips together. "Hmm," she replied.

Mixell felt her body tense, and he knew she was planning something. She was still quite athletic, as she had proven in the barn at Harrison's house a few months ago, and he felt her firm body as his arm pulled her close against him.

"Don't even think about trying anything," he said. "I swear to God, if you so much as twitch, I'll pull the trigger."

He felt Christine's body relax somewhat. "Alright, Lonnie," she said. "I'll play along as your hostage. I'm interested in seeing how this plays

out. You didn't plan on being discovered, so let's see how you weasel
your way out of here."

"What did I say about you opening your mouth?" He pressed the
pistol barrel more firmly against her head. "Besides," he said, "I've got an
extremely valuable hostage—the director of the CIA."

It was a short distance from the hallway to the exit, and they reached
it before other Secret Service agents or uniformed officers entered. However, a quick glance after cracking the door open revealed about a dozen
agents and officers in strategic positions outside the White House, plus
more moving into position.

Mixell's van wasn't far away, but he would be in the open during the
short journey to the vehicle. Even with Christine pressed against him,
she would block only half of the agents. There would be others behind
him with a clear shot, if they were willing to take it while Mixell had a
pistol pressed against the CIA director's head.

After considering his options, Mixell devised a plan.

He called out, "I promise to release the CIA director, unharmed,
once I'm safely away. All you need to do is drive the Gordon's Wholesale
van up to this door. The keys are in the van."

When there was no response, Mixell directed Christine to reiterate
his command.

Christine pressed her lips together again. "Hmm . . . hmm," she replied.

"Very funny," Mixell replied. "You're allowed to talk now. Tell the
agents and officers to do as I've directed."

"They don't work for me."

"I know that," Mixell growled. "But if you don't prove your worth as
a hostage, you're worthless to me and I'm stuck here. Do you know what
happens next?"

"I can do the math."

"Then you better start talking."

"How's this—I'll have them bring the van up and let us go, after
they've verified the White House has been evacuated? The president is
already safely away, and once everyone else is safe, it's just a building.
You can blow it up if you want."

"You're not in any position to negotiate."

"Actually, I am." Christine twisted her head toward Mixell, so she could look him in the eye. "If you want to leave here in anything but a body bag or handcuffs, you'll need my help."

"Fine!" Mixell replied. "Just get the van up here and have them agree to let us go."

Christine called out to the Secret Service agents and police officers, repeating Mixell's demands, and after a few rounds of back and forth followed by a moment of silence, a Secret Service agent replied.

"Agreed."

The minutes ticked by as Mixell waited, and although the delay felt excruciating, he was able to savor the moment. With his arm wrapped tightly around Christine, he could feel her body trembling. Her bravado was an act; she was scared to death.

He was going to enjoy ending her life—slowly and painfully.

The van engine started, and a moment later the vehicle pulled to a halt with the passenger door beside the White House exit. The driver stepped from the van, leaving the engine running, then Mixell opened the passenger door and dragged Christine into the van behind him, staying low in the vehicle until he was in the driver's seat.

"Close the door," he ordered Christine as he kept the pistol aimed at her.

After she closed the passenger door, he said, "Place the side of your face against the dash."

Christine did as Mixell ordered, then he pressed the pistol barrel against the other side of her head and sat up in his seat, putting the van in gear.

The Gordon's Wholesale van sped down the South Lawn driveway until it exited the White House grounds.

69

WOODMORE, MARYLAND

Jake Harrison and Khalila Dufour were monitoring the rapidly unfolding situation from Mixell's rental property in Woodmore, debating what to do next. An aerial surveillance drone had picked up the white van Mixell was driving, following from a sufficient height to remain undetected. As long as Christine remained a hostage inside the vehicle, law enforcement was hesitant to engage Mixell, fearing an unfavorable outcome.

Shortly after the van departed the White House grounds, an explosion was reported in the District. On their cell phones, a video feed from the NCTC revealed a massive crater in the South Lawn, but the White House itself remained intact. After several queries, Harrison was assured that Maddy was safe.

Harrison and Khalila tapped into the aerial drone's surveillance video as Mixell's van worked its way through D.C. and merged onto Interstate 395 southbound, disappearing into the Third Street Tunnel a moment later.

The drone repositioned near the exit of the almost one-mile-long tunnel passing beneath the National Mall and Capitol Reflecting Pool, monitoring the possible routes: Mixell could continue west on I-395 toward Virginia, turn east onto I-695 toward Maryland, or slip into the D.C. neighborhoods via Virginia Ave SW or South Capitol Street SW. Unfortunately, white was the most popular van color in the country, with about a half-dozen white vans entering the tunnel in proximity to the Gordon's Wholesale van.

The aerial drone was ordered to descend to obtain a better view of the vehicles exiting the tunnel, close enough to discern who the driver was and the markings on the van. The wait seemed interminable, with white van after white van emerging with no driver matching Mixell's description or adorned with the Gordon's Wholesale insignia. Harrison had become convinced that Mixell had somehow slipped away when the van finally emerged from the tunnel.

Mixell was driving, but there was no sign of Christine. He had either killed her and dumped her body in the tunnel, or perhaps he had knocked her unconscious, and she was hidden behind the van's dashboard after slumping in her seat.

The van traveled east on I-695, and the chat thread associated with the surveillance video postulated where Mixell was headed, focused on where and how to engage him while minimizing the risk to the CIA director. As Harrison watched the van merge onto the Baltimore–Washington Parkway, he realized where Mixell was going.

He dialed the NCTC, requesting Jessica Del Rio, the supervisor overseeing the Mixell investigation. When she answered, he said, "Mixell doesn't know we've located his hideout. He's headed back to his rental home here in Woodmore. We can set up an ambush and take him out when we get a clear shot. Don't engage him along the way. Let him think he's slipped cleanly away."

Jessica agreed and directives flowed out from the NCTC to the various law enforcement agencies, quickly reaching the FBI agents and police officers at Mixell's rental home. Harrison and Khalila conferred with Singleton, the lead FBI agent, identifying several locations where personnel might get a clear shot when Mixell stepped from the vehicle, depending on where he parked the van.

Harrison wasn't a trained sniper, but he trusted his marksmanship more than that of the FBI agents and police officers at the property, and Singleton agreed that Harrison would take the premier hiding spot, offering the highest probability of a clear shot once Mixell arrived. Khalila took the best location on the other side of the driveway.

He was no stranger to danger and adrenaline, but his pulse raced at the thought that Christine might already be dead. He took a deep breath and slowed his breathing, and his heart rate followed.

70

WOODMORE, MARYLAND

In the vicinity of the rental property on Enterprise Road, there was no indication of law enforcement presence. The roadblocks at the intersections of Lottsford Road and Central Avenue had been cleared, all vehicles had been removed from Mixell's rental property, and Harrison and Khalila, plus eight FBI agents, were hidden on the farmhouse grounds.

Harrison lay on his stomach behind a fallen tree that had been swallowed by the underbrush, having cleared a small hole in the foliage to provide a clear view of the gravel driveway. On the other side of the driveway, Khalila knelt at the edge of a backyard patio, hidden behind a worn wooden partition with several small gaps offering a view of the other side of the van once it arrived.

Singleton had provided Harrison with a rifle to improve the accuracy of his shot, should he take it once Mixell arrived. The rifle hadn't been sighted in to adjust for rifle and shooter bias, but Harrison figured it wouldn't matter. The driveway was only thirty feet away.

Unfortunately, Singleton had made it clear that Mixell would be arrested; this wasn't a CIA operation with the authority to kill an enemy combatant. Mixell would be killed only if Christine's life, or those of law enforcement personnel, were threatened. The FBI would take the lead in Mixell's arrest and Christine's rescue, with Harrison and Khalila providing backup if anything went wrong.

Time passed slowly while they waited for Mixell's arrival. Harrison monitored the drone surveillance video, showing the van entering the outskirts of Woodmore. After it turned onto Enterprise Road, Harrison turned the video off and focused on the end of the driveway where it met the street.

A moment later, a white van with the Gordon's Wholesale logo emblazoned on the side turned into the driveway and approached the house. Mixell was driving, and there was still no sign of Christine.

The van coasted to a halt, and Mixell opened the door and stepped onto the gravel driveway, then walked toward the house. When he reached the front door, four FBI agents swarmed from around both sides of the house with weapons drawn, converging on him.

Mixell turned around with a shocked expression and raised his hands in the air. As he was being forced to the ground by the FBI agents, Harrison emerged from the tree line and moved swiftly toward the van, opening its passenger side door. The interior of the vehicle was empty—there was no sign of Christine.

He headed toward Mixell as the FBI agents finished their search, verifying Mixell had no weapons or explosives strapped to his body. Mixell had been babbling the whole time, asking why he was being arrested. When the agents pulled him to his knees, Harrison suddenly stopped.

This wasn't Mixell.

The man had a remarkable resemblance to Harrison's former best friend, but it definitely wasn't Lonnie Mixell.

Harrison joined Khalila and the FBI agents gathered around the man, stopping beside Singleton. "This isn't Mixell," he informed him.

"What's your name?" Harrison asked the man.

The man, trembling in fear, replied, "Robert Keeshan."

Keeshan went on to explain that he was a model and was here because he had been hired for a body-double gig. No details had been provided other than there was a work party at this address, and that he was supposed to drive this van here and knock on the door. At the party, he was supposed to remain aloof and minimize the engagement. He was impersonating a new hire at the company and no one should realize that a body double had taken his place.

Harrison glanced at the Gordon's Wholesale van.

"Where did you get the van?"

"I did a vehicle swap in the I-395 tunnel in D.C."

"We're looking for the man you're impersonating, Do you know what car he left the tunnel in?"

Keeshan nodded. "He left in mine. A blue Ford Taurus."

"What's the license plate number?"

"I don't have it memorized."

Singleton turned to Harrison. "We'll look it up. It won't take long."

"Was there a woman with the man you swapped vehicles with?" Harrison asked.

Keeshan nodded. "She left in the car with the man."

Khalila joined the conversation. "Didn't you think there was something strange about having to swap vehicles in the 395 tunnel?"

"I . . . I didn't ask questions. I need the money. Why he wanted to be impersonated is none of my business. I figured the guy was having an affair. He was with an attractive woman, and they were clearly an item—he had his arm around her waist. She seemed nervous, as if they were sneaking off for a tryst while I covered for him at this party."

"We've got the license plate number," Singleton announced. "It won't be long before we find the vehicle."

71

ALEXANDRIA, VIRGINIA

Thirty minutes earlier, Lonnie Mixell had started the engine in Robert Keeshan's blue Ford Taurus, watching the Gordon's Wholesale van pull back into traffic and head toward the I-395 tunnel exit. He had picked a perfect spot for the vehicle swap, inside a traffic tunnel hidden from overhead surveillance. More important, however, was that unlike many highway tunnels, I-395's Third Street Tunnel had a wide emergency shoulder on the right side, where the vehicle swap could occur without impeding traffic.

After the van pulled back onto the Interstate, Mixell had waited a few minutes to let aerial and satellite surveillance assets focus on the white van during its journey to the farmhouse in Woodmore, pulling their attention away from the I-395 tunnel exits.

While he waited, Mixell realized he had a dilemma on his hands and a critical decision to make. After departing the White House, he had detonated the C-4 and traveled into the tunnel, where the first phase of avoiding apprehension had gone according to plan; the vehicle swap with a body double had been an insurance policy in case law enforcement had somehow correlated the explosion to him and the Gordon's Wholesale van before he had time to ditch the vehicle.

At this point, he had planned to head to Union Station where subway, train, and bus lines from Maryland, Virginia, and the District converged. The Ford Taurus would be left in the parking lot where it would be tracked down by law enforcement, while he disappeared amongst the more than seventy thousand people entering and departing Union Station each day. However, the woman sitting beside him had thrown a wrench into the plan.

The last element of Mixell's revenge had been focused on Christine, who would be dealt with once Harrison had suffered sufficiently from Angie's demise. Eliminating Harrison would be easy, Mixell figured, because they would eventually meet—each man was tracking down the other. Christine, on the other hand, was well guarded by her CIA protective agents and would not be personally involved in the attempt to apprehend him.

The challenge of capturing and tormenting Christine had unexpectedly been solved, but replaced with a sticky dilemma. He could not bring Christine with him while he escaped through Union Station; there would be too many opportunities for her to slip away or alert law enforcement or security personnel along the way. It had been difficult enough to ensure Christine didn't attempt to escape during the vehicle swap in the tunnel or to alert Mixell's body double, who clearly didn't want to know what was going on.

After assessing the issue, with one hand on the steering wheel and the other pointing a pistol at Christine in the passenger seat, Mixell realized he had two options. The first was to execute his escape as planned, which meant a quick death for Christine—a bullet to the head and her body deposited somewhere. However, that was a distasteful solution, as Christine's death would be far too easy. He wanted to draw things out, savoring the moments in which Christine grappled with the terror and pain as her life slowly slipped away.

Mixell had made his decision, then pulled into the heavy traffic on I-395. Instead of taking the exit back into D.C. toward Union Station, Mixell stayed on the busy interstate, headed into Virginia.

The blue Ford Taurus ground to a halt at the back of a warehouse in Alexandria. Situated on the bank of the Potomac River and bordered on one side by Oronoco Bay and the other by Founders Park, the car was sufficiently hidden from view. During the short drive from Washington, D.C., Mixell had fleshed out his plan for Christine.

For just a moment, he reflected on the decision he had made in the I-395 tunnel. He had chosen a plan in which there was likely no possibility of escape, yet he harbored no regret. His plan for revenge—the thoughts that had haunted him for eight long years in prison and each night since his release as he drifted off to sleep—would have a satisfying ending. One that would include both Christine and Harrison.

While the hatred for his former best friend could not have been more intense, he harbored some degree of remorse for Christine. However, she was the one who had decided her fate, choosing to side with Harrison instead of him, or simply staying out of the issue. To the contrary, she had done everything within her power to hunt him down.

Mixell put the car in park and stepped from the vehicle, keeping his pistol aimed at Christine as he walked to the passenger side door, then opened it.

"Out of the car," he said, "and on your knees."

There was fear in her eyes as she complied, but to her credit, she did an admirable job containing the emotions and thoughts that were undoubtedly swirling inside her mind as she knelt on the ground before him.

Mixell walked behind her and placed the pistol barrel against her head.

"You're going to rot in Hell!" she said.

Leaning toward her, he whispered in her ear. "Not just yet."

He shifted the pistol in his hand, grabbing onto the barrel instead, then smashed the pistol grip into the side of her head, knocking her to the ground. After verifying she was unconscious, he lifted her over his shoulder and headed toward the warehouse.

72

K-571 *KRASNOYARSK*

Captain Second Rank Gavriil Novikov leaned over the fire controlman's shoulder, studying the data fusion display on his console. *Krasnoyarsk* was thirty miles west of the Strait of Hormuz, having halted its pursuit of the American aircraft carrier. A few miles to the east, a formidable sonobuoy barrier had been laid by several squadrons of P-8A Poseidon submarine-hunting aircraft. With the sonobuoy field on one side of the aircraft carrier and the mined strait on the other, the American warship sailed on a north-and-south track, pacing back and forth as it awaited resolution of its fate.

It would not have to wait long.

Three friendly submerged contacts appeared on the western edge of the fire control fusion plot, heading east toward the aircraft carrier. The Akulas had arrived, ready to execute the plan formulated as they had pursued the carrier east; a new operational message had been received by all four submarines during their last trip to periscope depth.

Novikov had to admit that the tactic he had devised and convinced Russian Fleet leadership to implement was both novel and counterintuitive. Normally, if attempting to penetrate a sonobuoy field, stealth was paramount. The trek through the sonobuoy field would be treacherous, with the submarine attacked and likely sunk if it was detected. To maximize the probability of survival, the crew would shift to the much quieter electric drive and rig the ship for Ultra Quiet. The pace through the sonobuoy field would be slow and tedious, like an animal sneaking up on its prey, moving carefully through the grass until it was close enough to pounce.

The Akulas headed toward the American aircraft carrier, past

Krasnoyarsk as Novikov kept his submarine far enough away from the sonobuoys to remain undetected. As the Akulas approached the sonobuoy field, they slowed to ahead one-third, but kept propulsion shifted to the noisier steam-turbine main engines. It would not be long before they would need maximum speed.

The three Russian attack submarines continued east while Novikov moved *Krasnoyarsk* into position for its part in the plan, ordering his submarine to periscope depth, but keeping the scope lowered to avoid discovery by periscope detection radars.

Krasnoyarsk cruised beneath the water's surface at five knots, waiting until the Akulas reached the point where they would likely be detected by the sonobuoys. All three Akulas suddenly shifted to ahead flank, beginning a high-speed run through the sonobuoy field.

Turning to his Watch Officer, Novikov ordered him to raise the radar mast. A moment later, after the mast pierced the water's surface, *Krasnoyarsk* was ready to execute its part in the plan.

Novikov's proposal to penetrate the sonobuoy field had flipped traditional tactics on its head. Instead of creeping slowly past the sonobuoys, hoping to avoid detection, the Akulas would travel at maximum speed, not caring whether they were detected or not. They would be attacked, of course, but *Krasnoyarsk* and its loadout of anti-air missiles had changed the equation. Any attempt to sink the Akulas would be defeated, with HAAWCs launched from the P-8As shot down. Until *Krasnoyarsk* ran out of anti-air missiles, the Akulas were invincible.

But *Krasnoyarsk* had only fifteen anti-air missiles remaining, so the Akulas had to penetrate the sonobuoy field quickly and reach the open water beyond, where they could not be tracked until a new sonobuoy field was laid.

As the Akulas approached the sonobuoys, Novikov knew it would not be long before the P-8As, monitoring the sonobuoys as they circled high above, detected the high-speed submerged contacts and sent torpedoes their way.

"Energize the radar," Novikov ordered.

Krasnoyarsk was now at risk of detection, but was also safe from attack until it ran out of anti-air missiles. Additionally, the P-8A crews would be focused on the Akulas, which were speeding toward the American aircraft carrier.

Not long thereafter, the radar operator reported three new contacts descending toward the Akulas. Novikov launched three anti-air missiles, and the HAAWCs were destroyed before the torpedoes were released. Moments later, another round of HAAWCs were launched, followed by another round shortly afterward.

It was anticlimactic, as the HAAWCs had no defensive measures and no ability to even detect the incoming missiles, and all nine HAAWCs were destroyed. By the time the last mangled HAAWC splashed into the water, the three Akulas had exited the sonobuoy field and traveled beyond its detection range.

It would not be long before the American aircraft carrier was within firing range.

73

USS *THEODORE ROOSEVELT*

On *Theodore Roosevelt*'s Bridge in the ship's Island superstructure, Captain Ryan Noss had watched in dismay as three consecutive rounds of HAAWCs were shot down, their remnants splashing into the ocean. The three approaching Russian submarines, classified as Akula by the P-8A crews monitoring their sonobuoys, had now cleared the buoy field and were beyond detection range. The submarines had undoubtedly changed course after speeding past the buoys, so the P-8As now had no target solution to guide additional HAAWCs toward the approaching threats.

The P-8As were busy laying another layer of sonobuoys closer to the carrier, and Noss watched as the buoys splashed into the sea, but it likely wouldn't matter. The Akulas would be within firing range before the area was sufficiently populated with buoys.

Noss turned to his Officer of the Deck, ordering him to turn east, bringing the ship as close to the minefield as possible, buying a few more minutes as the Akulas closed on their target.

The ASW commander apparently had come to the same conclusion—that the sonobuoy fields wouldn't be populated fast enough—and Noss listened to the speaker on the Bridge as the ASW commander ordered a half-dozen MH-60Rs aloft. Since the helicopters had proven quite vulnerable to the anti-air missiles, they had been held in reserve, with the ASW commander depending instead on the P-8As, which flew at an altitude beyond the range of the Russian missiles.

However, with the P-8As temporarily ineffective, the MH-60Rs were being pressed into action. Many, if not all, of the anti-submarine helicopters would be shot down, but hopefully the Russian guided missile

submarine would run out of missiles before the carrier ran out of helicopters, and three MH-60Rs would survive long enough to detect and
kill the approaching Akulas.

Noss felt the carrier banking to starboard as it commenced a turn to
the north. They had traveled east as far as possible, with the minefield
less than two thousand yards away.

There was nowhere else to run to.

74

USS *MISSISSIPPI*

Five thousand yards east of the minefield stretching across the Strait of Hormuz, the fast attack submarine USS *Mississippi* loitered at periscope depth at the northern end of the Gulf of Oman. In the Virginia-class submarine's Control Room, Commander Brad Waller was seated in the Captain's chair waiting for a path to be cleared through the mines, monitoring the situation as additional messages were downloaded from the Radio broadcast. To the west were five more fast attack submarines, waiting in line behind *Mississippi* for their turn through the minefield. Not far from the strait in the Arabian Sea, specialized mine-clearing ships were en route, but were still over a day's journey away.

Two weeks ago, *Mississippi* had been stationed near Vladivostok, monitoring Russian Pacific Fleet activity, when several nuclear-powered submarines had sortied from the Russian port. Waller had latched onto the first one, trailing it as it journeyed southwest before losing track of the submarine in the busy Malaysian shipping traffic. Disappointed in their performance, Waller and his crew had been given a second chance, waiting to come to *Theodore Roosevelt*'s aid. The only thing standing in the way was the minefield blocking the strait.

Waller stood and stretched his legs, surveying the Control Room watchstanders. Only a third of the consoles were manned. He had maintained his crew in a normal watch rotation, waiting to shift to Battle Stations once the minefield was cleared, hoping to keep his crew fresh for the tense battle likely ahead.

"Conn, Radio." The report emanating from the Control Room speakers broke Waller from his thoughts. "New intel message received. Mine clearing is almost complete. Only six more mines to go."

"Is an ETC provided?" Waller asked.

"Conn, Radio. Negative. No estimated time of completion is mentioned."

Waller gritted his teeth. USS *Michigan* and its SEAL detachment were making progress, but would they complete the task in time for *Mississippi* and the other fast attack submarines to defend *Roosevelt,* or would the carrier be sent to the bottom before assistance arrived?

75

WASHINGTON, D.C.

In the Presidential Emergency Operations Center deep beneath the East Wing of the White House, in a bunker built to protect the president from aerial attack, the president and his advisors were gathered around a table in the executive briefing room. The White House above was still being swept for other bombs Mixell might have planted, with the president conducting business inside the PEOC until it was deemed safe for him to return to the surface.

Joining the president at the table were his Chief of Staff Kevin Hardison and National Security Advisor Thom Parham, while on the phone were FBI Director Bill Guisewhite, CIA Deputy Director Monroe Bryant, and NCTC Supervisor Jessica Del Rio. The topic of the conversation was the effort to locate Mixell and Christine.

Bill Guisewhite provided the latest information. "Mixell swapped vehicles inside the 395 tunnel, which we didn't realize until the van arrived at the house he'd been renting. After the vehicle swap, the van was driven by a body double Mixell had hired in case he was tracked from the White House. The bad news is that we didn't have aerial surveillance of the tunnel exits at the time Mixell departed in the new car; our assets were following the white van. The good news is that we know the color and model of the car he switched into, and its license plate number. We'll locate the car shortly after it passes a speed or traffic light camera. We've also got law enforcement on the alert. We're searching for the vehicle with every means possible."

"Is there any indication of Christine's condition?" the president asked.

"Our last intel was when Mixell swapped vehicles inside the tunnel. Christine appeared unharmed at that time."

"What about the explosives Mixell planted?"

"We're almost done searching the White House for additional bombs. As you know, we were able to move the C-4 eggs from the kitchen onto the South Lawn before they were detonated. We also located the Secret Service Uniformed Division officer who escorted Mixell into the White House, who was locked in the kitchen walk-in freezer with one of your staff. Both are fine. When Mixell was discovered inside the White House, he wasn't far from the kitchen, but we don't know where he went or what he did after locking the officer in the freezer. We don't suspect he planted other bombs, but we're conducting a thorough search just in case."

The president nodded his understanding. "Anything else on this topic?"

"Not at this time," Guisewhite replied.

The teleconference was ended and a new one initiated, this time with acting Secretary of Defense Peter Seuffert, Secretary of the Navy Sheila McNeil, and Chief of Naval Operations Admiral Joe Sites, who were prepared to brief the president on the situation in the Persian Gulf.

"The current scenario is perilous," Sheila McNeil announced. "*Theodore Roosevelt* is being engaged again by the Russian submarines, with our ability to sink them being thwarted by anti-air missiles launched by the SSGN. We've lost several MH-60Rs—they can't get close enough to drop their torpedoes—and the weapons launched by the P-8As have been shot down before the HAAWC wing kits release the torpedoes."

"How are we going to protect our aircraft carrier?" the president asked.

"We have six fast attack submarines on the other side of the minefield. The SEAL detachment aboard *Michigan* has been working the issue, and we hope that a path through the minefield will be cleared soon, which will allow our fast attack submarines to engage. We're running out of time," McNeil admitted, "but the mine-clearing task is almost complete."

"I understand," the president replied. "Keep me up to date as events unfold."

76

STRAIT OF HORMUZ

Two black mini-subs sped through the murky water, passing shadowy mines on each side, plus above and below, as they traveled through a tunnel carved through the minefield. In one SDV, Senior Chief Russ Burkhardt sat beside Kurt Hacker, while the other SDV transported Michael Keller and Dave Narehood toward their destination—the final four mines that needed to be cleared, which would open a path large enough for the waiting fast attack submarines to pass through. Both SDVs were traveling at maximum speed, and it wasn't long before the last four mines materialized in the distance.

By now, the process of clearing the mines had become routine: attach a limpet to a mine, set the timer, then retreat a safe distance before the limpet detonated. A safe distance had been determined to be about one hundred yards, but that wasn't what occupied Burkhardt's thoughts as they approached the remaining four mines—they had only two limpets left.

After mapping the minefield at the beginning of the effort and identifying how to most efficiently cut through the barrier, then assessing their inventory of limpets, they had determined that they would be two limpets short and had prepared for the final challenge. The remaining four mines were the last to clear because they were arranged in pairs, one above the other. While the SEALs cleared the previous mines, working their way toward the final four, the machinist mates aboard *Michigan* had fabricated two unique hand winches, one for each SEAL team.

Burkhardt shifted propulsion to neutral and let the SDV coast to a halt near the bottom of one pair of mines, while Keller stopped his SDV near the bottom mine in the other pair. In the back seat of each SDV, alongside a limpet, was a manual winch that had been modified, adding a third hook. After setting the SDV buoyancy to neutral, letting it hover in the water nearby, Burkhardt and Hacker slipped from the front seat, retrieved the modified winch, and kicked their fins, sending them toward the lower mine in their pair. Nearby was a thick anchor chain rising through the water toward the higher mine they would need to destroy.

Hacker connected one of the winch hooks to a link in the anchor chain and a second hook to another link farther up, then cranked the winch. Slowly, the upper link was pulled down until it reached the winch. The third hook, which served only to keep the chain link in its new position, was slipped into the upper link and the winch was relaxed, allowing Hacker to remove the original hook from the link, extend the winch, and slip the hook into position several links higher again.

It was a painstaking process, pulling the higher mine down link by link, and Hacker and Burkhardt took turns with the manual labor. Soon, a dark bulbous shape took form above, and Burkhardt and Hacker kept at it until both mines were at the same height, about ten feet apart. After releasing the upper hook this time, Hacker connected it to the anchor chain of the mine beside them, then began cranking the winch, pulling the mines toward each other.

While formulating the plan to destroy two mines with one limpet, the SEALs had been concerned that bringing two mines so close together would set one or both of them off. After the mines had been described to the Navy's mine experts and been identified, the SEALs had been assured that neither mine would detonate due to proximity to another. It would take a reasonably large surface ship or submarine to trigger a mine's magnetic field fuze. However, the SEALs had been cautioned not to depress a contact spike as the mines were brought together.

Burkhardt monitored the mines as Hacker slowly pulled them toward each other, and the process was stopped when the two mines were about three feet apart. With the contact spikes extending about twelve inches, that left a one-foot gap between the two. Not far away, Keller and Narehood were completing the same process, running just a few minutes behind.

Hacker swam back to the SDV and retrieved the limpet while

Narehood did the same. Next came the real challenge—or question. What was the best strategy for using a single limpet to destroy two mines? These limpets had shape-charge warheads, designed to blow a hole deep into a ship when attached to the bottom of its hull. After deliberating the issue, the SEALs had decided to attach the limpet to one of the mines, with the second mine in the line of fire, attempting to kill two birds with one stone. Hopefully, the limpet shape charge, combined with the detonation of the first mine, would be sufficient to destroy the second.

Burkhardt helped Hacker attach the limpet to the mine, slipping it carefully between the nearest contact spikes, then fastened a strap around the mine, holding the limpet in place. Hacker set the limpet timer, then the two SEALs waited until Keller and Narehood finished their preparations and provided the awaited signal. Hacker activated his timer, as did Keller, and the four SEALs swam back to their respective SDVs.

After retreating in their SDVs a safe distance away, they waited as the timers counted down and both limpets detonated.

It took a while for the water to clear, and it was a welcome sight when it did. The last four mines blocking the path through the minefield had been destroyed.

Both SDVs turned and sped back toward *Michigan* to deliver the news.

77

ALEXANDRIA, VIRGINIA

As the haze cleared from her vision, the first sensation Christine became aware of was pain. The right side of her head, where Mixell had struck her with his pistol, throbbed, and her shoulders ached. After collecting her senses, she realized she was dangling from a rope tied to a ceiling beam, the ends fastened around her wrists with her arms extended above, while her feet dragged on the floor.

Christine pulled her feet beneath her and stood, taking the strain off her shoulders. Looking around, she realized that she was in the warehouse that Mixell had parked behind. It seemed to be a storage facility, because it was mostly filled with stacks of crates with open alleys between them. One side of the warehouse appeared to be an open area where shipping vehicles could be loaded or unloaded. Mixell had pulled the Ford Taurus into the building through a now-closed large garage door opening, taking up a portion of the open area.

Night was approaching, the day giving way to dusk. Through grimy windows, it was gray outside, with the inside of the warehouse lit by yellow light bulbs hanging from the ceiling.

A sound of metal scraping caught Christine's attention, and she turned to spot Mixell squatting beside a toolbox on the floor, sorting through its contents. After pushing a hammer aside, he extracted a pair of flathead nail-puller pliers and examined it closely, opening and then closing the sharp ends. He seemed dissatisfied with it, because he tossed it back into the toolbox and kept rummaging through the tools. He dug around some more, finding a scoring knife with a sharp, hooked end.

"This will have to do."

"What are you planning?" Christine asked.

Mixell glanced up at Christine. "How was your nap?" he asked as he stood and approached her.

"I had a nightmare—about a deranged childhood friend who was attempting to destroy everything he once held dear."

"If that's your attempt to prevent what's about to happen, you're going to have to do better."

"What do you plan to do with me?"

"Kill you," he replied.

His nonchalant answer, delivered with barely a thought, it seemed, sent a cold shiver up Christine's spine. "What would you gain from that?"

He stared at her dispassionately before replying. "My God, Chris. You still don't get it. What do you think all this has been about? What do you think I've been attempting to achieve since being released from prison?"

Mixell stepped closer to Christine and placed the sharp blade against her cheek. "Revenge, Chris. Revenge." A maniacal gleam shone in his eyes as he continued. "Revenge against the man and country who betrayed me." A look of disappointment suddenly overcame him. "I'll admit things haven't gone according to plan regarding my revenge against this country. According to the news on the radio, the president survived again; my little Easter egg plot failed. Brenda is going to be very upset."

"Brenda Verbeck? The former Secretary of the Navy?"

"That'd be her," Mixell replied. "She's got quite the vindictive streak. She paid me handsomely for the effort, ten million dollars up front, ninety million more upon successful completion of the task. It's too bad I won't receive the rest. On the other hand, I suspect I won't need it."

There was a hint of resignation in his voice, and Christine concluded that Mixell didn't have high hopes of leaving the warehouse alive. That didn't bode well for her, either.

"As to my revenge for what Jake did to me, the ante has been upped; Trish is dead and you chose to side with Jake. You're very much part of this now." He glanced at the floor, where there was a red patch beneath Christine's feet. "Do you know where you are?"

Christine shook her head.

"This is the warehouse where Trish was killed. This is the very spot where she died." He lowered his voice. "The same place you will die."

"Killing me won't bring Trish back."

"It won't," Mixell admitted, "but that's not the goal. You'll pay for helping Jake, and he'll suffer even more while he watches you die. I'll let you in on a little secret. Jake truly loved you, not Angie. He never admitted it, but I knew. Angie was just your replacement, the next best thing."

"I'm afraid you haven't been kept up on current events," Christine replied. "Jake hates me, blames me for what happened to Angie."

Mixell laughed. "Now that's a nice twist. He feels so guilty about Angie's death that he can't own it all himself. He blames you as well? This is even better than I had hoped."

He leaned closer to Christine. "But don't worry. He still loves you despite his act, and he'll suffer even more tonight. Do you know how much I'm going to enjoy the look on his face while he watches you die?"

"How are you going to manage that? Send Jake an invitation card with the warehouse address?"

"Almost," Mixell said. "I'm going to call him, and he's going to come here, alone, in a futile attempt to save you." He pulled his cell phone out. "What's his number?"

"Go to hell, Lonnie!"

Mixell's voice dropped a notch when he spoke again. "I'm going to ask you one more time, Chris. What is Jake's number?"

Christine pressed her lips tightly together. "Hmmm," she replied.

Mixell punched her in the face as hard as he could. Her head snapped back from the powerful blow, and her body, tied to the beam above, swayed back and forth from its force.

She slowly pulled her head erect, but there was a dazed look in her eyes as blood trickled down her chin from split upper and lower lips.

"I tell you what, Chris. The third time's the charm." He brought his hand up, holding the scoring knife at waist height. "If you refuse to give me his number, I'm going to carve you to pieces." He waited until her eyes focused on the knife. "What is Jake's number?"

Christine replied defiantly, "I'm not going to let you have the satisfaction of making Jake watch me die."

Mixell punched the hooked blade into Christine's abdomen, twisted it, then yanked it out, tearing a small chunk of flesh with it. Christine cried out in pain, squeezing her eyes shut and clenching her jaw as blood flowed from the wound. Once the pain subsided somewhat and she looked at Mixell again, he detected indecision in her eyes.

"Again?" Mixell asked. "Or are you going to give me Jake's number?"

She provided no answer, so Mixell jammed the knife into the other side of her abdomen, cutting out another small piece of flesh. This time, a muffled scream leaked from her mouth and she kept her eyes shut for a longer period of time. Blood was flowing from both puncture wounds, and perspiration had begun to bead on her face.

"More?" he asked.

"Please, Lonnie. Just stop."

Mixell punched the blade into the center of Christine's abdomen, then yanked it out, and this time her body convulsed for a few seconds and a moan escaped her throat.

He stepped closer to Christine and whispered in her ear. "Here's the deal. If we invite Jake to our party tonight, there's a chance, however slim, that you survive somehow. If we don't call Jake"—he placed the knife against her neck—"we can end things right now."

Mixell waited a moment for Christine to consider her fate, then asked again. "Would you like to provide Jake's number?"

This time, Christine slowly nodded, and the phone number followed.

Mixell typed the number into his cell phone, then tapped the *Call* icon.

In the NCTC parking lot, Harrison and Khalila were walking toward the facility's entrance when Harrison's phone vibrated.

"Harrison here."

"Jake, how are you doing, buddy?"

Harrison froze, unsure if he had correctly identified the caller's voice. "Lonnie, is that you?"

"Who else would it be?"

"What have you done with Chris?"

"Don't worry, she's healthy enough at the moment."

"If you hurt her, I swear to God, I'll—"

"Oh, I'm afraid that I'm going to do a lot more than just hurt her."

Mixell's voice was filled with a kind of amusement, bordering on outright glee. "With your assistance, however, she'll suffer far less."

"What do you want?"

"I want you to finish what you set in motion when you turned me in. Angie's fate has been resolved. That leaves you and Chris."

"You sick bastard. Where are you?"

"Easy, buddy," Mixell replied. "That's no way to speak to someone who's got a knife pressed against Chris's neck."

"How is she? Let me talk with her."

"Just for a moment."

After a short wait, he heard Christine's voice. "Jake?" She sounded scared, but when she continued, her words came quickly and with conviction. "Don't worry about me. When you come, bring the entire HRC and kill this—"

Harrison heard what sounded like a punch, the sound of flesh hitting flesh. He knew Mixell had hit her, which filled him with a white-hot rage.

"Where are you, Lonnie?"

"You know where to find me. Same place you killed Trish."

"It was your bullet that killed Trish!"

"The same place *you* killed Trish," Mixell repeated, seemingly believing his delusional reimagining of what happened. "Her death is entirely your fault, and it's time you made amends for what you did. But I want you, and only you. If anyone else shows up, I'll cut Chris to pieces. Do we have an understanding?"

Harrison considered Mixell's offer and what it portended for his and Christine's fates.

"We have an understanding," Harrison replied. "I won't be long."

78

USS *MICHIGAN*

In the guided missile submarine's Control Room, Captain Murray Wilson watched the battle unfold, attempting to discern what was happening from the icons on the combat control consoles and the various displays selectable on Conn monitors. *Michigan* remained in a thin sliver of waterspace spanning the strait just west of the minefield, which USS *Theodore Roosevelt* also occupied above. Farther west, the waterspace had been divided into six operating areas, each owned by one of the six fast attack submarines that had recently passed through the minefield into the Persian Gulf.

The plan was simple in concept. The entire width of the Persian Gulf west of the strait had been divided into six areas, and no Russian submarine could approach *Theodore Roosevelt* close enough to launch torpedoes without being engaged by one of the American fast attacks. Unfortunately, to prevent blue-on-blue engagements, the Americans could not take advantage of their superior numbers, at least not in a way that truly mattered.

In an ideal situation, the battle would pit a single Russian submarine against two American fast attacks simultaneously. But two U.S. submarines operating in the same waterspace required a stratum separation scheme, with one submarine operating shallow and the other deep. However, the Persian Gulf was too shallow to accommodate this scheme, which meant each American submarine was on its own within its operating area.

As Wilson studied the sonar displays and various consoles, the Russian strategy became clear. The Akulas were operating closely together on the north side of the gulf, attempting to slip by along the Iranian coast. An Akula had entered each of the three operating areas to the north. In those three areas, it'd be a one-on-one battle between Russian and American submarines.

Wilson brought *Michigan* to the northern side of the Persian Gulf to better monitor the battles as they unfolded, and also so *Michigan* could serve as a stopgap if one of the Russian submarines prevailed and a nearby fast attack wasn't available.

The Akulas had slowed down upon detecting their American adversaries surging toward them as they exited the minefield, and each engagement had settled into the classic cat-and-mouse game as each submarine crew tried to determine a firing solution while both submarines frequently maneuvered. Eventually, the two submarines in the northernmost operating area engaged, with both launching torpedoes. After Sonar reported the dual launches, Wilson listened to the broadband sonar speaker for an indication of the battle's outcome. Not long thereafter, the sound of a single explosion rumbled from the speakers.

"Sonar, Conn," Wilson called out to the microphone above the Conn. "Can you determine which submarine was hit?"

"Conn, Sonar. Analyzing." A moment later, Sonar reported, "Loss of fifty-point-two-Hertz tonal in the northern operating area. The Akula has been sunk."

The tension in *Michigan*'s Control Room eased somewhat, as one of the three Akulas had been dispatched. As Wilson focused on the other two areas with Russian submarines, Sonar delivered a new report.

"Conn, Sonar. Gained a new contact in operating area Foxtrot, classified Yasen class."

Wilson shifted his attention back to the northernmost operating area, where the Akula had been sunk. It appeared that the Yasen-class submarine—*Krasnoyarsk*, based on the submarines that had surged from Vladivostok—had joined the fray. As capable as the Akulas were, *Krasnoyarsk* was three decades newer, with much more capable sensors and tactical systems.

The replacement Russian submarine would be a more challenging opponent than the previous Akula, and Wilson monitored that operating area more closely than the others. *Krasnoyarsk* and its opponent engaged in maneuvers and analysis as each crew attempted to discern an adequate firing solution. Eventually, dual torpedo launches were detected, and Wilson waited tensely as Sonar reported both submarines increasing speed as they attempted to evade the incoming torpedoes. Time ticked away and there was no explosion; both submarines had survived.

Moments later, an explosion emanated from the speaker selected to broadband sonar, and Sonar determined the explosion came from operating area Delta. Further analysis indicated that another Akula had been sunk. The southernmost of the three engagement areas was now clear of Russian submarines, with the third Akula still lurking in operating area Echo and *Krasnoyarsk* in Foxtrot.

Then another explosion rumbled from the Conn speaker.

Sonar analyzed the remaining acoustic frequencies in that area, then reported, "No longer detect U.S. submarine tonals in operating area Foxtrot. Yasen-class tonals remain."

Wilson took a deep breath and let it out slowly. *Krasnoyarsk* had sunk the U.S. fast attack. It now had a clear lane to approach *Theodore Roosevelt*. The fast attack in the adjacent area to the south would not be able to engage, since it was still dealing with the third Akula.

In normal situations, U.S. submarines could not enter a friendly submarine's operating area without permission and a stratum separation scheme. However, today's engagement was not a normal situation. Wilson had no order or authorization to do so, but made the call.

"Helm, ahead standard. Left full rudder, steady course two-eight-zero."

He was taking his submarine into operating area Foxtrot. For *Krasnoyarsk* to approach within firing range of *Theodore Roosevelt*, it would have to get past *Michigan*.

79

ALEXANDRIA, VIRGINIA

Darkness had fallen by the time Khalila's car ground to a halt on Pendleton Street, just before the right-hand curve leading to Harrison's destination, a warehouse built on the bank of the Potomac River. There were no pedestrians in sight, and no cars either at the moment, now that darkness had enveloped the city.

"Are you sure you want to do this alone?" Khalila asked.

"You heard Mixell," he replied. "This is between me and him. Promise me you'll stay out of this."

Khalila nodded solemnly. "I'll wait here. Call if you need me."

Harrison pulled his pistol from its holster as he stepped from the car, then moved swiftly along the curve in the road, where Pendleton transitioned to North Union Street. Not far from the warehouse, he stopped in the shadows across the street from the building.

A single door and several multi-paned windows spanned the side of the building facing Union Street. Harrison checked the warehouse for evidence of a security system—cameras or motion detectors—but didn't spot any telltale signs.

As he prepared to cross the street to engage Mixell, his thoughts drifted back to a scene in his house in Silverdale, Washington. Christine had just departed after offering him a job at the agency.

After he closed the front door, Angie leaned against the wall, tears in her eyes.

"I know you have to take this job," she said. "Lonnie will eventually come after you, and the sooner he's back behind bars or dead,

*the better. But be more careful this time. Maddy and I can't afford
to lose you."*

Tears fell down Angie's cheeks.

*Harrison wiped them away. "Nothing's going to happen to me.
We'll find Lonnie and either kill him or put him in prison again,
and this time he won't get out.*

"I'll be safe. You and Maddy will be safe. I promise."

The memory left a bitter taste in his mouth. He had failed Angie. He
wasn't going to lose Christine.

Harrison crossed the street and stopped against the building, then
peered into the nearest window, hoping to get a clear shot on Mixell and
end tonight's ordeal quickly. The window was too filthy to see through,
so he wiped most of the grime away with his sleeve, enough to get a
decent look. The interior was filled mostly with stacks of crates, plus the
blue Ford Taurus that Mixell had switched into while in the I-395 tunnel. There was no sign of Mixell or Christine, however.

He moved to another window, and then another with the same result. The only items visible were the stacks of crates and the Taurus.
Mixell must have positioned himself and Christine, or perhaps the
crates as well, so that Harrison wouldn't have a clear shot from outside
the building. While looking through the next window, however, Harrison spotted a rope tied to a ceiling beam, rising from behind one of the
stacks of crates. The rope was taut and swayed slightly on occasion, and
Harrison concluded that Christine was tied to the beam.

Harrison completed his survey of the warehouse from the remaining windows, and Mixell and Christine were hidden by the crates from
every vantage point. He would have to deal with Mixell the hard way.

He approached the warehouse door and tried to open it, but it was
locked.

Pulling the cell phone from his pocket, he called Mixell.

"I'm here," he said when Mixell answered. "The door is locked."

"I'll call you when I'm ready," Mixell replied, then hung up.

80

USS *MICHIGAN* • K-571 *KRASNOYARSK*

USS *MICHIGAN*

The atmosphere in *Michigan*'s Control Room was subdued, with orders and reports being calmly passed between operators and supervisors as Wilson's crew focused on refining a target solution for the Russian guided missile submarine. Designated Master one, *Krasnoyarsk* was a quiet submarine indeed, held only on tonals detected on *Michigan*'s towed array, which added to the difficulty of developing an adequate firing solution, due to having to wait several minutes after each maneuver for the array to stop snaking back and forth.

Complicating the matter, *Krasnoyarsk* was maneuvering frequently as it headed toward *Theodore Roosevelt*. Whether it was because *Krasnoyarsk*'s crew had counter-detected *Michigan* or was maneuvering prudently in the vicinity of the American fast attack in the operating area to the south, Wilson didn't know. Either way, each time *Krasnoyarsk* maneuvered, it invalidated the firing solution Wilson's crew had been developing, since the Russian submarine's new course and speed were unknown.

Being the first submarine to fire was normally an advantage, and Wilson considered firing with a poor target solution. However, if *Krasnoyarsk* hadn't yet detected *Michigan*, Wilson would be throwing away a significant advantage he held over his adversary. Additionally, if the firing solution turned out to be inadequate, the torpedo would need a steer command from *Michigan*'s crew to turn it onto an intercept track with the target. Unfortunately, the guidance wire sometimes broke during launch or while paying out as the torpedo sped toward its target, so Wilson couldn't count on being able to send a course update to the torpedo after launch.

After considering the matter, Wilson decided to side with patience—continue to prosecute *Krasnoyarsk* until he had an adequate firing solution.

K-571 *KRASNOYARSK*

In *Krasnoyarsk*'s Central Command Post, Captain Second Rank Gavriil Novikov moved from supervisor to supervisor, checking on his crew as they traveled through the perilous water toward the ultimate prize, the American aircraft carrier trapped between the Russian submarines and the minefield blocking the Strait of Hormuz. It was obvious that a path had been cleared through the minefield for American submarines. However, it must not have been large enough to allow passage of the one-hundred-ton aircraft carrier, since it remained in the thin sliver of water on the Persian Gulf side of the minefield. For the time being, it was still trapped.

Regarding the current attack by the four Russian submarines, what was happening in the adjacent water to the south was unclear. Novikov's best assessment was that at least one Akula had been sunk—the one *Krasnoyarsk* had replaced. The Akula in the operating area to the south was still alive; Hydroacoustic held the sonar signature of the Russian submarine and the American submarine it was prosecuting. Whether the third Akula, the farthest one south, was still in play, Novikov couldn't determine.

What was far more important was whether there was another American submarine between *Krasnoyarsk* and the aircraft carrier. That the U.S. Navy overall held a significant numerical advantage over the Russian Navy was obvious, but how many American submarines had surged into the Persian Gulf was unknown. It was prudent, Novikov had decided, to assume that at least one more U.S. submarine stood between *Krasnoyarsk* and its goal; sinking the aircraft carrier would not be so easy. The next report over the Command Post speakers confirmed his assessment.

"Command Post, Hydroacoustic. Hold a new contact, designated Hydroacoustic two-one, bearing one-zero-zero. Analyzing frequency tonals."

As Novikov wondered which class of submarine he was facing, Hydroacoustic followed up. "Command Post, Hydroacoustic. Contact two-one's tonals correlate to Ohio-class submarine."

Novikov pondered the unusual report. He had expected to face another fast attack, not a guided missile submarine. Carrying 154 Tomahawk missiles and a specialized SEAL detachment, the American guided missile submarines were valuable assets and would not be employed in standard submarine warfare unless there was no other option.

This was relatively good news. All four of America's guided missile submarines had their keels laid in the 1970s, and although their tactical systems had been modernized, their hull-mounted acoustic sensors had been fabricated in the 1970s as well. The submarine's crew would have to rely more on its modern towed array rather than the somewhat antiquated bow array.

However, the American SSGNs had a notable advantage their fast attack counterparts lacked. SSGN commanding officers were Captains on their second submarine command tour, having previously commanded another submarine, and only the most successful officers were selected to lead SSGN crews. Novikov and his crew were facing a submarine hampered by its aging technology, but aided by an experienced, hand-picked Captain.

Novikov nodded subtly to himself, then announced, "All stations, track Hydroacoustic two-one."

His crew settled into the task, and after determining the contact's bearing rate, Novikov decided to maneuver for the next leg of analysis.

"Steersman, left full rudder, steady course zero-one-zero."

USS *MICHIGAN*

Lieutenant Commander Tom Montgomery monitored the target solutions being generated on the combat control system consoles while listening over his headset to reports from Sonar and the other Control Room watchstanders.

After responding to another report over his headset, he announced, "Possible contact zig, Master one, due to downshift in frequency."

Wilson glanced at the nearest time-frequency plot. Either the Russian submarine crew had detected *Michigan* and was beginning the prosecution phase, or the maneuver was part of its random course changes as it advanced toward *Theodore Roosevelt.*

He waited while the Fire Control Party sorted out what *Krasnoyarsk* had done. Montgomery eventually announced, "Confirm target zig. Contact has turned to port."

Wilson examined the time-frequency plot in more detail, attempting to determine the magnitude of the Russian submarine's turn. Based on the frequency shift, there had been a fifteen-knot downshift in speed. Assuming *Krasnoyarsk* had been traveling toward *Michigan* at ahead standard, that meant the Russian submarine had turned broadside to *Michigan,* attempting to maximize the change in bearing rate for its fire control algorithms.

Michigan had been detected, and *Krasnoyarsk*'s crew was beginning to refine its solution.

Wilson approached his Executive Officer. "We need a firing solution, soon."

K-571 *KRASNOYARSK*

After ordering several more maneuvers, Gavriil Novikov waited impatiently while Captain Anton Topolski, his First Officer, shifted between the fire control consoles, analyzing the data from Hydroacoustic.

Krasnoyarsk had just detected the American submarine on its bow sonar array. With the American submarine now held on two different sensors, the target solution came into focus. Once their adversary's course was refined to within ten degrees and its speed to within a few knots, they would be ready.

Topolski, who was hunched over the shoulders of the two men at the fire control consoles, tapped one michman on the shoulder. "Set as Primary." The michman complied, and Topolski announced, "Captain, I have a firing solution."

Novikov ordered, "Prepare to Fire, Hydroacoustic two-one, tube Two."

The Central Command Post watchstanders began executing their launch checklists, and as Novikov prepared to retreat to the back of the Command Post to supervise preparations, he hesitated. Typically, submarines fired torpedoes on a corrected-intercept solution, with the torpedo fired at a lead angle that took into account the target submarine's course, speed, and range, so that the torpedo and target eventually ran into each other.

But if the target submarine detected the torpedo when it was launched instead of when it went active a short distance away, it would immediately maneuver to a new course, invalidating the corrected-intercept course loaded into the torpedo, and the torpedo would be dependent on a course steer sent over its guidance wire. If the American submarine was close enough to track *Krasnoyarsk,* which Novikov suspected it might be, a corrected-intercept shot wasn't the best tactic.

He decided to determine which scenario he was dealing with. To his First Officer, he ordered, "Close, then open tube Two outer door."

Topolski looked up. "Sir?"

In preparation for battle, Novikov had opened the outer doors for every torpedo tube. Cycling a door would emit an unnecessary acoustic transient.

"Cycle tube Two outer door. I want to know if our opponent has us on its sensors."

Topolski passed the order to the Torpedo Room, and the outer door for tube Two was closed, then opened again.

USS *MICHIGAN*

Murray Wilson studied the sonar display, watching Master one on *Michigan's* port beam, drifting aft. Montgomery signaled that he had gathered enough information on *Michigan's* current course and was ready for a maneuver when a report from Sonar came across the Control Room speakers.

"Conn, Sonar. Receiving metallic transients from Master one. Possible torpedo door mechanisms."

Wilson acknowledged Sonar's report, then called out, "Firing Point

Procedures, Master one, tube One." Montgomery didn't yet have a firing solution, but whatever solution he had would have to do.

As the personnel in Control executed their checklists, Wilson changed course. "Helm, right full rudder, steady course one-two-zero." If *Krasnoyarsk*'s crew was preparing to fire, it was best to maneuver, placing *Michigan* on an optimal evasion course for a corrected-intercept shot.

K-571 *KRASNOYARSK*

"Contact maneuver," First Officer Topolski called out. "Hydroacoustic two-one is turning away, reversing course."

Novikov had received the answer to his question. The American submarine was close enough to detect a torpedo launch and would immediately maneuver. It was time to dispense with finesse and shift to brute force.

"Cancel Fire," he announced, followed by "Prepare to Fire, three-torpedo salvo, tubes Two, Three, and Four. Tube Two fired first." After glancing at the target's estimated range, he added, "Set salvo spread at twenty degrees."

That should be wide enough to bracket the American submarine no matter which way it turned.

After estimating the American submarine's new course, Novikov's crew completed preparations quickly and the reports followed.

Topolski called out, "Solution updated."

"Torpedoes ready," followed from the Weapons Officer.

The Watch Officer announced, "Countermeasures armed."

Novikov gave the order. "Fire tubes Two, Three, and Four!"

USS *MICHIGAN*

Michigan's Fire Control Tracking Party was zeroing in on a firing solution for the Russian submarine when Sonar's report blared over the Control Room speakers.

"Torpedo in the water, bearing two-four-zero!"

Wilson acknowledged Sonar's report, then examined the geographic display. A red bearing line appeared, radiating from Master one. As-suming the torpedo was fired on a corrected-intercept course, *Michigan* was already on an optimal evasion course. All that was needed now was speed and countermeasures.

"Helm, ahead flank! Launch countermeasures!"

The Helm rang up ahead flank and Lieutenant Resor launched one of *Michigan*'s decoys. A white scalloped circle appeared on the geographic display, recording the location of their countermeasure.

Wilson returned his attention to getting a torpedo into the water. His crew was still at Firing Point Procedures, but his Executive Officer hadn't determined a satisfactory solution. With *Michigan* increasing speed to ahead flank, they would likely lose Master one due to the turbulent flow of water across the submarine's acoustic sensors. They needed to launch a torpedo soon.

He stepped from the Conn and stopped beside Montgomery, ex-amining the solutions on the three combat control consoles. With the frequent maneuvering by both submarines, the three solutions were all over the place, failing to converge on a similar course, speed, and range of their target. As Wilson evaluated his options, he was interrupted by another announcement by the Sonar Supervisor.

"Torpedo in the water, bearing two-four-two!"

A purple bearing line appeared on the geographic display, followed by another announcement and a magenta bearing line.

"Torpedo in the water, bearing two-four-four!"

Their adversary had launched at least a three-torpedo salvo. Wilson responded immediately.

"Check Fire. Quick Reaction Firing, Master one, tube One."

Wilson canceled the normal torpedo firing process, implementing a more urgent version, which forced his Executive Officer to send his best solution to the torpedo immediately. The Russian Captain wouldn't know how well-aimed the torpedo was, and it was better to give him something to worry about instead of letting him refine his solution and send updates to his torpedoes over their guidance wires.

Montgomery shifted his gaze between the three combat control con-soles, then tapped one of the fire control technicians on the shoulder. "Promote to Master."

After the target parameters were sent to Weapon Control, Montgomery announced, "Solution ready!"

Lieutenant Jescovitch, hunched behind another fire control technician at the Weapon Control Console, reported, "Weapon ready!"

"Ship ready!" Lieutenant Resor announced.

"Shoot on generated bearings!" Wilson ordered.

Wilson listened to the whir of the torpedo ejection pump as the torpedo was impulsed from the tube, accelerating from rest to thirty knots in less than a second. Inside the sonar shack, the sonar technicians monitored the status of their outgoing unit.

"Own ship's unit is in the water, running normally."

"Fuel crossover achieved."

"Turning to preset gyro course."

"Shifting to medium speed."

Michigan's torpedo was headed toward its target.

Wilson examined the three sets of torpedo bearing lines on the geographic display, with new lines for each torpedo appearing every ten seconds. One set of torpedo bearings was marching aft, the bearings to the second set were steady, and the third torpedo was drawing slightly forward. *Michigan* was bracketed by two torpedoes, with a third running down the middle.

Stuck between two torpedoes and a third running up the middle, Wilson's only option was to pick a course that would place *Michigan* an equal distance between two of the torpedoes, hoping that the submarine would be far enough away from both torpedoes that each would fail to detect *Michigan* as they passed by.

After estimating the torpedo courses as best as possible, Wilson ordered, "Helm, right ten degrees rudder, steady course zero-seven-zero! Launch countermeasures!"

As *Michigan* turned eastward, Lieutenant Resor launched a second torpedo decoy-jammer pair. Wilson watched intently as all three torpedoes closed on *Michigan*.

K-571 *KRASNOYARSK*

Gavriil Novikov was monitoring his torpedoes—all three were running as expected—when Hydroacoustic called out, "Torpedo in the water, bearing zero-three-zero!"

The American submarine crew had counterfired, as expected.

"Steersman, ahead flank!" Novikov ordered.

Novikov evaluated whether the torpedo had been fired on a corrected intercept course, which would take into account *Krasnoyarsk*'s current course and speed and require an urgent maneuver, or whether the torpedo had been a shot in the dark, on the bearing where *Krasnoyarsk* had been when its torpedoes were launched. Maneuvering for a corrected-intercept firing when it was actually a simple line-of-bearing shot could accidentally turn *Krasnoyarsk* into the path of the more poorly aimed torpedo. He decided to wait a moment, long enough to determine the bearing drift of the incoming torpedo.

More bearing lines appeared on the fire control displays, drawing slowly forward.

The torpedo had been fired on a corrected-intercept course, but the target solution had a slight error in either *Krasnoyarsk*'s speed or course. Not a bad shot, Novikov conceded. But not good enough.

Now that Novikov had identified that the incoming torpedo had been fired on a corrected-intercept course, he knew which way to turn.

"Steersman, left full rudder, steady course two-one-zero."

The Steersman complied and *Krasnoyarsk* reversed course. Novikov monitored the torpedo bearings, which drifted rapidly aft after the turn. The torpedo would pass safely behind the submarine.

Turning his attention to his opponent's fate, *Michigan*'s acoustic trace was brightly lit on the Hydroacoustic display. The American submarine was traveling at ahead flank, attempting to evade the torpedo salvo. After comparing the bearings of his three torpedoes to those of his adversary, Novikov was convinced that one of his weapons would lock onto its target.

Michigan would not get away.

USS *MICHIGAN*

Murray Wilson studied the geographic display on the nearest combat control console. The torpedo behind them had closed to within three thousand yards and would catch up to *Michigan* in four minutes. The torpedoes on each side would pass by without detecting the submarine, but they were doing their job. Wilson couldn't maneuver in either direction without turning into the path of one or the other.

Wilson sensed the tension in the Control Room. The low murmur of orders and reports between watchstanders had ceased, the quiet in the Control Room pierced only by Sonar's announcements, reporting the bearings to the three torpedoes. One by one, the watchstanders in Control looked toward Wilson, wondering if he would find a solution to their dilemma.

There was nowhere for *Michigan* to turn to evade the torpedoes, and it couldn't go up or down, either. The Persian Gulf was too shallow. With *Michigan* measuring about eighty feet from keel to the top of the sail, there was barely a hundred feet to the surface and another hundred feet beneath the keel. There was simply nowhere to go.

Lieutenant Commander Montgomery reached the same conclusion.

"Sir," he said. "Recommend Emergency Blow."

"That won't work," Wilson replied. "There won't be enough of a depth change. We'll remain in the torpedo's detection cone once it clears the bubble cloud from the Emergency Blow. However . . ." Wilson paused as he stared at the navigation display, wondering if he could implement a strategy that had proved successful once before.

He tapped the Quartermaster on the shoulder a second later. "Overlay bottom contour."

The petty officer complied, and after several push-button commands, depth contours appeared on the display. Each level of the ocean bottom was displayed in a different color, increasing in brightness from a dark blue to bright yellow as the water depth increased. Ahead and just to starboard was a small bright yellow patch, indicating an area about a hundred feet deeper than the surrounding bottom.

"What's the bottom type?" Wilson asked.

The Quartermaster retrieved the requested information from the navigation database, then replied, "Mostly quartz sand and calcium carbonate mud, with intermittent coral reef formations."

Wilson immediately ordered, "Helm, right full rudder, steady course zero-seven-zero. Dive, make your depth two-five-zero feet."

The Helm and Diving Officer acknowledged, followed by a report from the Quartermaster. "Sir, charted water depth is three hundred feet."

"Understood," Wilson replied. Stepping onto the Conn, he called out loudly, "Attention in Control. I intend to put *Michigan* on the bottom in the deepest spot we can reach before the torpedo catches up to us. If we're lucky, we'll end up in a spot we can sufficiently hide in, hoping the torpedo chasing us either loses us in the bottom clutter or locks onto a nearby coral reef instead. Carry on."

Turning toward the Quartermaster again, Wilson ordered, "Energize the Fathometer."

The Quartermaster complied, and the submarine's Fathometer began sending sonar pings down toward the ocean bottom. On its display, the distance beneath the keel steadily decreased as *Michigan* sank toward the gulf bottom until the Diving Officer called out, "On ordered depth, two-five-zero feet."

The middle torpedo was only two minutes behind them. *Michigan* would reach the shallow patch at about the same time. Wilson's eyes shifted between the combat control console display and the Fathometer readout as the torpedo behind them closed the distance.

"Conn, Sonar." The Sonar Supervisor's report echoed across the tense Control Room. "Torpedo bearing two-five-zero has increased ping rate. Torpedo is homing!"

Wilson said nothing, his eyes fixed on the Fathometer. Suddenly, water depth began decreasing rapidly, reported by the Quartermaster. "Six fathoms beneath the keel . . . Five fathoms . . . Four fathoms . . ."

They were passing over a coral reef. But how high would it rise and how sturdy was it? With the submarine traveling at ahead flank, hitting even a coral formation could inflict significant damage to the submarine's rudder.

As the Quartermaster called out, "Zero depth beneath the keel," *Michigan* shuddered, knocking some of the personnel standing in the

Control Room off balance. Wilson grabbed onto the Conn railing, his eyes still fixed on the Fathometer. The Diving Officer turned toward the Captain, looking for direction. *Michigan* was barreling along the ocean bottom at ahead flank speed, receiving who knows what kind of damage. Meanwhile, the torpedo behind them kept closing.

"Conn, Sonar. One minute to torpedo impact."

Sonar's report was barely audible above the racket as *Michigan* plowed along the ocean bottom, but the loud scraping sounds suddenly ceased.

Wilson immediately called out, "Helm, back emergency! Dive, bottom the submarine! Don't break the bow dome!"

The Diving Officer turned back quickly toward the Ship Control Panel, simultaneously ordering the two planesmen in front of him, "Three down, full dive fairwater planes."

Wilson felt tremors in *Michigan*'s deck as the ship's massive seven-bladed propeller began spinning in reverse. *Michigan* tilted downward three degrees as it slowed, and a shudder traveled through the ship's hull as the submarine rammed into the ocean bottom again.

"Thirty seconds to torpedo impact!"

As the submarine's speed approached zero, Wilson called out, "Helm, all stop!" and the Helm twisted the Engine Order Telegraph to the ordered bell. The tremors beneath Wilson's feet ceased, and *Michigan* came to rest with a slight tilt to port. The racket of the submarine's grounding was replaced by a serene silence, interrupted only by the high-pitched pings of the torpedo behind them.

"Ten seconds to impact."

A few seconds later, a deafening explosion rumbled through the Control Room, followed by hollow tings echoing through Control as chunks of coral bounced off *Michigan*'s steel hull.

After checking with Damage Control Central, verifying there had been no reports of serious damage to the submarine, Wilson began issuing orders.

"Rig for Reduced Electrical Power." Picking up the Conn microphone, he pressed the button for the Engine Room. "Maneuvering, this is the Captain. Unload and secure both turbine generators as soon as possible. Also shift the reactor plant to natural circulation and secure all seawater pumps."

The Engineering Officer of the Watch acknowledged Wilson's order, and throughout the submarine, all nonessential equipment was secured, reducing the electrical demand to within the submarine battery's capacity. Additionally, anything that could transmit sound through the water, indicating that *Michigan* was still operational—primarily machinery noises from electrical generators, pumps, and propulsion-related equipment—was ordered shut down. If they wanted to survive, they needed to convince their adversary that their torpedo had sunk *Michigan*. That meant the submarine not only had to *play* dead on the gulf bottom, but *sound* dead.

As the crew secured nonessential electrical loads, the ventilation fans drifted to a halt, and an uneasy silence settled over the Control Room. The nuclear-powered submarine's battery was small by diesel submarine standards. Even if they successfully simulated a sunk submarine, they could not sit on the bottom for long.

K-571 *KRASNOYARSK*

"Command Post, Hydroacoustic. Explosion in the water, bearing zero-seven-zero. Loss of wire guide, tube Three."

Novikov didn't need Hydroacoustic's report to know that one of their torpedoes had exploded. The sound was audible through the steel hull as the shock wave rumbled by. The middle torpedo in the salvo had caught its target.

A moment later, Hydroacoustic followed up. "Loss of tonals from Hydroacoustic two-one."

The report dispelled any doubts of whether the American submarine had been sent to the bottom. *Michigan* was no longer a concern.

Turning his attention back to the directive he had received while *Krasnoyarsk* was still moored in Vladivostok, Novikov issued his next set of orders.

"Steersman, left full rudder, steady course zero-nine-zero. Slow to ahead standard."

Krasnoyarsk turned east again, closing on the American aircraft carrier.

81

ALEXANDRIA, VIRGINIA

After ending the call with Harrison, Mixell approached the front door of the warehouse and unlocked it. Slowly, with his eye on the door and his pistol drawn, he backed up to where Christine was tied to the ceiling. He stopped behind her, then slid the pistol into the small of his back. After pulling the scoring knife from his pocket, he cut the rope around Christine's wrists. He caught her with his left arm and held her against his body, then slid the knife back into his pocket and pulled out his cell phone.

He called Harrison, letting him know he could enter the warehouse. After ending the call, he swapped his phone for the pistol.

A moment later, the warehouse door opened and Harrison entered.

Harrison stopped after his first step inside the building. Mixell was holding Christine in front of him in a firm grip. He was a head taller than Christine, and he held her in his left arm so that her face was the same height as his, with her feet dangling in the air. The front of Christine's body from the waist down was drenched in blood, oozing from three wounds in her abdomen, with a small red puddle collecting on the ground beneath her.

But what captured Harrison's attention the most was the pistol in Mixell's right hand, its barrel pressed against Christine's head. Mixell was doing his best to recreate the scene in this warehouse a year ago, but in reverse, with him holding Christine hostage instead of Harrison holding Trish.

"How is this going to play out, Lonnie?" Harrison asked calmly, keeping his pistol down by his side, attempting to avoid any provocation that would force Mixell to pull the trigger. Mixell, however, seemed not to care that Harrison was armed.

"You have no idea?" Mixell asked. After a short pause, he said, "I'm sure you do. You were never the brightest bulb on the Christmas tree, but you undoubtedly know what's going to happen tonight."

"Just let Chris go," Harrison said, "and we can settle this between us."

"Not a chance," Mixell replied calmly. "You're going to watch Chris die, just like Trish. And up until the moment I kill you, you'll live with the realization that Angie and Chris are dead because of you. Because of what you did to me. You betrayed me! A brother!"

"If I could take everything back, I would."

"It's too late for that. You ratted me out, and as the saying goes—'With actions come consequences.' Besides, Chris deserves her fate. She joined you, turning against me."

"She was just doing her job," Harrison replied. "Surely, you see the difference between what I did and what Chris has done."

Indecision suddenly played across Mixell's face. But then his features hardened.

"Chris did more than just her job. She went out of her way, pulling you into the hunt. If she had just let you and me settle things, she wouldn't be here tonight."

Harrison focused again on the pistol pressed against Christine's head. She was terrified, but Harrison pushed that fact from his mind, wondering instead if he could get a clear shot. Mixell kept Christine in front of him, however, exposing barely half of his face, making himself an almost impossible target. Even if Harrison could raise his pistol and aim before Mixell pulled his trigger, he could easily hit Christine instead.

The only way to save her, if that were even possible, was to let Mixell take his revenge out on him instead.

He lowered his pistol and knelt to place it on the ground.

"Oh, no-no-no!" Mixell shouted. "Do you realize where I'm standing!

This is where you held Trish hostage and where a bullet took her life. Keep the gun and take the shot!"

Mixell moved his face back and forth slowly behind Christine's head, teasing Harrison as he exposed more, then less, of his face. Harrison again considered taking a shot, but it was just too risky. He was too far away and the odds of hitting Christine were too high.

He placed his pistol on the ground, then stood. "Let Chris go," he said.

"Pick up the gun!" Mixell yelled.

"Just let her go, you bastard! You can do whatever you want to me, but let Chris go!"

"Pick up the damn gun!" Mixell shouted again.

"I won't," Harrison replied.

Mixell tamped down on the fury building inside him. He wanted nothing more than to have Harrison put a bullet into Christine's head, the same way Mixell had taken a shot at Harrison, accidentally killing Trish. However, he had planned ahead in case Harrison refused. He would watch Christine die the same way Angie had.

"Step away from the pistol," Mixell ordered.

After Harrison took a few steps back, Mixell wedged his pistol into the small of his back and pulled the hooked blade from his pocket, pressing it against Christine's neck.

"Does this scene look familiar?" Mixell asked.

He had always found knives irresistible, and as he considered the turn of events tonight, he realized that nothing had really changed. Harrison had simply chosen a different way for Christine to die. Besides, there was no better way to remind Harrison of what he had done to Angie. And he was about to kill the woman Harrison loved even more.

Mixell pressed his face against the nape of Christine's neck and took a deep breath. Her scent was a combination of perspiration and fear, which he found quite pleasant.

Quietly, he said, "Chris, are you ready to die?"

She didn't reply, but the bravado she had displayed in the White House and earlier this evening had evaporated. He could feel her body trembling in fear, and her breathing had turned rapid and shallow. With his arm wrapped tightly around her body, he could feel her heart pounding in her chest, her pulse racing. He sensed that it was taking everything Christine could muster to hold things together. At that moment, he was filled with admiration, and he remembered why he had been attracted to her years ago.

As a kid, Christine had been fearless and determined, eager to prove that she was just as smart and capable as the boys she hung out with. Reflecting on what Christine had accomplished in her life, he concluded that she was the smartest and most accomplished of them all. Christine was, without a doubt, an incredible woman.

For a fleeting moment, he regretted what he was about to do.

He tightened his grip on the knife, its tip resting against her neck, then shoved it in.

Christine must have sensed her pending demise, because just before Mixell shoved the knife into her neck, she tried to twist free, attempting to pull his arm away enough to let her slip down and out of his grasp. Mixell held onto her, but instead of slicing into her neck, the knife dug into the base of her jaw.

Harrison could hardly believe what he was seeing—the scene in his house in Silverdale repeating itself, only this time with Christine. He screamed at Mixell to stop, at the same time knowing his words were useless. Mixell would not rest until Christine lay slain at his feet.

His words had no effect, but Christine's attempt to wrest herself from Mixell's grasp provided an opportunity. Mixell's face and the right side of his body were exposed as Christine tried to twist away from the knife cutting into her face. Harrison retrieved his pistol and trained it on Mixell, hoping to take a head shot. But Mixell's face was still partially blocked by Christine's, so Harrison went for his body instead.

Christine screamed in agony as the knife dug into her face, nicking her jawbone before sliding up her right cheek. She felt the blade cutting deep into her flesh, scraping across bone before the knife's hooked tip caught momentarily on her cheekbone.

She had no idea of what was happening around her, unable to focus on anything but the searing pain as the knife sliced through her flesh. Mixell must still have had her in his grasp, because there was no sensation of ground beneath her feet. The only thing her mind could focus on was the warm blood streaming down her face and neck, plus the mind-bending pain as Mixell freed the knife from under her cheekbone, ripping the blade up toward her eye.

Through the haze of pain and fear, Christine heard a pistol being fired, and Mixell's body jerking as the bullet hit its target. Thankfully, the knife stopped moving, but Mixell still held her firmly. Her feet hit the ground, then she was dragged back behind a stack of crates, where Mixell dropped her onto the concrete.

Standing behind the crates, Mixell released the knife and retrieved his pistol from behind him. He had taken a round in his upper right chest, but the wound didn't appear serious.

Christine was crawling slowly away, leaving a trail of blood on the floor, and Mixell debated whether to finish her first or shift his attention to Harrison. He decided to focus on Harrison, who was armed. Christine could be dealt with later.

He heard Harrison's rapid footsteps; he was repositioning, undoubtedly taking cover before Mixell got a clear shot. He peered around the stack of crates, firing a round just before Harrison slipped behind a pallet of crates about thirty feet away.

Movement to the side caught Mixell's attention. Christine had regained her feet and was staggering toward a nearby stack of crates. He wanted to finish her off while he held her in his arms, feel her body go limp as she took her last breath. But he would have to move into the open to grab her, giving Harrison a clear shot.

Regrettably, things would not end tonight exactly as he had hoped. But he could at least let her suffer a little while longer.

He shifted his pistol and fired twice, putting two bullets into Christine's back.

* * *

Harrison watched in dismay as shots rang out, followed by Christine's body shuddering as two bullets hit her, then she dropped onto the concrete floor.

He screamed at Mixell, but he wasn't sure what he was saying, the words tumbling from his mouth. He started firing at the crates Mixell was hiding behind, knowing that it wouldn't change Christine's fate. Anger and hatred consumed him, and he suddenly found himself racing across the warehouse toward Mixell, rapid-firing his Glock. He kept squeezing the trigger until the pistol stopped firing, then he released the magazine and reached for another one, slamming it into the pistol grip.

Mixell took advantage of the short pause, peering around the crates. He brought his pistol to bear, but Harrison swerved to the left just before Mixell fired, and the bullet missed. The shift further exposed Mixell, offering Harrison a clear shot. Both men fired almost simultaneously, and Harrison felt a bullet punch into his left shoulder.

At the same time, Mixell's head jerked backward, accompanied by a puff of pink mist blossoming behind his head.

Mixell collapsed to the ground as Harrison raced toward him. He knew Mixell was dead, but he kept shooting him until the second magazine was empty.

Harrison stopped and stood over Mixell's body, breathing heavily as the frenzied haze gripping him faded. Then his thoughts and eyes focused on Christine. She hadn't moved since she hit the ground.

Quickly, he was beside her, kneeling. She was alive but unresponsive. Her skin was pale and her breathing was fast and shallow. He retrieved his cell phone from his pocket and called Khalila, requesting help.

"I'll be there in a moment," she said. "I called the NCTC after I dropped you off. Backup and medical are already here, only a block away."

Harrison hung up, then removed his shirt, hoping to stem Christine's bleeding, but there was so much blood that he wasn't sure which wounds were the most critical—those in her back, abdomen, or face.

He folded his shirt and placed it on the ground beside her, then gently turned Christine over, placing the bullet wounds in her back atop his shirt, so the weight of her body would help curtail the bleeding. He assessed the wounds in her abdomen, which weren't bleeding as heavily as the ones on her back, then resisted the urge to look away after examining the damage to her face. Mixell's knife had torn through almost the entire right side of her face.

As he knelt beside her, applying pressure on the abdomen wounds with his hands, he realized that Mixell had been right—he had never stopped loving her. He had truly loved Angie, but his feelings for Christine had never subsided, they had simply been placed aside. He had often wondered what would have happened if Christine had called before he proposed to Angie. But he had always avoided answering that question. Now, as he knelt beside Christine, he knew why. He hadn't wanted to admit it, but he would have said goodbye to Angie and resumed his relationship with Christine.

Khalila burst through the warehouse door, followed by law enforcement and medical personnel. A team of four paramedics rushed across the warehouse and knelt beside Christine.

"What happened here?" the lead paramedic—Ali Rosenberg, according to her name tag—asked Harrison.

After he described Christine's wounds—the obvious ones to her face and abdomen, plus the two bullets entering her back—Ali asked Harrison to give them some space.

He backed up but hovered nearby until Khalila stopped beside him and placed her hand gently on his shoulder. "Let the EMTs take care of her. There's nothing more you can do."

They retreated a short distance as Harrison watched helplessly. He wasn't a physician, but he'd seen enough battlefield injuries to understand how serious Christine's wounds were and what the paramedics were doing as they attempted to stabilize her.

Ali performed a rapid trauma assessment, checking Christine's ABCs: airway, breathing, and circulation. "I've got a weak pulse," she announced, "and her breathing is labored."

In addition to Christine's fast and shallow breathing, she had also started gasping for air, even though she was unconscious. Harrison knew it was a bad sign; Mixell's bullets had punctured one or both of her lungs.

Ali listened to Christine's chest with a stethoscope, then reported, "No lung sound on the right. Get me a needle decompression kit!"

Her partner handed her the kit, and Ali jabbed the needle into Christine's right side, between her second and third ribs.

"Needle's in," Ali announced as blood and air spurted from the open end of the needle, relieving the internal pressure on Christine's right lung.

Another paramedic intubated Christine, connecting the thin tube to an oxygen bag placed over her mouth and nose, which was squeezed every few seconds. Now that Christine's compromised breathing had been addressed, Ali assessed her other wounds.

"Get me chest seals and gauze."

After Ali pressed gauze over the abdomen wounds, two other paramedics carefully rolled Christine onto her side so they could assess her back.

"Get chest seals on those bullet wounds," Ali ordered, "and get a backboard and a C-collar now!"

One of the bullet wounds was in the center of Christine's back, and care would be needed to ensure any spinal injury wasn't exacerbated during transit. Harrison cursed silently to himself. In his haste to stem her bleeding, he hadn't paid attention to how close the entry wound was to her spine before turning her onto her back.

The requested equipment quickly arrived, and Christine was carefully placed atop and secured to the backboard, and a collar was fastened around her neck to immobilize her head. As she was prepared for transport, one paramedic assessed her vitals while two other paramedics inserted IVs—one for fluid and another for medication—into her veins.

"Her blood pressure's falling," Ali announced. "Start a norepinephrine drip now!"

The medication was quickly injected into one of the IVs, then Christine was lifted onto a stretcher and wheeled toward the warehouse exit.

Harrison followed as she was loaded into an awaiting ambulance. He wanted nothing more than to go with her, but Ali placed a hand on his chest, stopping him from entering the vehicle.

She climbed inside with Christine, and as the rear doors closed and the ambulance sped away, Harrison watched numbly until the vehicle disappeared in a distant intersection.

82

USS *MICHIGAN* • K-571 *KRASNOYARSK*

USS *MICHIGAN*

On the bottom of the Persian Gulf, it was quiet in *Michigan*'s Control Room as Murray Wilson wondered if they had fooled *Krasnoyarsk*'s crew.

Standing on the Conn, bathed in yellow emergency lighting, Wilson discussed the situation with his Executive Officer, four department heads, and the Chief of the Boat. The first order of business was ensuring all noisy equipment had been secured, followed by a detailed inspection to determine what had been damaged during the less-than-graceful bottoming. The department heads departed to inspect their spaces, augmented by teams of personnel assigned and tasked by the Chief of the Boat.

Meanwhile, Wilson kept a keen eye on the Sonar display on the Conn and the tactical displays on the combat control consoles. The Weapons Officer had reported that they had lost the towed array during the bottoming, but the spherical array in the bow remained operational.

On the spherical array, they still held *Krasnoyarsk* via surface reflections—no direct path tonals were received—which was good news. If *Michigan*'s sonar could not directly see *Krasnoyarsk*, then the Russian submarine's sonars could not directly see *Michigan*. Wilson had indeed found a depression at the bottom of the gulf deep enough to hide in, and the Russians would have to rely on surface reflections, with their weaker acoustic signals, to detect and locate *Michigan* if they suspected it had survived.

Without the ability to maneuver the submarine and assist the combat control algorithms, it was difficult to determine what *Krasnoyarsk* was up to. However, all three operators manning the combat control consoles independently estimated that the Russian submarine was headed east, which made sense. It was resuming its pursuit of *Theodore Roosevelt*.

More important to Wilson and his crew was the path *Krasnoyarsk* took as it traveled through operating area Foxtrot. Wilson had bottomed *Michigan* in a depression almost due east of *Krasnoyarsk*, which meant the Russian submarine would pass by a short distance away. This was bad news, and good news.

The bad news was that the probability that *Krasnoyarsk's* crew would detect *Michigan* playing possum on the sea bottom increased as the Russian submarine drew nearer. The good news was that if *Krasnoyarsk* failed to detect and realize *Michigan* had survived, Wilson and his crew would be in an ideal attack position after the Russian submarine passed by.

As Wilson filled in the details of the plan forming in his mind, there was a high-pitched chirp from the Conn speaker, signaling that someone was calling the Conn over the submarine's sound-powered phone system. Wilson had ordered his crew to refrain from using the usual communication systems, which blared reports from speakers throughout the submarine, directing them instead to use the much quieter phone system.

Wilson picked up the handset and placed it to his ear. "Captain."

"Captain, Engineer. We've completed our inspection of the Engineering spaces and there is no noticeable damage."

Wilson acknowledged the Engineer's report, then awaited results from the rest of the submarine, which soon arrived. Aside from the towed array and the bottom Fathometer, *Michigan* had sustained no other damage, as far as they could tell.

Lieutenant Commander Montgomery, still in charge of the Fire Control Tracking Party, approached. "Master one will be at CPA in five minutes."

A glance at the nearest tactical display indicated that *Krasnoyarsk* had remained on an eastward course and would soon reach its Closest Point of Approach. It was unclear exactly how far away the Russian submarine would pass, but the estimates being generated on the combat control consoles placed *Krasnoyarsk*'s CPA at between one thousand and two thousand yards.

A submarine operating normally would definitely have been detectable at that range. Whether *Michigan* was quiet enough, with most of its machinery deenergized, was the critical question. A single burst of noise could give *Michigan* away. Shutting a watertight door too forcefully or dropping a wrench onto the submarine's metal deck plates could be heard thousands of yards away, depending on how quiet the surrounding ocean environment was.

Wilson settled into the Captain's chair on the Conn, then ordered the Chief of the Watch, "To all stations, no one is authorized to move or touch anything, aside from console controls, until further notice."

The order went out over the sound-powered phone system, and throughout the submarine, personnel movement ceased.

The watchstanders in the Control Room waited tensely as the Russian submarine drew closer to *Michigan,* with Montgomery periodically announcing the estimated distance to their adversary.

After reaching twelve hundred yards, Montgomery announced, "Master one is at CPA."

Wilson shifted his gaze between the Sonar monitor and the tactical displays, searching for any indication that *Krasnoyarsk*'s crew had realized that *Michigan* was resting on the bottom a short distance away and hadn't been sunk. *Krasnoyarsk*'s tonals and bearing changed steadily, consistent with a contact remaining on the same course and speed.

Montgomery kept reporting the distance to *Krasnoyarsk* as the submarine continued east, and the tension in the Control Room gradually eased. But Wilson realized they were approaching the most dangerous point, since *Krasnoyarsk*'s most capable sensor trailed behind the submarine.

Wilson reminded the Control Room watchstanders, "The towed array is passing by now."

Krasnoyarsk remained steady on an eastern course as Montgomery reported the distance to the Russian submarine in one-hundred-yard intervals. When the Russian submarine opened to three thousand yards and its towed array was about two thousand yards away, with no discernible reaction from *Krasnoyarsk,* the tension in the Control Room began to fade.

Wilson stood, signaling it was time to get back to work. To the Chief of the Watch, he ordered, "Inform all personnel that normal Battle Stations Torpedo duties may resume. Maintain all communications via the sound-powered phones."

The word was passed, and after another glance at the target solution for *Krasnoyarsk*—it was still headed east at about fifteen knots—Wilson decided to prosecute the Russian submarine while in *Michigan's* partially crippled state. The turbine generators had been secured, with the battery supplying all vital engineering and tactical loads. The lineup was sufficient to engage an adversary, but full propulsion was not possible without the turbine generators and the reactor coolant pumps they powered. However, Wilson's plan to sink *Krasnoyarsk* and avoid counterfire required no propulsion. He gained the attention of the Control Room watchstanders and explained.

"I plan to engage Master one while still in a reduced electrical status. Restoring the electric plant to a normal full power lineup requires bringing the turbine generators online, and I don't want to risk their tonals being detected. I also don't want to let Master one open range much farther before engaging. For my plan to work, we need to shoot soon, while Master one is still close.

"As I'm sure you've just noted, without the turbine generators, we can't evade at ahead flank. But even with full propulsion available, starting from all stop, we wouldn't be able to evade an incoming torpedo if we're fired upon from a range this close. Instead, once we shoot, we'll drop back down into the depression we're currently hiding in. It worked before and hopefully it'll work again if Master one counterfires. Any questions?"

There were none, so Wilson announced, "Firing Point Procedures, Master one, tube Two."

The Executive Officer stopped briefly behind each of the combat control consoles, examining the target solution on each one, finally tapping the middle fire control technician, who sent his solution to Weapon Control.

Montgomery called out, "Solution Ready!"

The Fire Control Technician at the Weapon Launch Console sent the course, speed, and range of their target to their MK 48 torpedo in tube Two, along with the desired search presets.

The Weapons Officer announced, "Weapon Ready!"

Lieutenant Resor reported, "Countermeasures are armed. Ship Ready!"

With *Michigan* one button push away from launching a torpedo, Wilson issued the critical order, bringing the guided missile submarine off the bottom.

"Dive, engage Hovering. Set depth at two-five-zero feet."

The Diving Officer relayed Wilson's order to the Chief of the Watch, seated at the Ballast Control Panel, who dialed in 250 feet and energized the submarine's Hovering system. Blue circles illuminated on the Ballast Control Panel, indicating that valves in the hull were opening. The Chief of the Watch called out periodically as the submarine's hovering pumps pushed water from *Michigan*'s variable ballast tanks, increasing the submarine's buoyancy.

At the forty-thousand-pound mark, *Michigan* began righting itself from its port list, then rose from the sea floor. Shortly after rising above three hundred feet, Sonar reported, "Gained Master one on the spherical array, direct path."

Wilson had bottomed *Michigan* on a course of zero-seven-zero, pointed in what was now *Krasnoyarsk*'s direction. Now that *Michigan* was rising above the nearby coral reef, its bow sonar array had a clear view of the Russian submarine and the torpedo tube openings in the bow were likely clear of the reef. Wilson had ordered a depth of 250 feet—an extra fifty feet higher than they would likely need—just in case.

"On ordered depth, two-five-zero feet," the Diving Officer announced.

After one final assessment of the tactical situation, Wilson confirmed *Michigan* was ready to launch its torpedo. Although he had explained his plan to drop back into the depression they'd been hiding in, *Krasnoyarsk* likely wouldn't be able to counterfire at all.

Wilson was hoping that Russian torpedoes had similar safety features as U.S. torpedoes. One of those safeguards was Anti-Circular Run, or ACR, which would prevent torpedo launch if the course being sent to the torpedo would turn it around after launch, placing the firing submarine in the torpedo sonar's acquisition cone. As intelligent as modern torpedoes were, they couldn't discern friend from foe and would lock onto any target that met the criteria. As a result, ACR interlocks were incorporated to ensure a torpedo, once launched, was disabled if it turned far enough so that it was looking back at the firing submarine.

With *Michigan* almost directly behind *Krasnoyarsk,* the Russian submarine would likely be prevented from counterfiring until it had turned far enough to clear the ACR constraint, so that its torpedo could turn in *Michigan*'s direction without seeing *Krasnoyarsk.* That would take time. Time Wilson hoped the Russian submarine crew wouldn't have.

Satisfied that the tactical situation was satisfactory, he issued the order.

"Match sonar bearings and shoot!"

The torpedo was impulsed from tube Two, and Sonar monitored the torpedo, ensuring it was operating correctly. Once the final report was received, Wilson issued the next command, moving *Michigan* to a safer position.

"Dive, set Hovering to four hundred feet."

The order was relayed to the Chief of the Watch, who adjusted the Hovering system depth setting, then monitored its operation as water was flooded into the variable ballast tanks.

Slowly, *Michigan* sank back into the bottom depression.

K-571 *KRASNOYARSK*

"Command Post, Hydroacoustic. Torpedo launch transient, bearing two-nine-zero!"

Before Novikov could react, Hydroacoustic called out, "Torpedo in the water, bearing two-nine-zero!"

Novikov spun toward the hydroacoustic display. A bright white trace was burning in on their towed array aft beam. Based on the intensity of the trace, the torpedo was close.

The American submarine hadn't been sunk, after all. *Krasnoyarsk*'s torpedo must have hit something else, or perhaps had not fatally damaged their adversary.

"Steersman, ahead flank!"

As the steersman rang up maximum propulsion, Novikov selected the optimal evasion course. They were already headed away from the torpedo, which was almost directly behind them, so only a slight change in course was required.

"Steersman, right full rudder, steady course one-four-zero. Launch torpedo decoy!"

Krasnoyarsk swung around as a decoy was launched, which gave Novikov hope until Hydroacoustic's next report. "Torpedo has gone active!"

The torpedo going active so soon told Novikov it had been fired from close range, which meant it would lock onto *Krasnoyarsk* before the submarine could open distance from its decoy. It would also catch up to *Krasnoyarsk* soon. He had to get a torpedo out quickly.

"Counterfire, bearing two-nine-zero, tube Five! Set short-range tactics."

A target solution would not be sent to the torpedo. Instead, it would be fired down the bearing of the torpedo launch.

"Torpedo is homing!"

Novikov remained focused on preparing their torpedo for firing. The torpedo tube was flooded and muzzle door already open. He waited for the Weapons Officer's report, which was delayed for some reason.

"Torpedo not ready!" the Weapons Officer finally called out. "Circular Run Interlock is engaged!"

Novikov glanced at *Krasnoyarsk*'s heading as it settled out at the ordered evasion course: one-four-zero. With the torpedo course after launch set at two-nine-zero, the torpedo could not be launched until *Krasnoyarsk* turned another forty degrees.

"Thirty seconds to impact!" Hydroacoustic reported.

"Steersman, right hard rudder! Steady course one-nine-zero!"

Novikov added an extra ten degrees to the turn to ensure the interlock cleared.

The Steersman yanked the rudder control hard right, kicking *Krasnoyarsk* back into another turn to starboard.

"Fifteen seconds to impact!"

Novikov checked the submarine's course, assessing how long before the interlock cleared. He figured it would take another twenty seconds.

They didn't have twenty seconds.

Novikov realized that *Michigan*'s Captain had planned it perfectly, waiting until *Krasnoyarsk* had passed by, firing from close range, giving Novikov and his crew insufficient time to respond before the incoming torpedo caught up to them.

Ten seconds later, the Command Post was filled with the deafening sound of an explosion. *Krasnoyarsk* jolted forward violently, knocking Novikov to the deck. As he pulled himself to his feet, the flooding alarm sounded from Compartments Eight and Nine. The normal white lighting in the Command Post extinguished a moment later, replaced by yellow emergency lights. Novikov felt his submarine slow and tilt upward as the sea poured into the aft compartments. With two compartments flooded, not even an Emergency Blow could keep them afloat.

Krasnoyarsk was going to the bottom.

USS *MICHIGAN*

"Conn, Sonar. Detect torpedo explosion, bearing one-six-three."

There was no need for Sonar's report, since the sound of the explosion had just reverberated through *Michigan*'s hull.

Moments earlier, *Michigan*'s Chief of the Watch had taken manual control of the Hovering system, slowing the eighteen-thousand-ton submarine's rate of descent as it approached the sea bottom. *Michigan* had landed with a dull thud accompanied by only minor metallic groans from the submarine's structure.

Another low rumbling sound passed through *Michigan*'s hull. Sonar reported their assessment. "Conn, Sonar. Master one has impacted the sea floor."

It appeared that their adversary had been sunk, eliminating any immediate threat to *Michigan*'s safety, so Wilson focused on returning his submarine to full operational status.

Picking up the Conn microphone, he contacted the Engine Room. "Maneuvering, Conn. Shift the electric plant to a normal full power lineup."

The Engineering Officer of the Watch acknowledged the order, and Wilson waited until the turbine generators had been brought online and full power restored.

"Dive, set Hovering to two hundred fifty feet."

The Diving Officer complied and *Michigan* rose from the bottom of the Persian Gulf again. After they cleared the coral reef, Wilson ordered, "Sonar, Conn. Report all contacts."

A moment later, Sonar reported, "Hold only Virginia-class submarines to the south and *Theodore Roosevelt* to the west. Hold no foreign warships."

It looked like the third Akula had been sunk.

Although *Michigan* didn't own operating area Foxtrot, Wilson decided to keep his submarine in the area in case another Russian submarine attempted to approach within firing range of *Theodore Roosevelt*. However, he decided it'd be prudent to let the U.S. ASW commander know that *Michigan* was in Foxtrot, so friendly forces didn't accidentally attack.

"All stations, Conn," Wilson announced. "Make preparations to come to periscope depth."

83

WASHINGTON, D.C.

It had been a long night as Harrison sat beside Khalila in a waiting room at George Washington University Hospital, the closest Level I trauma center to Alexandria. The surgery addressing the wound to his shoulder had taken barely an hour, and he was none too worse for the wear aside from a dull ache in his shoulder and his left arm in a sling. The hours passed by at an agonizingly slow pace as two teams of doctors attended to Christine's knife and bullet wounds, plus the savage damage Mixell had done to her face.

Harrison was no stranger to tense situations, and controlling his nerves while on a mission had never been an issue, but his right knee jittered uncontrollably as he awaited the outcome of Christine's surgery. Khalila said little as she sat beside him, but eventually placed a hand on his knee and pressed down firmly until the jitters subsided.

It was 6 a.m., ten hours after Christine had been wheeled into the operating room, when two doctors entered the waiting room and approached Harrison and Khalila, who rose to greet them and presented their agency IDs. Christine's parents were deceased and she was an only child with no living relatives, so the hospital had agreed to the agency's request that Harrison be briefed on Christine's condition.

The physicians introduced themselves; they were the lead doctors of the two teams that had tended to Christine's injuries. Norah Aller had led the general surgery effort to treat the wounds in her back and abdomen, while Alex Warren had led the maxillofacial surgery team dealing with her facial injuries. Norah was the first to brief.

"Christine's general wounds—from the bullets and knife—have been addressed, but there are complications. She suffered significant damage to several vital organs and she also lost a lot of blood, which placed additional stress on her body. More critically, one of the bullets entered her spinal column."

"Is she . . . ?"

"Her spinal cord is intact," Norah replied. "However, there was significant tissue damage and the resulting inflammation will put pressure on the spinal column fluid, which could impact her brain. As a result, we've placed Christine in a medically induced coma."

"For how long?"

"It's hard to predict, Mr. Harrison. We don't even know if Christine will—" Norah stopped midsentence, pausing for a moment as she considered her words. "We've done everything we can, and the rest is up to her. She's relatively young and in excellent physical shape."

A lengthy silence followed as Norah let Harrison and Khalila absorb the details of Christine's condition, then she turned to Alex Warren, who had led the other team of doctors.

"Although not as serious as the wounds and subsequent stress to Christine's organs," he began, "the damage to her face was traumatic. However, she was fortunate in some respects. There was no damage to the parotid gland and the knife missed the cervical branch of the facial nerve. But the buccal nerve was severed and the zygomatic muscles were—"

Harrison interrupted. "I don't understand what you're saying. Can you explain in plain English?"

Warren nodded. "Basically, several muscles and nerves that control the movement of Christine's mouth and nose, along with facial sensation, were severely damaged. The muscles have been sutured back together and the prognosis is good. The nerve damage, however, is more serious. Nerve coaptation—suturing severed nerves back together—is a more difficult procedure and the recovery is often not one hundred percent. A ninety percent recovery is probably the best Christine can hope for."

"A ninety percent recovery—what does that mean?"

"Her speech and facial expressions may be impacted. And then there's the significant superficial damage. This type of injury can be difficult for someone like Christine to deal with."

"Why is that?"

"Well," he answered uneasily, "she was a beautiful woman."

"She still is."

Warren nodded slowly. "Of course."

Norah and Warren asked if Harrison had any other questions, but Harrison had none at the moment. His mind and body felt numb as he grappled with the specter of Christine's death. Mixell had taken Angie from him, and now Christine's life hung in the balance.

Harrison watched as the two doctors departed the waiting room. As he stood beside Khalila, the ache in his chest and the emotion threatening to overwhelm him must have been evident on his face, because she pulled him into an embrace.

"I can't lose her," he said.

"I know," Khalila replied, hugging him tightly.

"She's going to live," she said. "Just believe."

84

WASHINGTON, D.C.

In the West Wing of the White House, today's meeting was being held in the Cabinet Room, a short distance down the hallway from the Oval Office, its eastern windows overlooking the Rose Garden. This was CIA Deputy Director Monroe Bryant's first meeting in the Cabinet Room, sitting in for Director Christine O'Connor, who was still in a coma. Seated near one end of a large oval conference table beside FBI Director Bill Guisewhite, Bryant took a moment before the meeting began to soak in the room's rich history and traditions.

Built primarily in the Georgian revival style, the room was adorned with neoclassical ceiling molding, French doors topped with arched lunette windows, and a fireplace on the north side of the room, above which hung a painting depicting the signing of the Declaration of Independence.

In the center of the east side of the table, the president sat in his customary spot in a chair two inches taller than the others, with Vice President Bob Tompkins sitting across the table. The cabinet members were seated according to the date the department was established, with Secretary of State Marcy Perini seated on the president's right, the secretary of the treasury on the vice president's right, and acting Secretary of Defense Peter Seuffert on the president's left. Additional cabinet members and White House staff were spread out on both sides of the table.

Before the meeting began, the president took a moment to acknowledge Bryant's attendance, then inquired about Christine.

"How is she doing?"

"No change," Bryant replied, "but we're hoping for good news in the next few days. The inflammation that led to Christine's medically induced coma is subsiding."

The president nodded solemnly. "I understand. Keep me informed when her condition changes."

After a glance from the president, Chief of Staff Kevin Hardison announced the first topic on the meeting agenda: Russia.

Turning to Bryant, Hardison said, "Looks like you're up first."

Bryant cleared his throat, then began. "Mr. President, we've completed our investigation into the assassination of former Secretary of Defense Tom Glass. We've concluded that the order came from Josef Hippchenko, the director of Russia's Foreign Intelligence Service, in response to our proposed economic sanctions against Russia. However, the directive undoubtedly came from the Kremlin itself. A complete report will be provided by the end of this week."

"Thank you, Monroe," the president said. "We'll table the discussion of our response options until the other Russian issues are discussed."

"SecDef," Hardison announced, "you've got the next topic, Russia's invasion of Ukraine."

Seuffert took his cue. "It appears that the intent of Russia's invasion was to seize the southeastern region of Ukraine, creating a contiguous land corridor between Russia proper and Crimea. They've done that, and the invasion has ground to a stalemate. It appears the plan now is to hold onto the territory until Ukraine wearies of the fight and decides to concede the land. We don't expect the war to tilt significantly toward one side or the other in the foreseeable future."

The Secretary of Defense's summary of the war kicked off a short discussion of additional potential economic sanctions against Russia, which the president entertained for a while before suspending the conversation. "Let's cover the remaining issue before we debate our response to Russia's transgressions."

Seuffert continued with an overview of Russia's attempt to sink the Theodore Roosevelt strike group, which resulted in the loss of four American surface warships and one fast attack submarine. "We gave Russia a bloody nose in the process," Seuffert remarked, "sinking the same number of combatants. They lost five nuclear-powered submarines, which is enough of a repercussion, militarily, I think. If we're ready to discuss response options, I don't recommend additional military action. We should invoke even more restrictive economic sanctions, strangling the government's income flow."

"No," the president replied. "Russia placed those warships in harm's way and suffered the consequences. Russia also needs to suffer repercussions for their actions, and I'm tired of more sanctions. I want a plan to hit Russia where it hurts. Something more than just a bloody nose."

"I understand, Mr. President," Seuffert replied. "We'll craft some options for you."

"What about Iran," the president said, directing his words to Secretary of the Navy Sheila McNeil, "and the role they played in Russia's Persian Gulf attack by mining the Strait of Hormuz?"

McNeil shifted uncomfortably in her chair. "I was going to recommend a similar approach as the one SecDef offered for Russia, which you just rejected. We attacked Iran, essentially unprovoked, destroying their new uranium enrichment facility, and we could consider Iran's participation in the Persian Gulf their retribution and call things even."

"In this case," the president replied, "I agree. We've set Iran's nuclear weapon aspirations back at least five years, which is a significant accomplishment. Regarding the assistance they provided to Russia in the Persian Gulf, sometimes it's wise to let your opponent get the last word. Otherwise, the conflict may never cease and even escalate. Let's call things even with Iran and move on. Are there any objections or alternate ideas?"

None were put forth, so the president turned to Hardison again, who brought up the last major topic of today's meeting: Mixell's attempt to assassinate the president.

Responsibility for the matter rested with FBI Director Guisewhite, who briefed everyone on the plot details, including the innovative element that some of the men and women around the table hadn't yet heard about—how Mixell managed to get the C-4 explosive into the White House.

"C-4 Easter eggs," someone commented after the revelation. "Now that's a novel idea."

"We're lucky it didn't work," the president said. "We're fortunate that Christine O'Connor recognized Mixell before he was able to slip away and detonate the eggs while they were still inside the White House."

There was a short pause as the president's thoughts seemed to dwell on Christine's fate. Then a few additional items were discussed over the next hour before the meeting was adjourned.

85

WASHINGTON, D.C.

Jake Harrison's car screeched to a halt, slightly askew in a visitor's parking spot at George Washington University Hospital. The engine had barely sputtered to a stop before the car door was opened and Harrison was hurrying up the sidewalk toward the hospital entrance.

A half hour earlier, Harrison had finally received the call he'd been waiting for—Christine's doctors had determined that she had sufficiently recovered, and they had weaned her from her medically induced coma. She'd been moved from intensive care to a normal hospital room, and was now lucid and accepting visitors.

Harrison flashed his agency ID at the woman at the information desk near the entrance, then proceeded to the fourth-floor ward, where he stopped at the nurse's desk, asking which room Christine O'Connor was in.

"She's in room 4106," she replied, "but she's not accepting additional visitors."

"Additional visitors? Who's with her now?"

"I'm not at liberty to discuss this with you. But if you'd like to have a seat in the waiting area, perhaps you can talk to Christine's visitor when she departs. If you'd like, however, I can let Christine know you're here."

"Please do."

After the nurse made the call, Harrison grudgingly retreated to the visitor's lounge, selecting a chair offering a view of the hallway leading to Christine's room. Twenty minutes later, a woman exited the room. He recognized her immediately—she was Joan McDonnell, Christine's best friend since the two had met on Penn State's gymnastics team as freshmen. Both had majored in political science and ended up with careers in Washington, D.C.

Joan headed directly to the visitor's lounge as Harrison rose to greet her. She said nothing as she approached, simply stopping in front of him before embracing him in a long, tight hug. When she pulled back, there were tears in her eyes.

"How is she doing?" he asked.

"As well as can be expected," she answered, wiping the moisture from her eyes with her hand. "She's still weak and talking is very difficult for her. Her face is heavily bandaged, and I can barely understand what she's saying. It's going to take a while for everything to heal."

"Why isn't she allowing additional visitors? The nurse said you were the only one she's authorized. Does she know I'm here?"

"She does."

"And she doesn't want to see me?"

"Not right now."

Harrison's heart sank in disappointment, unsure whether Christine didn't want to see him because she blamed and hated him for what happened, or because she simply wasn't ready to deal with people's reactions to her injuries.

"You just need to give her time," Joan said. "What happened to her that night was incredibly traumatic, both physically and psychologically, and it will take a while for her to process everything."

"You're right," Harrison said glumly. "I'll give her however much time she needs."

86

USS *MICHIGAN*

As *Michigan* leveled off at periscope depth, the top of its sail four feet beneath the water's surface, Murray Wilson peered through the submarine's periscope, searching for Russian warships. There were no visual contacts, although he knew that lurking beneath the surface of the Black Sea were three other U.S. Navy guided missile submarines.

Although *Michigan* was frequently called upon to deploy its SEALs, its 154 Tomahawk missiles, stored in seven-pack launchers in twenty-two missile tubes, were employed less often. This morning, however, *Michigan*'s crew, along with the crews of the three other guided missile submarines in America's arsenal, would participate in a rare event. At the designated time, all four submarines would launch their entire complement of Tomahawk missiles.

In the early morning hours, Ukraine had completed preparations for a counterattack into the swath of Ukrainian territory occupied by Russia. To soften the Russian defenses, the assault would be led by a targeted strike of more than six hundred Tomahawk missiles.

Wilson stepped back from the periscope, turning it over to Lieutenant Brittany Kern as an announcement came over the Conn speakers. "Conn, ESM. Hold no threat radars."

Kern acknowledged ESM's report as Wilson pulled the 1-MC microphone from its holster and issued the order his crew had been awaiting.

"Man Battle Stations Missile."

The Chief of the Watch, stationed at the Ballast Control Panel, twisted a lever on his console, and the loud *gong, gong, gong* of the submarine's General Emergency alarm reverberated throughout the ship.

As the alarm faded, the Chief of the Watch picked up his 1-MC microphone, repeating the Captain's order. "Man Battle Stations Missile."

Michigan's crew streamed into the Control Room, taking their seats at dormant consoles, energizing them while supervisors gathered behind their respective stations.

Wilson stepped from the Conn, leaving the safety of the ship in Lieutenant Kern's capable hands, then headed down the ladder to Operations Compartment Second Level.

Like the Navigation Center behind the Control Room, which had been converted into a Battle Management Center, Missile Control Center had also been transformed during the submarine's conversion from a ballistic missile submarine to an SSGN. The refrigerator-sized computers had been replaced with servers one-tenth their size, and the aft bulkhead was now populated with four workstations: two Mission Planning Consoles, a Launch Control Console, and a fourth workstation that displayed a map of *Michigan*'s operating area, which was overlaid with one green and several red hatched areas.

Wilson stopped behind the Launch Control Console beside Lieutenant Ryan Jescovitch, the submarine's Weapons Officer. Glancing at the fourth console, Wilson verified *Michigan* was within the green area— the submarine's launch basket—where all 154 of *Michigan*'s Tomahawk missiles were within target range.

Jescovitch reported to the Captain, "Five minutes to launch window. Request permission to launch Full Salvo."

Wilson replied, "Permission granted. Launch Full Salvo."

Following Wilson's order, there was no flurry of activity. Jescovitch simply turned back toward the Launch Control Console, his eyes focused on the time display as it counted down the remaining five minutes. At ten seconds before the scheduled launch, the launch button on the Launch Control Console display, which had been grayed out until this point, turned a vivid green. The Launch Operator announced, "In the window, Full Salvo."

Lieutenant Jescovitch replied, "Very well, Launch Operator. Continue."

Finally, the digital clock on the Launch Operator's screen reached 00:00:00. The Launch Operator pressed the green button, and *Michigan*'s automatic Tomahawk Attack Weapon System took control.

"Opening tube Three," the Launch Supervisor reported as the green indicating light for the missile tube turned yellow. Shortly thereafter, the indicating light turned red. "Hatch, tube Three, open and locked."

A few seconds later, the Launch Operator reported, "Missile One, tube Three, away."

The first of *Michigan*'s Tomahawk missiles had been ejected from the submarine, the missile's engines igniting once it was safely above the ocean surface. Another missile followed every five seconds, with the Tomahawk Attack Weapon System automatically opening and closing the Missile Tube hatches as required. *Michigan*'s Tomahawks were streaking north; Ukraine's counteroffensive had begun.

87

WASHINGTON, D.C.

It was 11 p.m. on the East Coast of the United States when the Tomahawk missiles were launched from the SSGNs in the Black Sea. Inside the Situation Room in the West Wing, the president and several members of his cabinet and staff were seated around the table and chairs along the room's periphery, watching events unfold on a ten-foot-wide monitor on the far wall. The president said nothing as the symbols representing the Tomahawk missiles traversed the Sea of Azov and moved ashore, striking their targets moments later.

In the southeastern region of Ukraine, a red line demarked the front line in the war between Russia and Ukraine, with Russia still controlling a corridor of territory connecting Russia and the Crimea. A few kilometers to the northwest of the red line were two concentrations of green icons representing Ukrainian forces marshaled for a surprise assault, with one strike force situated southeast of Zaporizhia and another south of Pokrovsk.

There was no movement from the green icons as American and Ukrainian military commands assessed the effectiveness of the Tomahawk strikes. It would take hours for detailed assessments, but a preliminary call would have to be made within the next few minutes, with Ukraine's military hierarchy deciding whether to commence their offensive or not.

Moments later, the green icons started moving—southeast from Zaporizhia and south from Pokrovsk—with both forces aiming to reach the northern shore of the Sea of Azov, cutting off over a hundred thousand Russian troops in the land corridor between the two assaults. It was obvious that the Tomahawk attack had been successful, and the preliminary results soon flowed into the Situation Room. The Russian formations at the two points of attack had been obliterated by the precision strikes.

CIA Deputy Director Monroe Bryant, seated at the table with the president, sensed an air of satisfaction in the room, with the United States delivering payback for Russia's assassination of Secretary of Defense Tom Glass and its attacks in the Persian Gulf. However, he wasn't exactly sure why he had been invited to the Situation Room for tonight's event, given that the CIA had played no role in it.

"That'll be all for tonight," the president announced.

As people started filing out of the Situation Room, the president turned to Bryant. "Stay for a moment."

The Situation Room emptied aside from the president and Bryant, plus Vice President Bob Tompkins, Chief of Staff Kevin Hardison, and FBI Director Bill Guisewhite. Once the conference room door was closed, the president spoke.

"There's the matter of Brenda Verbeck to resolve." Turning to Guisewhite, the president asked, "What do you have, Bill?"

"Just Christine's testimony about what Mixell told her in the warehouse in Alexandria—that Brenda had hired Mixell to assassinate you. We haven't been able to identify any messages between Verbeck and Mixell, nor trace any payments to him from her accounts or from those of her family, associates, or business partners. If she's the one who hired Mixell, she's covered her tracks well."

"Again," Bryant announced.

The president raised his eyebrows, and Bryant explained. "During the incident with Rolow, Verbeck revealed to Christine that she was the one who coerced him into eliminating the two Navy personnel who could have exposed her brother's sale of centrifuges to Iran. On two occasions now, Verbeck has been tied to murder. Does she need a third strike?"

The president reflected on Bryant's comments, then replied, "I'm confident that Christine isn't lying. And unless she's hallucinated both of these conversations, we have a very serious problem on our hands—what to do about Brenda Verbeck."

There was silence around the table until Vice President Tompkins spoke. "Letting Brenda walk after the previous incident was a mistake. The issue needs to be addressed, but nothing official. The initial concern remains: letting the press and Congress know that a senior member of the president's administration was involved in these plots is a potentially devastating revelation this close to the election."

"I agree," the president acknowledged. "I've reflected on this matter considerably over the last few days and have made a decision. Considering that Brenda hired Mixell to bomb the White House and assassinate me, which is undoubtedly an act of domestic terrorism, I have decided to classify Brenda as an enemy combatant."

Bryant did his best not to reveal his surprise at the president's decision. After a quick reflection, however, Bryant conceded that the classification was certainly within the president's prerogative.

The president turned to Bryant. "Do you understand how I want this matter handled?"

"I do," Bryant replied.

"How soon can this be taken care of?"

"Not long, Mr. President. Not long at all."

88

LURAY, VIRGINIA

Discovered in 1878 by Andrew and William Campbell, along with Benton Stebbins, after the trio detected a rush of cold air from a limestone sinkhole, Luray Caverns are the largest and most popular caverns in the eastern United States, featuring enormous chambers filled with towering stone columns, shimmering draperies, and crystal-clear pools. Designated as a Registered Natural Landmark, Luray Caverns also features a half dozen other attractions, including a one-acre maze of eight-foot-tall evergreen hedges.

It was almost noon when Brenda Verbeck's silver Mercedes-Benz SL roadster coasted into a parking spot near the maze entrance. It had been an hour-and-a-half drive from her home in Potomac, Maryland, making the trip after receiving a message from Christine O'Connor, who had requested a meeting at noon today to discuss a sensitive matter. Brenda was twenty minutes early, so she ordered a cup of coffee from the Stalactite Café and took a seat with a view of the maze entrance.

Standing by the entrance were two men in suits—CIA protective agents by the look of them—and Brenda noticed that they were preventing guests from entering the maze. It was almost noon when she finished her coffee and moved toward the entrance. The two men scrutinized her as she approached, but made no attempt to stop her from entering.

Once inside the maze, she pulled her cell phone out. She had never been through this maze and had no intention of wasting time. After launching a map app, she selected the satellite view and zoomed in on the maze. It took only a moment to identify the quickest way to the center, where she would meet with Christine.

A few minutes later, after spotting no one else in the maze along the way, she reached the center via one of its two entrances. It was an open space containing a large square fountain. On one side of the fountain sat a man, not Christine O'Connor as Brenda expected. She recognized him—one of the two CIA officers who had arrived at Rolow's home during her and Rolow's confrontation with Christine. Brenda wasn't sure what type of officer he was, paramilitary probably, by the look of him. But she remembered his name: Harrison. Jake Harrison.

Brenda stopped before him. "I don't believe we've been formally introduced," she said, extending her hand. "Brenda Verbeck."

Harrison stood and shook her hand, introducing himself as well, confirming that she had correctly recalled his name. He gestured to the edge of the fountain and waited for Brenda to sit before joining her.

"Thank you for coming," he said. "Unfortunately, Christine sends her regrets. She's unable to attend today, and I've been assigned to meet with you instead."

"I heard about what that terrible man, Mixell, did to her," Brenda said. "I'm so glad he's dead."

"I'm sure you are," Harrison replied.

"How is Christine doing?"

"She's recuperating."

"Well, please pass on my wishes for a speedy and full recovery."

Harrison smiled. "Of course."

"What did Christine want to talk about?"

"I don't know what she would have said to you, but I'll probably be more direct. You got away with murder before, but this time your luck has run out."

A chill raked Brenda's flesh. The topic of today's meeting had unexpectedly taken a precarious turn.

"Could you be more specific?" she asked tersely.

"Your interactions with Mixell are no longer a legal issue."

"Mixell? I've never had anything to do with him. I've never even met him."

Harrison stared at her, not even bothering to counter her claim. Then her thoughts snapped back to Harrison's comment. "What do you mean it's no longer a legal issue?"

"We finally get to the crux of the matter," he replied. "The president considered some sort of financial retribution, arranging for all of your assets to be seized. However, you come from a rich family, and the impact of losing your personal fortune would not have been terribly traumatic. So, the president made a more draconian decision."

Harrison's last sentence hung in the air before he explained. "I regret to inform you that you've been classified as a terrorist—an enemy combatant."

"What does that mean?"

"It means, Brenda, that the rules of combat apply to you. There will be no arrest, no lawyers, no courtroom drama."

It took a moment for Brenda to process what Harrison said and its implications.

"Are you going to kill me?"

"No," Harrison answered, "I'm not going to harm you. The last time we met, in Rolow's home, I stopped Khalila from killing you, remember?"

"I do," Brenda replied, relieved. "And I'd like to offer a belated thank-you for intervening."

"You're welcome," he said as he stood. "But I won't stop Khalila this time."

"This time?"

Harrison looked across the courtyard, and Brenda's eyes followed his gaze. Khalila was standing at one of the entrances, glaring at Brenda.

Khalila flexed her wrists, and a knife dropped into each hand from inside her sleeves.

"Goodbye, Brenda," Harrison said as he headed toward the other exit.

Brenda sat transfixed on the stone ledge, her body momentarily refusing her mind's command to flee. Not that it would have mattered. Harrison would surely block the other exit, and Khalila had already closed half the distance between them, moving swiftly toward her.

89

FAYETTEVILLE, IOWA

It was a clear blue day with the temperature in the mid-seventies as Jake Harrison sped down Interstate 80 in his airport-rented sedan. As the car slowed for the exit to Fayetteville, where he, Mixell, and Christine had grown up, his thoughts raced ahead to his pending meeting with anticipation and dread.

Now that the threat from Mixell had been eliminated, protecting Maddy in a gated and guarded condominium complex was no longer required, and Maddy had accompanied her grandparents when they returned to their summer home in Iowa. Harrison had agreed that Fayetteville would be a nice place for Maddy to spend the next few weeks until he figured out where they should move. There was no way they could return to their house in Silverdale, Washington, where Maddy's mother had been slain in the dining room, her blood staining the wood floor.

After Christine had received confirmation that her wounds were healing well and that there were no complications, she had also decided to return to Fayetteville. However, her mom and dad had passed away years ago and the house she had grown up in was now owned by the Andersons, so Christine had asked Harrison's parents if she could stay with them. She had asked that they not reveal this to Jake, at least for a while, but Maddy hadn't received the memo and had mentioned to her dad one night on the phone how much she was enjoying spending time with Christine.

Harrison had been surprised when he learned that Christine had asked to stay with his parents, but upon reflection, it made sense. Other than the home she grew up in, Christine had spent more time at Harrison's house and farm, by far, than anywhere else in Fayetteville. The barn behind the house, especially, held fond memories. He and Christine had often spent time in the loft when they were kids, talking as their feet hung over the edge of the opening overlooking the farms in the distance. After they began dating, they had sometimes escaped to the loft to do more than talk.

He recalled the first time he had planned to ask Christine to be his girlfriend. They had been sitting at the edge of the loft, their feet dangling over the edge as usual, and as they talked, he had placed his hand on hers, attempting to hold her hand. But Christine had misinterpreted his action and moved her hand to the side to make room for his. He could still remember the crestfallen feeling that had swept over him when he concluded that she had rejected him.

They had eventually sorted things out and started dating, and only later did Harrison learn that Christine had been clueless that day in the loft. Although Harrison's thoughts had turned romantic once they were teenagers, she was still in friend mode and hadn't understood what he was doing when he tried to hold her hand.

Harrison spotted his house in the distance and soon pulled into the driveway, past a black SUV parked alongside the curb. He wondered who the vehicle belonged to, then realized that Christine would have protective agents with her in Fayetteville.

He entered his childhood home, greeted first by his mom, then by Maddy, who came running down the hallway and jumped into his arms. He held her for a long moment; she was so much like her mother, exhibiting almost unbridled exuberance.

After learning that his dad was out running errands, Harrison sat down at the breakfast table, catching up with his mom and Maddy. His daughter filled him in on the new friends she had made in the neighborhood and that she had made plans to get together with one of them this afternoon. It wasn't long before she had to head over to her friend's house, and she hugged and kissed her dad goodbye.

Once Maddy departed, the conversation turned to Christine.

"How is she doing?" he asked.

"She's in relatively good spirits, it seems," Nadia replied. "But it's hard to know, sometimes, what people are really thinking and feeling."

"Where is she?"

"In the barn."

"Has she said anything about my request to meet with her?"

Nadia shook her head.

"Well, then," he replied, "we'll see how things go."

Nadia hugged him as he stood. "Good luck."

He left the house via the back door, immediately spotting a pair of protective agents at the barn's entrance. They apparently knew who he was, because neither man challenged him as he entered the barn. Christine wasn't anywhere on the main floor, so he climbed onto the second level. At the far end of the loft, Christine sat at an opening looking out across the farmland, her legs dangling over the side.

She must have heard him climb onto the loft, because she glanced over her shoulder, then slid to the left, clearing a spot for him to join her. Harrison would have preferred to sit on her left instead of right side, avoiding the matter of her injury if possible, but Christine either hadn't thought about it or perhaps didn't care.

Harrison sat beside her. There was a narrow white bandage about one inch wide on the right side of her face, running from the base of her jaw to just under her eye, covering the wound as it healed. She had been advised to keep it protected from direct sunlight for the first year, since the sun's ultraviolet rays could cause extra collagen to be produced as the wound healed, resulting in a thicker and darker scar.

While the bandage had no effect on her appearance as far as Harrison was concerned, Christine looked quite different compared to the last time he had seen her. She had lost a good deal of weight; with the injury to her facial muscles, it must have been painful to eat.

"Chris, I'd like to talk with you," he began slowly, "but if you'd rather be alone . . ."

"It's okay," she replied. "I've been alone with my thoughts for the last few weeks, and I could use the company." Her words were somewhat stilted, but not as much as he had expected.

She gazed across the farmland in the distance, and Harrison joined her.

"It feels good to be back in Fayetteville," she said. "It brings back memories of when things were simpler and more carefree. Before we carried the weight of the world, it seems, on our shoulders. I even miss the mean tricks your brothers and the other boys played on me on occasion."

"Well, you were the only girl in the gang, and some of the boys wanted it to remain a boys-only club. In their minds, it was your periodic participation fee."

"Yeah," she said, "I kinda figured that out, and I didn't really mind. I do have one regret, though. I always wanted a cool nickname, but you guys refused to give me one. I made up a few imaginary ones for myself over the years, but I'm thinking—I've got the perfect nickname now. How about . . . Scarface?"

"That is *so* not funny," Harrison replied.

Christine tried to laugh, but the sound came out distorted. The muscles in her face hadn't fully healed.

There was a long silence, and Harrison sensed Christine's mood turning serious.

"Your parents said you wanted to talk with me, and I'm sure it wasn't just to reminisce about our childhood. We've both had a lot of time to think about things, so why don't we get started?" She turned to him. "I'll go first."

She fell silent for a moment, and Harrison sensed the emotion gathering in her chest.

"I'm so sorry for everything that's happened to you," she finally said. "Angie's death, Maddy's injury, and Mixell almost killing you twice. You were right—all of it was my fault, dragging you into the effort to track Mixell down when it wasn't essential. I risked Angie and Maddy—and you—because of my selfish desires. You said you didn't want to have anything further to do with me, and I don't blame you."

She turned away, staring into the distance, unwilling to meet his eyes.

Harrison was stunned by her last sentence. How could she possibly believe he didn't want anything more to do with her? Then he realized that they hadn't spoken since Easter Sunday on the phone, when he had warned her about Mixell's C-4 egg plot. When Christine's life had hung in the balance in the Alexandria warehouse later that evening, he had been forced to confront his conflicting emotions, and everything had changed.

He wasn't sure where to begin. His feelings for her ran far deeper than he could ever express, driven by more than physical attraction. He had buried those feelings during his marriage to Angie, and now that they had resurfaced, they were stronger than they had ever been. As he sat beside her in the loft, he realized that Christine was simply an incredible woman, and nothing that had happened in the past would change that.

"I don't blame you anymore," he said. "You got caught up in a chain of events that I started when I turned Mixell in. I still think it was the right thing to do, but the events that followed were the result of my actions. Both of us made decisions that had unforeseen and horrific consequences. But we both did what we thought was right at the time, and that's the best I can ask of myself and of you."

Harrison placed his hand atop hers, and she let him curl his fingers under her palm and hold her hand tightly. When she turned to face him, moisture glistened in her slate blue eyes.

He recalled the time, in this very spot, when he had tried to hold her hand, but she had moved hers away. Had he been successful, he was going to try and kiss her.

He leaned toward Christine, stopping a few inches from her face. "Will it hurt if we kissed?"

She smiled and caressed the side of his face with her hand. "There's one way to find out."

Then she closed the remaining distance.

* * * THE END * * *

AMERICAN CHARACTERS

UNITED STATES ADMINISTRATION
Kevin Hardison—chief of staff
Marcy Perini—secretary of state
Tom Glass—secretary of defense
Peter Seuffert—acting secretary of defense
Sheila McNeil—secretary of the Navy
Nova Conover—secretary of homeland security
Thom Parham—national security advisor

CENTRAL INTELLIGENCE AGENCY
Christine O'Connor—director (DCIA)
Monroe Bryant—deputy director (DDCIA)
Frank McKinnon—deputy director for operations (DDO)
Tracey McFarland—deputy director for analysis (DDA)
Becky Rock—deputy director for support (DDS)
Jake Harrison—paramilitary operations officer (former SEAL, code name Riptide)
Robert Wilson—paramilitary operations officer (former SEAL, code name Leviathan)
Steve Hile—paramilitary operations officer (former Delta Force, code name Pile Driver)
Eric White—paramilitary operations officer (former Delta Force, code name Cutlass)

Bob Lesher—paramilitary operations officer (former Night Stalker, code name Falcon)

Khalila Dufour—specialized skills officer, National Clandestine Service (code name Stingray)

OTHER U.S. GOVERNMENT AGENCIES

Bill Guisewhite—director of the Federal Bureau of Investigation

USS *THEODORE ROOSEVELT* (NIMITZ-CLASS AIRCRAFT CARRIER)

Ryan Noss (Captain)—Commanding Officer

Dolores Gonzalez (Captain)—Combat Direction Center (CDC) Operations Officer

Michael Beresford (Lieutenant Commander)—Officer of the Deck

USS *MICHIGAN* (OHIO-CLASS GUIDED MISSILE SUBMARINE)—BLUE CREW

Murray Wilson (Captain)—Commanding Officer

Tom Montgomery (Lieutenant Commander)—Executive Officer

Ryan Jescovitch (Lieutenant)—Weapons Officer

Brian Resor (Lieutenant)—Officer of the Deck

Brittany Kern (Lieutenant)—Officer of the Deck

Keith Ressler (Lieutenant)—Officer of the Deck

USS *MICHIGAN*—SEAL DETACHMENT

Jon Peters (Commander)—SEAL Team Commander

Tracey Noviello (Lieutenant)—SEAL Platoon Officer-in-Charge

Russ Burkhardt (Special Warfare Operator Senior Chief)—SEAL Platoon Leading Chief Petty Officer

Michael Keller (Special Warfare Operator Second Class)

Kurt Hacker (Special Warfare Operator First Class)

Dave Narehood (Special Warfare Operator First Class)

USS *ASHEVILLE* (LOS ANGELES–CLASS FAST ATTACK SUBMARINE)

GARY WATSON (Commander)—Commanding Officer

RUSTY IDLEMAN (Lieutenant)—Weapons Officer

USS *MISSISSIPPI* (VIRGINIA-CLASS FAST ATTACK SUBMARINE)

BRAD WALLER (Commander)—Commanding Officer

OTHER MILITARY CHARACTERS

JOE SITES (Admiral)—Chief of Naval Operations (CNO)

MEDINA FALLS

SARAH GREENWOOD—waitress at Irina's Diner

GEORGE GREENWOOD—Sarah's father and owner of Irina's Diner

IRINA GREENWOOD—Sarah's mother

TRENT MCENTYRE—Sarah Greenwood's ex-boyfriend

GLORIA POTTER—rents cottage to Jake Harrison

NICHOLAI GHERKIN—customer at Irina's Diner

LEONID ROMANKO—customer at Irina's Diner

MIKHAIL GOERGEN—customer at Irina's Diner

CARVER CONSTRUCTION

JACK CARVER—Carver Construction owner

CRAIG DANIELS—Carver Construction supply manager

BETH WALTERS—Carver Construction secretary

CBS

BONNI SHUFF—CBS local TV reporter

ED LIPSKA—CBS local TV cameraman

NICOLE FLEMING—CBS national reporter

GEORGE WASHINGTON UNIVERSITY HOSPITAL

Norah Aller—general surgeon

Alex Warren—oral and maxillofacial surgeon

OTHER CHARACTERS—MALE

Lonnie Mixell—former Navy SEAL (aliases: Mitch Larson / George Banks / John Fonda)

Vance Verbeck—technical director, U.S. Navy Artic Submarine Laboratory

Dan Snyder—former CEO, Snyder Industries

Bob, Ray, and Tim Snyder—Brenda Verbeck & Dan Snyder's brothers

Ken Singleton—FBI agent

Alex Martin—Virginia state trooper

Fred Rogers—Capitol Talent Agency customer agent

Robert Keeshan—Mixell's body double

Dave Gordon—Gordon's Wholesale owner

OTHER CHARACTERS—FEMALE

Brenda Verbeck—CEO, Snyder Industries / former secretary of the Navy

Angie Harrison—Jake Harrison's wife (deceased)

Nadia Harrison—Jake Harrison's mother

Madeline (Maddy) Harrison—Jake Harrison's daughter

Jessica Del Rio—National Counterterrorism Center (NCTC) supervisor

Ashley Tobin—Secret Service agent

Ali Rosenberg—paramedic

Cheryl Payne—Woodmore, Maryland, property owner

Joan McDonnell—Christine O'Connor's best friend

RUSSIAN CHARACTERS

RUSSIAN ADMINISTRATION

DMITRY EGOROV—president
ANDREI GRIGORENKO—defense minister
MARAT TRUTNEV—foreign minister
ANTON KRAVTSOV—chief of staff
JOSEF HIPPCHENKO—director of the Foreign Intelligence Service (SVR)
DANIL MOROZOV—ambassador to Iran

K-328 *LEOPARD* (AKULA-CLASS NUCLEAR ATTACK SUBMARINE)

MAKSIM SIDOROV (Captain Second Rank)—Commanding Officer
LEV IVANOV (Captain Third Rank)—First Officer
ARTYOM YEGOROV (Captain Lieutenant)—Central Command Post
  Watch Officer

K-571 *KRASNOYARSK* (YASEN-CLASS NUCLEAR ATTACK SUBMARINE)

GAVRIIL NOVIKOV (Captain Second Rank)—Commanding Officer
ANTON TOPOLSKI (Captain Third Rank)—First Officer
PETR DOLINSKI (Captain Lieutenant)—Central Command Post Watch
  Officer

OTHER MILITARY CHARACTERS

NIKOLAI VOLKOV (General)—Chief of the General Staff

Pavel Klokov (Admiral)—Commander, Pacific Fleet

Alexei Sokolov (Major General)—Commander, 2nd Guards Motor
Rifle Division

IRANIAN CHARACTERS

IRIS *JAMARAN* (MOUDGE-CLASS FRIGATE)
BEHZAD AHMADI (Commander)—Commanding Officer

OTHER CHARACTERS
KOORUSH SHIRVANI—Iranian minister of foreign affairs
BEHROUZ KHAVARI—Natanz Replacement Centrifuge Assembly Center supervisor
SAEED MASUD—Natanz Fuel Enrichment Plant director
AMER SARSOUR—Natanz security guard
KARIM RASHIDI—CIA field officer

NATO CHARACTERS

JOHAN VAN DER BIE—secretary general
SUSAN GATES—British prime minister
LIDWINA KLEIN—German chancellor
FRANÇOIS LOUBET—French president

AUTHOR'S NOTE

I hope you enjoyed *Vengeance*!

As I mentioned in a previous author's note, I hadn't planned to write a military thriller series. *The Trident Deception* was a bucket list project for me, but when St. Martin's Press expressed interest in the book, the first question they asked was whether I was writing a sequel. My literary agent explained what the correct answer was, which I provided, and I was offered a two-book contract with the plan for additional books if the first two were well received.

However, the character set in *The Trident Deception* was designed to tell a specific story, and wasn't well suited for a military thriller series, so I introduced Jake Harrison in Book 2 (*Empire Rising*) and gave him a backstory involving Christine. By Book 4 (*Blackmail*), it had become clear that Christine was the favorite character by far (followed by Wilson), which surprised me. Even more surprising was the question I received the most from readers: When were Christine and Harrison going to get together?

The answer at that point in time was—*never*, because Harrison was married and not the type of character to have an affair or leave his wife for another woman. But it was also *never*, because I hadn't really thought about it. The characters were designed to move the various plots along, and I hadn't considered a plotline involving the characters themselves— I write military thrillers, not chick lit.

Blackmail was the middle book of a three-book Russian-aggression trilogy, and as I mapped out the next few books, three things became clear. First, I had exhausted all reasonably plausible ways that Christine could get into trouble, and that needed to be addressed. Second,

I needed a new adversary after three books involving Russian shenanigans, and I also decided to answer that oft-answered question about Christine and Harrison's relationship—would they get together, and if so, how?

Books 6, 7, and 8 were designed to address all three issues, moving Christine to the CIA, where she would have less opportunity to get entangled in dangerous situations, and introducing Mixell, who would serve both as the tie-in to the main plots in the trilogy while also serving as the catalyst to resolving the Christine-Harrison question. It was a challenge to add a character-driven element to what is unarguably a plot-driven series, but I hope you enjoyed the Harrison-Mixell-Christine storyline in the last three books.

I also have to give a shout-out to Khalila, who turned out to be a very well-received character, to the point that my editor floated the idea of a new series centered around her. But by that time, I had already fleshed out my next series—see the next paragraph.

Finally, to all of you: Thanks for reading, and I hope you'll check out my new military science fiction novels set a thousand years in the future. The genre is technically sci-fi, but I like to think of the books as military thrillers in a sci-fi skin, something I think many of you would enjoy. I hope you'll join me in the Nexus House / Colonial Fleet series!

ABOUT THE AUTHOR

Lynne Campbell

Rick Campbell is a retired Navy Commander who spent more than twenty years on multiple submarine tours. On his last tour, he was one of the two men whose permission was required to launch the submarine's nuclear warhead–tipped missiles. Campbell is the author of several novels, including *The Trident Deception* and *Deep Strike*. He lives with his family in the greater Washington, D.C., area.